About the Author

Unable to sit still without reading, **Bella Frances** first found romantic fiction in her grandmother's magazines. Occasionally stopping reading to be a barmaid, financial advisor, teacher and of course writer, her eclectic collection of wonderful friends have provided more than their fair share of inspiration for heroes, heroines and glamorous locations. Bella lives in the UK but commutes for international pleasure – strictly in the interests of research!

Susan Stephens is passionate about writing books set in fabulous locations where an outstanding man comes to grips with a cool, feisty woman. Susan's hobbies include travel, reading, theatre, long walks, playing the piano, and she loves hearing from readers at her website susanstephens.com

New York Times bestselling author **Teri Wilson** writes heartwarming romance with a touch of whimsy. Three of Teri's books have been adapted into Hallmark Channel Original Movies, including *Unleashing Mr Darcy* (plus its sequel *Marrying Mr Darcy*), *The Art of Us* and *Northern Lights of Christmas*, based on her book *Sleigh Bell Sweethearts*. She is also a recipient of the prestigious *RITA* Award for excellence in romantic fiction and a recent inductee into the San Antonio Women's Hall of Fame.

Sports Romance

Sports Romance:
In The Saddle

BELLA FRANCES

SUSAN STEPHENS

TERI WILSON

MILLS & BOON

First Published in Great Britain 2025
by Mills & Boon, an imprint of HarperCollins*Publishers* Ltd
1 London Bridge Street, London, SE1 9GF

www.harpercollins.co.uk

HarperCollins*Publishers*
Macken House, 39/40 Mayor Street Upper,
Dublin 1, D01 C9W8, Ireland

Sports Romance: In The Saddle © 2025 Harlequin Enterprises ULC.

The Playboy of Argentina © 2015 Bella Frances
At the Brazilian's Command © 2015 Susan Stephens
It Started with a Diamond © 2017 Teri Wilson

ISBN: 978-0-263-41718-0

MIX
Paper | Supporting
responsible forestry
FSC™ C007454

This book contains FSC™ certified paper and other controlled sources to ensure responsible forest management.

For more information visit: www.harpercollins.co.uk/green

Printed and Bound in the UK using 100% Renewable Electricity at CPI Group (UK) Ltd, Croydon, CR0 4YY

THE PLAYBOY OF ARGENTINA

BELLA FRANCES

For my mother, with all my love.

CHAPTER ONE

IN THE LAZY warmth of a summer afternoon, Rocco 'Hurricane' Hermida stepped out of his helicopter onto the utterly perfect turf of the Buenos Aires Campo Argentino de Polo. From her vantage point in the crowd Frankie Ryan felt the air around her ripple with the flutter of a thousand eyelashes. If awe was a sound it was the reverent silence of grown men turning to stare at their own demigod. No doubt the polo ponies were stamping and snuffling and shaking their shaved manes adoringly, too. Yet all *she* could feel were the unbidden tremors of hurt and humiliation and—damn him to hell—shame.

With every step he took across the springy grass his fabulous outline sharpened. A little taller, definitely more muscular. Could his hair be longer? It had seemed so shockingly defiant all those years ago. Now it just trademarked him as none other than Argentina's own—her finest, proudest export.

Wind whipped at silk skirts and hands flew to hair and hats. The crowd swelled and leaned closer. For a second her view was obscured, but then there he was again. Clearer and nearer. Ruggedly, shockingly beautiful. And still making her heart pound in her ears—after all these years.

He turned, cast his profile; it was caught on camera

and screened all around. The scar through his eyebrow and the break in his nose—still there. A hand landed on his shoulder, and then there at his side was his brother Dante, as blond as Rocco was dark—twin princes of Darkness and Light.

It really was breathtaking. Just as they said in the media. Only even more potent in the flesh. The dazzling smiles of their happy conspiracy, the excitement of the match, the thrill of the crowd. How intoxicating.

How sickening.

How on earth was she going to get through the next four hours? The party afterwards, the gushing hero-worship? All over the man who had looked her in the eye, kissed her full on the mouth and broken her soft, trusting heart.

Easy. It would be no problem at all. How hard could it be to watch a little polo, sip a little Pimm's and keep well out of trouble?

Tipping too large sunglasses onto her too small nose, she took a seat on the high-rise bleachers and crossed her jiggling legs. Maybe she shouldn't have come here today. She could so easily have made this stopover in Buenos Aires and not taken in a polo match. It wasn't as if she was obsessed with the game itself. Not anymore.

Sure, she'd grown up more in a stable than in a home. And yes, once upon a time becoming a polo player had been her sixteen-year-old heart's desire. But she'd been naive back then. Naive enough to think her father had been kidding when he said the best thing she could hope to become was a rich man's secretary, or better still a rich man's wife. And even more naive to throw herself into the arms of the most dashing man she'd ever seen and almost beg him to take her to bed.

Almost beg? That wasn't strictly accurate, either.

At least in the ten years since then she'd got well past palpitations and hand-wringing.

She spread out her pale Celtic skinny fingers, frowned them steady. Looked at the single silver ring with *Ipanema* carved in swirling writing—a gift for her fourteenth birthday, worn ever since. She rubbed at it. She still missed that pony. And she still hated the man who had stolen her away.

But at least Ipanema's line was alive and well. She was the dam of two of the ponies on Rocco Hermida's string. His favourites, as he made no secret of telling the world's press. And rumoured to be being used in his groundbreaking genetics programme. *And* about to carry him onto the field and to victory at this charity polo match. Well, that was what everyone here thought anyway. To the home crowd there was not a shred of doubt that Argentina's darling was going to triumph over the Palm Beach team. Totally. Unquestionably. And, with his brother at his side, the crowd would be guaranteed eight chukkas of the most mouthwatering display of virile man candy in the whole of South America.

But Frankie Ryan wasn't drooling or licking her lips. Oh, no.

She was rolling her eyes and shaking her head. As much at herself for her stupid reaction—thankfully she now had that under *total* control—as at the flirty polo groupies all around her.

The fact that Rocco Hermida was here, playing, was completely irrelevant. It really was.

He probably didn't even remember her…

Which was actually the most galling thing of all. While she had burned with shame and then fury on learning that he'd bought Ipanema, and had then been sent off to the convent, *he* had appeared in her life like a meteor, blazed a trail and as quickly blazed off. He'd never been back in touch. He'd taken her pride and then her joy. But she had learned a lesson. Letting anyone get under her skin like that was never going to happen again.

She had a perfectly legitimate reason for being here that had nothing to do with Rocco Hermida. She might look like a tourist today, but she was full of business. Landing a job as product development manager at Evaña Cosmetics, after slogging her guts out as an overgrown intern and then an underpaid assistant just so she could sock it to her old man was a dream come true!

She could think of worse things than travelling to the Dominican Republic and then Argentina in search of the perfect aloe vera plantation. And she could think of much worse things than an overnighter in Buenos Aires to lap up the polo followed by a weekend at her friend Esme's place in Punta del Este to lap up the sun and the sea.

Bliss.

She got another drink—why not? As long as she was fresh enough to start on her presentation tomorrow she could have a little downtime today. It might even do her good to relax before she went out on her last trips. She still had plenty of time to put it all together into a report before the long flight home and her moment in the boardroom spotlight.

It was *such* a big deal. She'd spent so long convincing the directors to take this leap of faith, to look farther than their own backyard for organic ingredients, to have a unique selling point that was *truly* unique. So while she could play the tourist here today, the last thing she'd do was jeopardise it by getting all caught up in Rocco damn Hermida.

She began to thread and weave through the contrasting mix of casual *porteños* and glamorous internationals. On the other side of the giant field, spread out like bunting, she spotted the exclusive white hospitality tents. Esme would be in one of them, playing hostess, smiling and chatting and posing for pictures. As the Palm Beach captain's wife, she was part of the package. Frankie could imagine nothing worse.

An announcement rang like a call to prayer, and another headshot loomed on the giant screens. There he was again. The default scowl back in position, the dark hair swept back and landing in that flop across his golden brow. He was in the team colours, scarlet and black, white breeches and boots. As the camera panned out, she instinctively looked at his thighs. Under the breeches they were hard, strong and covered in the perfect dusting of hair. She knew. She remembered. She'd kissed them.

For a moment she felt dazed, lost in a mist of girlish memories. Her first crush, her first kiss, her first broken heart. All thanks to that man. She drew her eyes off the screen again, scowled at it. Muttered words under her breath that her mother would be shocked to hear, let them slide into the wind with the commentator's jabbering biography—a 'what's not to love?' on the Hurricane—and the brassy notes of a gaudy marching band.

The first chukka was about to start. The air around her sparkled with eager anticipation. She could take her place—she could watch this—and if he turned her stomach with his arrogance she could cheer on Palm Beach. Even if two of his ponies *were* from Ipanema, the Rocco Hermida on those screens was just an imprint of a figment of a teenage girl's infatuation. She owed him nothing.

If only it was that simple.

He was electric.

Each chukka was more dramatic and stunning than the one before.

He galloped like the wind and turned on a sixpence. His scowl was caught on camera, a picture of composed concentration, and when he scored—which he did, ten times—a flash of white teeth was his momentary gift to the crowd.

And of course there was Dante, too. Like a symphony, they flew up and down the field. Damn, damn, *damn*, but it was utterly, magnetically mesmerising.

They won. Of course. And as fluttering blue-and-white flags transformed the stadium and the crowd hollered its love she scooted her way out. Head down, her face a picture of 'seen it all before, can take it or leave it, nothing that special', she made her way round to the ponies—the real reason she was here.

The grooms were hosing down the last of them when she slipped through the fence, and watery arcs of rainbows and silvery droplets filled the air. She sneaked around, watched the action. She loved this. She missed it. Until this moment she hadn't realised how much.

Everyone was busy, the chat was lively and the whole place was buzzing at the fabulous result. Of course the Palm Beach team were no pushovers, and Esme would be satisfied, but the day belonged to Rocco Hermida. And Dante. As expected.

As soon as she had taken a little peep at the two ponies she wanted to see she'd head off, have a soak in the tiny enamel bath in her hotel's en-suite bathroom. She would use some of the marketing gifts from the last plantation: a little essential oil to help her relax, and a little herbal tea to help her sleep. She'd been on the go for twenty-four hours. Even if she did make the party tonight, which

Esme seemed so determined she would, sleep was going to have to feature somewhere.

No one was paying her any attention. She didn't blame them. Small and slight and unremarkable, she tended to pass under most people's radar. Unlike the polo scene groupies, who were just like the ponies—all perfect teeth, lean bodies and long legs. Treated as a boy until she'd re-alised herself that being a girl was a lot more fun, she'd run with her brothers, ridden the horses and wandered wild and free all over the farm. Until the day that she had flown out of the stables to hunt for her brothers and run straight into Rocco Hermida.

She would never forget that moment.

Rounding the corner, she'd seen him, blazing like sunshine after thunder in the shadows of the muddy lane. He'd stood and stared. She'd slammed to a stop and gawped at him. She had never seen anything more brilliant, more handsome, more menacing. He'd looked her over, taken his time. Then he'd turned back to Mark and Danny and wandered away, rattling off questions in his heavily accented English, turning her life on its head, oblivious.

Now he was responsible for this world-class string of ponies, his world-class genetics programme and a whole host of other businesses. But polo was his passion. Every-one knew that. And the giant horse transporter with 'Her-manos Hermida' on it, parked at the rear of the *campo* and drawing her closer, was an emblem of how much care he put into his ponies.

It was immaculate. A haven. Ponies were hosed down, dried off and resting in their stalls. Gleaming and proud. She walked amongst them, breathing in their satisfied air. Where were her girls? She was so keen to see the mix of thoroughbred and Argentinian pony, trained to world-class perfection. She knew she'd recognise Ipanema's progeny—the ponies he'd kept on the string were her living image. She felt sure she would feel some kind of connection with them.

'*Que estas haciendo aqui?*'

Right behind her. Frankie started at the quiet growl. Her stomach twisted. Her whole body froze.

'Did you hear me? I said, what are you doing?'

Words stuck, she willed herself calm. 'Just looking,' she finally managed.

'Turn round.'

She would not—could not.

'I said, turn round.'

If she'd been in the heart of an electric storm she couldn't have felt more charged. The voice she hadn't heard for years was as familiar as if he had just growled those unforgettable words, 'You are too young—get out of here!'

A pony turned its head and stared at her with a huge brown eye. Her heart thunder-pulsed in her chest. Her legs felt weak. But from somewhere she found a spark of strength. He might be the most imposing man she had ever known, but she was her own woman now—not a little girl. And she wouldn't let herself down again.

She turned. She faced him. She tilted up her chin.

He stared, took a pace towards her. Her heel twitched back despite herself.

'I knew it was you.'

She forced her eyes to his even as the low growl in his voice twisted around her.

He was still in his playing clothes, his face flushed with effort and sweat, his hair mussed and tousled. Alive and vital and male. She could hardly find the strength to stand facing him, eyeing him, but she was determined to hold her own in the face of all that man.

'I came to see Ipanema's mares.'

Her words were stifled and flat in the perfectly climate-controlled air. Another pony stamped and turned its head.

'You came to see *me*.'

Her eyes widened in shock and she spluttered a laugh. 'Are you joking?'

He stepped back from her, tilted his head as if she was a specimen at some livestock market and he might, just might, be tempted.

He raised an eyebrow. Shook his head—the slightest movement. 'No.'

He was appalling, arrogant—outrageous in his ego.

'Look, think what you like—and I'm sorry I didn't ask permission to come to a charity match—but, *really*? Come to see *you*? When I was sixteen I had more than my fill of you.'

A rush of something dangerous, wicked and wondrous flashed over his eyes and he closed the gap between them in a single step. His fingers landed on her shoulder, strong, warm and instantly inflaming. He didn't pull her towards him. He didn't need to. She felt as if she was flush against him, and her body sang with delight.

'You didn't get your fill—not at all.' He curled his lip for a moment. 'But you wanted to.'

The coal-black eyes were trained right on her and she knew if she opened her mouth it would be to whimper. She clamped it shut. She would stare him out and then get the hell away from him.

But his hand moved from her shoulder, spread its warming brand up her neck.

'Frankie… Little Frankie.'

He cupped the back of her head, held her. Just there. She jerked away.

'What?'

If she could have spat out the word with venom she would have, but she was lucky to get it out at all, the way he was simply staring at her.

'All grown-up.'

He took another step. She saw the logo of his team in red silk thread: two balls, two sticks, two letters *H*. She saw the firm wall of muscle under his shirt—hard, wide pecs, the shadow of light chest hair framed in the V. She saw the caramel skin and the wide muscular neck, the heavy pepper of stubble and the rich wine lips. She saw his broken nose, his intensely dark eyes, his questioning brows. And she scented him. Pure man.

That hand was placed on her head—and it felt as if he was the high priest and this was some kind of healing ritual.

One she did not need to receive.

'Yes, all grown-up. And leaving.' She pulled away. 'Let me past. I want to go.'

But he held her. Loosely. His eyes finally dropped to absorb every other possible detail. She could feel his appraisal of her sooty eyes too big for her face; her nose too thin; her mouth too small; her chin too pointed. But instead of stepping back he seemed to swell into the last remaining inch of space and he shook his head.

'In a moment. Where are you staying?'

She wavered—rushed a scenario through her mind of him at her cute little hotel, in her tiny room. Filling up all the space. The picture was almost too hot to hold in her head.

'That doesn't matter. I'm only here for a day or so.'

He was in no hurry to move. She looked away, around,

at the empty glass she somehow still clutched in her hand. Anywhere but at him.

'I think you should stay a little longer. Catch up.'

There was nothing but *him*—his body and his energy. Ten years ago she had dreamed of this moment. She had wept and pined and fantasised. And now she would rather die than give him the satisfaction.

'Catch up with what? I've no wish to go over old ground with you.'

'You think we covered ground? Back then? In that tiny little bed in your farmhouse?'

His words slipped out silken and dark.

'You have no idea, *querida*, how far I would have liked to have gone with you.'

He caught a handful of her bobbed hair and tugged. She flinched—not in pain, but in traitorous delight.

'How far I would go with you now...'

He smoothed a look of hunger all over her face. And her whole body throbbed.

'You've got no chance,' she hissed.

A smile—just a flash. Then his mouth pursed in rebuttal. A shake of his head.

It was enough. She put her hands on him and shoved. Utterly solid—she hadn't a hope. He growled a laugh, but he moved. Stepped to the side.

His tone changed. 'Your horses are resting. They played well. In the stalls at the top. Take your time.'

She pushed past him, desperate to escape from this man, but two steps away she stopped.

She swallowed. 'Thank you.'

'The pleasure is mine, Frankie.' He whispered it, threatened it. 'And I aim to repeat it.'

He left her there. She didn't so much hear him go as feel a dip in the charge in the air. The ponies looked round at her—sympathising, no doubt, with how hard it was to share breathing space with someone who needed his own solar system.

She found her mares. Saw their Irish names—Roisin and Orla—and their white stars, but most of all their infamously wonderful natures, marking them out as Ipanema's. She could never criticise what he had done with them—the effort and love he poured into all of his stock was legendary. And she was proud that Ipanema's bloodlines were here, in one of the best strings in the world. If only Ipanema was still here, too…

Her brother Mark would be delighted. His own expertise was phenomenal in the field of equine genetics and this line had put their stud farm on the map. She knew he kept in touch with Rocco, sharing professional knowledge from time to time, while her father had fumed silently every time his name was mentioned. His suspicions had never been proved, but he'd never let her forget that he had them. Oh, no. And he'd punished her by sending her off to the convent to learn to 'behave'.

But she'd been away from Ireland five years now. Away from that life and forging her own. Madrid was her home; Evaña was her world. Her father had passed the business to Mark and all her contact with beautiful creatures like these was sadly limited to the infrequent trips she made to see him.

She kissed their polished necks and they whickered their appreciation, soothing her heated blood before she went back out into the day.

Sometimes animals were a lot easier to deal with than people. Actually, animals had *always* been easier than people. They had their moods and their own personalities, of course, but they never judged, never made her feel like the slightly gawky, awkward tomboy that everyone else did. Especially Ipanema. Being given her as a foal to bring on had changed her life completely.

She'd loved that pony, and Ipanema had loved her right back, and when she'd been sold to Rocco her heart had taken its first battering.

She stepped out into the warm afternoon. The thrill and roar of the crowd had died down, but the celebrations were only just beginning. There was to be a party at the Molina Lario Hotel later, hosted by the champagne sponsors. Esme had told her to join her there.

It's only the most talked-about event in the charity polo circuit after Dubai and Deauville! You need to let your hair down—there's more to life than work!

But Rocco would most likely be there. And her reserves were running low. Maybe she'd call it a day, lap up the night safe in bed and swerve the whole unfolding drama attached to seeing him again.

She pushed her glasses back up her nose and wound her way round to the flotilla of white hospitality tents, her legs more obedient, less shaky now. But she should have known better than to think she was home free. At the edge of the field and up on the screens were four tall men in red, black and white, four in blue and yellow. All were standing on the podium, and every eye was drawn to them. Even hers.

Round about them were all the beautiful people. She hung back, watched.

A cheer… The cup being passed over, held up. Dante beaming his easy, confident golden smile. Rocco curling his lip. The crowd adoring.

They stepped down and into the flow of people— mostly girls, she noticed. Well, they were nothing but obliging! Letting themselves get all wrapped up in them, posing together in a spray of champagne, moving to another little group. Another pose, a squeeze, kisses on cheeks.

She'd seen it all before, of course—most recently in the pages of various magazines and in online news. But watching it like this she felt a flame of anger burst inside her. Anger at herself for still being there! Still gawping. She was a respected businesswoman now. Not a stupid, infatuated little girl!

She turned and began a fast path out. She'd get a cab, get away, get her head straight.

Her flat-heeled sandals moved swiftly over the grass, her stride long in her cotton sundress. Molina Lario was getting less and less attractive by the moment. More of that? No, thanks. Esme would understand. She knew her feelings for the arrogant Rocco ran to pathological disgust—she just didn't know why.

No one did.

The one thing she could thank him for, she supposed, was igniting that fire for her to get the hell out of County Meath. When she'd watched him swing his rucksack over his shoulder and walk away from her, down the single-track farm lane, through the dawn light and rain dust, she'd realised he was heading back into a world wide open with choices and chances. She didn't need to be tied to County Meath, to Ireland, to the narrow options of which her dad thought her capable.

She'd taken a cold hard look at herself. Skinny, flat chested, unattractive and unkempt. Her dressing table cluttered with riding trophies instead of make-up. And when she'd stopped wailing and sobbing into her pillow she'd plotted her escape.

And now here she was—out in the world.

And here she would stay—proving them all wrong.

Head down, she reached the gates.

Just as a figure in black stepped alongside her. Large, male, reeking of strength.

'Señor Hermida asks that you join him.'

A rush…a thrill thrummed through her. For a moment she felt the excitement of flattery. Tempted.

But, no. That way disaster lay. She was headed in a whole different direction.

She didn't even break her step.

'Not today. Or any other day, thanks.'

She eyed the gate like a target board, upped her pace. Lost him.

Almost at the gate, she felt his presence again.

'Miss Ryan, Señor Hermida will collect you later for the party. 10:00 p.m. At your hotel.'

She spun on her heel, ready to fire a vicious volley of words right back. But he was walking away, obscured by the hundreds of people crossing in front of her. As obscured as her own feelings at seeing the Hurricane.

So sure he'd mean nothing to her, she'd turned up as if it was all in a day's work to bump into him. But skulking about in the crowds, sneaking among the horses when she could so easily have done things properly…? She should have asked Mark to set it up. That was what someone who truly wasn't fazed would have done—brushed off what had happened between them and joined him for a drink and a chat for old times' sake…

Instead of spontaneously combusting when he'd come up behind her.

He was dangerous. The last thing she needed.

Her career was her life. Not ponies. Or polo. Or dark, intense men who lit up her body and squeezed at her heart.

She emerged onto the pavement like a hostage set free. He didn't know her hotel. And he didn't know *her*.

Collect her later? Arrogant fool. One overbearing father and two extremely alpha brothers did *not* make Frankie Ryan anyone's pushover.

She would be swaddled in Do Not Disturbs and deep, deep sleep. He could just cross her off his list and move to the next name. There were bound to be hundreds.

CHAPTER TWO

'So MANY GIRLS, so little time,' Dante mouthed, and winked at him over the heads of the two dancers from Rio who had just wound themselves around him.

Well, that was him taken care of for the evening—or the next couple of hours at least.

Rocco had just peeled a sweet little blonde from hm. Normally his preferences did run to sweet little blondes, but tonight... He strode to the wide windows that ran the length of the Art Hotel penthouse—Dante's go-to joint for post-match partying. Tonight he was well off his game.

He braced his hands on the glass and stared out across Palermo to the outskirts, where he knew her hotel was. One phone call and he'd found out everything he needed to know. One phone call that had confirmed she was in town long enough for him to scratch the itch that had started all those years ago.

The blonde put her arms around his waist again. He was losing patience with her, but she would be well looked after—by someone else.

He looked round at his team members and friends. All getting into the party spirit one way or another. For Rocco the party wouldn't start until he had Frankie Ryan in his arms. Then and only then would he get rid of this tension that had built almost to a frenzy since he'd seen her sneaking into the transporter.

He checked his watch.

Too early, but he had a feeling she wasn't going to be waiting on the steps of her hotel wearing an expectant look and a corsage. No, something told him that she was going to be a little less easy to convince than the now-sulking blonde, who'd finally realised he wasn't just playing hard to get.

He called his driver. He couldn't wait anymore.

'Dante—I will catch you up.'

His brother, busy, lifted an arm in acknowledgement. He hadn't told him he'd seen her at the match. Wasn't in the mood for questions. Why? Because he barely understood himself why this slip of a girl, now a woman, had occupied so much of his head for so long.

The last time Dante had raised the subject with him, after a particularly broody day in Dublin when he'd failed to make contact with her, it hadn't gone well. He'd called her Rocco's 'Irish obsession'. It was probably the only time they'd failed to agree on anything. He'd admit it now, though. He was definitely obsessing about her now.

He checked his phone, his money and, for the first time in a long time, his appearance. He knew how he looked. He wasn't coy or stupid. Normally it was irrelevant. There were far, far more important things in this world—like loyalty, like honour. Like family...

And if he was honest, that penthouse full of beautiful women back there...? None of them interested him more than the skinny, hazel-eyed Irish kid he'd met ten years earlier. A little bit of closure on that particular puzzle would be good—it had been a long time coming.

He swung into the back of the sedan. An hour earlier than he'd suggested and the city was limbering itself up for the night ahead. The party at Molina Lario would be good, for starters. But he was feeling post-match wired and just this side of in control. He spread his arms across the back of the seat, watched the sights of his town slip past. A bit of Barcelona here…a look of Paris there. The spill of people on wide streets, corners alive with café culture. Vibrant, creative and free.

But he was no romantic fool. Yes, he loved it. Loved it that he had run its streets and slept in its parks. Loved it that he had survived. Was grateful that he had survived when so many others had fallen or, perhaps worse, were living the legacy of those years in prisons or still on the streets. He would never, ever forget or take that for granted.

But all he had—his wealth, his businesses, his health, his adoptive family—all of that he would trade right now for one more day with Lodo. One more chance to shield him and protect him and cherish him—better than he'd managed last time…

The car cruised to a stop. They were here. He hadn't been in this part of town for years. Villa Crespo was outside Palermo and on the up, but he would have preferred that she'd stayed closer to the centre, where the worst that could happen was pickpocketing. He got out. Looked around. It seemed quiet enough. The hotel was traditional—a single frontage villa. Ochres and oranges. Cute, he supposed. He went inside.

The concierge was startled to see him, and he jumped up from his TV screen, gave him the details he needed. Her room, first floor; her visitors, none; and her movements, she'd been in her room since her return earlier.

He ignored the old cage elevator and took the stairs three at a time. If she felt about him the way he thought she did they could stay in her room. No problem. Or they could hang out for a while and then go on to another party, or back to Dante's pad, or even to the estancia. It had been a long time since he'd taken a woman back there. But he felt even now that one night with Frankie Ryan might not be enough. An undisturbed weekend? That might just about slake this thirst for her.

He stood outside her door.

Dark polished wood. Brass number five.

He knocked. Twice. Rapid. Impatient.

Nothing.

She should be getting ready, at the very least.

He knocked again.

Still nothing.

He'd opened his mouth to growl out her name when the door swung open.

And there she was.

Bleary eyed, hair mussed and messy, one bony white shoulder exposed by the slipped sleeve of her pale blue nightdress, her face screwed up against the light from the hall.

He'd never seen anything more adorable in his life.

'Frankie.'

He stepped forward, the urge to grab hold of her immense.

But she put a hand to her head, set her features to a scowl and opened her mouth in an incredulous O.

'What—what are *you* doing here?'

He still couldn't believe how sleepily, deliciously gorgeous she looked. His eyes roamed all over her—the eyemask now awry, the milky pale skin and the utter lack of anything under that thin jersey nightdress. It clung to her fine bones and tiny curves. As beguiling as he remembered, though maybe her breasts were rounder, fuller...

'What are you—? Why are you—? I told your guy I wasn't coming.'

He dragged his eyes back to her face. Heard a noise at the end of the corridor. The concierge was peeping, making an 'everything all right?' face, wielding a pass key. Rocco nodded, put up his hand to keep him back.

'Let me in, Frankie.'

She seemed almost to choke out her answer. 'No!'

'Okay, I'll wait here—get dressed.'

'I'm. Not. Coming.'

He was slightly amused. Slightly. The irony of the situation was not lost on him.

'We've been here before, *querida*, only last time it was you on the other side of the door. Remember?'

And there it was—that wildness he had seen all those years ago. That almost wantonness she'd exuded that he'd found exhilarating, intoxicating. She leaned out into the corridor, to check who was there, then looked right up at him. He drew his eyes away from the gaping lines of her nightdress, followed her gaze.

'I can't believe you're actually standing here!'

'It would be better if I came in. As I recall, that was your preference last time.'

'I was *sixteen*! I made a mistake!' She blazed out her answer.

Then she gripped her arms round herself. All that happened was that the neckline of her nightdress splayed open even more, letting him see right to the tip of one small high breast. He reached forward, gently lifted the fabric and tugged it back into position, ignoring her futile attempts to swat his arm away.

'Why don't we discuss that inside?'

His hand hovered, then retracted. He badly wanted to touch her, but he was nothing if not a reader of women and he sensed she was going to need more than a pep talk to get her on-message.

'You made yourself perfectly plain the last time we met. And I don't have any wish to spend any more time with you. I *told* your guy. I couldn't have been plainer.'

'The last time we met was four hours ago. You were in my horse transporter. You came looking for me.'

She was so wild, standing there in next to nothing. He was getting harder and harder just looking at her. Memories came of her slipping into his bed, waking him up with her naive little kisses and her hot little body. Him literally pushing her out of his bed—like rejecting heaven.

Her eyes blazed. 'I came looking for our bloodline, not *you*! You arrogant ar—'

He put his finger on her lips where they framed the word he knew she was about to launch at him. Her eyes widened even more.

'Don't belittle yourself, *querida*.' He lowered his voice, stepped closer. 'Go inside, get dressed, and I will take you to the party and tell you everything you want to know about your ponies.'

But lightning-quick she grabbed for his hand and tried to pull it away. The sleeve of her nightdress fell lower and the pull of the fabric strained on her breasts. Her nipples, twin buds, drew his eyes—and, damn it, the flame of heat coursed straight to his groin.

'I call it as I see it, and I see you as an—'

He couldn't hold back. She fired him, inflamed him. He wanted to taste her so badly. He had to contain her, have her mouth under his.

She lifted her arms to push him and he scooped her wrists together, pinned them behind her. Then he heaved her against him and crushed her insolent mouth. Fragile but strong, she strained and stiffened and held her lips closed. Which just drove him wilder! He could smell her desire. He could taste her passion. So why was she so intent on keeping him back?

He gripped her head and stared into her eyes.

Her hands flew to his wrists. She dug in her nails. She flashed and fumed and forced out her breath through the clenched teeth in her mouth. But she didn't pull back, and he needed to *know*. He grabbed her hips and ground her into his hard, throbbing length, felt her sweet mound and watched her shocked face.

And he saw. Oh, yes. *Oh. Yes.* She told him. Her eyes closed. Her head dropped back and she moaned. Dark and deep and long.

That was it. All he needed to know.

He thrust her away, spun her round, slapped her backside.

'Get in there. Get dressed. Meet me outside. You have half an hour.'

He'd had to get back onto the street—get some air. Calm his blood.

So he'd been right all these years when he'd wondered if he was idolising a memory. If she really had fired him up as fast and hard as his youthful body had ever experienced.

He really should have been given a medal after that weekend. The utterly overt way she'd tried to seduce him had been sweet, but he doubted her family had thought so. And they hadn't known the half of it.

From the first moment when he'd seen her in filthy jodhpurs to her sidling up beside him at dinner as he'd tried to keep focussed on the deal he was supposed to be there to cut with her brother, her face covered in make-up she'd clearly had no notion of how to apply, and wearing a dress—which had seemed to cause her family some amusement. To the full-blown assault of her coming into his room.

Kiss me, Rocco.

That look in her eyes…the shadow between her open wet lips. He had wanted to—so badly. She'd blown his mind. But of course he had chased her away. What kind of guy took advantage of a girl five years younger, barely aware of her own sexuality, acting as if she'd never even been kissed? And there was the fact that her family's hospitality to him had been beyond reproach… She was off limits, and then some.

But in the predawn light she'd woken him again. Naked. In his bed. The memory still packed a punch.

He had been disorientated, but harder than he had ever thought possible. Seconds, maybe minutes had passed as they'd found each other, and he'd done things he should never have done. But thank God he had stopped in time—before it had gotten out of hand. She had begged and wailed and made it even harder for him to send her away. So in the end he'd left himself. After one look back at her, wrapped in a sheet, all eyes and white skin. One look that he had never erased from his mind.

He pushed up off the sedan's door, walked, paced down the street. He had already drawn attention to himself. He should be waiting in the car. A crowd was starting to gather—people who were wondering what the hell the captain of the polo team that had just won the biggest charity match ever seen in Palermo was doing, tonight of all nights, outside a midrange hotel in Villa Crespo.

He checked his watch.

Forty minutes.

And then he knew.

She wasn't coming.

He stared up at the first-floor windows. Maybe a curtain twitched.

The throng of interested happy people watched and waited. The concierge wrung his hands at the door.

Rocco turned away from the crowd. Got into the car. Nodded to his driver and was driven off through the streets.

What kind of stupid game was she playing? They had unfinished business. A hot physical agenda to work through and close down. It was that simple—that straightforward. Where did all this chasing feature? He was *Rocco Hermida*. He didn't *chase*. Not like this. Not like a stupid adolescent.

If she wanted him the way he knew she wanted him she could damn well quit her coy little act and juvenile games. She could come and get him. And she would.

He smiled grimly at the passing scenery as he made his way back to Recoleta. Yes, she would. He would lay money on it. His Irish obsession? *Su obsesion Argentina!* *Her* Argentinian obsession. She was right in it with him. Up to her neck.

Frankie pulled closed the curtain as the sleek black car skirted the corner and vanished. She stepped back into the shabby-chic room and sat down on the edge of the bed. In a short silk shift, her arms and legs bare but slick with oil, she looked as good as it got.

Her hair was washed, conditioned and straightened into a sleek, shiny bob. Her face was clear, the dark circles camouflaged by the miracle concealer her company were just about to launch. She had lined her eyelids with shadow the same blue as her dress and coated her lashes in black. Lip gloss plumped her lips and the lightest hint of bronzer dusted her cheeks. She'd come a long, long way from the pony-mad teenager who'd tried to bag Rocco Hermida.

So why had she not quite been able to follow through?

One look at the television screen showing the pictures the rest of the world would be watching—well, the rest of the polo world—had confirmed it all. Rocco, Dante and their teammates. Pictures of the match, of the cup being presented, of the fans in and outside the stadium. Of the women who'd featured past and present on the arm of the Hurricane. A never-ending cornucopia of beautiful blondes. One after another after another.

The TV programme was admittedly more focussed on his love life than on his sporting prowess, but still Frankie had been utterly transfixed by the flow.

And when the final pictures of the piece had showed the team heading off with a troupe of polo groupies to a luxury penthouse in a luxury *barrio* this very evening she had sat down and sighed. *Really?* It was one thing to offer yourself on a plate to a playboy aged sixteen. It was another thing entirely to do it when you were twenty-six. Especially when she had more than a hunch of what would follow.

He'd unleashed something in her that no other man could. He had barely touched her and she had almost screamed with need. He had kissed her and it had been all she could do not do jump into his arms and wrap herself round him. And when he'd put his hands on her hips and ground them together…

The ten years she had waited had flashed and were gone and she was back in his arms, in his bed, with that first white-hot flame of passion. But all she'd gained in the past four hours was the knowledge that he saw her as unfinished business. Was she really going to let herself become that? An arm-candy statistic? Would it be *her* face that flashed up next? Entering the Molina Lario at his side for the whole world to see? The whole world, including her father...

She had battled her way out of the black fog of depression, had rebuilt herself piece by piece, layer by layer, after her father had stripped her bare of everything she'd ever cared about. Hidden her away and punished her. The bruise of the slap that had landed across her cheek had faded so much faster than the bruise that had bloomed across her heart for all those years.

Was being Rocco's 'Irish squeeze' going to be her legacy? Her mother would have a fit and her father would roll his 'I told you so' eyes.

She lifted up the remote control and changed the channel to some glitzy, ritzy soap opera—probably much like Rocco Hermida's life. And what would *her* part be? The beautiful heroine? Hardly. More like the kooky best friend put in as a comedy foil. Because that was the other thing—she didn't really measure up as his type of leading lady. She was distinctly lacking on all the fronts he seemed to major in—like big hair and big breasts. And, though her confidence was never rock bottom now, it was hardly skyscraper high, either.

A tiny part of her did wonder, even if she arrived at Molina Lario with Rocco, was sure she would leave with him, too? After all, she'd never managed to stay the course with any previous man.

She was twenty-six. She was doing well for herself. She didn't need to create a whole load of heartache. So she'd waited ten years to see if he was still as hot as she remembered? Answer—yes. What was the next question? Was there going to be a day after the morning-after? Answer—no. Conclusion—*put all thoughts of Rocco Hermida out of your head. And don't spend the next ten years in the same state of perpetual wonder as the past ten.*

There were bound to be other men who could light her up like he did. Surely!

Frankie turned the television off altogether and sighed. Her phone flashed and she leaned across to the bedside table to check it. Esme.

Hey, beautiful. We need you! Come shake off your jet lag and meet the Palm Beach boys. Told them all about you so you'd better get here soon! No excuses! X

She stared at the message. She could pretend she hadn't seen it. She could turn her phone off and read her emails instead. But, knowing Esme, she'd turn up and drag her out anyway. So should she? Meet the Palm Beach boys? Maybe that would be just the thing to cure this once and for all. To go. Confront her demon. Let the dream shatter for good. And maybe she'd even get herself worked up over some other handsome man who was just a fraction less arrogant, less dominant, less utterly overwhelming.

The phone lit up again.

The car's on its way. Tango time! X

That was decided, then. She stood up. In her silver sixties slingbacks she made all of five-five—'the height of nonsense', as her father had used to say, and not in a good way. But whatever she was, she was big enough to play in the playgrounds of the *porteños* and their Palm Beach buddies.

She could pull this off. Of course she could. If she could lift herself out of the blackest depression and keep it at bay for all these years she could damn well paint on a smile, slip in and hang out with her best friend.

Esme knew more than anyone that parties weren't her thing, but this was a watershed moment. A mark of her own maturity. She had weighed it all up and traded a night or an hour with Rocco 'Hurricane' Hermida. She had so much more to get from life than an empty inbox and a roll in his hay.

She slipped on the Bolivian silver earrings she'd bought at a market in the Dominican Republic, grabbed her clutch. Incredible that two days earlier she'd bought these earrings, totally unaware that Rocco Hermida would hurricane his way back into her life. But there was nothing surer that in two days' time, regardless of what happened, he would be hurricaning his way back out of it.

Just remember that, she told her wild side. *Remember that and stand well back.*

CHAPTER THREE

THE GLAMOUR OF polo had never held any attraction for Frankie. Sure, she'd learned how to dress, how to style her hair—okay, she'd learned how to plug in straighteners—and since working at Evaña Cosmetics for the past four years she'd grudgingly warmed to the wonders of make-up.

But the hats and the heels, the sponsorship deals and the general buzz about anything related to the ponies or the players she could still, if she was honest, pass on.

Tonight, though, entering the grand Molina Lario Hotel—a French-style mansion house renowned for its exclusive, excessive entertainments—she lapped up the atmosphere and soaked up the vibe. People there exuded something purposeful, joyful and wholly sensual—and it seemed to chime with the city itself. There was passion in the air and there was anticipation all around. She could smell it. She could taste it. Would it be possible, just for a night, that she could actually live it?

She skipped up the carpeted stairs. Cameras flashed ahead, but none flashed at her. She was a nobody. And that suited her perfectly. She glanced at the anything-goes glamour. This was South America meets Europe. It was relaxed, but it was sexy. It was just how she felt. And for once she felt that she'd actually nailed the look.

She wandered through to a lounge that exuded a quiet buzz. Clutches of people were laughing, sipping and looking around. Glasses of Malbec. Bottles of beer. Canapés of steak; morsels of cured meat. Waitstaff in long white aprons and fabulous smiles.

No sign of Esme, but she was in no rush. She wandered back through to the main reception area. An alluring orb of Lalique glass gifted light to the huge oak table below, heaving under the weight of champagne. Its impressive spread drew her closer. Long-stemmed flutes in columns and rows fizzed and popped with tiny clouds of bubbles—*perfect*. That would be her tipple of choice tonight.

Marketing screens were strategically but discreetly placed all around, and here and there the people who made headlines were positioned in poses, eyes on the cameras and smiles for the crowd. The double-H logo of Hermanos Hermida caught her eye and flipped her stomach. So she was immune to him? She was going to pass on him? Really?

Yes, really.

She wasn't naive enough to think that when she saw him her heart wouldn't leap and her blood wouldn't flame. But she was smart enough to know that these were physical reactions. They would pass. And she was *not* going to be held in thrall by her passion for a playboy. Not with the world looking on. Not with so much to lose and so little to gain.

She sipped at her drink and rubbed at her silver ring. A roar of laughter and energy flooded the hallway. A crowd approached along the red carpet. And there he was.

Tall and dark, the flop of hair his instant brand. Blue shirt, dark trousers and a body that her fingers clawed at themselves to touch. Air and energy thrummed around him. Simmering, menacing, mesmerising. Faces turned awestruck and adoring.

Frankie turned away, clutched at the table and steadied herself.

She'd half expected that he would come for her. Chilled when he didn't, she looked back. He and his brother were surrounded by lights, laughter, a myriad of love. He looked at her—just for a moment. Long enough to let her know that he had seen her and had dismissed her.

Was that it? Had she had her moment in the sun? Had he already moved on?

Of course.

She was ridiculous to think otherwise.

Suddenly her 'New Frankie' plan seemed preposterous. She put down the flute, saw the huge smudge of lip gloss on its edge and rubbed at it almost apologetically. Esme must be here somewhere. She would find her and camp out with the Palm Beach crew. That had been her plan all along, and she owed it to Esme and to herself to follow through. It was either that or go back to the hotel. And, really—was she going to give in *that* easily?

Still aware of the Hermida circus to her left, she turned her back and fumbled in her bag, found her phone. Thank God for distraction. And a text from Esme.

Hurry up! Tango Bar—Hugo waiting. ;-)

There were lots of Hugos in the world of polo, but only one on the Palm Beach team. He was nice, she supposed—a tall, square-jawed picture of health and handsomeness. And he played well—really well. But the thought of small talk with such a big guy held very little appeal.

She clicked off her phone and dropped it back in her bag. Still, if she was going to make a go of the evening, she'd better fill it with something other than the mouth-watering sight of Rocco.

Her eyes slipped away of their own accord, to see if she was even on his radar, but he was now in front of the screens, his arms round some girls, gaze straight ahead. The understated scowl of a smile just added to his allure and made her recoil like a sulky cat. So she was *that* disposable?

Tango music drifted up the stairs, meaning that she was going to have to walk past the impromptu photo-shoot to get to it. She could do that. Sure she could.

Trying to paint 'not bothered' all over her face, she tilted up her chin and began her stalk past. A photographer stepped back to get a better shot and she had to swerve swiftly to avoid him. Her ankle twisted in her shoe and she swallowed a yelp of pain.

Big biceps reached out, steadied her. She looked up, startled, into the face of Dante Hermida. Like a sunbeam of happiness he sorted her stumble, flooded her path with smiles.

'Hey—are you okay?'

His touch was disarming, warming, lingering just that second more than necessary.

Solid—like a brother's.

'Fine. Thanks.'

'Are you sure? You seemed in a bit of a rush, there.'

Frankie opened her mouth to speak, but a figure immediately loomed up, put an arm across Dante's shoulder, steering him round.

'I'll take over here.'

Rocco. Like an unexploded bomb.

His brother didn't lose a beat.

'You reckon?'

Rocco didn't even reply, just exuded danger.

Frankie stared from the bemused smile of Dante to the intense frown of his brother. Like a wall of testosterone. One of them was hard to cope with, but two was ridiculous.

Looking past them was not an option. Rocco's eyes demanded hers. Her heart thundered in her ears. Resolve began to crack and crumble.

She spoke up into the rock-like face. 'Thanks—that's kind of you, but I'm going to meet my friends.'

Dante laughed, thumped Rocco on the back.

'You win some…'

Rocco continued to stare. One second more and she would cave in completely. She had to go. She dragged her eyes back and, head down, she bolted. Distance was her only hope. Because there was something he did to her that nobody else could do.

He entranced her. Absorbed her. All she could see were those eyes. She could still feel the touch of his lips. Longed for them.

It was frightening just how much.

She rattled down the sweep of stairs, glanced back— couldn't not. He was staring down. In the sea of people his eyes were trained on hers.

She kept going. Another close encounter? Another lucky escape? Why did it feel as if the hunt was on—that it was only a matter of time?

The Tango Bar was dark and the caress of the music was mesmerising. Simple piano melodies and the undercurrents of slow-burning passion thrummed through the room. She scanned the shadowy space for Esme and within moments had tracked down her party. Another bunch of golden-skinned, smiling sunbeams, not even dusky in the gloom.

Esme was in her element, surrounded by handsome men like cabana boys, and their attention was forced on Frankie as Esme spotted her. Introductions flew past in a good-natured blur and ended with her being set up with Hugo.

Which should work—if she managed to stop her three-sixty swivels, checking who was coming and going from the bar. If she could settle with her champagne and enjoy the company—because it was fun! Everyone was having a good time. Her, too. Damn right she was!

Anyway, Esme wasn't great with no, so she would stay—as long as she didn't pull a muscle forcing this smile—and then slink off back to her adorable little bed. She'd get up for brunch and then catch some sights or work on her presentation before she joined Esme to take the short trip to Punta.

Rocco *who*? He'd be so far in the past by then that she might even need to be prompted to remember him. And that was good. It *was*. What was bad was this unhealthy obsession that had gripped her in the past few hours. It was like being sixteen all over again.

But she was twenty-six. In Argentina. On a business-with-pleasure trip. She was accomplished, confident… *ish* and worldly. She caught herself starting another head twist and forced a redirect onto the dance floor. Surely this next round of dancing with these outrageously sensual dancers would focus her on something other than Rocco Hermida.

She sat on the edge of her small wooden seat, watching Buenos Aires at its best. This passion was what she'd felt all evening. *This* was why this city was alive as no other. Lingering looks, perfect posture, movements laced with stark innuendo. The trail of the male dancers' hands over their partners and the mirrored responses. Truly, she was spellbound.

When the first round of tunes had passed a dancer approached her, and she rose as if in a trance to join him on the floor. Esme whooped behind her and she suddenly wondered how she'd got to the edge of the floor, in the light grasp of this man, when she was pretty likely to make a fool of herself.

Those dreaded Saturday-morning dance lessons might turn out to be useful after all. Six months of her life, dragged there by her mother, who'd been worried she would turn into a boy completely.

There had been no way Frankie would signed up for the local Irish-dancing classes, for fear any of her classmates would see her. But she had reluctantly agreed to a block of ballroom lessons, which everyone had found strange at the time. Strange—but no one had complained. And she might have kept it up—it had been quite fun— but her Saturday mornings had been precious. They'd been for ponies and stick-and-ball practice. So, age fourteen, she'd put her foot down and refused to return. Stubborn, she supposed. At least that what everyone had said she was.

And proud.

So she kept her head up now and moved in the way he directed, basic steps coming back to her moment by moment. She'd been so charged since she'd arrived in this city she felt as if she must be oozing passion, and this dance was just what she needed to get some of it out. She stepped as he stepped and turned when he threw her, spilled herself back into his arms.

Right back. Right in front of Rocco.

There, at another small table at the side of the floor,

he was sitting. Watching. One arm over the back of the chair, strong legs splayed open. Face in a scowl of such intensity. He stared right into her eyes. She felt her legs almost buckle. But she was scooped up and she finished the dance. Clearly a novice, but she hadn't disgraced herself. Except for that moment.

The music stopped. A kiss of her hand and she was escorted back to her seat. Everyone whooped at her bravado, high-fived her first-timer success, and she sat flushed and alive and breathless.

And then he was up. On his feet. Walking onto the floor. Walking around a female dancer. Stirring up the crowd. As the melody started, the place buzzed and bubbled expectantly.

'He dances as he plays,' she heard Hugo say. 'And he used to box. Lightning reflexes—fearless and utterly controlled. What a guy.'

He was everyone's hero.

His partner—blond hair slick and tied at the nape of her neck, short red low-cut dress, nude high heels—dipped her eyes and her head and answered his sensual commands. Wound her body slowly with his, stepped in quicksilver paces and flicked lightning-fast kicks. Rubbed her hands all over him. And he stood there. Directing her. Absorbing her. Tall, straight, thoroughbred man. They were electrifying.

Frankie's heart pulsed. It was too much. Too much to bear. She shoved herself up from the table and pushed her way out through the crowd. Hating her stupid, ridiculous reaction to watching this man! He was just a man! So why had she given him this power over her?

She raged as she made her way upstairs and along a dimly lit porticoed hallway to the ladies' room. A five-minute break and she'd go back to Esme, tell her she was done for the night, and then head off to her bed. It was still only 2:00 a.m., and they'd all be out for hours, but she'd had enough. She would work on her presentation tomorrow, meet up with Esme and then head for Punta. Then her last trip out to the Pampas and then back to Madrid. She couldn't wait.

She brushed her hair, reapplied lip gloss and scowled at herself. Enough was enough. She was back in the game. Time to take control properly. Today could be chalked up to a bad trip down memory lane, but it ended here. Now.

She pushed the doors open to go and let Hugo down gently and bid Esme good-night.

But one step out into the quiet corridor and her arm was tugged, her hand clasped and off she was dragged. Rocco took four strides and turned into a dark alcove. He hauled her round and threw her down onto a hard velvet love seat as if he was still choreographing a dance. She fell down and her head fell back.

'Is *this* what you want, Frankie? You tease me, stand me up—then flaunt yourself all around this party— dancing like an orgasm is waiting to explode from your body! And you think I'll just stand back and watch?'

She gripped the sides of the seat and faced him. Her dress had ridden up and her bare legs skittered out in front of her. She breathed and fumed through angry teeth and stared up at his furious face, still working out what had just happened.

'I thought more of you than that. All these years I have respected your memory. I never had you pegged as a little tease.'

She saw her own hand flying out in front of her to slap him. But he grabbed it and hauled her to her feet. The love seat dug into the backs of her legs. His body was flush with her front. His fury was too close, too real.

His hand still circled her forearm and she tugged it free. 'Let go of me! Let me *go*. Go and dance with your blonde. I don't want anything to do with you—I don't want my name associated with you!'

He fumed, dipped his head closer to her. All she could see were glittering black eyes.

'So that's it? You want my body and my bed but you don't want anyone to know? You're still trying to play the good girl? Even though it's obvious to anyone here tonight that you are desperate for my touch.'

As he spoke he trailed one featherlight finger over her cheek. She shuddered. Feverish.

He drew his head back an inch and smiled like the devil.

'*Desperada,*' he whispered.

Then he reached behind her and squeezed her backside, pulling her into furious contact with his pelvis again.

She opened her mouth, but the raging defence she'd intended to spit out died in her throat. There was no defence. She burned for him. She ached for him. She had to have him or she would never, ever be complete.

She reached for his face. Grabbed hold of his head in her hands and pulled it down—pulled down that mouth she had dreamed of and kissed it.

She thought she might drown.

Her fingers threaded and gripped his hair. His cheekbones pressed into her palms. Hot wet lips pushed against hers. His tongue darted into her mouth and her legs gave way. He licked and suckled and smoothed his tongue over hers.

He grabbed her head with one hand and the cheeks of her backside with the other. He pulled her flush against him. Hard against him. She moaned his name and he silenced the sound. He breathed her in and she breathed him. Her hands flew around, grabbing hair and shirt and skin. She moaned again and again. His mouth was on her throat, kissing and biting, and then moving back to her lips. She snaked her leg round his waist, heaved herself up as close as she could.

He walked them two paces, then slammed her against the wall.

'You little wildcat. You crazy little wildcat.'

They were the first words he'd said, his breath in her ear as he held her against the wall with his body and ran his hands over her, up and under her dress. He found her panties and tugged them to the side, slicked fingers across her soaked, swollen flesh. The bullet of pleasure careered to her core and she bucked. Once, twice.

'Rocco…' she cried into his shoulder.

'Here? In this hallway? We wait ten years and it is to be *here*?'

He barely touched her and she cried out again—almost a scream.

Over his shoulder she saw a figure, but she didn't care.

He must have sensed it, for he immediately slid her to the ground and sorted out her dress. She stood like a rag doll. He tilted up her chin, smoothed her hair, looked at her with eyes blazing and glinting and fierce.

Then he cupped her face and bent down for a kiss. Slower, softer, but still a kiss that killed her. He tilted his brow to rest it on hers and held her close in his arms. She felt the heat, the strength, the fire of this man all around her.

'I want you so badly. I want you like I've never wanted any other woman. *Ever.*'

He pushed back from her, still holding her head, stayed nose to nose with her.

'You are with me now. The games are over.'

He kissed her again, fiercely branded her mouth with his tongue. Then he stepped back, ran one hand through his hair and took her hand in the other.

'Come. We will go to my home.'

She started to move in a passionate trance, her legs and her head swimming and weak.

'Wait—I need to tell Esme. I'm with her.'

'Brett Thompson's wife? I told her already. I told her you were leaving with me. Told her *and* Hugo. As if I would let you spend another moment with *him*.'

She processed that. 'You did what? When did you do that?'

He looked down the hallway, tension and command rolling off him. 'You'd left your table. I asked where you had gone. They presumed to the restrooms, so I told them you wouldn't be returning—we had unfinished business.'

She stalled and her eyes flew open.

'You said *that*?'

'What? Was there really going to be another outcome, *querida*? Did I force your tongue into my mouth and your legs around my waist?'

Without waiting for an answer, he led her off down the plush carpet of the hall.

Oil-painted bowls of fruit and soft amber lamps lined their path. At the end, the giant Lalique chandelier marked the entrance and the exit. The table below it was cleared of champagne, its gleaming oak surface smoothly and proudly uncluttered. A few people still milled around. More rested in armchairs, their voices lower, softer, tired.

And outside the night was turning to day and the day was only beginning.

CHAPTER FOUR

Rocco HAD THREE HOUSES and one boat. His town house in Recoleta was mere streets away. They could walk it. His estancia, La Colorada, was two hours away by car. His seafront villa in Punta del Este was a short helicopter trip away. And his boat was somewhere off the coast of Cayman.

His head rolled options like dice as he palmed the small of Frankie's back and escorted her out.

He wanted unrestricted, uninterrupted access and time with this woman. He deserved it—he needed it. And so did she.

He glanced at her and she turned big hazel eyes up to him. He put his arm round her shoulders and squeezed her into his side. She reached up and touched his chest, scraped her fingers across the new wound that throbbed under his shirt. Better than any physio, she would be the ultimate remedy for every last thumping bruise and cut from today's match.

'How long until you go back to Europe?'

He nodded to the doorman and walked her down the carpeted steps. His car rolled into view. He checked each way and across the street. Nobody. He checked behind them. Clear. He always checked. He was always his own security, but he was hers, too—for now.

'A week. We go to Punta del Este later today—Esme and Brett and me. Then I have a business trip to the Pampas on Thursday. Flying back on Friday.'

So she was heading to Punta, too?

'They'll be going to the Turlington Club party,' he said, almost to himself. So was he. He never missed it.

But if the world was heading to Punta, he would be heading in the opposite direction. With Frankie.

'I'll take you to Punta. Tomorrow.'

Dice rolled. Decision made.

She stopped right there on the pavement, a flare of anger replacing the passion that had flooded her body. 'I told you my plans. There's no way I'm changing them.'

'No? You've already changed them. You're here now. Are you really saying that you'd rather lie on a beach with your friend than climb into bed with me?'

He trailed a thumb across her jaw as her mouth pursed, framed a retort, then slid into a sexy smirk.

She dipped her eyes, then fired him a look. 'I'll give you a day of my time. After that I'm back on plan.'

He couldn't help but smile back. He didn't normally deal well with independence—women were all about love, not combat. But for the few hours they were going to have together, it wasn't going to be a deal-breaker. So far it had even added to her allure. *So far...*

He kept his hand on her jaw.

'I'll take your kind offer of a day.'

He stepped a little closer to her, gripped her chin a little more firmly and watched as she dragged a breath in through bared teeth.

'And since that's all you're offering, we're not going to waste a moment. I've got a place round the corner...'

His eyes dropped to her mouth. Wet lips.

'If you behave yourself I'll take you to your friends

so you're…"back on plan". Does that meet with your approval?'

Her narrowed eyes signalled that she knew he was mocking her.

'It does.'

'Excellent. Our first compromise. We'll head straight to my town house, then.'

He held open the car door and waited. She fired him a look that told him he'd only won the first round. Then she slid inside. He scanned the street again and joined her.

The moment he closed the door they slammed together across the leather.

Seconds later and the flames roared around them. A pyre of passion.

But she hauled herself back, splayed her hands on his thighs and looked up, straight into his eyes.

'Just for the record, I wasn't playing games. I went to the party because I didn't want to let Esme down—not to flaunt myself in front of you. If it hadn't been for her I'd still be tucked up in my bed. So consider yourself lucky.'

Still in combat.

He grabbed her bare arms, his fingers closing round them easily. He stifled a chuckle. Nodded seriously. 'Oh, I do—I do.'

But suddenly he was struck by just how close they'd come—how far they'd journeyed. How easily they could have lost this opportunity. How hard he needed to pursue her just to scratch this itch.

He added quietly, 'I think there's more than luck at work here. It was always going to end this way with us.'

The car moved slowly; the darkness loomed. Her heaving breaths answered him. Her skin looked silvery smooth, each slim arm still braced on his thighs. She was mesmerising.

He grabbed a handful of silky hair and tugged her head back. He wanted to savour every second, to devour her, to linger over every moment like an eight-course, wine-matched gourmet meal—to swallow her whole.

He met her mouth as she reached for his—succulent as watermelon, sweeter than syrup.

He tasted. Lost himself. Scooped her like sauce onto his lap and let her soak against him.

He sat back as she straddled him…as they went up in flames again.

Seconds more and the car turned a corner, then stopped. They were here.

He reached for the door handle, caught the flash of the driver's eyes in the mirror, held her as he stepped out of the car and strode to the iron gates.

Still dark, the straight path to the curved, domed entrance was softly illuminated with studs of light. His finest home. His proudest purchase. Every step proof of how far he had come from thieving street child to national hero. Normally he lingered, savoured. But not tonight. Tonight he marched with his treasure. Past the low sweet-scented bushes, the spiky-headed lavender and geometric box hedge. None of that mattered.

He had waited for her. And now she was here. Right here in his city, in his house, in his arms.

The heavy half-glazed door reflected them as they stepped up. She looked tiny, slight, and for a moment he remembered the girl she had been. So full of energy, so bold and uncompromising. She might have grown up, filled out slightly, but under her subtle make-up and silky hair and the well-cut dress, she was still that refreshingly natural, honest creature he'd first laid eyes on in that muddy lane.

And finally he was going to take her in the way he had

longed to take her. He could hardly bear any more heat at his groin right now. He was slightly out of control—he could feel it.

His hand was steady as he pressed the keypad, but that was sheer force of will. The door swung open into the high domed entrance. Lamps glowed like sleepy sentries down the hallway. Palms bent their heads in welcome. Portraits calmly considered them. It was as if the whole house was waiting.

He felt her step in beside him.

'Mother of God, what a place…' she breathed.

She was turning three-sixty, gazing at the glass, the gilt, the marble, the grand sweep of carpeted stairs. But the normal flush of pride, the pause and then the proud history lesson, didn't ease from his lips.

'Upstairs,' he said.

He caught her as she turned back to him, hoisted her weightless body into his arms and strode to the stairs.

'Oh, yes,' she said.

She didn't lie back—not Frankie. She grabbed his head, tried to kiss him.

It was the sheer force of the habit of climbing those stairs that got him to the top without missing a step. She was insatiable. He could hardly contain her as she slid her legs round his waist, held on to his head and licked and tongued her way across his face.

He had to stop—couldn't take another step with this erotic creature writhing all over him. He had to take her *now*. Here in the hall.

In a heartbeat he'd scooped his arm up her spine, bent her backwards and laid her straight down on the floor. Her eyes flew open with the speed of his move, but the wicked flash of joy told him she was even more fired up.

'You don't want to take this slowly, do you, *querida*? You haven't got the patience.'

'You can go slow with your blondes.'

She blew in his ear, her hot breath sending him into a fury of desire for her.

'But I haven't got all day, so get a move on.'

He braced himself just to look at her. No one spoke to him like this—*no one*. He would never tolerate any mention of previous partners, never entertain censorious comments. But she did it. And he was loving it.

'You think…?'

She lay still. Just for a moment. Her hair was a spill of the darkest rum, her eyes diamond black in the hollows of her satin-skinned face. Mesmerising. Absorbing. So beautiful.

Something hovered between them in that second. Heavy, humid, portentous.

And then, like a tide taken at the flood, they grabbed for each other.

She pulled at his shirt—fingers grabbing, nails scratching. Vaguely aware of his wound throbbing, he filled his hands with her. Hauled her dress up and over her hips. She tried to scrabble towards him, to get at more of his clothes, but he had to see her and touch her. *Had* to.

He pinned her to the ground with his hand and stared at her slender bones, at the tiny triangle of her panties. She was so delicate, so feminine… Another jolt of lust made him even thicker. Even harder. He grabbed the fine fabric that covered her in his fist and tugged. She yelped and breathed out hard. But she still clambered to clutch at him as he balled the shredded silk and tossed it aside.

'I *liked* those,' she said.

'You put them on knowing I'd take them off. Didn't you?'

'You're so hot for yourself—aren't you, Hurricane?'

He grinned at her again—couldn't help it. She fired him up to be a little more rough, a little more bold.

'I'm hot for *you*.'

He pulled her dress right up to her waist, exposed her nakedness to his hungry eyes.

'You're perfect.'

She was. Exquisite. The neat V of dark hair drew his gaze, and as the words left his lips he parted her flesh and slid his fingers home.

Like a wild beast calmed, she stilled, threw back her head, closed her eyes and moaned. She was swollen and soaked. Just as he'd known she would be. As he'd always remembered. Her clitoris was engorged, begging for his touch, and he circled and slid his finger over it just once. Her cry echoed off the walls and went straight to his heart.

'I've got to taste you, *hermosa*.'

Hands to her hips, he slid her swiftly up the silk rug. She hauled at her dress, dragged it over her head and unhooked her bra. She lay back in the moonlight, clothes cast around under the domed ceiling. She was some bewitching fairy or nymph, clouding his head. Entrancing him. Robbing him of sense.

He lifted her hips, held her open under his gaze, drinking in the moonlit sight of her that he'd never had a chance to see properly in those few stolen minutes years ago. Then he bent his head until his lips and tongue lay between her splayed legs. And then he lapped her, tasted her and relished her.

She had orgasmed in seconds that first time. Caught him completely by surprise. And herself. He doubted she had even known what had happened. He'd catapulted himself out of bed in shock.

But this time as her legs tensed, her arms gripped his

and she burst apart, pulsed and jerked in his mouth. As her cries echoed in the hallway he held her in place and licked at her until she thrashed her arms and legs and begged him to stop.

'Rocco—Rocco, please!'

The words rang out, almost dragging him out of his frenzy. And then he was lifting her, hugging her up, plastered against his body, striding along the hallway, taking them both to his suite. She hung her head on his shoulder, lay limply in his arms.

'Is that what it takes to calm you, Frankie? I must remember that…'

She felt so soft in his arms, lying back quietly as he paced past closed doors. Light was beginning to flood in through the huge stained glass window that marked the end of the hallway and the door to his suite.

'I'm only taking a moment…' She smiled, then tipped up her face, softened by dawn's golden light.

God, she was even more beautiful like this. He didn't think he could wait another second to have her.

He kicked open the door. Three paces and he laid her down on his bed. She leaned up on her elbows, completely naked. He zoned in on her tiny curved breasts, pink nipples erect and inviting. His hands fumbled like a teenager with his belt, his fly, his shirt buttons.

Her chest heaved up and down with hard, shallow breaths, then she kneeled up and grabbed at his shirt, hauled at it. Kissed him.

'Back in the game—*Hurricane*.'

Sweat beaded between them—he didn't know from whom. They made noises…breathed and gasped and murmured each other's names. She was licking at his nipples, her fine little fingers running over his flesh, tracing the fresh scar that had begun to bleed.

'Oh, my God—did I do that? I'm *sorry.*'

He kicked off the last of his clothes, pulled a handful of condoms from the drawer and scattered them on the bed.

'Doesn't matter. Come here. Lie down.'

He grabbed her by the wrists and held her as he kneed her legs apart and then tipped her down.

She strained, held herself taut as he positioned her. Her eyes were on him. His erection. He was so swollen it stood proud, huge, and just the sight of her staring made him nearly lose his grip.

'Rocco, my God…my God.'

She leaned up, licked her wet lips and raised her eyes to his. He felt like a god. *She* did that to him.

His fingers peeled a condom packet apart and she reached to take the condom out. Then she cupped his straining sac and began to roll it delicately. Too delicately.

He'd had enough. His control was shot. He couldn't wait any more.

He shook his head. 'Lie back. Let me do this, Frankie. Come on, *hermosa.* Come *on.*'

She did as she was told. But her eyes drank him in. Every part of him.

Finally he was just where he wanted to be, leaning over her as he'd wanted, as he'd imagined. Finally he was getting to hold her under him and nudge the tip of his shaft inch by inch into her hot, sweet heaven.

She was so slight, so slender. But so ready. And even if he'd had an ounce of self-control left—even if he'd wanted to take it slowly—she had other plans. She slid down to meet him, her eyes never leaving his even as her body took him in and her hands smoothed their way around to his backside.

And he slid home.

The strain not to take her hard and fast nearly broke him, but he lifted her hips and took it as slowly as he could. He felt her fingers frame his face…looked down, opened his eyes. She was staring with those huge eyes, deep and dark and so full of secrets. She licked her lips and drove him on with her hips. Her breasts jiggled as he thrust into her and he knew then that this was the most erotic experience of his life.

'Rocco, baby, this is too good…too good.'

She squeezed her hips even more, and just the perfect tilt of them sliding together nearly killed him. She called out to the day-brightened room as she lost it. He was losing it with her. This was it. The wait was over.

He grabbed her wrists with one hand and pinned them above her head, held her down. Then he threw each of her legs round his waist and hauled her by her hips as close as he could get her. She curled back on the bed, for once his supplicant, and he leaned over her, stared into her and ground himself free.

Released.

It was immense.

He came and didn't stop coming. And she was there, squeezing him home.

Cradling her in his arms, he rolled over and spread her like silk over his body while he crashed back down to earth. His heart hammered and his vision struggled to return. The edges and curves of the white plaster cornice slowly took shape around the dark grey ceiling high above him. The blackout blinds were high on the windows, letting in the morning's brightness.

It was days since he'd been here. Weeks, maybe even months since he'd had a woman here. And he'd never, ever had a girl like Frankie here. Anywhere. *Ever.*

He squeezed her to his chest, almost as if checking she was real.

'What do you think? Worth the wait?' he said finally.

She lay still. 'I hate to burst your bubble, but I think it might need to be the best out of three.'

He smiled. *Trust her...*

She smoothed her hands over his chest, pressed her fingers into the bruise that now bloomed like a map of the world over his right pec.

'Is that sore? Am I hurting you?'

He snatched at her skinny little wrist as she fired him one of her wicked grins.

'The purple skin and burst stitches don't give you a clue?'

She batted her eyes and lowered her head. Kissed the bruised flesh—little whispers of touch with that fiery mouth.

'Is that better?'

He threaded his fingers through her hair, caught them up in a tangle and worked it free.

'I'll live. Come here.'

He wanted to feel her close against him. He was acting out of character, but having her wrapped over him felt so damn good. He loved women—of course he did—but he knew the chemistry, the bonding, the whole emotional fallout attached to the aftermath of lovemaking could lead to expectations he was never going to fulfil. But this moment he had waited for. And he was going to savour it.

'Makes a change from the last time, when you tried to kick me out of bed.'

'At least one of us had our head screwed on.'

He leaned up on his elbow to look at the sleek cat that lay across him.

'You know how crazy that was? You tested me to the

max. I've never been so tempted, and you were—what?—sixteen? Have you *any* idea how wrong that would have been?'

'Didn't feel wrong at the time, though, did it?'

She twisted her head round to look at him, pressed another whisper-kiss to his chest. Nothing about her felt wrong. Then or now.

He shook his head. 'Your family didn't strike me as being the most freethinking. It was a miracle that we weren't caught.'

She turned her head, pulled herself away. Lay back on the bed beside him and stared up at the ceiling.

'We were. Caught. Actually.'

'What? Are you kidding me?'

He shifted up. No way. *No. Way.* He would have known—he would have been called to account. There was no chance her brother would have continued to do business with him—no way their professional or personal relationship could have withstood that type of interference.

She twisted her head. 'Oh, don't worry—I denied it. Until I was hoarse. And Mark doesn't know—at least I think he doesn't. But my dad—let's just say he has suspicions…deep suspicions.'

Damn. He hadn't considered that.

'Angel—I'm sorry. I'd never have left you to handle that on your own had I known. What happened?'

She sighed, and he saw her twist at the silver ring on her finger.

'I don't know. I don't know if we woke him with our noise or if he was just awake anyway. But after you'd got your stuff together and walked out I went to go back to my room and he was there—at the top of the stairs. He asked me outright what the hell I'd been doing.'

He remembered every second of that night. Stifling her cries with his mouth as she came in his hand from those few fevered touches. Pinning her down and then reality crashing round him as he'd realised what the hell had just happened—what the hell he'd been about to do. Trying to get out of bed, pulling on clothes that were icy and damp, buttoning himself up over the erection that wouldn't go down. Heaving on his boots as she'd still tried to tempt him back to bed. Finally grabbing her shoulders and hissing at her to stop, to leave him, she was too young!

But she hadn't given up. Naked, driving him wild. He'd hauled the sheet off the bed and wrapped her up. As he'd yanked the door open and tried to remember which way was out the farmhouse's narrow windows and dark passages had lent him no clue.

Finally he'd stumbled down to the kitchen, past the sheepdogs lying in front of the fire's dying embers, heard the tick of an old clock, heaved on the rusty bolts that had held the door closed.

She'd come down to stand in the doorway to the hall with a haunted look—as if the heart had been ripped out of her. He'd stopped then—aching to go to her, to make her feel better, to take away the hurt, take away his own hurt.

But he'd been young—only twenty-one! He'd spent so long getting to that point, working through his own pain. La Colorada had finally been ready. His polo career had been taking off. He hadn't been able to stay there, to ally himself to a woman—a *girl*. He'd been only just beginning to taste the chance of a sweet future. It would have been madness to go to her.

So he'd turned back to the door, hauled it open and stepped out into the early-morning rain. She'd come right out into the daylight, onto the huge slabbed courtyard, called his name one final time. But he'd just slung his bag onto his shoulder, taken one final look at her, wrapped up like temptation's gift. And then gone.

'He was just standing there—then he went into the guest bedroom, saw you were gone and the state of the room. Saw me in the sheet.'

She turned her face away.

'He slapped me and called me a whore.'

Rocco sat up, but she'd turned onto her side. He scooped her in close, feeling the shock of those words.

'Hermosa, lo siento mucho,' he soothed, furious that he had not known this.

'It's fine,' she said—too brightly. 'I lied. I said you must have left ages earlier. That I'd just pulled the sheet off. I don't know what else I said. I made it up.'

He kissed her shoulder, cursed his stupidity. Of *course* they had been heard. They'd been wild for each other—then and now. And he'd thought they hadn't been. *Stupid.*

'It's not fine. I apologise.' He pulled her back and turned her round, right round, until her head was tucked under his chin. He rocked her, hating the thought of her hurting. 'What did he do? Were you punished?'

She gave a hollow little laugh.

'If you can say being sent away to a convent for two years is punishment, then, yes, I was punished.'

He struggled to get his head around this, but knew he had no small part to play.

'And he made sure that Mark sold Ipanema. That she went to you was coincidence, but it made it all the harder.'

Rocco squeezed his eyes closed, feeling her pain.

'I see. *Now* I see. I didn't think… Angel, I'm sorry. If you'd got in touch I could have sorted it— I could have spoken to him. I wish you'd let me know.'

'You made it quite plain that the last thing you wanted was for me to get in touch, Rocco. Anyway, it's totally in the past—it's fine. I served my time.' She laughed. 'Honestly. It's done.'

He pulled her close. He couldn't deny that. Any more than he could deny how deep the scars of childhood could wound. How hard they were to heal. His own were like welts under his skin. No one could see them, but they were always there—always would be. Despite the 'luxury' of enforced therapy for five years. Five years until he'd learned to say what they wanted to hear: that he *didn't* hold himself responsible, that it *wasn't* his fault his baby brother had died.

Who else was to blame if not him? Who else had dragged him from doorway to doorway, scavenging, begging, stealing and worse? Who else had got caught up with the gangs, the drug runners and the killers?

He glanced past Frankie's scooped silhouette to the tiny battered photo of Lodo that he carried with him and placed at his bedside wherever he was. Precious life snuffed out before he'd even turned four years old. Being responsible for him, letting him down, losing him—it was the hardest lesson he had ever learned. But he had learned it. And he would never ever forget it.

The knowledge that Martinez, Lodo's killer, had never been held to account was like a knife to his ribs every day. But he would make it happen. One day.

He felt Frankie stirring, trailing hot little kisses over him and moaning with hot little sounds. She wriggled against him and he reacted instantly, his mouth seeking hers, his hands cupping her breasts and his knee shifting open her thighs. He positioned himself between her legs, so ready to slip inside her.

'You owe me,' she said as she rolled beneath him, 'and I'm here to collect.'

He smiled as she slid her tongue into his mouth. He owed her, all right, and he was going to pay her what he could. But the guilt that was already unfurling from his stomach was telling him he was never going to give her what she really wanted.

He reached for another condom, turned Lodo's picture face down and held her tight in his arms as he sheathed himself.

So if he wasn't going to give her what she wanted, what the hell kind of game was he playing? Because he knew that with every kiss, every stroke, every whispered word, while she might be calling it payback, he was storing up a whole load of brand-new trouble.

She slipped around him, climbed on top, and his body responded hard and fast again. He might have been able to hold back the tide in her farmhouse but as he slid himself into that gorgeous sweet place he'd been dreaming of for years he felt the world reconfigure.

Trouble?

Totally.

CHAPTER FIVE

HER EYES WERE SUNKEN. Her chin was grazed. Her thighs were weak and sore. Frankie hung on to the porcelain sink and stared at the wreckage.

Making love could do *this* to a person? She'd thought she might be glowing, radiant—rosy cheeked at the very least. The shadows under her eyes looked like a sleep-deprived panda's. Was there any product on earth that could work actual miracles? Not any that she had in her bag. Nothing that Evaña sold could even come close.

She stared round the 'hers' bathroom in this glorious suite. It was easily the prettiest she had ever encountered. Antique silver gilt mirrors dotted the shimmery grey marble walls. Sweet little glass jars held candles and oils, and there were feather-soft white folded towels. Lush palms and filmy drapes. A huge bath like a giant white egg cracked open was set on a platform atop four gilded feet. She pondered filling it, but surely it would take hours?

And how many hours were left in the day? Had she really been in bed for ten of them? A good, convent-educated girl like her? Though in the eyes of her father she was 'just a whore'.

She shivered in the warm humid air at the memory of that slap, those words. The stinging ache on her cheek had been nothing to the pain of Rocco's walking away. And when he'd never come back, when all she'd been left with was a crushing sense of rejection, she'd had no fight left. Her father's furious silence... Her mother's hand-wringing despair... Going to the convent in Dublin had almost come as a relief. *Almost*.

Then finding out that her beautiful Ipanema had been sold...

Mark had come to tell her. She'd been sitting there in her hideous grey pinafore and scratchy-collared blouse in the deathly silent drawing room that was saved for visitors. The smell of outdoors had clung to Mark's clothes—she'd buried her face in his shoulder, scenting what she could, storing it up like treasure.

He thought she'd be happy that the handsome Argentinian she'd been so sweet on—the one who was now scooping polo prize after prize—was Ipanema's new owner. He'd known it would be upsetting, but she had always been going to be sold—surely she'd known that? She was their best, and they needed the money now that Danny had walked out on them and Frankie's school fees were so high. It wasn't as if she was home anymore, riding her every day after school. And Rocco Hermida was easily the best buyer they could hope to find—notoriously good with animals, and miles ahead in equine genetics. Soon there would be more Ipanemas. Wasn't that great?

She'd painted on her smile until he left, knowing that she had nothing now. Not even the smell of fresh air on her clothes.

Dark days had followed. She'd moved listlessly through them. She'd lost her appetite, become even thinner, lost her sparkle, lost her motivation for everything. No one had been able to believe the change in her. Herself least of all. One minute naive, innocent, unworldly. Next moment as if she had been handed the book of life and it had fallen open at the page of unrequited love.

Because it *had* been love. She, in her sixteen-year-old heart, had known it was love. And he didn't love her back. She had laid herself bare, body and soul, and he had played with her a little, then tossed her away.

The only ray of sunshine had been Esme. Relentlessly digging her out of her dark corners—relentless but never interfering. Just like now.

Frankie pulled out a bath towel, shuddered at her own selfishness.

What must Esme be thinking? Her best friend, whom she hadn't seen for years, had been so excited to hear that she was coming all the way from Madrid—had sent a car to collect her, planned to show her such a good time at the Molina Lario, over the weekend in Punta…

She had managed one brief reply to Esme's text to say she was 'Fine! Xxx', and then her phone had been powered off. She cringed, wondering what she must have made of Rocco's dismissive statement that they had 'unfinished business'. It would be news to Esme that they had any business at all!

Frankie Ryan was not a party girl—never mind a one-night stand girl. She was a no-nonsense career girl. A don't-ever-give-them-anything-to-criticise girl. She hated anyone knowing her business, judging her or in any way getting past the wrought iron defences she had spent the past ten years erecting all around her.

Well done, she thought as she stared at her own mess. *Well done for walking straight into the lion's den.* She looked at it—his den. The extravagant opulence. Everything in prime fin-de-siècle glory. Silvery marble and gilded taps, Persian rugs and domed cupolas. And Rocco Hermida...prowling.

She'd walked right in, lain right down and made sure that the whole world knew. So much for wrought iron. Everyone could see right through it.

She'd told him far too much last night. Given too much of herself away. She didn't want this to be a pity party. She wasn't here for his sympathy. She'd never breathed a word about that night to another living soul. Denials to her father, and her mother too shocked even to ask. Mark and Danny both oblivious. Rocco needn't have known.

But it was done now. She couldn't take it back. As long as he didn't think he *owed* her or anything. That would be too much to bear.

She padded to the shower, turned on the jets and jumped back as water blasted from all angles. Then she adjusted the taps, stood determinedly under the slightly too cold spray and scoured herself. You could take the girl out of the convent...

She patted herself dry and swaddled herself in a robe. Used a brand-new toothbrush that made her think of all the other brand-new toothbrushes that would come after she'd gone.

One-night stand.

Whore?

Absolutely not. She was tying up loose ends. She was filing away memories and then moving on. She was here on business and she was having some pleasure. What was so wrong with that? People did it all the time! She just hadn't got round to it until now.

Rocco was an expert at it. Had been from the very first moment she had met him. A roll in the hay and then off down the lane. She was going to learn from that. Surely, if nothing else, she would *learn* from that. Because she'd be damned if she was going to be the one huddled in a sheet with a broken heart this time.

It only took Dante twelve hours to track him down. In person. Rocco was walking back from the kitchen with two bottles of water and a decision about exactly where to eat lunch in his mind. He'd worked up a king-size appetite, and as soon as Frankie came out of the shower he was going to feed her, nourish her, make sure she had enough fuel for them to continue where they'd left off. It was pretty much all he had head space for just now.

He'd done too much thinking in the past few hours— watching her as she slept, biting down on his anger. He should have done more at the time. He should have checked she was all right. He should have at least figured out that the reason she'd never been mentioned was that she'd been sent away in disgrace.

Damn, but this just proved his point. Being responsible for others was a non-negotiable non-starter. Lodo, Dante—and now this. Nothing good came of it but feelings of guilt, regret, that he could have done more.

What concerned him most was that even though she had every right to hate him and hold him responsible she had come here—after all this time. And no matter what she claimed—that it was a business trip, that she'd wanted to see the ponies—she had tracked him down. And right now she was in his bedroom.

That part wasn't the problem—not at all. And she didn't seem like the kind of woman who'd turn needy and emotional. But still, you never knew… Sometimes it was the wild ones who were the most vulnerable.

So he had to be crystal clear that this was a short-term party for two. With no after-party. Of course, that would be a whole lot easier if he wasn't so turned on by her.

If he'd been able to get her out of his system like every other woman before. But that wasn't looking as if it was going to happen any time soon.

'Hey, *guapo*!'

Rocco paused, and scowled at Dante as he sauntered in from the grounds.

'What are *you* doing here?'

Dante's easy golden grin slid over him, for once jarring his mood.

He didn't want to be disturbed—didn't want to have to think through or account for what he was doing. He just wanted to enjoy it while it lasted.

'You didn't seriously think I would stay away? Took me a while to track you down, though. Never thought you'd hole up *here*.'

He drew a hand through his dark blond hair, reached for one of the bottles of water.

'There's more in the fridge. These are for us.'

'*Us*? As in *la chica irlandés*? So she's still here?'

He whistled. And grinned. And removed his hand when he saw that Rocco wasn't going to relinquish the bottle.

'Ah. So we're still working through the obsession?'

He nodded his head. 'We're getting there.'

Dante was smirking, prowling about, checking things out.

'You got plans?' Rocco cracked the lid on his water, necked half of it, tried to swallow his irritation at the same time.

'Well, the party's moved on—everybody's in Punta. Waiting on *you*.' He tossed away his jacket and eased himself onto a sofa, looking as if he was just about to film a commercial. As usual.

'Don't let me hold you back. I've got stuff to do at the estancia. Might take me the weekend to fix—'

Dante ignored him, cut in. 'You know you've created a whole lot of buzz? The way you acted last night. But hey, it's cool. I'll get out of your hair. Leave you to work all the knots out. God knows you've been coiled up with it for years. A whole weekend, though? Impressive.'

'You're reading too much into this.'

'What about Turlington?'

'What about it?'

Dante pulled out his phone, started to browse through it as if he had all the time in the world. That was the thing about Dante—he made easy an art form.

'Oh, nothing. Except you've never missed it yet. And there will be a lot of disappointed people there if you don't show up.' He grinned at his phone. 'In fact there will be a lot of disappointed people if you *do* show up with *la chica*. What's her name again? Frankie?'

'Yeah, that's me.'

They both turned round. And there she was. Framed in falling sunbeams from the hallway, golden all around. She walked towards them into the kitchen. And if he'd thought she'd looked sexy in her little blue dress, it was nothing to seeing her decked out in one of his favourite blue shirts. Scrubbed clean, hair sleek, bare limbs.

Had she done the buttons up wrong just to add to the whole 'tumbled out of bed' look? His eyes zoned straight in on the asymmetric slices of fabric that skimmed her toned, succulent thighs.

She strolled right up and took the bottle of water that was dangling limply from his hand. Then she unscrewed the top, tipped the bottle head against his, winked, said, 'Cheers!' and took a long, slow sip.

His eyes zoned in on her throat. Swallowing the water. It killed him.

He'd really thought that some of her allure would have rubbed off by now. Didn't feel like it. Not the way he was warming up. He turned away.

Dante beamed at her as if she was some kind of clever child who had taken its first steps or said its first words. Then he did exactly what he always did: he stood up and sauntered over as if he was being called to the stage to collect a prize—all easy charm and sunshine smiles.

'I'm Dante. *Absolute* pleasure to meet you, Frankie. Again.'

He kissed her right cheek, kissed her left cheek. Held her by the shoulders and gave her a long once-over. Nodded.

Rocco sank the rest of his water and watched from the corner of his eye.

She was smiling that smile. She could be so intense, but when she smiled her face lit up like *carnival*.

'Pleased to meet you, too, Dante. *Again.*'

'Dante's just leaving.' He took his empty bottle and fired it into the recycling bin. It clattered noisily.

Dante didn't miss a beat.

'Yeah, I'm heading to Punta, Frankie. We always head there after the Molina party. It's the Turlington Club party tomorrow night. I'd be happy to take you.'

It was the usual chat, but seeing the flash of dipped eyes and the curve of a smile made him bristle. Was she flirting? Was Dante flirting right back? Whatever—it was pushing his damn buttons. That was all it was. He should know that. What was *wrong* with him? He should calm the hell down.

She opened her mouth to reply but he cut in. 'As I said,

I have to call in at La Colorada. So I'll let you know later if I'm going to make it up to Punta.'

'How about you, Frankie? What would you rather do? Go and muck out horses with the Lone Ranger here, or drink cocktails at Bikini Beach with me?'

Rocco felt his fingers grip Frankie's shoulders. 'Frankie came all the way here to *see* the horses, so I reckon that answers your question.'

'And I thought she was here to see you…'

The swine threw his head back and laughed. Round One to him.

Rocco palmed her back as he steered her down the hallway, with Dante's chuckling words ringing in the space. 'I'll see myself out, then. See you at the Turlington Club, Frankie—save me a dance.'

How many times had Dante tried that routine on one of his girls? And how many times had Rocco found it entertaining? Countless. Watching their eyes widen, wondering who to look at—wondering if Dante really *was* flirting.

'You never said anything about going to your ranch.'

She had stopped dead, in that way that she did. Like a mule.

'No, I didn't, but I have to go there now.'

He paused. This could be the moment. At any other time, with any other woman, this *would* be the moment. As soon as they got possessive, bitchy or mean: *It's been great, but change of plans. Thanks for a wonderful time.* It would be that clean. The words would maybe sound harsh, but it would be short, sweet, simple.

He considered, but he just didn't want to. Not yet anyway. Another day should see all the knots worked out…

'But I've already told you I was only here with you for the day. I've come halfway across the world to see Esme.'

She was still with *that*? She couldn't see herself that the minute she'd landed it was *him* she'd tracked down? He was still coming to terms with everything she'd told him, but he was slowly getting there—she couldn't really be blind to the fact that it was *his* house she was standing in, in *his* shirt, after having *his* body all over her for the past ten hours.

'Punta is a two-hour trip. If you want to leave now I'll make the arrangements…'

She opened her mouth.

'I have to go to the estancia. Juanchi, my head gaucho, wants to talk. He's got a concern about one of the ponies on the genetics programme. It's up to you. Easy to get you to your friends, if that's what you want.'

She twirled a strand of hair, made a little face, shrugged. 'Okay. Sounds like a plan. As long as there are no more surprises.'

Sounds like a plan? No more surprises? He almost did a double-take. God, she riled him like no other woman ever could.

But even as she stood there he wanted to wipe the coy little look off her face with his mouth.

'That's the thing about surprises—you can't always see them coming.'

She slipped him a little smile. 'I suppose…'

'Take us—right now.'

He took the water from her hand, put it on the console table beside them.

'Bolt from the blue.'

He slid his hands round her waist, felt the faint outline of her ribs, pulled her towards him. She was still holding back. Still playing her game. He could feel it. No arms round his neck…no legs round his waist.

'This has been a very lovely surprise. Gorgeous.'

He stepped into her space, eased his thumbs to the underside of her breasts. Slowly, slowly rubbed the soft flesh, gently massaged.

'So what if it's only going to last a few more hours? A day? You go your way—I go mine.'

He kept up his sensuous caressing. She blinked her eyes, slowly, softened like butter in the sunshine.

'But there's no point denying that right now we're very…'

His hands slid to the sides of her breasts and his thumbs found her nipples. Little light touches to begin with, just how she liked it.

'Very…'

She closed her eyes.

'Hot for one another…'

Her head fell back and she ground out a long, satisfied sigh. 'Mmm…'

He nodded. Slid one hand to the hem of the shirt, gripped her hips, kept up the pressure on her nipples. Then he bent his mouth to the fabric, drew long and deep on each nipple, soaked his own shirt with his mouth, tugging those buds to hard points.

She was so easy to turn up and down, on and off. Like a geyser.

He stood back, admired his work.

'Lose the shirt,' he said.

For a moment she stood, dreamy and drugged. Then she fixed him with a look. Dipped her chin. Smiled like sin.

'Make me.'

He grinned. He couldn't help it. There she went again— matching him. Firing him up. Making him feel that here was a woman who could stand toe to toe with him.

Dammit, but he couldn't afford to let crazy thoughts like those into his head.

He grabbed for her. '*Make* you, Angel? In ways you've never even dreamed of...'

She tried to duck away but he caught her. She screamed with laughter as he hauled her close to him and silenced her with kisses like a crazy man. She caved. Totally caved. Couldn't get enough. She suckled his lip, his tongue, showered him with kisses.

She thought *she* was calling the shots?

He needed to be in complete control of this. Couldn't afford any slip-ups.

He tossed her over his shoulder. Her shirt—*his* shirt—rode up, and he held his hand over her bare backside, bringing it down just a little hard. Just a little warning—*he* was in control. And that was how it would stay.

CHAPTER SIX

FRANKIE WAS PREPARED for the long jacaranda-lined driveway. She was prepared for the still green lakes overhung with sleepy willows. The curved pillared entrance, the endless array of white-framed windows, the pops of colour from plants, pots and baskets—all of them were totally as she'd envisaged. She was even prepared for the unending horizons she could see on either side of the mansion-style ranch house, rolling into the distance, underlining the vastness of the lands, the importance of the estancia, the power of the man.

But she was not prepared for the huge lump that welled in her throat or the hot tears that sprang to her eyes when she saw the horses that galloped over to the fence to welcome their master home, racing alongside the car as he drove, happily displaying their unconditional love. Nor was she prepared for the uninhibited smile that lit up Rocco's face as he watched them.

The freedom they enjoyed shone out as they played in the fields surrounding La Colorada. It had been so long… so, *so* long since she had enjoyed that self-same freedom. After Ipanema had gone she'd never felt the same. She'd barely even sat on a horse—she'd thought she'd grown up, moved on from her teenage fixation with horses, moved on to her adult fixation with escape.

But here, now, it all came flooding back. Maybe it was just because she was so tired, or maybe it was a reflection of all that had come at her these past several hours, but she struggled to hold back a sob as memories of her happy childhood slammed into her one after another after another. A childhood that had been so completely shattered with the arrival of Rocco Hermida.

She twirled her ring and swallowed hard.

'I have to find Juanchi. You can wait in the house— relax until supper. Come on, I'll show you inside.'

Those were the first words he had spoken to her in the best part of an hour. They'd gone back to bed, both drifted off to sleep, and when she'd woken he'd been pulling on clothes with his phone clamped to his ear. It hadn't moved far ever since.

Her little vinyl carry-on case had arrived, its gaudy ribbon, scuffed sides and wonky wheel incongruous beside the butter-soft leather weekend bag Rocco had been chucking things into as he spoke.

Rattling out questions, he'd glanced at her, given a little wink, then turned his back and walked to the window, continuing to berate the poor director of some vineyard who was on the other end. His hand had circled and stabbed at the air as he'd punctuated his questions with a visual display of his frustration.

She'd showered and dressed quickly in what she'd thought might be appropriate—denim shorts and a pink T-shirt. What *else* would you wear to a ranch? She'd slipped her feet into white leather tennis shoes and thrown everything else in her case. Rocco had dressed in jeans and a polo shirt. He'd paced up and down. More gestures, more rattled commands, more reminders that the Hurricane was well named.

She'd looked around, making sure she hadn't forgotten

anything. She wouldn't be back there after all. Spotting her watch on the floor, where she must have thrown it earlier, she'd bent to pick up. Where were her new earrings? She'd glanced all around and then had seen them at the side of the bed, there beside a little photograph. She'd walked round and reached out to scoop them up, but her hand had closed on the tiny frame that lay face down instead. She'd placed it upright.

It had been a picture of a child. She'd lifted it up to have a closer look. A blurry picture of an infant, maybe two or three years old. Bright blond hair, kept long, but definitely a boy. Solemn dark eyes, only just turned to the camera, as if he really hadn't wanted to look. There had been something terribly familiar in the scowling mouth. Dante? She didn't think so.

She'd turned to ask Rocco. He had stopped his artillery fire of instructions for a moment, had been standing framed in the hugely imposing window, an outline of the blue day all around him—so light and bright that she hadn't quite been able to see his features.

She had smiled, held up the picture.

The phone had been dropped to the end of his arm, a voice babbling into the air unheard. He'd paced forward as a thunderous tension had rolled through the room. Something akin to fear had spread out from her stomach at the way he'd moved, the slash of his features and the dark stab of his eyes.

He had taken the photo from her without so much as a glance, but she had felt the wall of his displeasure as if she had run against it, bounced off it and been left scrabbling in the rubble.

Nothing. Not a sound, a word, a look.

He had pulled open a zip in the leather holdall, tucked the photo inside, zipped it back up and then lifted the phone to his ear. He had taken her earrings, dropped them into her hand and then moved back to the window.

The conversation had continued.

She had tried not to be stunned, tried not to be bothered. It was clearly something personal. He was clearly someone intensely private. But it had hurt—of course it had. How much more private and personal could you get than what they had shared these past few hours? She'd opened up to him, told him about her father's fury and her mother's disappointment. He'd told her—*nothing*. Didn't that just underline the fact that she'd served herself up and he'd selected the bits he wanted, then pushed back the platter, folded his napkin and was probably looking around for the next course.

Again.

She had to get smarter. Had to keep herself buoyant. More than anything else she had to make sure the black mood didn't come back.

She'd stuffed her watch and earrings inside her case with her other belongings, rolled it to the door and swatted him away when he'd attempted to lift it. She could look after herself. And then some.

Then the two-hour car journey. The icy silence punctuated by more intense conversations on his phone. Frankie had drifted in and out, picking up snippets about equine genetics and shale gas fields, decisions about publicity opportunities he wanted reversed. *Now.*

She had rummaged in her bag, pulled out a nail file. She'd filed her nails into perfect blunt arcs. The scenery had been flat—green or brown—and the company had been intently and exclusively business. Her phone was still dead and her guilt about not speaking to Esme properly still rankled.

The car had rolled on. She had gazed out of the window, anger and upset still bubbling in her blood. Then she had felt her hand being lifted. She'd looked round sharply. He had smoothed her fingers, squeezed them in his own—the gnarled knuckles and disfigured thumb starkly brown against her paper-pale skin. Still he hadn't looked at her, but he'd lifted them, pressed his lips to them, and she had known then that that was as much of an apology as she was likely to get.

Damn him. Fire and heat. Ice and iron. She shouldn't allow him to win her over as easily as that, but there was something utterly magnetic about this man. She needed to play much more defensively—protect herself as much as she could. Because every time she thought she'd figured this—*them*—out he shifted the goal posts again.

She could have been on a helicopter to Punta right now. He had offered to send her. Not to *take* her, of course—there was the subtle difference. And she had declined. She'd still have plenty of time to catch up with Esme when she got there. Her buying trip to the Pampas was not for days yet. She would make it to Punta tomorrow, the party was tomorrow night—it would be no time at all until this thing burned out between them. No time until she was off doing her own thing again.

If she kept her head it should all work out fine.

There had been more calls, more decisions. She'd sat wrapped in her own thoughts, no room for soft squeezes or stolen kisses. Had closed her eyes and drifted off to sleep, finally opening them as they'd arrived at this heart-stopping ranch.

'It's fine,' she said now, stepping out of the car, and feeling every one of her senses come alive with this place. 'You go and find Juanchi and I'll have a wander.'

For the first time since Dante had left Rocco seemed to look at her properly. He finally tucked his phone away in the pocket of his jeans, flipped his hair back from his eyes and scowled.

'Problem?' she said, with as bored an expression as she could muster. Diplomacy wasn't her biggest skill, and she knew if she really spoke her mind it might not be the best move. Not yet anyway.

'I've been neglecting you.' He looked at her over the roof of the car. 'So much to deal with—my apologies.'

Frankie shrugged. 'You're a busy guy,' she said. 'I really don't want to be in the way.'

He was looking around, as if Juanchi was going to spring out from behind a bush. He looked back. Looked totally distracted.

'I'll catch you up,' she said, walking off, waving her hand.

'Where are you going to go?'

'I'm a big girl,' she called over her shoulder, 'I'm sure I'll find something to occupy myself.'

'Wait by the pool. Round the back. I won't be too long.'

She answered that with another wave and kept walking.

CHAPTER SEVEN

FRANKIE STEPPED TOWARDS the house. Up close it was imposing, presidential. The drive swept before it in a deferential arc. Pillars loomed up, supporting the domed roof of the entrance and the terrace that wrapped itself like a luxury belt all around it.

She could imagine Rocco roaring up in a sports car, braking hard and jumping out, striding up to the doors, owning the whole scene. In fact, she didn't need to imagine it—she'd seen it all before, in that television report of Rocco. This was where he had been photographed with one of his blondes. Carmel Somebody…the one who'd been reported to be 'very close' to him.

She walked towards the door, noted the long, low steps, the waxed furniture and exotic climbers. Frankie stopped. She didn't particularly want to go wandering about in his house—she didn't particularly want to get wrapped up in any more of his life. Not when she was only passing through. Was it really going to help her to have another page in her Hurricane scrapbook? She already had a million different mental images of Rocco: making love, showering, sipping coffee at the breakfast table. She had hoarded more than enough to keep her going for another ten years. What she really needed to do was start erasing them—one by one. Otherwise…? Otherwise history was going to repeat itself.

Rocco wasn't looking for a life partner. He was looking for a bed partner and some arm candy. And so was she.

She turned on her heel. She'd go to the stables. She'd feel much more at home there.

It was strange how unlike her expectations this part of the estancia was. She'd grown up with so many stories of heartless South American animal husbandry. Horses whipped and starved and punished. But Mark had been vehement in his defence of Rocco. He had confirmed the rumours that had rolled through their own stables—of the Hurricane in the early days, sleeping with his horses rather than in his own home, spending more time and money on them than he did anything else. He'd been notoriously close to his animals, and notoriously distant with people.

It didn't look as if much had changed.

She picked her way along the side of the house, past the high-maintenance gardens and round to the even more highly maintained stables.

They were immaculate. Nothing out of place. All around grooms—some young, some old, Argentines and Europeans, men and girls—seemed lazily purposeful. Here and there horses were being walked back and forth to the ring, or beret-capped gauchos were arriving back from the fields with five or six ponies in lightly held reins. No one seemed to notice that she was there, or if they did they left her well alone.

Rocco was nowhere to be seen.

She walked past high fences, their white-painted wood starkly perfect against the spread of grass behind. The sun's heat was losing its hold on the day, but some horses and dogs still sought shade under the bushes and trees that lined various edges of the fields.

Rounding the corner of a low stable block, she saw him. Off in the distance, deep in conversation with an old, bent man. Juanchi, she supposed.

Even from here he was striking, breathtaking. His stride was so intense, yet it held the effortless grace of a sportsman. Every part of him was in harmony, undercut with power. Everything he did with his body was an art. Kissing, dancing, riding, making love. Being so close to him for these few hours she had learned his ways, his unashamed confidence, control and drive. He was everything she had spent the past ten years expecting him to be. Everything her broken teenage heart had built him up to be. More was the pity.

She stood back, watched, willed herself not to care. So he was Rocco Hermida? *She* was Frankie Ryan. He didn't have the monopoly on everything. She could kiss, she could ride and, now that she'd spent the past fourteen hours with him, she could claim to be quite an accomplished lover, too.

She supposed…

She didn't have much to compare him to—a few disappointing fumbles at university parties, a dreary relationship with a co-worker when she had first arrived in Madrid. But that was because she hadn't known her own body back then. It wasn't because Rocco and only Rocco could light her up with a single touch. Other men could do that—she just hadn't learned to let go yet. Now she would. She was sure.

But even watching him standing on the threshold of his immaculately appointed barn, a structure more at home in a plaza than a field, she couldn't deny he was captivating. He listened to the old man, gave him his full attention, nodded, then pulled the bolt closed on the barn and moved off with him. She watched them walk back out from the shadows cast by the building's sides into bright sunlight.

Respect. That was what he was showing. He respected this old man.

That intrigued her. Of all the qualities she'd seen in him—leadership, confidence, passion, determination, even brotherly affection to Dante—respect hadn't been visible. It showed something about him now, though. It showed that he was even deeper and harder to read than she'd thought.

They turned another corner and vanished from view. Her eye was drawn back to the barn.

Wouldn't it be fabulous if one of Ipanema's ponies was inside? No high-powered polo match to recuperate from, just waiting for a little handful of polo nuts and a hug. Wouldn't it feel fabulous to sit on one of Ipanema's ponies? Wouldn't *that* be worth a phone call back home?

She started across the yard, but the low groan of a helicopter coming in to land made her look to her left. And there, off in the distance, she saw them. All shiny chestnut coats and forelock-to-muzzle white stars. Her face burst into a smile that she could feel reach her ears—she would know them anywhere. Like a homing device, she made her way forward.

They were playing in the field with four other classic caramel Argentinian ponies. For a moment she wondered what it would be like to be able to see them, be with them every day. Hadn't that been her dream job once? What had happened to that girl? So desperate to get away from the choking darkness of depression and the oppressive judgement of her father, she'd moved away from everything else she held dear, too. She barely had any time with her mother or her brother Mark. She was in regular contact with Danny, thousands of miles away in Dubai, but that was probably because they'd recognised in each other the same desperate need to escape.

Two of the ponies noticed her leaning on the fence and began to trot over. She looked about. Maybe the grooms and gauchos were all crowded together inside somewhere, drinking maté, because the whole place seemed to have become deserted.

Would it be too awful to help herself to a saddle? To tack up one of the ponies? To climb on its back and trot a little? What would be the harm in that? It wasn't as if Rocco would even know. It wasn't as if he particularly cared what she was doing. Then or now.

He'd never made the slightest effort to find out anything about her after that night. It was all very easy to say now that he felt terrible, but really—how much effort would it have taken to ask after her while he was negotiating the sale of Ipanema? She'd never blamed him for her getting sent to the convent—she held herself personally responsible for *that*…had made herself personally responsible for everything! And maybe it was that—the tendency to be so hard on herself—that had made her slide so quickly into depression.

Well, not anymore. She would never go back there.

She spotted the tack room and sneaked inside.

Five minutes later she was up and over the wide, white-slatted fence. Five minutes after that she was hoisting herself lightly onto a pony. In a heartbeat she had covered the entire length of the field—just in a walk, then a trot. Then, with a look around her, to make sure there was still nobody caring, she tapped her heels into the sides of the adorable little pony and cantered to the farthest side.

In the distance she could see seas of green and yellow

grass. Brown paths cut through them here and there, and running east to west the blue trail of a stream. Gunmetal clouds had rolled across the sky. And that was it. She was alone, she was as free as a bird and she was loving every last moment.

The pony was a dream—the lightest squeeze with her thighs and it picked up speed, the lightest tug with the reins and it turned or stopped. Most of their horses before Ipanema had been show jumpers rather than polo ponies. Ipanema's grandmother had been a champion show jumper, her mother had carried royalty at Olympia and then Ipanema herself had been spotted as a potential polo pony. When her father had taken her to County Meath she had just won best playing pony at the Gold Cup at Cowdray.

Frankie had been put on horses since she could walk. At age four she'd been able to balance on one leg on the sleepiest pony as it circled the yard—until she'd got yelled at to get down. At age ten Danny had dared her to try fences as high as the ones she had seen at the show trials. Of course she had fallen, tried to hide her broken arm for fear of her father's wrath and then been taken by her long-suffering mother to get it put in plaster. Yes, she'd pushed every boundary growing up—and she was going to push another one now.

Nobody was around. She walked the little pony out of one field and into another. A long clear path lay ahead. She squeezed lightly and started to gallop. On through the pampas, with the seas of green on either side of her as high as the pony's withers. Dust blew up around her, clouding her path, but she trusted the pony and gave her her head.

It all came back—those daily rides with Ipanema, and before her all her other favourites from the yard.

Feeling the warm air whip past her cheeks, the excited thump of her heart and the sensation that she was leaving all her worries behind her, she realised that there was no release like this. No wonder the first thing she'd done after school was to race home, tear off her school uniform and fly to the stables. She'd never known how badly she missed it until now.

The countryside didn't change—just more and more of the same. At one point she was alongside the stream, but then five minutes later it was nowhere to be seen. The huge grey clouds had rolled closer and were underlit with gold from the sinking sun. Sunsets seemed to arrive so much faster here than in Ireland. She'd check the time, but her watch was still stuffed in her case with her earrings... and her hurt at his actions over that photograph.

Who could it have been? Who could have caused such a shut-down? She let the images flit through her mind: the cherubic cheeks, the shock of blond hair. Apart from the scowling mouth there wasn't much of a family resemblance...but then there was no family resemblance between her and Mark. More between her and Danny...

Anyway, she was thousands of miles away from any of them, and every strike of the pony's hooves was taking her farther away from Rocco, too. She needed the space. This was definitely a much better option than hanging around by the pool, waiting for his godlike presence, for him to condescend to speak to her. She needed to get her world back into perspective. She needed to make sure her defences were completely and utterly intact.

She slowed down, picked up the stream again, nosed the pony forward to have a drink. Smoothing her hand down the pony's soft, strong neck, she made a mental note to check out some stables in Madrid. Maybe she should go even further than that. Maybe she should re-evaluate her whole life plan. Did she *really* want to work her way through the ranks of Evaña? Or did she want to go back to her first love: horses? How could she break back into that world? Move back to Ireland? Go work for Mark?

A noise sounded above her, off in the distance. The pony's ears pricked up.

No, she didn't want to keep running. But she didn't want to go back, either. She had put so much into her career already, and had so much more to prove. To the company and to herself. She knew she'd chosen a deliberately hard path, but the payback from every small success was worth a thousand times more than any easy life back in Ireland. Only a few more days and she would get her next big break—or not. It was all to play for—and she was damned sure she was going to give it her all.

She tugged the reins ever so slightly. Time to get going again. Another gallop around and then she'd head back. She was pretty sure she could find her way. If those thunderous-looking clouds hadn't rolled in so quickly she'd have a glimpse of the sun to give her her bearings.

The pony picked up her heels and they started to canter. The noise above her continued to grow. She twisted her head—a helicopter. They were so common here. Like a four-door saloon, everyone seemed to have one. It seemed to circle above her, and then flew away.

She was thirsty—should have taken a drink at the stream herself. She looked around, trying to see where it was. It should be on her right, and if she could find it she could follow its path most of the way back.

A slight sense of unease gripped her. Grasses swayed in the breeze in every direction. The wind was picking up. More low clouds swollen with summer rain had now rolled right overhead, darkening the day and filling the air with warning. There was not a landmark to gift her any sense of where she was or where she should go.

The pony seemed quite content to trot on, but she was beginning to worry that it would trot on forever. Her legs were beginning to chafe on the saddle and a huge wave of tiredness washed over her.

Suddenly, as fat raindrops landed on her legs, her bare arms and then all about her, she thought she saw movement off to her left. She turned the pony round, sure she knew now which way to go.

The rain exploded in sheets of grey. She could barely see a foot in front of her. Her lashes dripped; rain ran down her face. She slid in the saddle and dipped her chin down to try and deflect what she could. She looked around, trying to make sense of her surroundings, but couldn't see anything except wave after wave of summer storm.

She tried to look for shelter—anything, even a tree— but there was nothing except the oceans of grass and rain. Rain didn't fall like this in Ireland. This was vicious, relentless, unforgiving.

Suddenly the pony was frisky. Movement again—and a figure appeared, riding right at her. She pressed her thighs, willed the pony on, but the pony was too excited. And in a heartbeat Frankie realised why.

'What the *hell* are you doing?'

Rocco. Like a freight train through the night he rode right at her. She tried to move away, but he pulled on his reins and spun to a stop at her side. The wildness, the rage on his face stole her breath. She pushed her soaked hair out of her eyes and bit back the shock and the swollen lump in her throat.

'What does it look like I'm doing?'

He jumped down and grabbed her reins.

'Get down.'

'Don't speak to me like that!' she yelled back. 'You're not my damn father.'

The rain was still lashing in sheets around them. She could barely see the planes of his tanned face but his eyes flashed fire through the silvery air.

'For the first time I realise what it must have been like to be your damn father!'

He circled her waist with his arm and heaved her off the horse. Landing against his side, she shoved him away.

'Get your hands off me. Stop treating me like a child.'

Her throat was sore from swallowed emotion, but she would not give him a hint of it.

He moved to reach for her, but then stopped. His hands were clenched into fists at his sides, his jaw was rigid, his mouth a grim slash. But his voice when he spoke was quietly, menacingly calm.

'You caused me to send out a helicopter when a storm was coming in. You caused panic at the estancia. You stole a horse and—'

'I did *not* steal—'

He held his hand up to silence her and she was so taken aback she stopped.

'You *stole*—' he emphasised the word again '—a twenty-thousand-dollar horse. A horse that is part of our genetics programme. Without a thought about anyone but yourself you took off into the country. And *that's* not behaving like a child?'

She heard his words, saw his fury and felt such a wave of shame.

'I didn't mean any harm.'

He stared at her.

'Look at you.' He reached across, roughly cupped the

back of her soaked head, wiped his thumb hard across her cheek. 'Soaked to the skin... Lost...'

She dug her teeth into her lip. She would not cry. *Would not*.

'I wasn't lost. If the storm hadn't come in I would have been fine.'

She could feel the ache between her legs from hours in the saddle, her skin was beginning to chill, and despite herself her teeth began to chatter.

He regarded her with such contempt—as if she was the most infuriating thing he'd ever had to deal with. Then he reached back to his own saddle to a blanket that lay beneath. He yanked it free and held it out.

'Here. You need to get rid of those clothes—for what they're worth.'

She looked at him.

'What? And then you'll wrap me up and make me ride home side-saddle in a blanket? This isn't some damned John Wayne film! I'm not your weak little woman!'

She grabbed the reins out of his hands and tried to climb back on the horse. Immediately she felt his arms around her, spinning her to face him.

'Weak little woman? You're as far from that as it's possible to be. God knows, you might want to try it some time.'

He stared down at her, his fingers gripping her shoulders. She looked into those eyes, at that mouth. She felt the tug of desire and desperately, *desperately* wished that she didn't. She knew that she wanted to slide her arms around his strong neck, wrap herself up in his hard, warm body. How could this physical draw be so strong? So irresistible? But she wouldn't give in—no way, not this time.

She turned her cheek. He tugged at her chin.

'Look at me,' he ordered.

She tensed, but slid her eyes back.

'Look at you? Now? Because it suits you?' She shoved at him. 'But from the moment I woke up at your town house, and then in the car, the last thing you wanted me to do was look at you. Or at your damned photo!'

'I was busy. I have to take care of so many things,' he growled out.

'You're not the only one with a life. With a past.'

He looked away, as if expecting the horses to agree that this was the most exasperating nonsense he'd ever had to endure.

'Frankie—I don't do this with women. I don't explain myself... I don't fight.'

'No? Well, maybe that's the problem. Maybe you should try explaining yourself once in a while!'

She knew she sounded shrewish and shrill. She knew her voice was wobbling with unspilled tears. She knew if she stood another second in his company she would submit to whatever he wanted—just so she could feel that soothing sense of completeness he gave her.

But where would that leave her?

'I'll follow you back to the ranch,' she said to the wind. 'And then I'll make my own way to Punta. Okay? Then you'll not need to look at me, or fight with me, or damn well come and "rescue" me.'

She tried to stuff her wet tennis shoe into the stirrup, tried to hoist herself up. Once, twice, three times she tried, but exhaustion wound through her, heavy and dark as treacle. She laid her arms on the saddle and hung her head, dug deep and tried again.

Then Rocco's arms. Rocco's shoulder.

He pulled her back, and she used the last of her energy to spread her fingers against him and push.

'Frankie, *querida*, stop fighting me.'

He scooped her against his body, his shirt wet but warm. He walked her three paces, holding her close, whispering and soothing. She had nothing left to battle him with, and as he pinned her arms at her side in his embrace she let all her fight go like a dying breath.

'I can't let you go back like this.' He clutched her in one arm and flicked out the blanket with the other. 'I can't stand watching you fighting against me so hard when there's no reason.'

'But there's *every* reason,' she whispered. If she didn't put up a fight now, God only knew where she would end up.

He cupped her face by the jaw and stared down, the angry black flash of his eyes softening as the raindrops suddenly lessened, then stopped, leaving a cooling freshness all around. Light settled.

'There's nothing to be gained. Not when this is what we should be doing.'

He gently brought his mouth down to hers.

Heaven.

Warm presses, soft, then more demanding. She answered him, echoed everything he did—how could she not? His tongue slid into her mouth; his hand slid under her T-shirt. He cupped her damp flesh and shoved her bra to the side. She burned for him. She clutched at him, at every part of him.

This hunger was insatiable. Terrifying. Thundering through her like the summer storm.

He reached into his pocket and pulled out a condom.

'Do I need to carry one everywhere I go now?' he breathed into her. 'What I have to put up with to get what I want…'

And just like that the soft, easy current she was slipping into so easily turned into a dangerous riptide.

She pulled back. 'What?' she whispered. 'What did you just say? What you *have to put up with*? You don't *have* to put up with me. Nobody's forcing you!'

He grabbed her roughly. Shook her shoulders.

'*Why* do you misinterpret everything I say or do? You and I... We are incredible together. And we don't have much time left. If you want to waste it fighting—that's your choice.'

He shook her again, and she felt her world wavering right there. He was right. They had only hours left. Hours she had dreamed of her whole adult life. But she wasn't going to mould herself into the image of the women he was used to. She was who she was.

'Apologise for how you treated me when I held up that photo.' She saw him physically bristle. 'I don't need to know who it is, but I didn't deserve that.'

He eyed her steadily. His eyes held the power and the vastness of the rolling skies above them, but she didn't look away.

'It is...he is...someone very close. Someone who is no longer here.'

She swallowed.

His eyes slid away, then back.

'I see,' she said. It had been all she needed, but hearing the words, she knew she had prised open a box that was kept very, very tightly shut. 'Thank you. I didn't mean to pry.'

She dipped her eyes, but felt his fingers gentle on her chin.

'And I did not mean to hurt you.'

Tenderly he touched his lips to her brow, pulled her against him and tucked her under his head.

The horses stood together, heads twisting, eyes wide. The grasses settled into a silken green wave, the sky cleared of clouds and then darkened and the warm summer day slid slowly into sleep.

They stood together, silent, breathing, thinking, kissing. And Frankie knew that, no matter what happened next, the rest of her life would be marked by this day.

CHAPTER EIGHT

ROCCO STARED AT the phone in his hand as if it was an unexploded bomb. Finally the PI he'd had on his books for the past ten years had uncovered something concrete.

So long. It felt as if he'd been waiting his whole life to hear it. And, no—it wasn't even confirmed—but, hell, it was as close as it had ever been. He'd pursued this last lead tirelessly, feeling in his gut that he was closing in. And to discover that Martinez—Lodo's killer—might have been living for the past ten years in Buenos Aires would be a twist of fate almost too bittersweet to bear.

He'd admit it to no one but Dante, but this news shook him to his core.

He fastened cufflinks and tugged cuffs. Glanced into the mirror and confirmed that his restless mood was reflected all over his face. The shadow from his imperfect nose was cast down his cheek and his scar throbbed—a reminder of every punch he'd ever slung in the boxing ring and on the streets. Every blow, every ounce of rage directed at Chris Martinez for what he had done. And at himself for what he hadn't.

It was the timing of this that was wrong—in the middle of the Vaca Muerta shale gas deal, which was worth billions and his biggest venture yet. That and the delicious distraction of Frankie. But it was too important to let a moment pass.

This was the closing in on a twenty-year chase—one that had started with him running for his life, dragging Lodo along behind him, as the shout had gone up that the gang were back and wanted revenge. And Lodo—trusting, loyal Lodo—had been right there behind him as they'd leaped up from their cardboard box beds and hurled themselves into the pre-dawn streets.

Why he had let him go, let his fingers slip, was the question he could never answer. It was the deathly crow that lived in his chest, flapping its wings against his ribs at the slightest memory of Lodo—a shock of blond curls, the curve of a child's cheek, the taste of *choripan*, the sight of graffiti, the swirl of Milonga music. Every part of BA held a memory, and it was why he would never, ever leave.

Even when that piece of slime Martinez was locked up or dead. Even then. Lodo was still there in those streets. The streets were all he had to remember him by, and nothing would drag him away. At least he understood that now—now that the counsellor's words had sunk in, twenty years after hearing them.

How could someone who was as blessed as he'd turned out to be have fought against it so hard?

He'd been 'saved' by Señor and Señora Hermida as part of their personal quest to 'give back' to BA after they had just managed to escape the big crash that had caused so much devastation to others. Been dragged to their estancia, sent to an elite school with Dante, given every last chance that he would never have had when he'd wound up abandoned, orphaned and nearly killed.

The years of his hating the privilege had taken their toll on his *madre* and *padre*—that was how he referred to his and Dante's parents. They deserved that at least, after tirelessly forgiving him time after time. Bringing him back every time he ran away, channelling his energies into pursuits like boxing and polo that had eventually turned out to be life-saving. They had understood that he couldn't just accept the endless stream of money that could so easily have been his—not that they'd allowed him to squander it. He'd had to work for every peso.

But he'd preferred a much harder path. Starting with only the blood in his veins and the sharp senses he'd been born with. Self-sacrifice, almost self-flagellation, had been way better than any golden-boy opportunities. He had self-funded every step of the way. For him there had been no other way.

And he had done well. Very well. He had everything he could ever want.

Apart from his own family. He would never have that. It was a fruit too sweet. There would be no wife, no child. No one to fill Lodo's place.

But he was a man. He needed a woman. Of course he did. And one who accepted the limitations of her role.

The scent of Frankie wound through from the dressing room. This whole situation had unravelled in a way he had not predicted. He'd thought a passion this hot was just after a ten-year build-up and would be over well within the time he'd allotted. That it was as much about finally sampling forbidden fruit as any genuine full-blown attraction. But he'd been wrong. He was nowhere near sated.

How long it would last was something he was not prepared to commit to—but he was not going to let her out of his sight. Not while she excited him and incited him so much. Pure sex, of course. But sex the likes of which he had never known. And, since all his relationships were effectively based on sex, the currency of this one was totally valid.

Longer term? No. Her expectations would be sky-high. She'd want an equal footing in everything. She'd fight him every step of the way if she felt something wasn't fair. And he had no time for that. He had no time to be looking after a woman like that. That level of responsibility was to be avoided at all costs. Hadn't he proved that? Wasn't his trail of devastation big enough? No. She'd exhaust him. Cause him sleepless nights—in every sense.

That whole episode with her taking the pony and disappearing was evidence enough. His jaw clenched at the rage he'd felt when he'd found her gone. What a fool he'd been. Wandering around the garden first, calling her name, imagining that she'd be lying there waiting—warm and welcoming. Then when he'd realised she wasn't there or anywhere in the house, that sick feeling of panic had begun to build.

He'd felt it countless times with Dante when they were younger—as teenagers out roaming around the city, or later when they'd both go out and Dante would disappear for days, getting lost in some girl. Forcing himself past the terror of losing him had been years in the achieving, but he'd schooled himself. He'd learned. *Dante* was in total control of Dante. Lodo—well, that had been a different matter.

And today he'd been feeling it all over again. Bizarre. He'd been dwelling a lot on Lodo these past few days. Dredging up all the pain again. He had to get hold of himself, though—put the plaster back over his Achilles' heel. And damn fast.

Hours later he was sitting alongside her in the helicopter— watching the raw excitement on her face as the came in to land on the perfect patchwork quilt that made up Punta del Este. The sea, the beach, the clusters of yachts, the million-dollar homes—all were laid out like a beautiful chequered cloth.

He loved this place. Loved that Frankie was here, sharing it with him.

He showed her round his house and the gardens he'd designed himself. Watched her natural interest and joy at the little hidden corners, the sunken nooks, the bridge that spanned the inner courtyard swimming pool—it was a pleasure to see unguarded happiness. He wasn't usually in the business of comparisons, but—again—her lack of artifice, her unedited honesty, was so striking up against some of the other women he'd dated. Refreshing as rain on parched earth. It fed something in him—something he hadn't even known he was hungry for.

And then, of course, there was the passion. As soon as they'd got indoors and he'd got a message that there was further news about Martinez, he'd taken her—fast and hard. Maybe too hard. But she'd responded; she'd given it right back. She was just what he needed right now. No mind games, no manipulation. Just *there*, answering his body with her own. The perfect partner while he worked through this news.

Now he paced to the bathroom door. Opened it. Saw her. Wanted her all over again.

She kept her gaze straight ahead, frowned into the mirror as she smoothed her hair with her fingers and clipped in the emerald earrings he'd had delivered. He would give them to her to keep when she finally left. He would give them to her to remember him by.

The memories he had left her with the first time…

His hands curled into fists as he thought of how badly she had been treated. He had been so oblivious. He was angry, and still coming to terms with seeing a side of her she managed to keep well hidden.

To the world she was wilful, too stubborn. But to him she was just a highly strung filly. As highly strung as Ipanema had been when she'd arrived from Ireland. Missing her farm, her spoiled life. All she'd needed was a bit of careful management and a strong hand. She'd respected that. Needed that.

Just like her mistress.

And now he found himself easily, instinctively handling *her*.

He didn't need to wonder too deeply about why. They were both meeting each other's needs. It was that simple. There was no deeper, darker agenda. It was what it was. And it was good—for now.

'Perfecto.'

He said it aloud.

She smiled a self-effacing little half smile. 'Thank you. But I'm not going to lie... The thought of being all over the press as your date is giving me hives.'

He walked to her, wrapped his arms round her as she stood staring into the mirror. He in black, she in white. Her lips were a stain of poppy red, her hair a patent shimmer. In spiked heels, she was just tall enough to tuck her head under his chin completely. He nestled her against him, enjoying the fine-boned feel of her.

'You'll be sensational.'

'I'd rather be a nonentity. Walls need flowers—that's where I prefer to plant myself. And the thought of the media and all those people staring at the photographs of me...'

She shuddered and he held her back from him, stared at her. 'All those people?'

'Well, people who know me. Okay,' she said, pulling away, 'my family. They'll judge. And not in a good way.'

'It's only a party, Frankie. I'm sure they have them in Ireland.'

'Sure they do—but I like to keep my invites on the down-low. It's easier that way.'

'I reckon we can pull off a party without it hitting the headlines.' He hooked his thumb under her chin, tipped it up gently. 'Don't you?'

She rolled her eyes, quirked her lips into a smile. 'I suppose so.'

'Good. So we'll just go for a little while. I may have to return to BA early tomorrow anyway. I have some business that can't be postponed.'

He regarded her carefully, feeling strangely sure that if he opened up to her she would hold his confidence. But, no. That was not an option. Never an option.

'I head out the day after…so that all works out, then.'

Her voice was strained. He understood instantly.

'No, Frankie. I am *not* saying goodbye. Not tomorrow or the day after.'

He held her within his outline, stared at them in the mirror.

'I'd like you to stay on in Buenos Aires—with me. Until…until we put out this fire between us.'

'Rocco—' she started.

He watched her steady herself, watched strain splinter across her face.

'I'm only in South America for a few more days and then I'm flying back to Europe.'

'So stay longer. We *have* to continue this thing that we've started. It would be crazy not to. What do you say? Think about it.'

He didn't want to think about it. He just knew it felt right.

He turned her in his arms. She opened her mouth, as always needing to have her say, but some things needed no discussion. This was one of them.

Careful not to smear her lipstick, he kissed her lightly. But he slid his tongue into her mouth—just as a little reminder that the slightest touch was all it took.

The party was exactly as he'd expected it would be. The elegant country club was bedecked with all sorts of champagne-themed nonsense, and golden fairy lights around the jacarandas that lined the driveway made the blue-flowered trees look like sticks of giant glittery candyfloss. A gold marquee squatted on the lawn at the front of the old colonial-style house that had now become the clubhouse. Grace and glitz cautiously circled each other before the electrifying dance that would come later.

He watched as Frankie warily eyed the obligatory press corps as their car curved round the driveway. He had to smile at how contradictory she could be. So confident, so combative—but also so anxious about being his date.

He smiled, squeezed the hand he'd held throughout the car ride even though his mind had drifted to the next stage of the Martinez investigation—a task he'd entrusted to Dante: one final check on the identity of the man they suspected of being Chris Martinez. He scanned his phone for about the thousandth time in the past hour. Still nothing. He slid it away, held her close, tucked under his shoulder, feeling her presence soften his frayed edges.

Shadows of other times flitted through his mind, startling him. Fleeting moments when the salve of another body had shored up the pain. One happy dark morning, before her breakdown, when he had crawled into the warmth of his *mamá*'s bed after his *papá* had left on the soulless search for work. Feeling her love as she'd closed her arms around him. And then, mere months later, he had been collapsing into the arms of the nuns at the hospital. Hiding in their long black skirts. Racked with the agony of guilt when he'd seen Lodo laid out in the mortuary.

Strange that the touch of a lover had brought of these feelings back. It never had before. The news about Martinez had affected him very deeply, it seemed.

'Here we go, then.'

He smiled. It was unusual for him to have a date who preferred to stay in the background. Refreshingly unusual. He tried to soothe the tension in the brittle grip of her fingers and the jagged cut of her shoulder under his arm as he steered her past the openly intrigued crowd. Fields of happy, curious faces turned towards them like flowers—as if they were the sun, giving light and warmth. To him, Frankie felt colder by the second.

He knew she'd rather be curled up in his lap on the couch, watching TV and making love, than stuck in the media glare with all these gilt-edged sycophants.

Carmel had loved the spotlight. And had stupidly thought she could use her media chums to manipulate him, dropping hints that they were 'getting serious'. Hearing that had sobered him up pronto. *Finalmento.*

And of course Carmel was here tonight—she'd never miss it. All flowing golden hair and shimmering curves in a red sequined dress. Holding court in the middle of the vast foyer. She caught sight of them entering, covered her shock well. But he knew that the extravagant tilt of her head, the slight hitch in her rich syrupy laugh and the twisting pose to showcase her fabulous figure were all for him.

Dante had warned him that Operation: Frankie Who? was well underway. Everyone was desperate to know about the girl who had caused the Hurricane to bail out of the post-match celebrations and go off radar. The fact that she was more shot glass than hourglass, and had never made a social appearance before that anyone could remember, was as baffling as it was irritating for them.

Baffling for him, too, if he was honest. He'd felt physical attraction before. But this was crazy—like a wild pony. Ten years breaking it in, and still it wasn't tamed.

'Look how much of a sensation you're making,' he whispered into her ear, lingering a moment, knowing just how to heat her up.

'The only sensation *I've* got is horror,' she shot back. 'They're like vampires, waiting for blood. Get your garlic ready. And stay close with your pitchfork.'

'Relax…' He smiled and steered her through with a few nods, a few handshakes, but it was clear for all to see that he was lingering with no one but Frankie. He'd need to work hard to ease these particular knots from her shoulders—especially since she was so damn independent in every other aspect of her life.

'Let's get a drink.'

He liked this club—this home away from home. It was old, but not stuffy. The rules were as relaxed as you could hope for, and the people easy.

He and Dante had spent so much of their time here, back in the day. Made fools of themselves, learned to charm, in Dante's case, or in his case, fight a way out of trouble. All in the relative safety of this club that had seen generations of polo-playing Hermidas. Generations who now posed with other serious-eyed teammates or proud glossy ponies, looking down at them from their brass frames in the oak-panelled club rooms. *Full-blood* Hermidas. He never forgot that he was there by invitation only. But he was grateful now—accepting. Indebted.

He led her through the gold-draped dining room, past the billiard room and out to the terrace. Dark, warm air flowed between open French doors and mingled with chatter and laughter and lights. On the lawn the marquee throbbed with a low baseline—incongruously, invitingly.

'Do you want to dance?' he asked, handing her a glass of champagne.

'No. Thanks.' She sipped it, looked around.

'You want some food?' He indicated the abundant buffet.

'Not hungry. Who's the girl in the red dress?' she shot out.

He looked down at Frankie's upturned curious face. So she'd noticed. Predictably, Carmel was on form.

'An ex-girlfriend. Carmel de Souza. She likes the limelight—and you're in it.' He sensed some kind of predatory emotion in Frankie, but for once in his life it didn't make him recoil. 'She once had plans that involved me, but I suspect she has all those bases covered by now. She's never single. *Ever.*'

'That's no surprise—looking as she does.'

'Relax. Looking as she does is a full-time occupation. And I *mean* full-time.'

'Really?' Frankie sounded slightly snippy. 'Doesn't she have a *proper* job? Something with a bit more… substance?'

He shrugged. What *did* she do? Shop? Party? Self-promote? She was her own industry.

'She looks good. She snares rich men.'

'So she's a man hunter? Is that it?'

'More of a husband hunter, to be honest. And with me that was never going to happen. It became a bit of an issue between us.'

She gave a derisory little sniff and he cocked a curious brow. Her eyes, turned up to him, were full of clarity, deserving truth.

'Is that something *you'd* struggle with?' It was as well to know. It had been a deal-breaker before. More than once.

'It's not something I've ever given much thought to.'

He felt his phone vibrate.

'Is that you stating your position, Rocco?'

She'd framed the question carefully, but it would have to wait. He whipped his phone out, saw the screen ablaze with messages and one missed call. Dante.

Dammit.

'What's wrong? Is everything okay?'

'Nothing. Just a call I need to return. Give me a moment.'

He stepped away from her on the terrace, which was glazed with more firefly golden lights. Tried to press Redial. The call wouldn't connect. He pressed again. And again.

He strode along the terrace, checking the phone for a signal. Chatter from the house and music from the marquee clouded the air. Still no connection.

He paced away from the clubhouse, took a flight of stone steps down towards the tennis courts. Nothing.

There was a couple necking in the shadows—he took a path to their left. A gravel walkway narrowed by high hedges studded with flowers, their petals closed in sleep. The trail of party voices was now dimmed, the lights less frequent. Only occasional glimpses of moonlight and his frustratingly inept phone gifted him any real visibility.

He tried one more time.

The phone lit up as a message came through.

Dead end. Sorry. Be with you shortly.

A peal of laughter sounded above the strains of dance music. A breath of wind rose and fell. Around him leafy bushes puffed out like lungs, then sank back. He stood staring at the message.

It couldn't be. He had been so sure. *So sure.* Had felt it so strongly.

He had thrown everything at this. Years of patience. Every favour called in. How much longer was it going to take? How could thugs like Martinez hide their tracks so well? He'd known even as a child that the Martinez brothers were in deep with Mexican drug lords. Why hadn't the police ever caught up with them? Surely not *every* cop was bent? But they'd evaded everyone, and every effort he had put in had hit a dead end.

But they were out there somewhere. And they were not invincible. He was not frightened of them. Not anymore.

He would find him—Chris—the one who had fired the shot.

His day would come.

He stood. Drew in a deep, deep breath. Squared his shoulders. Slipped the phone away again. Looked back at the clubhouse, the party.

Frankie. For a fleeting moment a knot loosened inside him. Like a drop of black molasses slipping from a spoon. Peace. Another strange, unbidden thought.

He banished it. He was getting sentimental—that was all. He needed to get his head clear, keep his focus.

He started back up the path. Dante couldn't be too much longer. He listened for a helicopter, but the wind was rising and the party was beginning to throb as parties did.

He got to the terrace, caught sight of the spill of people all staring inside, through the French doors. Strode inside.

He might have known.

There she was. Carmel and her circus. And pinned in the middle, like a church candle in a blaze of fireworks, was Frankie.

Carmel was working her red dress as only she could. Fabulous breasts up and out, tiny waist twisted, hair tumbling like a waterfall of silk. She would have dwarfed Frankie anyway, but right now she looked just as she had in the bathroom mirror—a pale ghost of who she really was.

She made his heart melt.

'I'm sorry to take so long.' He reached out for her.

'Rocco—darling.'

At the sound of his voice Carmel swirled, pouted her glossy best, offered him her cheek. He had no time for her games. But she was quick.

'I was looking after your date. You left her all alone, baby! Were you looking for *me*?' she added, stage-whisper loud.

Over Carmel's shoulder he caught a glimpse of Frankie's inky eyes trained straight at him.

'Did you get your call made?'

He nodded.

Carmel manoeuvred her way between them. She turned her back on Frankie, rubbed her breasts against him.

'Rocco, baby... Have you missed me?'

She pouted and preened.

A camera flash went off.

She never missed a moment.

He opened his mouth to put her in her place, but Frankie suddenly rounded those sequined hips and stood at his other side, shoulders back and determined little chin tilted.

'*Miss* you? How could *anyone* miss you?'

Cool, understated, but strong. Rocco's eyes drank her in.

Carmel did an uncharacteristic double-take. 'I beg your pardon?'

'Subtlety, honey. Try looking it up.'

Rocco smiled and raised an eyebrow at Carmel. He'd never seen anyone take her on before—never mind trump her.

Frankie slid her arm around his waist, swivelled back to Carmel. 'And, for the record, my *date* has all he needs right here.'

Carmel put her hands on her abundant hips and stuck her head forward, looking for all the world like a turkey in a burlesque show. She started gabbling in Spanish, clearly thinking Frankie wouldn't understand, and she was totally unprepared for the volley that was fired right back at her. Even *he* was surprised at the colour of the words Frankie was using.

'Come. Enough,' he said, putting his arm around her and dragging her outside as she continued to sling one shocking insult after another.

Her feet shuffled to keep up as he quickened his pace, and then he spun her right round, framing them in the French windows.

'Stop, now. *Enough!* Where did you even *learn* those words?'

He held her possessively, and when she still poured

forward mouthfuls of cheek he had no other option. He gripped her jaw and angled her mouth just where he wanted it. Heard the swell of gasps and gossip, saw the flashes of cameras as he lowered his head and kissed her quiet.

She gripped onto his arms, wavered on her tiptoes, until he felt the anger and fight ooze out of her. Fury died in her mouth to be replaced by the soothing heat that only they could build.

He pulled back and smiled at her. 'Finished?'

As her eyes fluttered open there was a lull in the music and he heard the noise of a helicopter's rotors in the distance. He looked up. Dante? He trained his eyes on the lights from its belly as it loomed closer.

What had he found out? Surely they were closer? Surely *someone* knew something about Martinez? He desperately wanted to know the details—still couldn't believe it was completely a dead end—but that would have to wait until they were alone. Right now he owed it to Frankie to soothe her tension and get her well away from Carmel and the rest of this circus.

He led her down through air thick with pulsing music and events that were yet to happen.

'Is there anyone you *won't* take on, *hermosa*?'

He smiled softly at her. She was still tense and tight-lipped, rigid shoulders still not relaxed under his arm.

She shrugged. 'She deserved it.'

He couldn't disagree with that.

'I mean—is it a party in *her* honour? Because that's how she was acting!'

He ran his hand up to her neck, rubbed softly, his fingers bumping against the heavy earrings that even in the gloom caught scattering light.

Suddenly she swung round. 'Are you mad at me?'

He frowned. 'Why would I be mad?'

She swung away. 'I don't know—for running my mouth off? But I can't take those kind of women. Acting as if they've got a mandate on life just because they're every man's fantasy.'

'You believe that? Even if I tell you that some of those curves feel like leather balloons and they're no more real than the those fake emeralds you've got hanging from your ears.'

She fired her hands up to touch them and framed her own face in shock. 'Are you *serious*? I thought these were legit! I've been terrified all night that I'd lose one.'

He laughed out loud. Put his hands on her shoulders, pulled her in and hugged her.

'I love that about you,' he said. 'Of *course* they're real. Totally genuine. Just like you.'

She mock punched his chest and he held her close. There was so much about her that he loved. Even apart from the way she felt in his arms and in his bed. He loved her total lack of artifice—seeing her next to Carmel had been such a startling contrast, suddenly making him see her own Achilles' heel, making him feel so protective of her.

Maybe there was more than sex between them.

Maybe they should talk it through—cards on the table.

Or maybe that would just get her thinking in ways that wouldn't be all that helpful. And he had so much of his own thinking to do now.

He lifted his head to the helicopter that was now thundering closer, recognised it as Dante's. Its lights lit up the lawn, the tennis courts and finally the helipad itself.

'Here comes Dante.'

They stood on the terrace, watched as he jumped out under the copter's whirring blades in a black tux, white shirt and black tie, blond hair slicked back. His movie-star looks were striking. He jogged up, hand raised in greeting, but as he climbed the steps and got closer Rocco saw the usual million-dollar smile was slightly subdued.

Dante glanced to Frankie in acknowledgement and in question.

Rocco shook his head—a warning to say nothing.

Dante nodded. 'Hey! How's the party?' He was an expert, slipping right into charm mode. 'May I say how beautiful you look?'

He took Frankie's hands, scanned her, kissed her cheek. Rocco tried not to care.

'Well said. There's a whole crowd of women in there, waiting for you to say that to them. Starting with Carmel. *We've* got more important things to do.'

Dante looked mildly amused.

'Of course you have. Life just keeps getting in the way, doesn't it?'

'Take it easy in there, handsome.'

'I'll call you. Later.'

They grabbed hands, slapped backs. Then Rocco watched him go. Straight back, easy stride, head high, holding knowledge he burned to know.

Three girls—tiny dresses, long legs—threw up their arms and ran to him. Dante slid them all under his shoulder, not missing a step. Rocco slid his own arms around Frankie, pulled her flush against him. Stood there. Just held her.

Once more the lure of music and dancing and hard-core partying held no interest. He couldn't wait to get himself and his toxic thoughts away—to lose himself in this woman. To mindlessly make love to her until he didn't feel any pain, until he had cleared a path to what he had to do next.

'You want to stay much longer?'

He nodded to the valets and cars crawling slowly by, dropping, parking, leaving.

'I think Dante's got it covered.'

He nodded, tucked her in close again, slid his hand up through the soft skein of her hair.

One thing and one thing only was clear to him now. He was going to tell her that she'd better arrange a leave of absence for a while, because he needed her here. He wanted her in his bed and in his life. He wanted to wake up beside her and come home to her for longer than just this weekend.

And, just like Martinez being held to account, it was non-negotiable.

CHAPTER NINE

NIGHT'S DARK CLOAK lay heavy all around. Frankie woke
with a start, for a moment lost, with no dawn-edged window, no lamplit carpet to guide her vision.

She was in a huge space, lightless. Black. Warm. Safe.
Rocco's room. Rocco's home.

She flung out her hand. No Rocco.

He liked total darkness when he slept. Blackout blinds,
no lamps. Just bodies—naked, entwined—and loving,
and snatches of deep, dreamless sleep.

Then daybreak.

But it was still so dark, so vividly velvety black. And
his empty space was cold. She clutched her arms around
her body and shivered.

Rocco had been more intense than ever in his lovemaking tonight.

Almost as soon as they had got home he had poured
them both large measures of whiskey. His he had thrown
down his neck in a single gulp, the stinging heat of the
liquor appearing to make no impact on him. He'd seemed
to waver over pouring another, glancing sideways at the
bottle before putting his glass down carefully. Then he'd
cast off his dinner jacket and tie and in two slow strides
had hauled her against him.

He had devoured her. It was the only way she could

describe it. It had seemed there wasn't enough of her for him. They'd kissed so fiercely her lip had been cut and he'd tasted her blood. It was only then that he'd stopped his wildness. He'd heaved himself back from her, arms locked and rigid, gripping her and staring at her with shocked concern that he'd hurt her. But she'd felt nothing. Nothing but bereft when he'd pulled himself away.

She'd grabbed his head and pulled him back, and then they'd formed that heaving, writhing mass of fire and passion and pleasure. Hot, slick heaven. No wonder she was shivering now.

She licked her bruised lip and wondered where he was…what time it was.

Her hands groped over the clutter on the table beside her, grabbing for her phone. Her fingers bumped against the glass of water Rocco had placed there for her, trailed over the emerald earrings she'd carefully removed earlier and finally closed around her smartphone.

Instantly it lit the room. 4:00 a.m.

The screen showed two missed calls.

Mark.

Her heart froze. What was wrong? He rarely phoned. He knew she was here. Had something happened to her mother? Her brother? Her father…?

She sat up straight and frowned as her eyes focused, trying to work out the time in Dublin. 10:00 p.m.? She opened her messages and clicked on the link that he'd posted. It took her straight to a news item.

Her brother Danny. In Dubai. A photograph of him walking with a beautiful redhead. So what?

She squinted at the text. *Married?*

The message from Mark was curt. Did she know anything about it? Their mother was in a state of shock.

No wonder! Danny did exactly as he pleased. Without

asking anyone's permission. And the last person, the *very* last person he would confide in was Mark.

Frankie hated the estrangement between them. It had lasted so long. What a waste—what a terrible waste that they'd never got past their bitter feud. She thought of Rocco and Dante and the inseparable bond between them—*her* brothers should be like that. They really should.

She stared at the space where Rocco should be lying. Stared at the untouched glass of water on the table beside it, at his watch beside that, and beside that…

The tiny battered leather-framed photograph of the golden haired cherub. It was gone.

She stared at the space where it should be—where he'd carefully placed it earlier. She'd hardly even dared to look in his direction when he'd sat on the edge of the bed, pulled it from his pocket and set it upright. Almost ritualistic, almost reverential. She'd felt the air seize up, as if some sacred event was happening.

Of course since then she'd run her mind over all sorts of possibilities. It definitely wasn't Dante. He'd been six years old to Rocco's eight when Rocco had been adopted. The child in the photograph was barely two or three. She wasn't given to flights of fancy, but she'd hazard that the child was a blood relative. Maybe they'd been separated through adoption? Maybe that was way off the mark, but there was *something* that ate at him from the inside— something that caused those growling black silences, that haunted glazed look, his overt aggression.

He'd been like that tonight. She'd sensed it. Sensed it in the way he'd lain in bed, holding her after they'd both lost and found themselves in one another.

After he'd poured himself into her she'd felt an instinctive need to hold him, cradle him. But he'd pulled away, closed down. Lain on his back, staring unseeing at the black blanket of air. Lost.

She knew she should encourage him to talk, the way he had encouraged her. She also knew getting past the hellhound that guarded his innermost thoughts would be a Herculean task. But it was the least a friend could do. The least a lover would do.

And that was the dilemma that she was going to have to face. What *was* she to him? What was he to *her*? And even if she worked that out, what future was there for two people who lived thousands of miles apart? He might say he wanted her to stay on, but even if she stayed a few extra days—assuming she could negotiate that with her boss—what was going to happen at the end? How horrible if he suddenly tired of her and she felt she'd overstayed her welcome, like the last guest at a party.

Distance was be the one thing that would give her clarity. Of *course* she wanted to stay on—he was addictive, this life was heavenly—but it was all part of the ten-year fuse that had been lit when they'd first met. And she didn't want to be blown to pieces once it finally exploded. She'd have to have this conversation with him. And before too much longer.

Her phone vibrated in her hand. Another message from Mark…another photograph. This time there was no mistake. Bride and groom. She dragged on the photo to enlarge it. The girl was beautiful, but with Danny that was nothing new. Whoever she was, and whatever she had, she'd hooked him. Danny looked…awestruck.

Wow. She had to show this to Rocco. Had to share her news.

She swung her legs out of bed, reached for a shirt and set off to find him along the cool, tiled hallway. At the far end she could see the eerie green glow from the courtyard pool. On the other side, the TV room was lit up, the flickering glare of the television screen sending lights and shadows dancing.

She took the long way—through the house rather than across the little bridge. The glass walls reflected light and made it hard to see anything.

But what she *did* see wounded her more than any torn lip.

He was sitting on a low couch, facing the screen. The light licked at the naked muscled planes of his body. One arm rested on the armrest of the couch, a whiskey tumbler full of liquor caught in his hand, and the other held something small, square—it had to be the photograph. He was staring at it, unsmiling, as a sitcom she recognised played out on the screen.

Parallel to the room, across the courtyard, separated from him by the illuminated water, the bridge and all that glass, she watched him. He didn't move. Not a single muscle flickered with life. He sat as if cast in marble.

Finally he lifted the glass to his lips and sank a gulp of whiskey.

She didn't need any close-up to see that he was upset. Her heart ached for him.

Through the glass rooms she went until she came alongside the doorway. She stood still.

'Rocco,' she said softly.

He knew she was there. She felt his sigh seep out into the room. He blinked and dipped his head in acknowledgement, then finally lifted his arm in a gesture she knew was an invitation to join him.

She moved, needing no further encouragement, and slid onto the couch, under his arm. He closed it round her and she laid her head on his chest.

His body was warm. He was always warm. She rubbed

her face against him, absorbing him, scenting the faint odour of his soap and his sweat. The powerful fumes from the whiskey.

He lifted the tumbler to his lips and drank. Less than earlier, but still enough for her to hear the harsh gulp in his throat as he swallowed. He put the glass down on the edge of the armrest and sat back, continued to hold her in the silence of the night.

'I woke up. My phone's been going off.'

He took another silent sip.

She spoke into his chest. 'Looks as though Danny got married. In Dubai. Mark sent some pictures that are in the news over there. He says no one had any idea. Mum's in a state.'

'He's a big boy,' said Rocco.

What could she say to that? He was right. There was no way anyone would have hoodwinked Danny. He was far too smart.

'I know, but I kind of wish he'd told us.'

'What difference would it have made? Would you have gone?'

She shrugged her shoulders, incarcerated under his arm.

'I might.'

The silence bled again. He took another sip.

'Are you planning on sharing that whiskey?'

'You want to drink to the happy couple?'

It wasn't a snarl, but it wasn't an invitation to celebrate, either. She pushed up from him but he didn't look at her. His face, trained now on the television screen, was harsh, blank.

She reached out her fingers, gingerly threaded them through his fringe, softly swept it back from his brow.

'I want *you* to be happy, Rocco.'

It was barely audible, but it was honest. Shockingly honest. And when he turned his hurt-hazed eyes to hers she began to realise how much she meant it.

'Come on. Come back to bed,' she said—as much a plea as an order.

She stood, reached for the tumbler, tried to take it out of his hand. And then her eyes fell on the leather-framed photo that he held in his other hand. He turned it then. Turned it round so that the plump-cheeked infant was staring up at him. He looked at it and his bleak, wintry gaze almost felled her. Then he turned it face down, lifted the glass and tipped his head back to drain the dregs.

'Come on, Rocco. Please.'

He held his eyes closed as he breathed in, soul deep, then opened them and stared blankly at the screen.

Frankie turned to see the characters' slapstick antics. They were trying to move a couch up a flight of narrow stairs—a scene she'd seen countless times before and one that always made her laugh. But not this time. Not in the face of all this unnamed pain.

She turned back to see the coal-black eyes trained back on the photograph.

'If you want to talk or tell me anything…? God, Rocco, I hate to see you like this.'

'Go back to bed, then.'

She swallowed that. It was hard. It would be hard hearing it from anyone. But from a man of his strength, his intensity, his power—a man who meant as much to her as he did…

'Not unless you come with me.'

He lifted the empty glass to his lips, sucked air and the few droplets of whiskey that were left. Like a nonchalant cowboy before he went back on the range.

'As much as you tempt me, I don't think that's a good

idea right now,' he said, glancing at the bottle on the bar to one side of the huge television.

She stood right in front of him, deliberately blocking his view of the silently flickering screen and the half bottle of whiskey that was just out of reach.

'Why not, Rocco? Why not talk or make love or even just hold each other?'

He shook his head slightly, made a face. It was as if all his effort was trained into just...*being*.

'Right now I don't trust myself. I don't want to hurt you again.'

'What do you mean, *again*? You didn't mean to hurt me—you got carried away. We *both* got carried away. You've got something carving you up. Rocco. Let me...'

'Just give me space, Frankie.'

She swallowed. He sounded exhausted, but he was brutal. She was brave enough to take him on, though. Him *and* his dark, desperate mood.

She wedged herself between his open legs, hunkered down, rested her arms on the hard, solid length of his thighs. This beautiful man—every inch of him—deserved her care.

'I don't think space is what you need just now.'

She looked up past the black band of his underwear to the golden skin and dark twists of hair, the ripped abs and perfect pecs, the strong male shoulders and neck and the harsh, sensuous slash of his mouth.

She trailed her touch down hard, swollen biceps, followed the path of a proud vein all the way to where his fingers lay around the photograph. Finally she traced her fingertips over his, and held his eyes when they turned to hers.

'What can be so bad? There's nothing that isn't better when it's shared.'

Slowly, boldly, she closed her fingers around the photograph frame.

'Can I see?'

His gaze darkened, his mouth slashed more grimly, but she didn't stop.

Gingerly, she tugged it from his grip. 'Is he your son?'

She had no idea where that came from. But suddenly the thought of an infant Rocco was overwhelming.

'You're opening up something that's best left shut.'

His voice was a shell—a crater in a minefield of unexploded bombs.

She climbed up closer to him, balanced on his thighs. Lifted the photo frame into her hands completely, laid her head against his chest and scrutinised it.

And he let her.

She felt the fight in him ease slightly as he exhaled a long breath.

She sat there waiting. Waiting…

Finally he spoke.

'He's my brother. His name was Lodovico—Lodo. He was three years old when that photo was taken. And he was four years old when he died.'

She held her breath as he said the words.

'I was his only family. Our *papá* had disappeared and Mamá had lost her mind. Nobody else wanted to know.'

His voice drilled out quietly, his chest moved rhythmically and the haunted black eyes of his poor baby brother gazed up.

'I was with him when he died. I didn't cause his death—I was only a child myself. I am not responsible.' The words came out in a strange staccato rush. 'But I *feel* it,' he added harshly, and a curl of his agony wound round her own heart.

She swallowed, shifted her weight, slid to his side and

under his arm. She held the photo in front of them, so they were both looking at it.

'I can say those words over and over and they still mean nothing. I've said them so many times. Meaningless. Of *course* I am responsible.'

'How did he die?'

It seemed baldly awful to say it aloud, but she knew she had hear it. She knew there was worse to come.

'By gunfire. Shot dead. A bullet aimed at *me*. Because *I* was the one running errands for a rival gang. And when the stakes are high, and the police are being paid to look the other way, and mothers have gone mad and fathers can't take the shame of not being able to provide…life is cheap.'

She sat up. He stared ahead. The credits were rolling on the television screen. His face was stone.

'But you just said…you were a child, too… How can you be blamed?'

'How can I *not* be blamed? If I hadn't become little more than a petty criminal—if I had found another way for us to live—if I hadn't got greedy and done more and more daring things…*terrible* things. If I hadn't let go of his fingers when he needed me most…'

His eyes crashed shut and his face squeezed into a mask of agony.

Frankie tugged him to her, desperate for his warm, strong touch as the hurt of his words and in his face gnawed at her resolve.

'What age were you—six? Seven? How could you have prevented *any* of those things happening?'

She stared up at him but he merely turned away, as if he'd heard it all before.

She placed her hands on his cheeks and positioned herself round to face him, held him steady in her grip.

'Rocco. You were a child. And you're *still* tearing yourself up over this?'

His face was a ridge of rock and anger.

She kissed him. She kissed the jutting cheekbone that he turned to her, the wedge of angry jaw, the harshly held crevice of his lips. She felt her tears slide between them and put her lips where they washed down.

'Rocco, baby…you were *not* to blame.'

His eyes were still closed to her but she didn't care. She couldn't stand to see her warrior in such pain. With tiny, soft presses she slowly covered his face with her lips, whispering her heart to him.

He kept himself impassive, cold and distant. He didn't push her away, but she could feel that he wanted to. As with every other time, she let her body guide her, not her head. He needed her. She needed to let him see how much. As instinctively as a flower faced the light, or curled its petals at night, she laid her body around him and soothed him.

And slowly he began to respond to her heat and light. He sighed against her whisper-soft kisses, melted into her cradling arms. He sat back against the couch and she climbed over him, slipped her legs around him to strengthen him, to imbue him with everything she could. The energy and emotion they had shared welled up inside her, and she knew she would gladly gift it all to him to ease his awful pain.

'Frankie…' he breathed into her neck as she lay over him.

His arms that had been lying limply at his sides, not quite rejecting her, now closed around her and held her tightly against him. She found herself rocking slightly, in that age-old movement of reassurance and care.

'You would never do anything to harm an innocent child. *Never.*'

His arms slid closer around her, holding her body and her head clasped against him. He had so much power and strength and yet he was so vulnerable, lying there in her arms.

'I would do anything to turn the clock back. I could have done so much more to protect him.'

'And who was protecting *you*?'

He sighed against her. 'I didn't need protecting. I needed to be reined in. Always have.'

She pulled back and stared at him, cupped her hands around his beautiful, broken face.

'Rocco, don't you even see what you're saying? You were a child, too. And what's even harder to take is that you were trying to be an adult—to make decisions that your parents should have been making for you.'

He recoiled at that, but she didn't stop.

'I can't pretend to understand what you've been through. But I *do* understand that you're adding to the pain of losing Lodo by hating yourself so much for something that wasn't your fault.'

He was still, his eyes level with her chest, not looking at her. The hair of his fringe had fallen down over his scar. She pushed it back and then gently lowered her head to kiss the reddened mark.

'I wish you would leave the hate. There's so much about you to love. Your body is covered in your history—even this crazy little scar. Fighting in the streets when you should have been learning Latin... I *love* it.'

He didn't move a muscle. She moved her lips to the flattened break in the bridge of his nose. Kissed it.

'And this *perfect* imperfect nose. Getting a polo stick in your face because you wouldn't give up...'

She curled downward, holding on tightly, not daring to open her eyes, letting her body guide her, remembering all the things he'd told her about his injuries. The bones in his shoulder were all out of alignment from his falls and fights. She lowered her lips and ran them along each bump and ridge.

Finally she placed her lips over his. Soft, firm, warm. The fires they had lit between them were always glowing, ready to flare into life.

'I love these lips.' She kissed him so softly. 'The pleasure they have given me…'

She felt something inside her contract as she spoke. Waves of emotion rolled and more words formed in her throat. She choked them back and used her mouth to show him how she felt. Softly pressing their mouths together, carefully sculpting and moulding and shaping. The familiar blaze was already taking hold, but this time something bigger, higher, sweeter sang out through the fire.

'Oh, Rocco…' she said as the waves began to break.

He stood up in one smooth movement. She held on as he began to walk, as he repositioned her, cradled her and carried her forward. She held on to the thick column of his neck and pulled herself close as he walked slowly back to the bedroom.

He opened the door and carried her in, walked right over to the bed and laid her down as if she were a silken cloth. He moved over her and stared down at her. She stared back. Up at his face, still intense—always intense—but softer now.

'You sweet, sweet girl,' he said as he slowly unbuttoned the shirt she'd thrown on.

She sat up, threaded her hands through his hair and pulled him down to her. She kissed him. Over and over.

That was all. Just kissed him. Feeling those lips that she'd come to cherish for the pleasure they gave. Kissing and holding and adoring him. Nursing him with her body. And her heart.

Those words welled up in her throat again. But she swallowed them down.

He touched her as if she was treasure, moved her carefully on the bed, began to stoke their sexual love with his mouth and his hands. She climbed higher and higher, beginning to lose track of where she ended and he began.

'Frankie, *carina*...'

He eased her legs open with his thighs and slid inside her. Huge and thick, he filled her completely, perfectly. Inches from her face she felt his warm breath. She ran her hands over the rough stubble of his jaw, felt the enveloping power of his body around her.

She knew the crescendo was coming, but each honeyed beat of the prelude was immense. So perfectly, precisely slowly he eased himself in and out of her. Rocco... her wounded soldier...her love. The words choked her as she kissed him and he kissed her back, murmuring sounds about how he treasured her until she knew she could hold on no longer.

Never, *ever* had she known the depths of such feeling for another human as their lovemaking throbbed to its final conclusion and she broke like a concerto of strings all around him and cried out the blissful joy from her heart.

He collapsed onto her, crushing her, winding her in the most perfect way possible. His hair-roughened limbs and stubbled jaw were her satin sheets. Their breath and sweat mingled. Light from the neglected hall doorway seeped into the room and soothed the night's edges with silvery strokes.

And together they lay, weary, slipping into slumbers and dreams, knowing that they'd crossed some giant divide and there was no longer any way back.

CHAPTER TEN

A WHISKEY HEADACHE was about the last thing Rocco needed as he prowled through the house, drinking water and rewinding the events of the previous night.

What the *hell* had he been thinking? Did he have a body double? What had gotten into him?

The party. And for the first time he could remember wanting to leave the Turlington Club early. Hell, he'd even had to be persuaded to attend in the first place. It had all looked the same—the crowd had been the same, the sponsors had laid on the usual fantastic spread. The only thing that had been different was his head. And Frankie. And those two things were probably connected.

Carmel… Trying so hard to eclipse Frankie and having it backfire so spectacularly. If anything had made him realise how much of a sham his relationship with her had been it had been seeing her beside Frankie, seeing how much of a contrast they were.

Carmel was all about Carmel. She never gave a damn about anyone else. He'd was only ever been there because he'd given her social credit—not because she'd actually loved him… He should have seen through that right at the start instead of being captivated by her body. A body that left him completely cold now. Now his 'type' ran to a whole different set of vitals.

He took another glug of desperately needed water. Dehydrated on top of everything else.

Dante and the news that there was no news. How the hell all this had ended in another blind alley, he still couldn't figure. As soon as Dante got here he'd go through the whole trail piece by piece.

He rubbed at his jaw, rasped his fingers through the stubble. He really needed to shave—he'd probably removed another layer of Frankie's skin this morning.

Frankie. Most of all Frankie. Was he losing control? He was still furious with himself for taking her so fast and hard, hurting her in his selfish need to bury his anger. He'd known he was being rough. They did 'rough' really well. But he'd pushed the limits, and 'rough' definitely didn't mean drawing blood.

And even after that she'd still come to find him. And he had stupidly told her all about Lodo. He felt like knocking his head off the wall to see if there were still any brains in there. When had he ever, *ever* opened up to anyone about his brother? It had taken his therapists five years to get him even to say his name, and he had blurted the whole thing out to *her* in one night!

What kind of crazy was going on with him just now? And how was he going to get back from where they'd ended up last night? Sex that had been tender, beautiful. The best tender and beautiful sex he'd ever had. The *only* tender and beautiful sex he'd ever had.

Dammit again. What was happening? He knew things had changed now. Not permanently—but she was a woman. She'd have expectations. Women *always* had expectations. And *he'd* paved the way for that.

Why was sex such a comfort in his life right now? Couldn't he just rein in his emotions as he had every other time and use sport? Boxing had sorted him out in his early teens, and polo had been his salvation right up until *she'd* walked back into his life.

He really had to get some kind of normal back in place. This just wasn't *him*. Using a woman to help him sift through all the debris in his head showed a lack of judgement.

It wasn't that he didn't trust her to keep the story about Lodo to himself—he did, of course he did. It was just that keeping things tight had worked so well up to now. The closed ranks of himself and Dante were perfect: There was no judging, no explaining. The last thing he wanted to do was *talk* about it. Women were always *talking* about it.

He reached the TV room and saw the whiskey bottle. At least half of it gone. And it hadn't even served its purpose, because he'd sunk it and *still* blabbed when she'd come in—when she'd wheedled it out of him.

He shook his head as he lifted the bottle and carried it back to join the others on the bar. It would be a long time before he'd touch it again.

He looked at the couch, saw the photo. Staring at it, he saw an image of them sitting together. She hadn't wheedled it out of him. She'd been great. She'd done exactly what he would have done if he'd seen her sitting in a mood like that. Exactly what he *had* done when she'd gotten herself in such a state about the media.

He picked up Lodo's picture. So he'd told her? He shook his head again. The only thing to do now was make the best of it.

He knew that it was only a matter of time before some nosy investigative journalist or unofficial biographer unearthed it and splashed it all over the media anyway. He'd buried as much as he could of his early life, but there was always someone willing to swap a story for cash. Hadn't he tried that himself in the hunt for Chris Martinez? He was still trying. It was all he had left.

And as soon as Dante came over, after they'd talked through in detail what he had and hadn't found, he'd be back on it—like the relentless bloodhound he was.

Although, he thought as he lifted the whiskey tumbler and made his way through to the kitchen, the hunt for the Martinez brothers was something he'd be keeping to himself. The contacts he'd had to establish, the risks he'd taken to scratch the underbelly of the world they existed in, to breathe that stench again—there was no way he wanted to share any of *that* with Frankie. He barely wanted Dante to be involved. He didn't want her exposed to it and, crucially, he didn't want to increase the risk by widening the circle of knowledge.

No, he'd shared more than enough with her already.

He put the glass in the gleaming empty dishwasher, turned to the coffee machine and started it up. There was no point in trying to claw back what had gone. All he could do now was keep a lid on the rest. And, yes, he'd asked her to stay on here—but after the events of last night maybe that wasn't such a great idea. Not while Dante was due and the chase was still on. Not when he seemed to be in the habit of opening up and blabbing about stuff that no one should have to carry apart from him.

He shook his head again. What *was* it about her that she had got him to open up like that? He'd never even come close to it before. Totally uncharacteristic behaviour. He had quite knowingly left Lodo's picture out in the bedroom, even after she'd asked him about it. With every other woman that picture had been tucked away. He did not sow the seeds of pity—he did not want to harvest their emotions. If he had any sense at all he'd shut his mouth and shut down this obsession that seemed less and less like unfinished business and more and more like an unsolvable problem.

He was getting used to her being here. He was loving the way their bodies were so utterly in tune with one another. He was loving the easy presence she had, sharing space with him. He was loving the ease that she brought to his life rather than the fuss and nonsense of someone like Carmel. But she had to know that there was never going to be anything more than this. She'd started to ask him last night, just before the call from Dante, and they had to finish that conversation soon.

He checked the time. Dante would have partied hard last night, knowing him, so it would be another couple of hours before he was ready to surface. He could get caught up on work, or he could sweat out this hangover with some serious exercise. An hour of running on the beach and then a session with the punching bag should sort him out. Maybe he should wake Frankie and ask her to come running with him? No, maybe not. He could do with some more thinking time. Because 'losing himself' in her just seemed to be adding to the list of problems, not solving any.

He ran for miles. Kept going well past the point where he normally doubled back. The surfers were out in force, riding the pretty big waves that spilled up and soaked him time and again as he pounded along the beach. A couple of riders passed, their horses galloping in the foam, and he made a mental note to take Frankie out riding in the surf before she left. She'd love it.

His head was still pounding, and still full of conflicting thoughts, but at least he'd cleared up one thing and he felt a hell of a lot better for it.

He trudged up from the beach, thinking about a long drink and a cool shower. Thinking about whether it should be alone or not. Thinking about Frankie and the conversation he was definitely going to have with her. Picking up from where they'd left off last night. God knew he had said it often enough in the past—no commitment past a sexual relationship. No expectations. And definitely no one getting any ideas about buying a hat. He liked her. A lot. But it was best if they were both really clear about what was going to happen next. He had to make sure she had no stupid notions brewing after last night.

But first he was going to get that drink.

He rounded the corner of the garden onto the terrace—right into the middle of a cosy scene.

Dante and Frankie. They were huddled together, staring at something. And the closeness of them, shoulder to shoulder, thigh to thigh on the swing seat, brought a bitter taste to his mouth. What was Dante playing at? Happy families?

'Oh, my God, he's not going to like this.'

'Not going to like what?' he asked, aware of the growl in his voice—aware and not giving a damn.

They both looked up sharply. Dante couldn't hide the moment of surprise on his face, but then, as ever, he slipped right back into easy charm.

'Hey, bro, that's some dynamo you're operating. Wall-to-wall private partying and a ten-mile run before breakfast? I've been here for ages, waiting for you. Good job Frankie was here to look after me.'

Don't let him wind you up, he told himself. But even though he knew Dante was deliberately baiting him, he still rose.

'You're here earlier than I thought,' he said, walking

towards them, still sitting there all cosy together. 'You should have messaged me. I'd have made sure I was here.'

'Well, normally I wouldn't rush, as you know, but with Frankie here just now I can hardly stay away.'

Frankie laughed and punched the side of his arm playfully. 'You're hilarious. You only just got here!'

And then Dante slid his arm around her and squeezed her against his side, blue eyes flashing and smile beaming. A look of complete joy on his face.

'This is still early for me, sweet cheeks. Normally my first meal after Turlington is dinner. Today I'm going for brunch. Impressed?'

Rocco was so, so *un*impressed. Dante had gone right past flirting and moved into some kind of buddy brother-in-law role. The last thing Frankie needed was any more in the way of invitations to be part of Team Hermida. Rocco needed to bring him up to speed on things—and fast.

'Frankie, can you leave us for a moment? Dante and I have a little business to discuss. In private.'

Which was true, but he could have handled it a lot less awkwardly than that, he supposed. The look that flashed over her face told him he'd hurt her, but she rose up with a serene little smile.

'I'll leave you to it. I'd better say goodbye, Dante— I'm not sure when I'll next see you. I have to get back to work soon.'

He stood, too, grabbed her shoulders and held her.

'Ah, parted so soon...I didn't realise. Sorry—I thought you were here for a while. Okay... Well, I'm sure this will only be a temporary goodbye—and it would be great to keep in touch anyway. Hermanos Hermida is always on the lookout for new cheerleaders.'

Had he lost his mind? What the *hell* was he doing?

Rocco watched as Dante pulled her in for a squeeze that lasted far too long, and had the fists in his hands curled into tight, angry balls. If that punching bag was at hand it would get a blasting!

Finally he let her go, and she sauntered off with that sexy little walk, wearing yet another of his shirts. Beautifully.

He turned to Dante.

'*Sweet-cheeks? Cheerleader?* What the hell are you up to, Dante? Since when do you lead *any* woman on to thinking they're going to be part of this family?'

Dante walked towards him.

'Relax. You're like a caged beast. I had to smooth over *your* clumsy move. What was all that about? Sending her away the way you did? Who treats the woman they love like *that*?'

He froze. Dante had sat down again and picked up a newspaper, flicked it open and started to scan through it. He lifted a cup of coffee to his mouth and sipped. As if he had merely asked him about the weather instead of firing a volley of emotionally charged bullets. And striking his target—bull's eye.

'You can forget *that*.'

'What?' he asked, flicking on, sipping on. 'Are you going to try to pretend you're *not* in love with her? It's as obvious as Carmel's fake boobs. Talking of which— you might want to break the habit of a lifetime and check out the latest media reports. If you say you're not in love, you'd better put out a press release.'

And he tossed him his phone.

Pictures of him and Frankie. His eyes scanned them— leaving the villa, entering the Turlington Club, and then the one that he himself had staged, kissing passionately. His eyes widened at how hot they looked. And then there were more—of them staring into each other's eyes, thinking they were unobserved, smiling and hugging. Okay, it *did* look like love caught on camera, but they were just lovers out together. It was no big deal. He'd been with other dates before and there were probably dozens of pictures just like these.

But as his fingers scrolled down he saw what Dante was pointing out. There *were* pictures of him with other women, but he held them at a distance and his face was rigid. And the headlines screamed, The Hurricane Has Been Tamed!

La Gaya—the Magpie—that was what they were calling Frankie, thanks to her striking dark hair and her pearl-pale skin—and to stealing from the nest of the glorious Carmel. *Brilliant*. Just what he needed.

He tossed Dante his phone.

'It'll blow over. No big deal. There's more important stuff to deal with. Like what did you find out?'

Dante dropped the humour like a soaked blanket.

'It was the longest of long shots. Might still be something in it, but I don't know. I got the feeling from our guy that they're doing as much fishing as we are. Someone's claimed to have shared a cell with a guy who knew Chris Martinez. Said he'd been inside and then released after only serving a couple of months. The talk was that he'd done a deal and been given a new identity. But that's all it was. Talk.'

'Sounds pretty likely, though.'

'Maybe. I'm not sure. But there was nothing else to get from the guy. He didn't have any more intel on Martinez. And he started to ask too many other questions. I reckon he was fishing for info about *you*.'

Rocco mulled that over. He'd been so careful about this. He didn't deal directly with investigators himself.

This was the first time Dante had stepped in for him but otherwise he always used a proxy, kept his distance, organised everything via a separate email account and phone number. The last thing he wanted was to bring any shame on the Hermida family. Not after all they'd done for him. So for all that he was picking through the detritus of a nasty world, he'd done it carefully—*very* carefully—up until now.

'Okay,' he said. 'Thanks.'

'What next?'

Rocco rubbed the back of his neck, stretched out his shoulders, flexed his hands. Shook his head.

'I don't know. I'll give it some thought.'

'Don't you think you should leave it for a while? It's not as if the trail is red-hot. Spend some time with Frankie and fix that before she goes. Don't leave loose ends, or you might…'

He frowned at Dante.

'Might what?'

'Lose her.'

They stared at each other across the table, the newspaper spread out between them like a matador's cloak. And Rocco was definitely the bull.

'I'm just saying—I *know* you. When you get information—*any* information—about Martinez you go into these moods, lash out at people. Like I just saw. And someone like Frankie isn't going to hang around to take it.' He put his hands up in a mock surrender. 'Just sayin'…'

'I've got it covered,' he said.

'I'm sure you have.' Dante reached for him, slapped his back, the way they always did. 'I'm going to head off now. Are you travelling back to BA today? Tomorrow?'

'Later today, if you want a lift. Frankie has a meeting

set up with a trader to check out some aloe samples before she flies back to Madrid.'

He nodded. 'I'll leave you two alone. Time must be precious.'

Dante lifted his phone, drained his coffee and pulled out his car keys. One final slap on the back and then he walked away, tripping down the steps as if he was dancing in a damn Hollywood musical. How did he make every moment of his life look like a movie? He pulled him out of his moods every time.

Rocco smiled to himself. God, he loved that man. He headed indoors. Time to shower, shave and then bundle them both back to La Colorada and their full and frank, no-holds-barred discussion.

Frankie finished the last part of her email and reread it for the tenth time. Her finger hovered for two whole seconds above the keyboard—and then she pressed Send.

Gone. Too late to do anything about it now.

She had taken almost two hours to think it through, come to a final decision and then write the damned thing. Two hours in which she had written out a list of pros and cons that had Rocco Hermida's name in both columns.

Staying here was a pro because it gave her more time with him—time to get to know him better, to explore every part of his fabulous estancia, to go riding, to take in the next polo match and to lie in his arms after it and revel in the gorgeous feeling of being Rocco's girl.

But staying here was also a con, because if she did all of those things it meant that she was going to fall deeper and deeper in love. And she wasn't stupid enough to think that was a two-way street—yet. It might be…in time. But after opening up to her last night, lifting the lid on his box of secrets, he'd slammed it shut again, nailed it down and buried it deeper than it had ever been.

He'd prowled through the house on the phone, moving into empty spaces and closing glass doors, literally shutting her out. He'd spent nearly all morning running on the beach, and a good part of the afternoon in the gym. He'd been curt, verging on rude when Dante had been there, and though he'd apologised he'd offered no explanation or softening. It was almost as if he was angry at himself for sharing his story, for making himself seem a little more human, a little more mortal than godlike.

And in a way that just added to the allure. He was *so* complex, so dark, so vulnerable. And she ached to help him slough off this crown of thorns he wore. She'd never felt more moved than when she was lying in his arms, making love in the early hours of the morning. It was like opening her eyes after the longest sleep, glimpsing a beautiful sunrise, seeing a glorious future—and then feeling darkness seep back as night fell prematurely, suddenly. Leaving her stumbling about in the dark, unable to find the light.

So what to do? What to do…?

In the end one thing had tipped the balance—he enriched her. But more than that he needed her. She knew how hard it had been for him to talk about his early childhood. Maybe he never had before. And if she didn't make an effort for him now she might never take the chance again. Because it *was* a chance. There was no guarantee that he was going to revisit any of that trauma with her or anyone else. It broke her heart to think that he carried that guilt. But it was so *him*. To shoulder everything himself. And keeping everyone else at a distance was probably the only way he could handle it.

Did she really expect him to treat her any differently

than any of the countless women she'd seen on those pictures that she and Dante had scrolled through earlier? She
knew what she felt, but getting him to a point where he
might admit the same was like trying to reroute a hurricane. It was only going to go where it wanted. And when
it hit land everybody had better stand back.

She sighed and clicked on her sent box to confirm
that the email had indeed been delivered. Knowing that
in approximately two hours' time her boss was going to
read it and probably go into some kind of tailspin himself.

The timing couldn't be worse. She was asking for
leave at a time when she should have been parcelling
herself up to be sent express delivery back to Madrid.
She could feel in her bones the resistance to her proposals already. The emails that had been coming from head
office were getting more and more cautionary. She could
detect a derisory sniff in the air, and now she was seven
days away from a one-to-one with her boss.

But she was going to use this extra time to polish her
proposal until it shone. Going organic was the only way.
Natural products were everywhere. There was nothing
to commend Evaña to the modern savvy shopper. If she
could develop an organic line and hook in a couple of
bloggers, they'd be off to a flyer. If not they were going
to continue to lose customers like skin lost elasticity, and
none of the big stockists would look twice at them. At
least this way the ageing geriatric company might have
a future. And if it had a future, so did she.

That *had* to remain her number one priority. Being
here with Rocco was enriching, but it wasn't real life.
Real life was waiting for her when she jumped out of the
metro in Madrid and picked her way along the *calle* to
head office and her moment in the spotlight.

She packed up her briefcase in readiness for their

early-morning helicopter ride. Rocco's helicopter... Rocco's pilot. Hopefully their journey would go by unnoticed. The last thing she wanted was any more media interest as a result of her being with him. Her poor mother was already contending with whatever it was that had tipped Danny over the edge and into wedded bliss. He was playing his cards very close to his chest, as he always did. But thankfully what had happened in Punta seemed to be staying in Punta—for now anyway.

She braced herself every time she got a message, thinking it might be her mother, wailing and crossing herself over her daughter's loose morals—or even more likely her father, who would be happy to finally be proved right.

She zipped up the black leather case, stacked it beside the gorgeous old desk in the study she'd settled herself in and smiled. Strange how she'd begun to see things slightly differently after hearing Rocco's words. For a moment she let herself bask in all the sweet things he'd whispered to her at night. Let herself feel that she was unique in a positive way, rather than freakily different from all the local girls. Feel proud of what she'd achieved rather than ashamed that she didn't want what had been mapped out for her. An inspiration, he'd called her once. And more than a tiny part of her wanted to believe that.

She traced her way back through the expansive masculine home. Polished parquet floors with silk runners spread out along long narrow hallways. Console tables punctuated the burgundy silk walls, highlighting fabulous black-and-white photographs of gauchos and dancers and patent-coated stallions. It was so *him*—so darkly, elegantly, brutally beautiful.

His bedroom threw the house's dark arteries into airy relief. High ceilings, wide windows and sumptuous silk carpets—and the bed that they had christened after that disastrous pony ride two days earlier.

She smiled, looked at it and straightened the pony-skin cushions, setting them against the vast wooden head-board. The little photo of Lodo was back in place on the bedside table. She picked it up and looked at it—really looked at it. What a beautiful boy he had been…but so solemn. God only knew what terrors he'd seen—what terrors Rocco had seen and continued to see. He might have clammed up again, but those flashes of truth had given her such insight—personal nuggets she'd hold dear and treasure.

She sighed. Blew out a huge breath she hadn't even realised she'd been holding. She glanced over at the door to the dressing room and her battered little carry-on and suit bags. She had to remember she was here for a pur-pose, and it wasn't all about taming the Hurricane—and the more she read the subtext of her directors' bulletins the more she felt the enormity of that task, too.

But she *could* nail this, she thought as she moved over and ran a hand down her best summer suit, smoothing down the fabric and straightening the seams. She could actually make a difference—not only to Evaña but to herself, too. She could talk terms with traders, strike reasonable deals and put the stats into a really slick pre-sentation. She could do some groundwork with bloggers and a beauty editor she'd begun to get friendly with. She really could pull this off.

And then she'd have banked more than enough to ride back to County Meath with her head high and her pride intact and demand a very long overdue apology from her father.

CHAPTER ELEVEN

TWENTY-FOUR HOURS LATER Frankie jumped out of the helicopter, kept her head bent, clutched her briefcase to her body and hurled herself across the parched grass to the driveway. Her heels stuck in mud-baked crevices and the rotors thundered over her head, throwing up the skirt of her dress. But she didn't care. She just wanted out of it. Out of the helicopter and away from her stinging reflections on the crucifying day she'd forced herself to relive on the hour-long flight back.

Coming in to land, she'd spotted riders cutting through the head-high grass fields and moving into the rougher countryside that she'd crossed herself a few days earlier. Clouds of dust swirled and settled as they rode through green-and-yellow grassland. Rocco was sure to be with them. She'd left him this morning, after another night of frenzied passion—another night when she'd longed to cry out her heart into the hot dark night, to whisper her love and bask in the emotions that rolled through her when she lay in his arms.

But she hadn't. She'd held back. She'd silently floated in oceans of happiness, but had been ever aware of the crashing waterfall that was right there, just out of sight, a glaring reminder to hold something back—her life raft.

She couldn't criticise Rocco for anything. He was attentive, considerate and caring. He worshipped her body, and he appeared to enjoy her mind, her conversation and her company. But he was as deep and as distant as ever. Every time she'd tried to sneak a look past his barricades he'd somehow made them higher.

And now, with the days ticking by, she was feeling more and more anxious that she'd made a terminal career mistake by asking for more time when the finance department was asking for more cutbacks.

But she'd left this morning determined to bring back some good news, to make the directors see that she really knew what she was doing.

Before that she and Rocco had breakfasted on the north-facing terrace, surrounded by huge potted urns of showy red flowers and under the arches of clambering ivy that softened the house and the wide, spare landscape. Silently, comfortably, they'd munched on freshly made bread, sipping strong coffee and planning their day, so full of promise and excitement.

Rocco had planned a morning of intense demanding phone calls to finally nail the squirming management of Mendoza Vineyard, and then an afternoon of wild riding across his land. He'd promised to wait until she returned so she could join him. That had been the plan. And she had been desperate to saddle up the other mare—Roisin—and see just how much like her mother she was. In fact she had jumped right into his lap with joy at the thought of it, and he had gifted her one of his rare laughs, his face lighting with happiness, his eyes sparkling with pleasure.

Frankie had never felt more alive. Today was going to be *her* day. She was going in well armed after her visit to the traders in the Dominican Republic. She knew what she wanted, the terms she could afford to offer. The processing plants were nearer at hand, and the botanicals they needed were all available locally, too. The opportunity to make genuinely organic products rather than to follow the market leaders with their petrochemical derivatives was just too good to miss. She could visualise the artwork, smell the creams and lotions, feel the luxury...

So where had it all gone wrong?

Along the wide, straight jacaranda-lined driveway she stumble marched. Sweat and dust and her own gritty determination were smeared all across her face. Her mascara had run about three hours earlier. She'd seen it when she had tried to stare herself calm in the bathrooms of the one-storey cubic office block. When she'd excused herself after an excruciating meeting between the trader who'd gathered all the samples she'd asked for and an audience she hadn't.

Staring into that mirror, her best suit a crumpled mess, her hair blown all over, she had felt again the crippling sense that she was once more a silly little girl playing in a big boys' world.

La Gaya—one of them had openly called her that. Magazines with Carmel de Souza's picture had been clearly laid out on the reception area's coffee table. One of the traders, his arms folded over his chest, had set his face in amused judgement. So *this* was the Hurricane's lover? Not much to see. Not compared to Carmel.

Either they hadn't known she was fluent in Spanish or they hadn't cared. The terms they'd offered had been unmanageable. The profit margins and her hopes of promotion had slid away like oil through her fingers as she'd contemplated their bottom line. It had been hopeless.

All this time, all this work, and the whole thing was now unravelling out of her control. And she suspected that more than some of the reason for the unreasonable terms was her relationship with Rocco. Who would take her seriously when she was, after all, just another morsel of arm candy?

She'd kept it together for as long as she could—she really had. She knew there was no place for emotion in business. Especially when she was there representing her company. So she'd taken it on the chin until she'd heard 'La Gaya' one last time. Then she'd stood up, snapped her tablet closed, braced her hands on the desk and fired at them with both barrels.

She hadn't come all the way across the Atlantic Ocean to listen to this rubbish. They were in business or they weren't. And the last thing—the *very* last thing—that a prestigious, established firm like Evaña would do was get into bed with a bunch of half-baked professionals like them!

She reached the lakes that marked the start of the house grounds proper. Willows overhung the water, fronds dripping down, gently scoring the water's surface. Huge puffy clouds bounced their way across the sky. So much nature and not a living soul to be seen. Good. That was just what she needed right now.

She pulled her phone out of her bag as she marched, checking to see if there were any messages. Not trusting herself to call Rocco, she had sent him a text.

I'll pass on the riding. See you later.

No kiss. She'd ignored his call and climbed back into the helicopter, feeling twenty-year-old pain all over again. Fury at not being taken seriously; rage that she wasn't considered equal. Like when she'd been her brothers' shadow, following them about the farm, until her father had caught her and sent her off to the kitchen, roaring at her that she was getting in the way—a liability, a pest.

She flung open the front doors and clicked her way along the parquet. Heels deadened in the rugs, she passed the photos of sullen gauchos, passed the console table now groaning under the weight of Rocco's boxing trophies. She'd found them the day before, in a box in the dressing room, and polished them up happily and set them out proudly as he'd watched, humouring her.

She pushed her way into the bedroom and stood there. And breathed. And stared around.

Rocco's bedroom. Rocco's house.

What was she *doing*? What on *earth* was she doing?

Still behaving as if she was six years old—running away from her problems. Hiding out in her bedroom until she stopped crying and then flying back outdoors on a pony or after her brothers, only this time being much more careful not to get caught.

But she wasn't in her own bedroom. She wasn't even in her own country. She was here because she'd contrived to be.

Like dawn breaking over frosty fields, suddenly everything sparkled with clarity. She walked to the bed and sank down.

She really had brought this on herself. The whole nine yards of it. The trip to South America. She'd been doggedly, determinedly desperate to come here. *Desperada*. He was right. She had done all this for *him*. Right from dreaming up the new range, so dependent on natural products... She could have gone to India or Africa. But no, she'd found the best plantations in Argentina. And no one had been able to persuade her otherwise.

She'd planned and plotted the whole thing. Including the polo match. How could she have been so blind that she hadn't seen for herself what she was doing? So she was *over* Rocco Hermida? *Hated* the man who had broken her heart and stolen her pony? Who was she fooling? She had *never* gotten over him. And every move she'd made in the past four days had guaranteed she never would.

Blind...? Stupid...?

Now she had to add those to the mix.

She was ambitious, yes—but even she hadn't realised how much. And now the whole thing was coming tumbling round her head. She'd veered off her career path and right into the path of the Hurricane. Even though she'd known it would be short-term, even though she'd been able to see the devastation that was bound to be wreaked.

She was all kinds of a fool. If she didn't act fast she was going to blow her future with Evaña. It was time she grew up. It was time she stopped waiting for Rocco. She'd chased her dream all the way here. And her dream was as out of reach as it had ever been.

Because what was *Rocco* doing? Was *he* pining in his bedroom, head under the pillow, wailing like a baby? No. Damn right he wasn't. He was out on the pampas, wind in his hair, riding up a storm. He was no closer to her emotionally than he had been that very first night.

She had seen into the depths of his despair, had tried to soothe and salve. She could see how much hurt he harboured and she could help him through it—she knew she could. But he would not let her in.

Lodo's picture was there. Rocco's mind was not. Every time she tried he backed right off.

She had gone out on a limb professionally and now, instead of ticking off her to-do list, she was actually unravelling all her efforts. She wasn't just putting things on hold, she was deconstructing them. Getting her face splashed all across the media and then erupting when an ill-mannered man made some stupid comments. Had she learned *nothing*? Had she left the farm, travelled round the world, fought her way to a position of relative success just to have it all shatter around her?

An inspiration?

A devastation, more like. She *had* to get her act together and salvage what was left. Get back on the career path. Limit the damage. Batten down the hatches and hold tight.

What a day! How long since he'd allowed himself the luxury of taking off for the afternoon? Riding out around his land, feeling free, feeling part of a bigger scene, a higher purpose? Feeling that the world was his and that peace was…possible. He'd wanted Frankie there—he'd waited for her—but there would be other times. Perhaps.

As he'd ridden out through dust clouds and stony streams he'd had time to think, to curse himself for not being as straight with her as he should have been. The emails she'd gotten from her boss had crushed her. Panicked her. Adding to that by laying it out that what they had was at best a one-week sexual odyssey had seemed too cruel. And the more time he spent with her, the more he began to wonder if this *might* actually work longer term… It might—but he had to be absolutely honest with himself and with her.

He wasn't the marrying type. He wasn't even the commitment type. And she was. She might not admit it, even to herself, but she was the type of girl who put down roots, built a nest, cultivated life in a way that he recognised. If things had been different he might have wanted it, too. Real depth…real values. A real person. She wasn't going to flit about like an overpainted butterfly, landing on flowers, looking for attention like all the other women he'd dated.

He paused at that. Had he dated them for that very reason? So there would be no genuine commitment? Possibly. But Frankie was different. So was he being fair to her? Because it wasn't going to end any other way. He'd made that promise to himself years back. Being responsible for other human beings was not something he did well. Hell, the only reason he and Dante were so close now was because of the utter devastation he had caused every time he'd run away.

Two years his junior, Dante had hung on his every word, so when his efforts to get back to the streets had become wilder and wilder, when he'd seen just how upset he'd made Dante every time he was dragged back to his life of luxury—all that emotional blackmail had been banked and paid out again in brotherly bonding. They'd used Dante as a weapon to tame him. But that manipulation, that responsibility for someone else was never going to happen again.

So had he given Frankie false hope with his drunken blurting about Lodo? Sharing his emotional detritus for her to pick over? Who knew? He'd expected her to be flying high on some emotional magic carpet the next day, looking for him to jump on and relive it all over again. He'd been on his guard for pitying looks, stage-managed conversations, trailing pauses. No way was he going to indulge in any review of *that* particular episode.

It was time to face up to having the inevitable conversation that had eluded them so far. To go on any longer without talking through the state of play was disingenuous. The last thing he wanted was for her to build their time together into more than a week of fantastic sex—to set any emotional store by the fact that they'd each had their confessional moments…in his case a once-in-a-lifetime confessional moment.

But he'd be fooling himself if he didn't admit how much he hoped she'd share his point of view and keep things ticking along as they were. If she was cool with a physical relationship—a monogamous physical relationship—he was right there with her.

He walked from the yard to the house, already thinking about where she would be. What they'd do as soon as they met. He'd decanted the 2006 and 2003 Malbecs from Mendoza—could almost taste the subtle soft fruits and the plump warm spices. A couple of steaks, the fabulous wine and then an evening together in exactly the same way they'd shared every previous one. Perfect.

The house was empty. Usually the gauchos and grooms inhabited the kitchen and the rooms on the south wing, but since Frankie had taken up residence they had made themselves scarce. Another unnecessary line in the sand, he thought, kicking off his boots, pulling his shirt over his head and twisting the lid from a bottle of water. People were reading more into this than they should.

He walked on through the house. Alone.

She'd have been back for a good two hours now. Hot tub? Terrace? Bed?

He drew a sharp breath through his teeth and felt himself tighten as every sweet little image formed in his mind. This separation, if only for a few hours, had done them good. He was half crazy with longing for her. Strange that she hadn't wanted to come out riding. He reckoned things at work had maybe piled up for her. He *had* monopolised her time, and after all she was here on business. Even if that business *was* a bit sparse.

He'd done a bit of digging. Just a bit. And he wouldn't be holding his breath that her efforts were going to pay off. Or *any* efforts. Evaña was a company heading in the wrong direction, and Frankie dragging herself along in the dirt as it stuttered to the end wasn't going to be her smartest career move.

But that was *her* business. There would be nothing to be gained by him voicing that opinion.

The bedroom was empty. He seized the chance and had a quick shower, soaping himself alone for the first time in days. Strange how he'd got so acclimatised to her being around… Strange that he didn't resent it.

In fact as he tossed the damp towel into the laundry bin and pulled on fresh clothes an irritation that he'd never felt before barked up, unbidden. Where the hell *was* she? She should have been there to meet him.

His calls through the house echoed back unanswered. He checked his phone, checked his messages, but there were none from her.

Five minutes later he found her. Coiled on the ancient leather sofa in his favourite room—the snug. It was the room that had been his bedroom when he'd first bought the estancia. His bedroom, living room and kitchen. He'd existed in there as he had slowly ripped out and rebuilt the place, brick by brick. He'd made this room habitable first, then a bathroom. Then the stables.

For a long time the stables had been way more luxurious than the house. His horses deserved that. They were his everything. He poured his love—what there was of it—into them. He owed them everything. Without them he was nothing. He owed them for every envious glance from a polo player, every roar of adulation from the crowd. For each and every sponsorship deal that had opened doors and fast-tracked him to his other business deals.

People didn't understand that. Leaving behind the

luxury of the Hermida estancia had been like fleeing a gilded cage. He'd been thought mad to walk away. But his parents had understood. And Dante. They had understood everything, supported him in everything. He'd left that 'safe house' with one pony—Siren, his eighteenth birthday present. And after that he'd headed to Europe. Met Frankie in Ireland. Life had taken off. He would never, ever repay that debt. But he would never stop trying.

Frankie. She had to have heard him coming in but she kept her head buried in her laptop, brows knitted and a strange swirl of tension all around her.

She still didn't look up.

'Hey...I missed you out riding.'

He walked over to her, the dusky evening already softening every surface, blurring the odds and ends of dark artisan furniture against the plaster walls.

He leaned over her, kissed the top of her head, lifted her chin with his finger and met her lips. He could taste slight resistance, but it was nothing that he couldn't melt in moments.

And he did.

She sighed against his mouth.

'I missed you out riding, too.'

He kissed her, revelling in the 'Hi, honey, I'm home' greeting between them. He could get quite used to this.

'I waited. But there will be other times.'

She pulled herself back, dipped her head, stared at the screen.

So she was in a mood—prickly, like a neglected pony, one who'd expected to be ridden at a match but had been swapped for another. Sulky and jagged. Playing hard to get. Okay. He could deal with that.

He lifted her laptop onto the couch and scooped his

hands under her arms, lifted her up. Her reluctant hands slid around his neck.

'So what happened? How was your day? Did it go as well as you hoped?'

Her eyes rolled and her mouth tightened into a grim little slash.

'Not quite. Walking into an AGM of the Carmel Fan Club wasn't quite what I had in mind.'

He frowned. 'What does *that* mean?'

This time she pulled herself totally out of his arms, slid back down onto the couch, lifted up her laptop again— as if it was some kind of guard dog and he should back right off.

'Just what I said. There was quite a welcoming committee—seemed as though the traders had got the whole company out in force to see how I measured up. I had to wait in the reception area—and guess what were all over the coffee table? Celebrity magazines dedicated to your airhead ex. It was heartfelt—it really was.'

'I'm sure it was coincidental,' he said, thinking how unlike her this spiteful tone was.

'*Are* you? Were you *there*?'

He looked at her. Weighed up the benefit of engaging in this. Decided against it.

He turned round, shook his head and went off to the dining room. The wine decanters were set as he'd left them. Each vintage the perfect temperature, opened to breathe for the optimum length of time. He lifted the 2006. It was mooted to be even plummier than the 2003, and he held it to what remained of the light. These were *his* wines now. And there would be better and better to come.

How long had he harboured a desire to be *that* Argentinian? The one whose heritage went so far back. The one who had fought and risen above hardship. One who didn't have to worry about a place to sleep, a mouth to feed. A reputation to uphold. How remarkable that with effort you could *buy* that kind of stability. And he had. Centuries of tradition, and he now held it in his hand. How proud would his *mamá* and *papá* be now? How proud Lodo?

He swallowed his self-indulgent reflections, selected two etched antique-crystal glasses and made his way back to Frankie. She would enjoy these. She would appreciate the effort and pride that had gone into them.

The room was darkening with each passing moment. He reached for the control pad and flicked a switch. Lamps in corners began to glow softly. He turned. The sheen on Frankie's dipped head gleamed. She looked *right*. There on that couch, in this room. Slowly, reverently, he poured, the full, fabulous scents wafting up as the liquid sloshed. He paced to her, handed her a glass.

'Try this.'

She made a face as though it was an old tin cup of stagnant water. Reluctantly held out her hand. Why did she not know what this represented for him? She was normally so attuned to him...

He watched as she swirled the dark red liquid round the bulbous bottomed glass as if it was a science lesson.

He did the same, but sank his nose in for a proper smell.

'What do you think of this vintage? This is the 2006 Malbec. The season went on until April that year. The aromas are immense—so balanced, no?'

Frankie stilled her eyes, cast her mouth into a tight little moue. 'Yes, it's amazing.'

Suddenly he felt a spark of anger.

'No, what's *amazing* is your churlish attitude.'

She did a double-take.

'What? What did you say?'

He sighed. How to phrase this without turning it into the drama she was clearly spoiling for?

'Frankie, the existence of Carmel de Souza in this world has nothing to do with you. I saw how you let her presence affect you at the party, but surely you're smarter than to let a photograph of her affect you at your *work*?'

Her back was against the huge armrest of the couch. Her legs were curled up, knees bent. He watched her from the corner of his eye as he stared straight ahead, twirling the gorgeous liquor round and round, examining the patina on the glass as it sank back down before being swirled up again.

'It's only *because* of that damn party that I'm feeling like this,' she said, cold steel jarring every word. 'If I hadn't been paraded about in front of all those cameras nobody would've even known who I was.'

She thrust her legs out, bare. She was wearing a T-shirt and shorts—not one of his shirts, he noticed. She gripped her laptop, held it steady on her lap.

'I went down there today as a professional and came back as nothing other than the Hurricane's current sex pet. And not a very impressive one at that.'

He raised his eyebrow—the only sign that he'd registered her statement. She needed to calm the hell down.

He swirled the wine one more time before drawing long on the scent and then finally tasting.

'I bought this vineyard today. I've always been a fan of their wines.'

She fumed. Obviously.

'Great.'

'Meaning…?'

'Meaning that it's all in a day's work for you to go shopping for a vineyard. Did anyone pile in to look at you and judge you? Make you feel as if you'd won last place in the celebrity-girlfriend competition? And that you were an idiot for getting your photo all over the front pages of some trashy magazine?'

'No, because the only person who judges me is *me*. I choose who I sleep with, and it's of no interest to me what anyone thinks of that.'

She reared up. The laptop slid to the couch. Her wine sloshed up the sides of the glass. She glanced at it and reached to put it on the side table, missed its edge in the gloom of the room. The glass wobbled and he lunged for it, caught it in his hand and righted it.

She opened her mouth, clamped it shut, then opened it again.

'That's all I am to you. Isn't it?'

Halfway to his mouth, he stalled the progress of his own glass. So there it was. The gauntlet thrown down. All hope of a mature, considered conversation was gone— Frankie's self-deprecating emotional show had just rolled into town.

'*Isn't* it?' She stepped down from the couch, the shrill tone in her voice a sword being drawn from its sheath.

He lowered the glass.

'We are currently lovers, if that's what you mean.'

She stood within the circle of his personal space. If he reached for her she would fit his body perfectly. He would curl her into him and lay his chin on her head. She would press her head to his chest and then plant tiny kisses on his neck. She would clamber up him like a cat and he would hold her, carry her, make love to her and know that he had never before and never would again find a girl like her.

But standing here right now, less than eighteen inches apart, it was like being on either side of a crevice. One wrong move and the whole thing would disappear down into a chasm. Gone.

'We are "currently lovers"?' she repeated, the low tone of her voice unmistakable.

He would not give her more. *Would not.*

He looked at her, at the damp, dusky lashes closed over the huge hazel eyes that had gazed into his, at the small soft lips that had given him every type of pleasure imaginable, at the silken swish of hair that had lain across his body night after night. At the selfless, giving, generous, loving girl that she was…

She loved him. He knew it then. As she stood there right in front of him. An iron hand squeezed his heart and a steel glaze crept all over his skin. She loved him and he could not love her back.

Not in the way she deserved.

'We can stay as lovers…like this…' His voice was strained, as though the decade-old tannins in the wine had welded it shut. The glass now dangled at the end of his arm, preventing him from holding her. He *should* hold her. He should comfort her. Every second that ticked by deepened the chasm. But still he held the glass in his hand, cupped the delicate weighted ball of crystal.

'Like what?'

One foot hovered over the edge.

He straightened his shoulders. Drew in a breath.

'Frankie…' he began, and he saw by the glimmer of hope that had flashed in her eyes and then slid down her face that she already knew what was coming next. If only he could save her, not pull her with him into the chasm…

'Frankie, we're great together…'

She closed her eyes. Clamped them shut as if trying to block him out.

'But…?' she breathed. 'We're great together *but*…?' Every syllable rang with the dreadful, sonorous clang of defeat. 'What are you telling me? What glib, half-baked reason are you going to trot out?'

'Angel, please,' he said, feeling the earth now leaving him, knowing that they were both falling.

She opened her eyes, looked at his arm, his shoulder, at a spot on the wall. In the distance he could hear the rumble of threatened thunder. A summer storm passing overhead. The land would be refreshed by morning, the air clearer and lighter. But he could already feel the aching black pain that would live in his heart as he rode the land, knowing she wouldn't be there for him to come back to.

'Shall I make it easy for you?'

She didn't sound angry anymore—just desperately, desperately sad.

'We're great together because we have great sex. But that's all there is and all there ever will be. We don't work on any other level.'

'That's not true,' he bit out.

She looked at him then. His Frankie. A dark sweep of hair hung over one eye, her stubborn chin was raised, her hazel eyes sunken and saddened.

'It is, Rocco. You're carrying around so much baggage, but everyone pretends it's not there. Even Dante— even *he* skips over all your moods and sulks. And God knows who you'd ever let get closer than him. A woman? A "weak little woman"?'

'We *are* close, Frankie.'

'I don't feel it, Rocco. Not close enough.'

In the past five minutes the gap between them had widened and stretched. They were still standing in each other's space, but light years apart—like dying stars in the cosmic darkness.

He swallowed. Words to beg her to stay—on *his* terms—words to beg her forgiveness for not being able to give her what she needed, words to erase the mask of pain he saw settle into the beautiful curves of her face, already gaunt and sunken—those words stuck deep in his throat. And his mouth sealed over them, bottled them up like uncorked wine.

She turned away as a huge sob forced her shoulders to shudder.

He'd save her. If he *could* save her. Give her the water and light that she needed. But she would always be parched of his love. His arms hung limp at his sides as she finally stepped from their space, bent for her laptop and left.

He stood in his room, the heart of his home, while the one chance he'd ever had of feeling true love slipped like a ghost from his grasp.

It always came back to this. It didn't matter about walls or wealth. None of that mattered. He'd never felt happier than in the warmth of his *mamá*'s bed until he'd felt the warmth of Frankie. A cardboard bed cuddled up with Lodo…sleeping on the beach with Frankie. It was people that mattered. But she mattered too much for him to give her only half a life.

The glass in his hand weighed cannonball-heavy. He lifted it now, looked at the delicate white patterns cut out of the paper-thin crystal. He looked at the barely touched, carefully nursed vintage wine that coated and glazed the sides of the glass. Looked at the space on the couch. Moments ago he'd cared more about scents and flavours than the beautiful woman who'd sat there.

And then, with all his might, he lifted it past his head and heaved it at the wall.

And watched as the rich red liquid streaked down the plaster.

CHAPTER TWELVE

SUNDAY MORNINGS AT home hadn't changed much in all these years. Frankie lay in her narrow single bed, staring at the low sloping ceiling as the scents of lunch wafted upstairs. Chicken and potatoes would be roasting; pan lids would be wobbling with vegetables boiling underneath. The windows would be steamed up and her mother's rosy face would be peering into the oven, or she'd be wiping her damp hands on the cloth tucked into her apron.

In the lounge, only ever used on high days and holidays, her father would be marooned in a sea of Sunday papers like a grumpy old walrus, occasionally barking out his horror at what he read to anyone who cared to listen. Such was their life—the cosy, comfortable, mundane life that they'd shared for almost forty years.

Why had she felt horror at the prospect of such a life? Why had she fought against it every step of the way? Casting her net as far from this place as she possibly could. Determined never to be *that* woman, *that* wife.

Why—when she knew, now that it was so far from her grasp, that it was as important to her as all her other dreams. Maybe even more so…

Perhaps not here on a farm in County Meath, but maybe on an estancia in Argentina. Or in a studio apartment in Madrid. Anywhere, in fact, as long as it was with Rocco.

She rolled around in the narrow bed, tucking her legs in sharply when shafts of cold air scored them. Her head was under her pillow, a balled-up paper handkerchief clutched in her fist. When would the crying stop? When would the misery of knowing she would never be with him again finally ease?

She felt the thickening in her nose and the heat behind her eyes that warned her of another outpouring. Two weeks she'd been like this. One week in Spain, and then she'd finally caved and taken leave, coming back here for the holidays.

That week in Spain had been a blur, of course. She'd caught the Madrid flight she'd originally booked, much to the discomfort of her fellow passengers and the aircrew, who hadn't quite known what to do with the agonised bundle of limbs she'd become, sleeping and weeping her way across the Atlantic.

Then, appearing for work, it had turned out she hadn't needed the extra time after all—though God knew they'd encouraged her to take it when they'd seen that their waterproof mascara wasn't quite so waterproof after all.

It was a miracle that she'd pulled herself together and finally got her moment in front of the board. Skirting over her lack of information about the Argentina growers, she'd made a one-sided, half-hearted presentation about the potentials of the Dominican Republic and openly accepted, when questioned that, yes, she *had* become 'overwrought' during her meeting with the Argentinian traders. And worse, yes—they probably could get better terms from India.

But Rocco Hermida wasn't in India.

He wasn't anywhere now.

And it was time she finally realised that. Since he'd walked out of her life she'd been chasing him. They were *his* steps she'd followed. *He* was the reason she'd cast her net so far and wide. *He* was the reason she'd taken a gap year, gone travelling, set herself higher and higher goals. She'd emulated him. She'd wanted to be worthy of him, even if she couldn't actually have him.

The only incredible part was how blind she had been in not seeing all this before. And, even more worryingly, persisting for all those years when she should have realised as he'd slung his rucksack over his shoulder that morning ten years ago that he didn't need her. Never would.

Tears burned and flowed again. The black jaws of agony yawned awake inside her again. She pushed her fist into her mouth to stop the howl. Her teeth scored her flesh, but the numb sting of pain meant nothing. She curled into a little ball and rocked herself into another day without him.

Eventually she became aware of someone moving about in the hallway. Her father, clearing his throat—his passive-aggressive way of telling her that she should be downstairs helping her mother.

Well, he was right about that. But that was *all* he was right about.

Since she'd come back they'd quietly circled one another, silently assessing but not engaging. She knew it upset her mother, but she was putting so much effort into not crying in front of them that she couldn't risk getting involved in any arguments with him. But it was coming. She could feel it.

Slowly she sat up, dropped her legs out of the bed, let them dangle in the chilly air. How many times had she sat just like this over the years? Countless. And here she was again. She stood. Her heart was strong. It could beat seventy times a minute. It had just taken the pummelling of her life and it was still beating. Life was going to get better. It *had* to.

She shuffled her feet into slippers, shrugged her shoulders into Mark's old Trinity College hoody and began to make her way along the hall.

'So you're going to join us?'

He was standing at the top of the stairs—just like he'd been all those years ago. Just standing there. Staring. Judging.

'Yes,' she said.

Something about his dark, solid, unflinching outline made her pause her steps. He was holding something in his hand.

'I *knew* I was right. All these years...'

There was barely any light in the top hallway. A tiny skylight and a four-paned window at the end. The flower-printed shade that her brothers had to dodge as they passed held only a dim lightbulb that daubed the walls and carpet in dark beige patches the colour of cold tea. Her father's anger radiated its own dark gloom.

She stared at him. The default denial—*No, Daddy, I promise I didn't*—sank to the floor. She had no use for it anymore.

'Yes. You were right. Does that make you happy?'

He seemed to take that like a blow, tipping his head back slightly with the shock of it. She couldn't see his face properly, but she could sense the intake of breath.

'Happy? How could any shame you bring on yourself make me *happy*? Then or now?'

'I've never done *anything* shameful.' She jerked her chin up at him. And she hadn't. There was no shame in love. 'But God knows you made me feel like I did. Treating me like an outcast—sending me away like that.'

'It was for your own good.'

'How can you *say* that? You ruined my life—selling my pony and imprisoning me in that convent.'

'Your life wasn't ruined by that—you were doing a good-enough job of that on your own. And you know we had to sell her. No one regretted it as much as I. But there was no option. Not with the run of bad luck we'd had with the others. And then Danny leaving. And anyway, the convent was the making of you.'

The convent was the making of you? He really thought that? The convent hadn't been the making of her—it had been her life outdoors, the farm, nature all around. It had been leaving home and travelling, choosing a job in a country where she barely spoke the language. Highest paths, toughest challenges, always proving herself. Hadn't it?

'You were wild. Ran wild from before you could walk. You needed some anchors and there were none strong enough. The nuns trained you to stand still and focus yourself.'

She almost had to steady herself as her world was suddenly whipped up in the air and reordered.

'I thought that you'd calmed down completely when you landed that job. But clearly not. The minute *he* appears you're all over the place again.'

He thrust forward a magazine, held it in his hand like a folded weapon. She stared at it. He thrust it farther.

'Read it. See what they're printing. And *then* tell me you're not ashamed.'

She lifted the magazine—the gossip section from his Sunday paper. She could barely make out the text, but his finger jabbed at a photograph and she could see by the stark colours exactly what it was.

The Turlington Club party. She was in white. Rocco was in black. She lifted it closer, tilted it to catch the gloomy brown light, and felt the fist around her heart squeeze a little tighter. Rocco was holding her as if they were dancing the most erotic tango. Bodies like licks of fire. Heat and light and passion bounced from the page. She turned away, clutching it, staring at it.

'It's him, isn't it? The one who came here. The hotshot…'

She stared at the picture. Stared at the man who was her whole world.

Her father was droning on and on. 'Coming here… turning your head like that…leading you on…getting you to do…'

She was suddenly jolted out of her gloom.

'Rocco didn't lead me on. What are you *saying*? It was me who tried to lead *him* on.'

The words her father was about to growl out hung in his mouth unsaid and he gaped.

She looked at him. 'Have you thought for all these years that *he* was the one to blame for what happened that night?'

Across the gloom of the afternoon they stared at each other. She was barely aware of the television being turned off, a door closing softly downstairs.

'It was me who went to him. *I* went to him. And then I went back to him last month.'

She saw him swallow—heard it, too. A gulp of shock.

For a moment he looked puzzled, even hurt. Then his face gathered itself into the storm that never seemed far away.

'Well, why have you come back here now?'

His voice was low and cold, like sleet landing on mud. But as she heard it and felt it all the darkness slowly began to melt away. She looked down at the magazine in her hand. She'd had all that. All that man. *Her* man. The only one who was right for her. All she'd lacked was the patience to help him see that, too.

'You know, Dad, I've no idea why I came back here. Not for your support or your love anyway.'

'Pfff!' he said. 'If we didn't love you we wouldn't care that you get yourself into all this trouble. You *and* your brother.'

For a moment he looked at her and she saw the shadows of worry and care etched deep. He was so hidebound by what others saw that he couldn't see that love was the most valuable commodity of all. He should be *happy* that Danny had got married in Dubai. So what if it wasn't a traditional wedding? It wasn't 'trouble'—it was love.

She thought of Rocco's hands holding her, his lips loving her. She thought of their nights and days. She thought of him gently teasing her out of her silly insecurities and stubbornly hiding his. She thought of him with Dante, his flashes of jealousy. His tiny keepsake photograph of Lodo. His overwhelming loyalty. And his love. He had such a capacity for love. He was frightened of it, but it was there in everything he did for them. And for her. He couldn't hide it. He loved her. He needed her.

'He loves me,' she whispered to herself. 'He understands me. He would never do anything to hurt me.'

'Well, if he loves you so much why are you here? Why aren't you with him? Why hasn't he made an honest woman of you instead of all this parading about, getting your picture in the papers, giving those gossips in the village something to say about you?'

She looked away from her father—out at the December sky.

'He made an honest woman of me the first day I met him. He showed me who I am and he made me learn about myself in a way that no one else possibly could.'

And he had. Her sexuality was part of her—a part of which she was now proud. They were perfectly matched, true partners, but each of them carried such huge scars that only the unflinching patience of true love would get past them.

'Well, I'll say it again—what are you doing here, crying in your bedroom? That's not going to solve anything.' He lifted the magazine out of her hands, stared down at the photograph. 'You might think that I'm some old fool, that I don't understand, but I'm not daft. You won't get far if you don't commit to one another properly. And I don't see much evidence of *that* if you're here and he's there.'

Frankie looked at her father. *Really* looked. When was the last time she had done that? He was of a different generation, but maybe he was no less well meaning or principled than she was. Maybe he did truly want the best for her. There were things that mattered to him that she couldn't understand. But she should respect them. For his sake.

'I love you, Daddy,' she said. 'I won't always agree with you, but this time I do.'

He hugged her gruffly, then pushed her away. No time for that kind of nonsense.

'Well, get on with you, then.' He shuffled around, put his hand on the banister and made his way down to the kitchen—to his Sunday lunch and his steady, uneventful life.

'You young people can be awful stupid at times.'

* * *

Rocco turned off the radio. Silenced the preamble to to-day's match. A resounding win predicted for Hermanos Hermida against their old rivals San Como. Dante was captaining for the first time. Rocco was glad. It was time he led the team on his own. He was a much more natu-rally talented player anyway—always had been. What Dante lacked in bloodthirstiness he made up for in con-summate skill. A fearless child, he had excelled in every sport.

Yes, he thoroughly deserved his place—and the win that was predicted to follow.

As for himself…? Rocco wasn't sure when or if he'd play again. He'd wanted to be there today, to lend Dante support. But right now he had come to the end of this particular road.

He sat back, ensconced in the leather bucket seat of his Lotus, tilted his head and closed his eyes.

You'd better get yourself sorted, man. You've just lost the best thing that ever happened to you and you're in danger of losing everything else if you don't dig your-self out of this pit.

Dante's words still rang in his ears.

He'd faced Rocco across the snug—having found him holed up there three days after Frankie had gone—when he'd run out of bags to punch and miles to run. When he'd been left with nothing more than a cluster of bottles to drain as he tried to drink the misery away.

'What do you think she'd say if she could see you now?' He'd looked at the mess on the wall—the vin-tage red-wine stain now dried and pink. 'Her hero. *Ev-erybody's* hero. God only knows what you did for her to give up on you.'

'What would *you* know?' he'd slurred back at Dante.

'You've never known what it's like to feel misery. Everything lands at your feet. Women, money, success...'

'You think? You think I've never known any pain? That just shows what *you* know. It's always been about you, Rocco. You and your *real* family. Your *real* brother. You never gave a damn about all the times I watched my mother in pain, waiting for news of where you were, never understanding why you'd do anything rather than be with us. And all we did was love you. You threw it back in our faces time and time again.'

He had been angry. Angrier than Rocco had known he could be. He'd sobered up in a heartbeat, watching him.

Dante had gone on, 'And how do you think *I* felt? Did you ever stop to think? Rejected over and over like that? Knowing that I was never going to be good enough for you? That I'd never hold a candle to Lodo's memory? You kicked me in the stomach more times than you'll ever know.'

'I...I'm sorry. Dante—I'm so... I'm just a mess. Not worth your love...'

At that Dante had reared up, his face a furious mask.

'Just *shut up*! Stop your self-pity. You're worth every bit of my love *and* our parents' love. And *her* love— Frankie's. You're just too damn stubborn and blind to see it.'

They'd ended up standing, facing each other like cage fighters. He'd so badly wanted to swing at him. So badly wanted to hurt him. Because he knew he was right. He'd acted terribly. Selfishly.

In the end Dante had walked away, shaking his head. And in that moment Rocco had made his mind up. His life as he knew it was over. He didn't want to be a playboy polo player anymore. He didn't even want to be a horse breeder. He didn't care about any of that. None of it mattered while he was hurting the people he loved. And he loved Frankie so much—so much it killed him to think what he'd done to her.

From the moment he'd seen her he'd loved her. He'd fought against it all these years, but he had. She sparkled, she shone, and she was as pure as a brilliant-cut diamond. She'd brought energy and passion and love to his life. She'd lit up the dark, solemn corners of his heart. She'd set fire to him that night in her bed—a fire that he'd never been able to put out. All the women he'd bedded since had been just an effort to smother that flame. But none of it had worked.

Seeing her at the Campo had just lent oxygen to the embers that had always been there. And he'd known then he'd had a second chance. He'd pursued her relentlessly, not taking no for an answer. She was *his*. He wanted her and he would have her. But only on his terms.

Who the hell did he think he was?

Standing in the wreck of his room, he'd thought about what he'd built up and now cared nothing for—his polo, his ponies, his estancia. She'd come farther than him. She might not have the baubles to show for it, the money, but she was honest. She had strength. Integrity. Compassion. And those were the things he'd suddenly realised he lacked.

He had so much to make up for.

The next day he'd gotten up, cleared up the squalor he'd created and started to sort everything out. He'd called in on Dante. Apologised and shared his plans with him: he was going to bow out of polo, get more serious with life, get more involved in his new businesses. And he was going to meet Chris Martinez. He didn't know how yet—but he was.

And after he'd done all that he was going to get

Frankie. He was going to lay his heart out for her. And if she didn't want him he would understand. He'd understand, but he wouldn't give up. He would prove to her that he was worthy of her. Somehow.

And now things had panned out just as he'd hoped. Even the tracking down of Martinez. The trail had heated up again and he'd stepped forward himself—no proxy. He'd wanted a face-to-face, and he wouldn't be wearing anyone's mask when it happened.

And now he was here. This was it.

To think it was all about to draw to its conclusion after twenty years on a pavement outside a modest villa, sandwiched between two high-rises in Belgrano. With the only criminals in sight the tourist-fleecing café owners.

For two hours he sat there, his fingers making slow drumrolls on the steering wheel. Two hours and then twenty years of hate would be gone. Twenty years of carrying a stone in his heart. Weighted, heavy, dungeon dark. And now, with one simple sighting, he'd stepped up to the light.

One look at the family that exited the dusty sedan and trooped into the house—a fifty-year-old man, his wife, his daughter and an infant that had to be his grandchild—and he knew he was free. Martinez looked aged, haggard. Weary. And suddenly the thrill of the chase was doused. He was finally hauling the past into the sunshine of this moment.

Chris Martinez hadn't caused the economic crash. *He* wasn't responsible for them ending up on the streets, for his father vanishing and his mother's breakdown. Rocco had chosen a path close to the dark side, sleeping on cardboard in doorways with Lodo. Stealing and mixing with criminals had only ever been going to end one way.

The Martinez brothers had been little more than children themselves—young men who'd gone deeper and darker than Rocco. But who knew what would have happened if Lodo hadn't died? If the nuns hadn't taken him in? If Senor and Senora Hermida hadn't shone a light in his life?

Lodo was gone. But there was so much to love and live for—so, so much.

His hand hovered over the car's door handle. It was time. He had to tie up this last knot.

He got out of the car and walked across the street. A tiny fence marked off the front yard from the pavement. He swung open the gate and walked four paces to the door. Gomez, the nameplate said. Knocked.

The young woman opened, the dark-eyed baby on her hip. She recognised him immediately and her mouth and eyes widened.

Behind her loomed her father—Chris Martinez, now Chris Gomez. They stared at one another and Rocco saw acknowledgement, acceptance and fear flit across his haggard face.

'I know who you are,' he said.

Rocco nodded. 'Then, you'll know why I've come.'

Martinez didn't flinch, but he stepped out onto the street, pulled the door closed behind him, shielding his home and his family.

Rocco could smell his fear, could see him digging deep for the strength he'd known he would one day need.

'I've changed.'

He stared at his face—looking for what he'd expected to see. Ugly snarling hate…brutality. But it was just a face.

'So have I.'

'I've watched you for years. I've waited for you to come—I knew you would find me.'

Rocco said nothing. There was nothing to say.

'I never meant for it to happen. I was afraid of them—They gave me a gun…' He dipped his head, shook it. 'I'm sorry,' he said finally, looking up.

Rocco looked into his sunken eyes, at his flabby face, his paunch and, behind the windows, peering out, his family.

'It was for me to forgive you.'

He held that gaze for long, searching seconds. This was the moment he had dreamed of for all these years. And now it was his…just seconds ticking by, two men united by one terrible moment and then separated on their own paths.

'It's done now,' he said, and walked away.

Rocco parked outside the cemetery. The late morning had seeped into noon brightness. The shadows had begun to lengthen. He pulled the tiny battered photograph from its leather frame. Lodo had lived for such a short time. If he'd survived…? Who could say? But he would treasure the moments they'd had together for evermore.

He should mark his time on earth in some way. A charity cup? A sponsorship? A garden? He would work that out. But now it was time to move into the present. He'd done all he could. He had to grasp his future with both hands—and fast.

He looked at his watch, worked out the time in Dublin. He knew she was there. Just as he knew it was only a matter of time now until he followed her.

But there was no way he could have forced himself back into her life until he'd cleared this path.

He could see that now. Finally. After the massive fight he'd had with Dante, which had almost ended in violence for the first time ever—and it was all thanks to Dante that it hadn't. His long-suffering brother had taken the verbal blows, the emotional abuse, and had walked away before he'd had to defend himself against the physical ones, too. A true brother.

He lifted his phone. His trips to Europe would be even more frequent now, so the jet he'd just bought was more a necessity than a luxury. The flight plan was already lodged: he'd be flying to Dublin later that day. But back to La Colorada first, to get everything organised with the horses. Although Dante was captaining HH, he had a ton of stuff of his own going on, too. Not least with this new mystery woman—the duchess he'd been pictured with on a yacht in the Caribbean.

He'd never known Dante so tight-lipped about a woman. And so sensitive. It made a change…

He pulled out into the midday suburban traffic, the urge to plant his foot to the floor immense. Anything to speed up this journey…the sooner to let his eyes light upon her sweet face.

God, he hoped she'd been okay. That last night— staying apart from her—had been one of the hardest things he'd ever had to do. Knowing that they were both in such pain and not being able or equipped to deal with it. She'd refused every offer of help—even a ride to the airport. But he'd insisted on that. As a concession, he hadn't driven the car himself. A concession that he'd rethought so many times. If he'd actually been at the departure gate with her could he really have let her go?

He didn't think so.

He pulled out onto the highway, sped along. Four hours and then he'd be on the jet. The best sixty million dollars he'd ever spent if he could bring her back home with him.

The straight, sandy driveway, its jacarandas weighted

down with purple blooms, the sky a streak of pale turquoise and the droopy green willows all welcomed him home. He spun the Lotus round and parked with a lot less care than usual. He felt teenager happy. Excited. As if he was going on a first date, but with the stakes so much higher. Incredibly high.

In through the doors and instantly he sensed it.

He stopped. Listened.

Nothing.

Only the steady tick-tock of the irritating antique clock that presided over the mantelpiece in the wide wooden vestibule. Underneath, the unlit fire was flanked by two towering palms in glazed urns. Corridors stretched off in two directions, the sheen of the parquet gleaming with hundred-year-old pride.

Silence.

It was lunchtime. He should be hearing the grooms chattering: the European girls, so highly strung, and all the gauchos—the young ones flirting and the older ones solemnly muttering. But there was nothing.

He walked on through the house. He couldn't dare think the thoughts he wanted to think. But the last time the house had been this silent was when he had thrown everyone out while he went on his three-day bender. And the time before that...

It had been when the staff had given him space. Space to share with Frankie.

He reached the snug, listening like a hunter, feeling as if he was following in the wake of something...of someone. But it was empty. He kept on, his footsteps now falling on the silk runners, deadening all sound apart from the thump of his heart in his ears.

His bedroom. He paused. Put his hand on the brass door plate and pushed. Cautiously he let his eyes fall into the space between the wall and the open door. His eyes landed on the rug, on the shaft of sunlight that lit the floor, moved to the wall by the dressing room. And there sat the tiny battered carry-on bag.

He threw open the door.

He checked the room, the dressing room, the bathroom, went out onto the terrace.

There was no mistake—*no mistake*—none. He picked up the bag and scanned every inch of it. It was Frankie's. He'd know it anywhere. And unless someone was playing tricks with his mind, it could only mean one thing.

Like a wild horse he charged back through the house, powering through doors, changing direction. Back to the snug, where the scent of fresh paint cut through the air. Where could she be? Where the *hell* could she be?

The main doorway was still open as he passed the ticking clock and stepped out into the sunshine, stared out all around. In the distance the grass-cutting tractors were trailing like giant beetles around the cultivated lawns surrounding the lakes. To the left horses grazed, staying near the trees for much-needed shelter.

And then his feet knew where to go, even if his mind didn't. In less than two minutes he'd skirted the house, run past the back terrace to the yard and the stables. Straight to the stalls of Roisin and Orla.

Dante might have chosen them for his string for today's match, but if he hadn't…

He stepped inside.

His heart stopped.

There she was.

Roisin's nose nuzzled into her hand as she turned her huge watchful eyes on him.

Frankie looked up, smiled.

'Hello, Rocco.'

He swallowed. 'Frankie.'

'Hope you don't mind me coming out here to see the ponies.' She ran the backs of her fingers down Roisin's white star. 'I never got a proper chance to get to know them last time.'

She turned her attention fully on the horse, smiled again and kissed her bobbing head, clapped her strong silky neck.

He watched her, transfixed. She was exactly as he remembered—but so different. Her sleek bobbed hair dipped over each cheek, almost obscuring her perfect petite nose and huge honest eyes. Her lips were parted as she murmured a reassuring string of soft words to Roisin. Then they tilted into another smile, which she turned to gift to him.

'You were right. I didn't come here for the horses last time. I thought I had. But it turns out there was a bigger attraction.'

His face eased into a smile. 'I knew it.'

She smiled, so softly, nodded in the half light of the stable.

'It's funny how things turn out, isn't it? Who would have thought that my grumpy old goat of a father would be the one to give me the best advice about love?'

'What advice was that, then?'

He moved closer, cutting out the sunlight that bathed her, casting her slightly into shadow. But she didn't need any sunlight. She *was* sunlight.

Even in the gloom he saw her smile deepen and her eyes sparkle with humour. She turned back to the pony, soothing her with slow, soft strokes.

'He said men can be very stupid sometimes. You in particular.'

He kept pacing towards her.

'Is that right?'

The pony whickered, looking for more affection, but she trained her eyes on his and kept them steady.

'Definitely.'

'He said *I'm* stupid? But I'm not the one who's fallen in love with a bad-tempered, jealous *porteño* with more bumps and scars than a beat-up car.'

She made a face, as if perusing him for the first time. Nodded. 'True, true... You could do with a new paint job.'

The heartbeats that passed were the sweetest of his life. He felt his cheeks almost split as a smile burst right across his face. He took another step closer.

'But he's right. I've been *very* stupid—falling in love with the cheekiest, most smart-mouthed little minx who ever climbed into my bed. Naked.'

'I was looking for something...' This time it was her turn to smile from ear to ear.

'Tell me you found it.'

She smiled coyly. 'Oh, yes. I found it, all right.'

'I think that's the first time I've seen you blush, Frankie Ryan.'

That crackle of heat began.

'It's too dark to see in here.'

'Maybe I just need to get a little closer to be sure, then.'

He was right beside the horse's withers.

'You'll have to wait in line. I came to see Roisin.'

He stepped right up, so they were almost toe to toe. He saw her chest rise as she drew in a sharp breath. Her lips parted slightly. His appetite for her roared into life. The hunger that would gnaw at him forever.

'You'll have all the time in the world to get to know her.'

He scooped his hand around her neck, felt the warm,

supple skin and silken hair. Sweet heaven, how had he lived these days without her?

'Oh, really?' she whispered, tilting her head back, her perfect wet lips opening in invitation.

He accepted. With the slowest, softest, sweetest kiss.

'Oh, yes,' he murmured, against her mouth. 'I'm not stupid enough to let you go for a third time.'

Thoughts of everlasting days and nights with his woman, his wife, swirled in his head—made him dizzy with his love for her.

Roisin stamped her foot. He grabbed Frankie by the hand, led her out into the sunlight.

'Come on. We've got two hours until we need to be at Palermo. It's Dante's first match as captain. He can help us celebrate.'

She stopped, narrowed her eyes at him. 'Celebrate? What…?'

He bumped his brow. 'Of course. How stupid of me.'

There in the middle of the yard she planted her feet like a stubborn mule. Folded her arms and scowled a grin at him.

And he did the thing he never dared hope he would do, but in his mind had been practising for twenty years. He dropped to one knee, held her pale skinny fingers in his hand, slipped the Ipanema ring off her right hand and looked up into that darling face. Her eyes, filled with trust and hope, and now glistening with tears, stared down.

'Frankie Ryan. Sexiest, smartest, kindest woman alive. Will you marry me?'

He touched her ring finger and held the tiny silver Ipanema band poised.

She cocked her head to one side. 'Can I think about it?'

'Will you do what you're told for once? *Please?*' he said, staring up into her smiling, crying face.

She pursed her lips, wiped her hand over her soaked cheeks, nodded her head. 'I actually think this once I can.'

Then he stood and swooped her into his arms. He clutched her to his chest and she clambered to straddle him even as he strode back across the yard to the house and the rest of their lives together.

* * * * *

AT THE BRAZILIAN'S COMMAND

SUSAN STEPHENS

For the fabulous Ms M, travelling
companion extraordinaire

PROLOGUE

THE TERMS OF his grandfather's last will and testament had shocked everyone but Tiago Santos, to whom they had come as no surprise. To inherit he must marry. It was that simple. If he did not marry within a specific timeframe the ranch he loved in Brazil, and had built up into a world-class concern, would be handed over to a board of trustees who didn't know one end of a horse from the other.

His grandfather had suffered from delusions of grandeur, Tiago recalled as he prepared to land the jet he had piloted from Brazil to the wedding of his best friend, Chico, in Scotland. Tiago must give up his freedom to marry in order to preserve the Santos name, which his grandfather had believed was more important than the individuals who bore that name.

'The name Santos must not die out,' his grandfather had stated on his deathbed. 'It is time for you to find a wife, Tiago. If you don't provide an heir, our family will disappear without a trace.'

'And if I marry and we're not lucky enough to have a child?'

'You will adopt,' the old man had said, as if a child could be so easily co-opted into his plan. 'If you refuse me this you will lose everything you have worked so hard to rebuild.'

'And the families who have lived on Fazenda Santos for generations? Would you disinherit them too?'

'Your bleeding heart is wasted on me, Tiago. Do you think I care what happens when I'm dead? My legacy must live on. Don't look at me like that,' his grandfather had protested. 'Do you think I won this land with the milk of human kindness? What's so hard about what I'm asking you to do? You're with a different woman every week— pick one of them. You breed horses, don't you? Now I'm asking you to breed on a woman and get a child to bear our name. You know what will happen if you don't. You don't even have to keep her. Just keep the child.'

There was no way to argue with someone on his death-bed, and for that reason alone he had held his tongue. But one thing was sure: whatever it took, he would save the ranch.

CHAPTER ONE

THE FIST CAME out of nowhere and smacked her in the face. Flat on her back in the hay, reeling from shock and fighting off oblivion, she blanked for a moment and then fought like a demon. Cruel hands grabbed her wrists and pinned them above her head. Before she drew her next breath a powerful thigh was rammed between her legs. Terror clawed at her throat. Pain stabbed her body. The man was kneeling on top of her. She was alone in the stables, apart from the horses, and it was dark. The band at the wedding party was playing so loudly no one would hear her scream.

No way was she going to be raped. Not if she could help it, Danny determined.

Fear and fury gave her strength. But not enough!

She couldn't fight the man. He was too strong for her. Pressing her down with his weight, he was grunting as he freed himself, breathing heavily in anticipation of what he was going to do.

Yanking her head from side to side, she looked for something—anything—to beat him off with. If only she could free one hand—

He laughed as she strained furiously beneath him.

She knew that laugh.

Carlos Pintos!

Everything had happened in a matter of seconds, blinding her to all but the most primal sense of survival, or she would have recognised her brutal ex. It sickened her to know that Pintos must have tracked her down to this remote village in the Highlands of Scotland. Were there no lengths he wouldn't go to, to punish her for leaving him?

Coming here to Scotland, she'd been running home—running away from Pintos—running for her life. But no longer, Danny determined fiercely. She had escaped her brutal lover, and had no intention of giving way to him now. This was over.

As hate and fear collided inside her an anger so fierce it gave her renewed strength surged inside her. Bringing her knee up, she tried to catch him in the groin. But Pintos was too quick for her, and he laughed as he backhanded her across the face.

She recovered to find him braced on his forearms, preparing for his first lunge.

'Boring then—boring now,' Pintos sneered as a guttural sound of terror exploded from her throat. 'Why don't you admit you want me and give in?'

Never.

The only thing that made it through her frozen mind was that if 'boring' meant refusing the type of relationship Pinto had demanded, then, yes, she *was* boring.

'Well?' he sing-songed, sending her stomach into heaving spasms as he licked her face.

It had only been after she'd been going out with him for a while that Danny had discovered that Carlos Pintos, a big noise on the polo circuit, was a violent bully. He was always charming in public, and she had been guilty of falling under his spell, but he became increasingly vicious when they were alone. He must have used that same charm to get through security at the wedding.

Exclaiming with revulsion, she whipped her face away from his slavering tongue, knowing she had only one chance. With his weight advantage Pintos was over-confident, and he was taunting her by drawing this out. Gathering her remaining strength, she snapped up and rammed her head into his face.

With a yowl he reeled back, clutching his nose, blood pouring through his fingers. She lurched away, but the deep hay slowed her progress as she scuttled crab-like across the stable. Grabbing hold of the hay net on the wall, she hauled herself up and hit the bolt on the stable door. Barging through, head down, legs heavy and as weak as jelly, she lumbered forward, setting her sights on an exit that had never seemed further away.

Having escaped the wedding party, Tiago was taking a brisk stroll around the home fields of the vast High-land estate. As heir to a ranch in Brazil the size of a small country, casting a professional eye over farmland was second nature to him. His public face was that of an international polo player at the top of his game, but his private world was the wild pampas of Brazil, where he bred horses—a place where men were worthy of the name and women didn't simper. The press called him a playboy, but he much preferred being outside in a chal-lenging landscape like this to the cloying warmth of the crowded house.

Quickening his stride, he headed around the side of the house to the stables. His friend Chico had done well, marrying the heiress of this estate, though Chico had his own slice of Brazil to add to the pot, so it was a good mar-riage bargain all round. Chico intended to breed horses here as well as in Brazil—priceless ponies that might have been said to be the best in the world if Tiago's hadn't

been better. He and Chico had often talked about expand-
ing into the European market, and he could tell that this
land had been primed and was ready for animals to raise
their young in the spring.

Which was more than could be said for him, Tiago
reflected dryly. Fulfilling his grandfather's demand that
he find a wife was still a work in progress. He liked his
freedom too much to settle down. The press referred to
his Thunderbolts polo team as a pack of rampaging bar-
barians. He gave the tag new meaning—though the public liked to think of him rampaging with a glass of Krug
in his hand and a beautiful woman on his arm.

He relaxed as he came closer to the stables, where he
would be as happy chatting to a horse as making small
talk in the ballroom. The courtyard in front of the block
was dimly lit, in contrast to the chandeliers set party-
bright inside the grand old house.

He was halfway across the yard when the door to the
stable block burst open and a small female, dressed in
some flouncy creation, tumbled out.

'What the—?'

Instead of reacting graciously as he ran to save her she
screamed some obscenity at him and, grabbing hold of
his lapels, roared at him like a tigress before angrily attempting to thrust him away. When this failed to make
any impact she stepped back and, holding herself defensively, glared at him through furious eyes.

For a moment he didn't recognise her, but then...

'Danny?'

He knew the girl. She was the bride's best friend, and
a bridesmaid at the wedding. He'd first met her at Chico's
ranch in Brazil, where both the bride—Lizzie—and Danny
had been studying horse-training under the heel of an ac-

knowledged master of terrorising students: his friend and teammate Chico Fernandez.

'What has happened here?' he demanded as she continued to glare at him. She was panting as if she'd run a mile. Then he saw her face was badly bruised. *'Deus*, Danny!'

Moving past her, he stared into the darkened stable block. Nothing seemed to be out of place, so he turned back to her.

'Danny, it's Tiago from Brazil. Don't you recognise me? You're safe now.'

Battered and bruised she might be, but her eyes blazed at this last comment.

'Safe with *you*?' she derided.

Fair enough. If she believed his press, she probably should run for her life.

But she didn't run. Danny stayed to confront him. She'd always had guts, he remembered, and had never been afraid to take him on when they'd met at Chico's ranch. But what had happened here?

'Why are you out here on your own?' And where the hell was Security? he wondered, glancing around.

'What's it to you?' As she spoke she touched the red bruise on her cheek.

'Quiet, *chica*... You need help with this.'

'From *you*?' she demanded. And then she shrieked. 'Watch out!' and, giving him one hell of a push, she alerted him to the shadowy form looming behind them.

Shielding her with his body, he countered the attack and knocked the man out cold.

Carlos Pintos!

He loathed the man. Pintos gave polo a bad name. A cheat on the field of play, as well as in life, he was also Danny's ex—who had brutalised her, by all accounts, he remembered now. Toeing the inert figure with the tip of his boot, he reassured himself that Pintos wasn't going anywhere before calling Chico on his phone.

A few terse words later, he turned back to Danny.

'Don't,' she said, holding up her hands as if to ward him off.

They'd had many a run-in during Danny's time in Brazil, but theirs had always been a good-natured battleground, where he teased and she flirted. It had never gone any further than that.

'*Thank you* would suffice,' he commented mildly. 'And please let me assure you that I have absolutely no intention of touching you.'

He was assessing her injuries as he spoke. Judging them superficial, he considered the subject closed— though the police would have to be alerted, and he would wait until he was sure Pintos was safely under lock and key.

'Thank you,' Danny muttered, frowning as she stared up at him from beneath her eyelashes.

Straightening his suit jacket, he brushed his hair back and then asked bluntly, 'Did he touch you?'

'What do you think?'

'I can see the obvious bruises, but I think you know what I mean.'

Grimly, she shook her head. 'He didn't do what you're thinking. You men all think the same.'

She was upset, but he wouldn't stand for that. 'Don't tar me with the same brush as Pintos. And you still haven't told me why you're out here on your own.'

'I was in the stable block checking out the horses,' she explained grudgingly.

He didn't believe her for a minute. Chico had staff to do that, and even Danny wasn't so closely welded to her job.

'I've lived here all my life,' she murmured, 'and I've always felt safe here. Nothing like this has ever happened before. And if you must know,' she added, flashing a glance up at him, 'I wanted to be alone. I wanted to think…away from the noise of the party.'

'I can understand you wanting some quiet time,' he agreed—he'd felt the same. 'But times change, Danny.'

'Yes,' she said ruefully. 'Everything changes. But I'm still here.'

He guessed she would miss her friend Lizzie now she had married Chico, and perhaps Danny's scholarship to train horses in Brazil hadn't been the golden ticket she'd hoped for. 'It takes time to establish a career—especially a career with horses.'

'And money,' she said. 'Lots of money that I just don't have. And if there's one thing I've learned it's that I can't have everything in life.'

'You're wrong. Look at *me*.'

She smiled at his arrogance, but he knew that self-confidence was the first step towards building any successful career. If he hadn't believed in himself, who would have?

'It's possible for you to do this too,' he said, and when she started to argue, he added, 'I admit I was in the right place at the right time, but I worked all the hours under the sun for that luck—as you do. I always had a vision of what my future would hold. You have the same. So go for it, Danny,' he advised. 'Don't hold back.'

If there was one thing he couldn't tolerate it was bullies, and he hated seeing what Pintos had done to this woman—stripping away Danny's spirit and leaving only the doubt underneath. He found himself willing his strength into her.

He'd never been in this position with a woman before;

communicating with women on a serious level had never been necessary. His life was full of women, and he had never wanted this type of interaction with one of them. But to keep Danny steady after her ordeal, he continued on with his theme.

'When we first met on Chico's ranch in Brazil you wanted your own horse-training establishment. Am I right?'

'Yes,' she agreed, but she was shaking her head. 'I was idealistic then. I hadn't thought through all the pitfalls ahead of me.'

'And you think it's been easy for me?'

His face was close. Her scent bewitched him. He was pleased when her flickering gaze steadied on his, telling him she was calming down.

"I worked hard and never gave up my dream. And neither must you, Danny. Never...*never* give up your dream.'

Her gaze strayed to Pintos.

'Don't look at him. Look at me.'

He was relieved when she did so.

'Thank you.' Her eyes were wide and wounded. 'Thank you for reminding me what I want out of life, and that he has no part in it.'

'Don't thank me. You're strong. You'll get over this.' He glanced at the creep on the floor. 'He won't be bothering you again. I promise you that.'

'I'm all right—really,' she insisted, with a smile that didn't make it to her eyes.

She didn't want his pity. He could understand that. Danny wasn't the type to make a fuss. She didn't cry, or cling to him. She'd been one of the boys in Brazil, only caring for her horses and for her best friend—today's bride, Lizzie. She had always lifted everyone's spirits on Chico's ranch.

He glanced again at Pintos in disgust. The creep had been so eager to recapture Danny he had forgotten to do up his flies. 'I'll stay with you until Security arrives,' he reassured her, seeing she was still frightened of the man. 'I'll hand Pintos over to them and then I'll take you back to the house.'

'There's no need for that,' she insisted, shaking her head as she hugged herself defensively.

'There's every need,' he argued. 'You shouldn't be on your own tonight. And you should get checked over.'

She shook her head slowly, as if she were reliving events. 'I can't believe I let this happen.'

'You didn't *let* this happen, Danny,' he said firmly. 'You've done nothing wrong.'

She glanced at him then, as if seeking reassurance. 'Maybe I should take it as a sign that my time here's done.'

'Then don't stay,' he said with a shrug. 'But just promise me you won't make any hasty decisions while you're upset.'

'Upset?' she scoffed. 'I'm over it.'

He doubted that. 'Good, but please sleep on it, and see how you feel in the morning. Maybe you'll feel differently then.'

'Or maybe I'll think *Clean page, new story.*'

'That's also a possibility,' he conceded.

'But I can't run away,' she said softly, almost to herself. 'I can't run away from Carlos or from anything else.'

'You don't have to,' he reassured her. 'Change doesn't always involve running away. Think carefully before you make any life-changing decisions. And don't go wandering around on your own in the dark in future.'

'Why?' Her eyes cleared suddenly and she repaid him with a piercing look. 'Because you won't be around to save me?'

He met that stare and held it. 'That's right. I won't.'

Danny's feelings were in an uproar. Yes, she was shocked by what had happened in the stable, but standing next to Tiago Santos was incredible, and unreal, and incredibly unsettling even without having Carlos Pintos at her feet. She had been violently attracted to Tiago in Brazil. From the very first moment she had felt a connection between them, and it was still there.

Which only proved what a hopeless judge of men she was, Danny reflected. Tiago was a notorious playboy, and when they'd first met she had treated him as such—teasing him, yes, because that was in her nature, but keeping a safe distance from him, all the same. And now Tiago was handing out life advice. Was he the best person to do that?

Surprisingly, tonight she would say yes—because tonight he was talking to her as Lizzie would, and his concern for her appeared to be genuine.

'Security's here,' he announced as two guards ran up. 'We'll go back to the house as soon as we've spoken to the police.'

'I don't need a chaperon, Tiago,' she stressed.

'That's good, because I'm not for hire.'

'Why don't you go back to the party?' she suggested, having no inclination to jump from the frying pan into the fire. 'I feel really bad, keeping you here.'

'You're not keeping me,' he insisted. 'We'll go back together. I have to know you're safe.'

'How much harm do you think can come to me between here and the front door?'

Tiago's answer was to stare at her in a way that told her he wouldn't be dissuaded, and in spite of his all too colourful reputation she had to admit she did feel safe with him. And she had to get over her schoolgirl crush fast, Danny cautioned herself. Tiago Santos was not for her.

'Just a few more minutes,' he said, staring at her with concern.

She smiled back at him, recognising that soothing, husky, faintly accented tone as the same voice he'd used to soothe his ponies in Brazil.

'You don't have to come back to the party, Danny. I'll make your excuses for you.'

'No, you won't,' she argued firmly.

Tiago raised a cynical brow over eyes that were dark and piercing. He was such a good-looking man it was impossible to remain immune to him. And he could read her like a book. He always had been able to.

The course she'd taken in Brazil had been so hard, and Tiago was a hugely successful polo international. She had always tried that little bit harder when he'd come to watch her working in the training ring. Her pride was holding her up now. He knew how shaken she was, but she didn't want him to think her weak.

As the seconds ticked by she longed for the sanctuary of her room. This situation was unreal, and she wanted nothing more than to strip off and stand beneath a shower, scrubbing every inch of her body clean. She had to get rid of Carlos's touch, and then hopefully forget she had ever been so stupid as to take up with a man like him in the first place.

She glanced at Tiago as he gave instructions to the security guards, thinking how different he was. Tiago's command of the situation was reassuring. He was everything the sorry excuse for a man at their feet was not.

Did the fates see any humour in the situation? she wondered. Tiago Santos, the world's most notorious playboy, was no playboy but a protector—strong and caring. He might look dangerous, but his character was different from the way it was described in his press.

'Where do you think you're going?' he called after her as she started back to the house.

'We've spoken to the police. Pintos has gone—'

'I'm heading your way, remember?' he said, catching up with her. 'Go straight up to your room and I'll tell Lizzie what's happened.'

'No, you won't. Lizzie's been upset enough tonight. She must have noticed I'm missing. She will have seen the lights of the police cars. This is her day, not mine. Let's not spoil it for her,' she said, desperate not to ruin Lizzie's day. 'Just tell her the fuss is over and there's nothing for her to worry about. Say I went to check on the horses and lost track of time. Tell her I tripped in the mud and had to clean myself up—I've gone upstairs to change my clothes and I'll be back at the party soon.'

'I'll do what I can,' Tiago promised. 'But I won't lie to her. Danny, you can't pretend nothing's happened,' he insisted when she scowled at him.

'That's not what I asked you to do. What?' she demanded impatiently, when Tiago continued to stare at her.

A faint smile touched his mouth. 'You might not be able to keep it a secret.'

'Why not?'

'You won't win any beauty contests tonight.'

She touched her face and groaned, remembering the bruises. She'd forgotten about them.

'Do you have anything you can put on them?' Tiago asked with concern.

'I'm sure there'll be something in the house.'

'Maybe I should call a doctor for you?'

'A doctor won't come out at this time of night—and why would we trouble one? Thank you for your concern—seriously, Tiago—but it's only a bruise, and bruises fade.'

'And you don't have to be strong all the time,' he fired back.

'What's it to you?' Biting back tears, and hating herself for the weakness, she confronted him in the way they had squared up to each other on so many occasions on the ranch in Brazil.

It was a terrible mistake to stare into Tiago's eyes. Her awareness of him only grew. But she couldn't allow him to patronise or pity her, if only because it was so dangerous to wonder, even for a second, how it might feel to have a man like Tiago Santos care for her.

The first thing she had to do was get over tonight. Bruises would fade, but the disappointment she felt in herself for not progressing her career as she would have liked, for not moving away from her home town, and most of all for getting mixed up with a man like Carlos Pintos, would take a lot longer.

'I should thank you properly,' she said, remembering her manners belatedly. If nothing else, Tiago had been her saviour tonight.

He shrugged it off. 'No medals, Danny. They'd only spoil my suit.'

He could always make her smile. The playboy was still in him, beneath that white knight's shining armour. She must never allow herself to forget that Tiago Santos possessed a glittering charm that had led many women astray. She must never be guilty of romanticising that charm, because there was another man underneath it.

Brutal tattoos showed beneath the crisp white cuffs of Tiago's immaculate dress shirt, and a gold earring glinted in what light there was. This was not some safe, mild-mannered man—a white knight racing to rescue the damsel in distress—but Tiago Santos: the most infamous barbarian of them all.

CHAPTER TWO

ANNIE, THE HOUSEKEEPER at Rottingdean, was waiting for them at the front door.

'Chico told me what happened,' Danny heard Annie inform Tiago discreetly as the housekeeper ushered her away. She saw him nod briefly.

'Before you go,' he called after her. 'Here's my card. If you need anything…'

'Your *card*?' She smiled at the incongruity of a barbarian carrying a card, but took it and studied it before looking up. 'I won't need anything, but thank you again for tonight.'

Tiago ground his jaw. He wasn't used to being on the receiving end of a rain check, she guessed as he turned to rejoin the party.

She scrubbed down in the shower, turning her face up with relief to the cleansing stream. So what excuse did she have for being in the stables on her own at night, in the middle of Lizzie's wedding party?

She'd been having a moment, Danny concluded. She had needed some quiet time to contemplate her life going forward now her best friend was married. The stables was where she had always sought sanctuary, even as a child. The horses were so quiet and mild they had always been a relief—a release from her troubled home life—and tonight had seemed a good time for her to re-evaluate in that quiet place.

The last thing she had expected was for a nightmare like Carlos Pintos to reappear. Thankfully, he would be locked away for a very long time now. The police had told her this. It turned out he was a wanted man, who had stalked and attacked several women.

So all she had to worry about now was Tiago Santos. *Oh, good,* Danny reflected wryly, wondering if she would ever get Tiago out of her head. While he was close by she could think of nothing else.

But where was she going with this? Shouldn't she toughen up and forget about men? Wasn't that safer? She would have to if she was ever going to give herself the chance of a career. And what was she waiting for as far as *that* was concerned? She had a prestigious diploma from Chico's training school in Brazil, as well as a life-time of experience with horses. It was time to make that count. It was time to start planning for the day when she had her own equine establishment.

With an impatient laugh she turned the shower to ice. Maybe that would wash some sense into her. She was a few hundred thousand pounds short of the start-up cash for her own place, with very little prospect of getting hold of such huge amounts of money.

'Danny?' Annie was calling from behind the door.

'Yes?'

'There's someone here to see you, hen.'

The familiar Scottish endearment made Danny smile. 'Just give me a minute and I'll grab a towel—'

It would be Lizzie. She would play down what had happened. She would change the subject and make Lizzie laugh. It was her best friend's wedding day, when everything had to be perfect. And it would be if Danny had anything to do with it.

'I can tell him you'd rather not see anyone if you'd prefer that, hen?'

Him?

'He's very concerned about you...' Annie waited, and then, receiving no reply, added, 'I think you should at least see him to reassure him that you're okay...'

Danny's heart went crazy. She was actually trembling. There was only one man who knew what had happened in the stable. And she had just vowed to cut him out of her life.

'I've brought you a clean dress. I'll just leave it on the bed, shall I?' Annie suggested. A few more seconds passed and then the housekeeper called out with concern, 'Are you okay in there, Danny?'

'Yes. I'm fine.' She put her resolute face on. 'I'm just coming... Could you ask him to give me a few minutes?'

'Will do, hen.'

And now there was silence. Was Tiago standing outside the door, or had he gone downstairs to wait for her? She stood listening, naked and dripping water everywhere, with the towel hanging limply from her hand. Wasn't it better to face him, talk to him, reassure him as Annie had suggested? Then she could finally put an end to this horrible episode. Tiago must understand that she was very grateful to him but that she didn't need his help going forward.

Securing the towel tightly around her, she firmed her jaw.

She was keeping him waiting. No woman had ever kept him waiting before. He had to remind himself that tonight Danny was a special case. She'd had a shock and he was supposed to be playing the role of understanding friend. At least that was how the bride had described him when he had passed on Danny's message. Chico had already told Lizzie what had happened, so obviously the bride was full of concern for her friend.

'Be gentle with her, Tiago'.

What the hell do you think *I'm going to be with her?* he had thought.

'Just do this one thing for me,' Lizzie had begged him with her hand on his arm.

'I will,' he had promised, finding a smile to reassure the bride. And he'd kept his word.

In his hand there was nothing more threatening than horse liniment to speed up the healing of Danny's bruises. Was that gentlemanly enough?

Danny looked at the dress Annie had left on the bed with dismay. It was the type of dress she'd seen in magazines, but it was hardly appropriate for someone whose life revolved around horses. It was lovely, and maybe any other night she would have loved to try it on. If she was honest, she would love to wear it—but not tonight, when she was feeling about as confident as a cockroach with a foot hovering over it.

The dress was bright red silk, and the type of dress to get you noticed, darted in such a way that it showed off the figure. It was a perfect dress for a wedding party, for dancing, for having fun. It was Lizzie's dress. She recognised it immediately and smiled, thinking of her friend picking it out for her to wear.

So what was she going to do? Tiago was waiting outside. Lizzie was waiting downstairs. She didn't want Tiago thinking she was weak, and she didn't want to worry her friend.

She put on the dress and left her hair loose. Slipping her feet into Lizzie's silver sandals—they were almost the same size—she checked herself over in the mirror. She tipped her chin up and sighed. The bruises didn't look too bad now, but they were still noticeable even though she had covered them with make-up. But there would be atmospheric lighting downstairs for the dancing. No one would notice, she hoped. She was definitely going to pull this off.

He could hear Danny moving around inside the room. Why the hell didn't she open the door? He rested his head against the wall, and then pulled away again. He thought about walking straight in, and then remembered he was playing the role of a gentleman tonight.

'Nearly ready,' she called out brightly, as if the evening had held nothing more for her than a garden party and a chance meeting between old friends. 'Sorry to keep you waiting!'

I bet, he thought.

She swung the door wide and for once he was speechless. A transformation had been wrought and for a moment he wasn't sure he approved. He'd seen Danny in breeches and a shirt often enough as she sat astride a horse. He'd seen her in a fancy bridesmaid's dress, demure and contained—and then bedraggled, muddy and bruised later, which had brought out his protective instinct. But this red clinging number—far too short, far too revealing…

'You can't be thinking of going down to the party dressed like *that*?'

The words were out of his mouth before he could stop himself. The irony wasn't lost on him. Danny was dressed as he expected a woman on his arm to dress—but this was *Danny*.

And, seeing the way she was staring at him now, he braced himself for the backlash he knew was on its way.

'I most certainly *am* going down in this dress,' she told him, her gaze steely. 'It's all I've got to wear—other than a bathrobe. Or I could make Lizzie think I'm in a really bad way and upset her even more than I have already by staying up here in my room all night?'

He slanted a smile, guessing none of those options would appeal.

'If you'd rather not be seen with me—'

'I brought you this,' he interrupted.

'What is it?' she asked suspiciously, thrown as she stared at the tube he held in his hand.

'I use it on the horses when they get bruises. It works miracles.'

She angled her chin to give him an assessing stare. 'Does it smell?'

A muscle in his jaw flexed as she brought the tube to her nose. 'I must admit I hadn't thought about that.'

'Perhaps I should?' she said with the suggestion of a smile. 'For the sake of the other guests, if nothing else?'

He raised a brow, forced now to curb his own smile. Having taken in the hourglass figure, the glorious hair hanging loose almost to her waist, and the tiny feet with pink shell-like nails enclosed in a pair of high-heeled silver sandals, he was appreciating Danny's indomitable spirit as he never had before. The fact that she could be so together after such an ordeal was hugely to her credit.

'Thank you, Tiago,' she said briskly, before he could process these thoughts. 'It seems I have a lot to thank you for tonight. And I do…sincerely,' she added, holding his gaze steadily for a good few seconds.

It was time enough for his groin to tighten. 'You're certain you're all right now?' He had to remind himself that his thoughts where Danny was concerned weren't appropriate.

'I will be when I get back to the party,' she assured him, glancing at the door. 'I'm keen to get everything back to normal for Lizzie as soon as I can. I'll just leave this here, if that's all right with you?' She flashed him a glance as she put the cream down on the table. 'I'll put it on tonight, when there's no one else around to smell it.'

He was unreasonably glad to discover she would be on her own tonight. 'Shall we?' he said, offering his arm.

'Why not?' she replied walking past him.

She walked ahead of Tiago, and all the way down the stairs she felt the heat of his stare on her back. The fact that they were both so aware of each other was exciting, but also dangerous, and she had no intention of allowing Tiago Santos to see just how much his presence rattled her, or that the sight of him close up was all it took to unnerve her.

No man could achieve his level of success by being an angel, though she supposed he couldn't be held responsible for the way he looked—those eyes, that mouth, the way he stood, eased onto one hip, as if life were his to survey at his leisure.

She had lived in Brazil for quite some time while she was training at Chico's ranch, and she had come to love the Brazilian people for their warmth and exuberance. Tiago had those same qualities in abundance, though she had to remind herself of the rumours that said he was a lone wolf and dangerous.

It was almost a relief to be enveloped in the noise and

exuberance of the party downstairs, where she headed straight for the top table and Lizzie.

'Wow—you look amazing,' Lizzie exclaimed, standing up to greet her. 'I'm glad I picked that dress—it really suits you. Are you okay now?' Lizzie added in a quieter tone, and then she saw the bruises. 'Oh, Danny! Your poor face!'

'Is it an improvement?' Danny touched her cheek gingerly.

'Don't joke about it. It isn't funny,' Lizzie insisted. 'Pintos is a monster. Thank God he's locked away.'

'Let's not speak about him again, okay?' Danny put her arm around Lizzie's shoulder. 'I don't want anything to spoil your wedding day.'

Lizzie ignored the warning. They were both too stubborn to be curbed so easily, Danny supposed.

'I'm just so relieved that Tiago was there to save you,' Lizzie exclaimed, glancing round to look for the man in question. 'Maybe he's not as bad as they say?'

'He's every bit as bad,' Danny argued as she stared at Tiago, who was talking to the groom.

'I can't imagine how Pintos crashed the wedding,' Lizzie went on with concern. 'He certainly wasn't on my guest list. Chico said he must have been playing polo somewhere in the British Isles and made that his excuse to come to Scotland to cause trouble for you. And the security people let us down. But there'll be no more mistakes, and Pintos won't do anything like that again.' Lizzie's face softened as she stared at Danny and shook her head. 'I feel so guilty about this.'

'Don't,' Danny said firmly. 'Pintos is evil, and I'm glad we're all rid of him.'

Lizzie smiled with relief. 'Thank you for coming back

to the party. That took a lot of courage, Danny. I was so worried about you.'

'You don't need to worry about me. I can look after myself.'

'But we've always looked after each other in the past, haven't we? And I wasn't there for you this time.'

'Lizzie,' Danny said in a mock-stern voice. 'This is your wedding day.'

'And you don't have to put on a front for me, Danny Cameron.'

'I'm not putting on a front. I'm letting this go. I won't allow Carlos Pintos to colour my life, or my thinking, or anything I do.'

'And he won't.' Lizzie gave her a hug. 'But I think there's another man who would like to…'

'Only because you're staring at Tiago. He thinks we're talking about him,' Danny pointed out, tensing as Tiago started heading their way.

She shivered as his shadow fell over them, and then was instantly annoyed with herself for reacting at all.

Tiago made a gracious bow to the bride, and then said, 'Excuse us, Lizzie. Shall we dance?'

Danny almost looked over her shoulder, to see who he was talking to. 'Me?'

'Of course you,' he said.

How could she refuse when Tiago was giving her a look she couldn't misinterpret—a look she had to act on immediately? Chico was hovering, and she had taken up quite enough of the bride's time.

Why make a fuss? she concluded. This was a party. It was no big deal if she had one dance with Tiago Santos.

'Seems I have to thank you again,' she said.

'Why?' He was frowning.

She couldn't speak for a moment as Tiago drew her

into his arms, swamping her with many emotions, chief amongst which was an intense awareness of him. This was more than she had expected to experience in one night. *He* was so much more. It was hard to breathe, or to register anything beyond Tiago's masculinity, and it took all she'd got to concentrate long enough to answer him.

'I'm glad you teased me away from Lizzie. I guess old habits die hard. We've practically been welded to each other since we were children.'

'And then Chico came along?' he guessed.

'That's right,' she admitted, smiling wryly.

'So you and Lizzie have been friends for a long time?'

'Yes, but I should have taken the hint faster that Chico wanted to be with his bride—so thanks for that.'

'Is that why you were in the stables earlier, Danny? Were you wondering how your life would go forward from now on, without Lizzie to confide in?'

'You're too smart,' she said. His intuition was unsettling.

'It's understandable,' he argued, drawing her into his hard-muscled frame so they could dance as one. 'You're bound to consider how this will change things between you, and we all need quiet times to sort out our heads. Did you come to a conclusion?'

She was coming to a few conclusions now. She wished she wasn't wearing such a provocative dress—it was giving Tiago all the wrong signals. He was making her wonder if she had come downstairs too soon.

Her body was rioting at the touch of Tiago's hands and the warmth of his breath on her skin. Having her hand in his was electrifying. Having him direct her movements, even in this harmless dance, was equally disturbing. She had to remind herself that dance was the lifeblood of Brazil, and that it was a means of expression that very few nations could use to such good effect. Right now Tiago and dance had combined to stunning effect.

And she had to keep it up for a little while longer, Danny reasoned, if only because Lizzie was watching them with concern. One dance with the most dangerous man in the room. She could handle that. She wasn't going to allow herself to be intimidated ever again—not by life, and not by Tiago.

They fitted together perfectly, considering Tiago was twice her size. He moved so well he made it easy for her. She found herself moving rhythmically with him in a way that was sexy, even suggestive, but it was just one dance, she reassured herself.

They were close enough to the top table for Lizzie to flash anxious glances their way, and she smiled back to confirm that everything was all right.

And it might have been had she not been moving closer and closer to Tiago. He didn't force her to. His touch remained frustratingly light. But the music was compelling her to do this. It was intoxicating, and the pulse of South America was soon running through her veins. She could feel his muscles flexing as he teased all her senses at once. If she moved away he brought her back.

There weren't many men who looked good dancing, but Tiago was one of them. Maybe because he was an athlete. His body was supple and strong. And he was Brazilian—dark and mysterious and sexy, with a passion he carried everywhere with him. She trembled as he dipped his head and his warm, minty breath brushed her face.

'I didn't know you were such a good dancer, Danny.'

'Neither did I,' she admitted.

His firm lips slanted in a sexy smile. 'It must be because you're dancing with me.'

She laughed at his engaging self-assurance.

'You were such a tomboy in Brazil.'

'I'm still a tomboy, Senhor Santos.'

'Tiago, please,' he murmured, in a husky whisper that raised every tiny hair on the back of her neck.

She couldn't deny she was disappointed to learn that Tiago still thought of her as a tomboy. She was a woman— a woman with needs. She was a confused woman, still recovering from the shock of an attack, but sufficiently recovered to know how deeply this man affected her. And dance was the perfect outlet for her emotions. Dance was a means of expression when words wouldn't come.

When the music faded and the band took a break she felt awkward suddenly, and glanced longingly towards the exit, where the double doors were open wide.

'Have you had enough?' Tiago asked.

She flashed a glance up at him. 'I'm sorry—am I being so obvious?'

'Too much too soon for you, I think,' he said wisely.

Once again that intuition of his was a warning of how easily he could read her. *Tiago* was too much too soon, and always would be, Danny suspected. If she had known how it would feel to be in his arms, how *she* would feel, she would never have agreed to dance with him.

'I do have one suggestion,' he murmured.

'Yes?' She glanced up and felt her heart turn over.

'Just wait a moment before you go. The DJ has taken over from the band, so have one more dance with me.'

She was just basking in the idea that Tiago enjoyed dancing with her when he spoke again.

'That way it will give Chico enough time to make Lizzie forget everything—including you.'

Danny's eyes flashed wide. His comment had stung. That was what happened when she dropped her guard around Tiago Santos. But he was right. She had to let her friend go and move on.

'If you're sure you don't mind dancing with me?' There were so many much prettier girls in the room.

'I'm sure,' Tiago confirmed with an amused look.

This was the type of thing she would have liked to discuss with Lizzie. They had both led such hectic, fractured lives as children, and had protected each other until their lives had been sewn together again by Lizzie's grandmother and by the housekeeper, Annie, both of whom had been determined that neither child would suffer because of their less than responsible parents.

'Shall I get you out of here?' Tiago suggested, after a short time longer on the dance floor.

She refocused fast. 'Sorry—was I frowning?'

'Yes,' he confirmed with amusement. 'I'm disappointed you can't concentrate on me.'

'Maybe that's why I'm frowning,' she suggested with a wry smile.

'Now I'm hurt.'

She doubted that. And she was willing to bet Tiago knew everything she was thinking. But she was starting to feel the strain of keeping up a bright and breezy front after what had happened in the stable.

'Are you serious about getting me out of here?'

'Absolutely,' Tiago said, steering her towards the door.

The other couples on the dance floor quickly closed over the gap they'd left and it was as if they'd never been there, Danny thought as she glanced over her shoulder.

'Don't look round,' Tiago advised. 'Keep on walking. No one will notice we're leaving—I'm thinking of Lizzie now—unless you draw attention to yourself.'

They wove their way through the tables with Tiago's hand resting lightly in the small of her back. His touch was like a lightning transmitter and the force field didn't let up—not even when he drew to a halt in the shadows beneath the staircase in the hall.

'I'll see you to your room,' he said.

She shook her head decisively. 'There's no need for that.'

'But I insist.'

The only explanation she could give for not putting up a better fight was that she was still in a state of shock. Why else hadn't she resisted his suggestion?

When they reached her bedroom door and Tiago opened it for her, he stood back.

'Goodnight, Danny.'

She held her breath as he ran one fingertip lightly down her cheek.

Why had he done that?

'Try to get some sleep,' he suggested gently before she could process that thought. 'This has been quite a night for you.'

In every way, she thought, still tingling from his touch as Tiago turned away.

'Goodnight, Tiago. And thank you…'

She watched him go, and only when his footsteps had faded and disappeared did she realise she was still holding her breath.

CHAPTER THREE

HE NEEDED A WIFE. Danny needed money. He had a plan. Danny was an intelligent, gutsy woman, and time was running out for the ranch. He would make her an offer. Every marriage was a bargain of some sort. People said they got married for love, but did they never sit back to think about the benefits to both parties? Not even when the occasional doubt crept in? Love might make the world go round, but without money the world and everyone in it would go to hell in a bucket.

He could offer Danny a shortcut to her dream, while marriage to her would secure the ranch for *him*. Getting the amount of money Danny needed for her venture must seem like a pipe dream to her—but for him…? Money was the least of his problems.

He'd ask her tomorrow. He'd lay everything out so she knew exactly where she stood. Their deal would be secured by a legal contract. And, as a bonus, he wanted her. He'd wanted her since Brazil.

He only had to think about the families who depended on him back in Brazil to know this was the right thing to do. When Danny met them she would agree too.

'Chico?' He had just spotted his friend in a rare moment away from his bride. It was time to put his plan into action.

'Yes, my friend…'

Chico Fernandez was another powerful polo player, with the dark flashing looks of South America.

Chico placed his arm around Tiago's shoulders. 'What can I do for you?'

'Danny works for you, doesn't she?'

'Danny?' Chico raised a brow. 'You're interested in Danny? She's a pretty little thing. I don't blame you. I'm glad you were able to help her today and, yes, she works here. Why do you ask?'

'I'd like to take Danny back to Brazil with me—if that's okay with you?' he asked dryly.

'Do I have any option?'

'No,' he said flatly, ignoring Chico's black look.

'So you want Danny to come work for you.' Chico's eyes narrowed. 'She's a great rider, and a promising trainer, but you don't need any more staff. What's going on, Tiago?'

'Danny wants her own place, and I think I can help her with that plan.'

'Really?' Chico stared at him suspiciously. 'Danny's had her problems—as you know. Are you going to add to them?'

'That is not my intention.'

'Don't hurt her, Tiago. Please remember that Danny Cameron is my wife's best friend.'

'I want to give her a hand up—that's all. I feel bad for her after what happened today.'

Chico frowned. 'I'll have a word with Lizzie—smooth the way for you.'

'That's all I ask, my friend.'

Danny collapsed with relief on the bed. It was one thing holding it together in public, but now she was here on her own…

Putting her arms over her head, she tried to pretend she didn't want to feel Tiago's arms around her—and a lot more besides. Could she really go through all that heartbreak again, with another polo player? Hadn't she learned her lesson?

Not that Tiago was anything like Carlos Pintos, but he was well out of her league. And how was she supposed to forget how it had felt to be in Tiago's arms on the dance floor? Or how she'd thrilled with pleasure when they'd moved together so effortlessly? How was she supposed to forget that?

She had to forget. She had to file it away with all the other good memories to pull out and reflect on whenever she needed a boost. Tiago was going back to Brazil soon. He would probably be gone by the time she got up in the morning.

While she'd stay here and nothing would change. She would still be working at Rottingdean when she was an old woman—still sending what money she could to her mother. It was never enough. Her mother had no idea about saving, or making do, or even working for a living. But if Danny stayed here she would never have the chance to build a nest egg. She would never own her own place—

So it was time to get moving—get on with life and make as much of a success of it as she could. She had more sense than to waste her time daydreaming about Tiago Santos.

She woke to a chilly grey dawn. Grimacing, she pulled the covers up to her chin. Chico and Lizzie had started improvements on the house Lizzie had inherited from her grandmother, but nothing had been spent on Rottingdean for years, and replacing the entire central heating system in the big old house was still a work in progress. The ancient radiators clanked noisily but gave off little heat—though Danny suspected she was shivering because she was tired as well as cold, having only dozed on and off through the night.

The reason for that was Tiago Santos.

So much for banishing the man from her thoughts! Tiago's touch on her body was as vivid now as it had been when he'd held her on the dance floor. She'd been warm in his arms.

She was a hopeless case, Danny concluded, swinging out of bed. Her only excuse was that Tiago Santos was the type of distraction that could make an arrow swerve from its course.

She showered, and grabbed a towel to rub herself down until her skin glowed red. Clearing a space on the steamed-up mirror, she examined her face. The bruise under her eye had turned an ugly yellow-green. Attractive! But at least the swelling had gone down, thanks to Tiago's horse liniment.

She laughed, remembering the look on his face when she had mentioned the stink. She knew that ointment well. They all used it. It had been a kind thought, but the sort of thing any man would do, she concluded wryly, throwing on as many layers of clothing as she had brought with her. She would have to put on everything she possessed to keep the bitter cold at bay.

It would be warm in Brazil.

'Oh, for goodness' sake!' she exclaimed out loud.

Glancing out of the window, she jumped back fast, seeing Tiago in the yard. So he hadn't gone back to Brazil yet...

With her heart beating like a drum, she took a second look. Tiago had stopped on his way across the yard to speak to a fellow guest, and was being his usual charming self. He made time for everyone, and even from this distance his smile made *her* smile.

It was such an attractive flash of strong white teeth in that stern, swarthy face. It was a smile that made her stomach clench and her limbs melt as she wondered, for the umpteenth time, what it would feel like to have a man like Tiago Santos do more than just hold her in his arms. She had experienced his concern and his friendship, and now she wanted more—she couldn't help herself.

Safe in the knowledge that he couldn't see her looking, she surveyed the well-packed jeans, the calf-gripping riding boots and the heavy sweater he was wearing today—which she found sexy, for some reason—under a jacket that moulded his powerful shoulders to perfection. The collar was turned up against the wind, and with his thick, wavy black hair blowing about he was an arresting sight.

And she should be arrested for what she was thinking.

She stood back quickly when he stared up, as if he could sense her looking at him.

Leaning back against the wall—out of sight, she hoped—she swallowed convulsively and closed her eyes, wondering if she had been too late and he had seen her.

What if he had? There was no law against looking out of the window.

She stole another look. Tiago had quite a crowd around him by this time. Even Lizzie's sophisticated wedding guests were thrilled to chat to a polo player of Tiago's standing, and particularly one whose success on the field of play was almost as legendary as his success with women.

To be fair to him, though, Tiago was also famous for turning his grandfather's failing ranch into a world-class concern. And his relationship with women was none of her business. Which, unfortunately, wasn't enough to stop her thinking about Tiago's women—all wearing outfits composed of cobweb-fine lace, or nothing at all, and smelling of anything other than horse liniment...

She should be going down to breakfast—not staring at one of the wedding guests, Danny reminded herself firmly. She was a home bird—not an adventuress on the hunt for a barbarian mate. She should be outside by now, exercising Lizzie's horse as she had promised Lizzie she would. There was nothing like a ride across the heather to blow the cobwebs from her mind.

Where was Danny? He was waiting to speak to her about his plan. Why hadn't she come down to breakfast?

He glanced at his watch impatiently. Had she made other arrangements? Had he missed her? Had she slipped away without him noticing?

Pushing his chair back, Tiago began to pace the room. Was he wasting his time in Scotland? His manager at the ranch had reported a group of trustees sniffing around Fazenda Santos. In its current condition the ranch was worth a fortune, but if men who didn't know what they were doing took it over it was doomed to fail. He wouldn't risk it—couldn't risk it.

Danny was his best hope if he was to comply with the terms of his grandfather's will, and she had mentioned her frustration at still being here at Rottingdean, where she had worked all her life. Surely she would accept his offer of a scholarship to train in Brazil? But what about the other part of his deal?

'Good morning, Tiago.'

He swung round with relief. 'So, there you are,' he said as she walked into the room

She seemed surprised. 'Were you waiting for me?'

'Yes, I was.'

'Well, here I am,' she said brightly.

A freshly showered Danny, with tendrils of honey-soft hair still damp around her temples, was an arousing sight that forced him to remember that what he needed was a short-term wife. His freedom meant too much to him to consider anything else.

'You seem recovered.'

'I am,' she said, frowning. 'Why wouldn't I be?'

'Good.' That suited him perfectly. 'I trust you slept well?'

Wrong question. His groin tightened immediately at the thought of Danny naked, stretched out in bed. It was important to keep this confined to business. He didn't have much time. But it wasn't easy when she leaned over him to scan the delicious-looking breakfast the house-keeper had laid out.

'I just came to say goodbye to you,' she said, grabbing a piece of toast. 'Annie said you had to get back today. I thought you might have left for Brazil last night.'

She was fishing. He took that as a good sign. 'Sit down?' he suggested. 'Eat breakfast with me. Why are you in such a hurry to get away?'

'Because I'm going riding in a minute. I don't have time to sit down and eat.'

'You'll need something to keep the cold out.'

Her glance flashed over his warm sweater. 'Don't worry about me. I'm wearing Arctic layers,' she explained.

She wasn't joking. She wore a thick-knit sweater with a fancy pattern, heavy winter breeches, and soft tan leather riding boots, which clung tenaciously to her shapely legs, hiding almost all the outline he had delighted in when he had danced with her last night. The thought of unpeeling her 'Arctic layers', as she'd called them, occupied all his thoughts for a moment.

'Why don't we ride out together?'

She stilled, with the toast hovering close to her parted lips. 'Do you have time?'

'I'll make time.'

'In that case…'

He caught her frowning as she headed for the door, as if she suspected there was more to this than a morning ride, but he didn't care what she thought now he had what he wanted.

His spirits lifted. He felt like a hunter with his prey in sight. And why feel guilty when he was about to make Danny an offer she'd be crazy to refuse? There was just one problem. Trying to appeal to Danny Cameron's calculating business brain might be difficult if she didn't have one.

She was quite likely to dismiss his plan out of hand. She would almost certainly consider a marriage of convenience to be selling out, as well as a serious betrayal of the marriage vows—and she'd have no hesitation in telling him. Unfortunately he didn't have the luxury of time to indulge in finer feelings. The thought of trying to do this deal with one of the women he customarily dated frankly appalled him. Even a night in their company could be too long. And where would he find another potential wife at such short notice?

'Riding out will give us chance to chat about your future plans,' he said casually as he held the door for her.

'Advice always welcome,' she said blandly, smiling up. 'But ride first, chat later,' she insisted.

Nothing about this was going to be straightforward, he deduced.

She hadn't planned on riding with Tiago. When Annie had told her he was eating breakfast she had considered going straight out, and then decided that would look cowardly. In keeping with her decision to toughen up, she had decided to face the hard man of the pampas to show him she was over yesterday, and not susceptible in any way to his undeniable charm.

'You're riding Lizzie's horse this morning?' he commented when they reached the stable yard.

'That's right,' she confirmed as they crossed the yard.

The horses were in adjoining stalls. She couldn't pretend that riding out with Tiago Santos wasn't a thrill. And it would look amazing on her CV, she conceded wryly. As if she needed an excuse to ride out with him!

They tacked up together. She tried not to notice how deftly Tiago's lean fingers worked, or how soothing and gentle he was with his horse.

'Are you ready?' he said, turning around.

Her heart-rate soared, and all she could think about was being held in those arms, how it had felt to be pressed up close against his body.

'Ready,' she confirmed, lifting her chin.

She had barely led Lizzie's horse out of the stable when her phone rang. She looked down at the screen and shook her head. 'Sorry, but I've got to take this.'

'Go right ahead.'

She walked quickly away from Tiago, concerned that her mother's torrent of words would alert him to her problem. It was always the same problem. Her mother was short of money again. It was the only time she ever called.

Taking a deep breath, she launched in. 'Did you get my messages? I was worried about you. It seems so long since I've heard from you. Are you sure you're okay? You're *not* okay?' Danny frowned with concern. 'Why? What's happened?'

She dreaded what her mother would say. It was never

good news. The type of men Danny's mother liked to go out with generally needed a loan. She held the phone tight to her ear as her mother repeated the familiar plea.

'It's just to tide him over, Danny. I told him you'd understand...'

Told whom? Oh, never mind. She wouldn't know the man, anyway.

'I knew I could rely on you. Thank you...thank you,' her mother was exclaiming.

'But I don't have that kind of money,' Danny said, horrified when her mother mentioned a figure.

Her mother ignored this comment entirely. 'Just do what you can,' she said. 'You're so generous, Danny. I knew we could rely on you.'

I'm such a mug, don't you mean? Danny thought.

'It's only a short-term loan. He's got money coming in soon.'

How often had she heard that? Danny wondered. 'I'll send you what I can,' she promised.

'I hear there's going to be a lot of money sloshing around Rottingdean now Chico Fernandez has taken control?'

She recognised her mother's wheedling voice and immediately sprang to her friend's defence. 'Chico hasn't taken control,' she argued, feeling affronted on Lizzie's behalf. 'Lizzie and Chico work in partnership, and their money has got nothing whatsoever to do with me. I'll send you what money I can when I've earned it.'

'Make sure you get your hands on some of their money,' her mother insisted, as if she hadn't spoken, and as if Danny were entitled to a share. 'You've got it good now, Danny. It's only fair to share your good fortune with others—with me—when things can only get better for you.'

Her mother's voice had grown petulant and childlike. An all too familiar feeling swept over Danny as she was tugged this way and that by a sense of duty to her mother and a longing to get on with her own life.

'Just one more thing before I go,' her mother said. 'I heard in the village that the repair work at Rottingdean is going to mean evacuating the house soon?'

'That's right,' Danny confirmed. 'It's great news that the old house is going to be given new life, isn't it?'

'I suppose so,' her mother agreed. 'But—and it's really hard for me to say this, Danny—I'm afraid you can't come back here to the cottage while the renovation work is being carried out.'

'Oh?'

'My new fella wouldn't like it, you see. You *do* understand, don't you?'

'Of course,' she said faintly, taking this in.

'I really think he's the one, Danny.'

Another one who was 'the one', Danny mused wearily. 'Just take care of yourself, Mum,' she said softly. She would pick up the pieces of her mother's life when it all fell apart again, somehow. And as for her own—

'You won't forget to send that money, will you?' her mother pressed.

'I promise,' Danny said.

'You're such a good girl.'

Danny shook her head at the irony of her penniless self, bailing out some unknown man, and then the sound of horses' hooves clattering across the cobblestones distracted her. 'Mum—I've got to go. I promised to exercise Lizzie's horse.'

'Just don't forget to send that money, will you, Danny?'

'I won't,' she said again as Tiago rode round the corner, leading her horse.

She cut the line and focused on him. He took her breath away. He looked so good on a horse. He was so at home, so at ease in the saddle, that just watching him was a treat. But she felt anything but at ease, and was already beginning to doubt her sanity at agreeing to ride out with him.

'Important call?' he asked.

'My mother.'

'Nothing more important than that.'

She murmured in agreement, thinking that Tiago looked like a visitor from another, more vigorous planet, with his deep tan, thick black stubble and his wild jet-black hair secured by a bandana for riding. And that gold earring was glittering in the grudging light of the early-morning sun. More marauding pirate, than wealthy and respectable rampaging barbarian...

'Something has amused you?' he asked as he handed over the reins of her horse.

'Just happy at the thought of riding out.' She concentrated on mounting up and curbed her smile.

Just riding out with Tiago would be an adventure—but he didn't need to know that. He made her feel things she had never felt before. Maybe she was a little bit in love with him? *Ha!* Much good *that* would do her.

He gave her an assessing look, but made no further comment as he led the way out of the courtyard.

He was feeling confident as they rode out together. He always felt confident, but Chico had filled him in on Danny's family background, which had led Tiago to believe that if Danny thought she could keep her mother secure *and* have a real chance of starting her own training centre one day her answer to his proposition would be yes.

Urging his horse forward, he headed for the open countryside.

He raised the issue a short time later, when they'd reined in. 'Would you be prepared to leave the country for a good job? Would you be able to leave your mother, for instance?'

'Oh, yes,' she said at once. 'I think she'd be relieved if I left her alone for a while.'

And just sent her money, he thought, remembering what Chico had told him about Danny's mother's constant demands for cash.

'And you? What would you like to do—ideally?'

'Me? I'm still considering my options.'

He ground his jaw as Danny turned her horse, shifted her weight, and took off again. What options was she talking about? Had someone else offered her a job?

He would not pursue her like some desperate adolescent.

Reining in again, he watched her ride. She rode like a gaucho with one hand on the reins, leaning back in the saddle, working her hips, looking as relaxed as if she were sitting in an armchair. She'd learned that in Brazil. She was fearless, he thought as she sped across the brow of a hill. He liked that. He liked Danny. A lot.

He couldn't believe how fate was smiling on him. If he played this right he could have a very enjoyable year with Danny Cameron. Once that year was over she would be free to do as she liked, with all the money she could possibly need, and in the meantime he would enjoy her in his bed.

The only fly in this almost perfect ointment was Danny Cameron herself. He couldn't imagine Danny following meekly where he led. Getting her to agree to a contract of marriage might be tricky, and would certainly require the utmost diplomacy on his part. She might not agree to marry him for cash, but she *would* agree to marry him. He would find a way.

Collecting his reins, he rode after her. The prospect of catching her heated his blood. He needed a result fast. He needed a wife fast. And here she was, perfect in every way: great with horses, and useful on a ranch. What more could he ask of a woman?

CHAPTER FOUR

'YOU'RE QUITE A RIDER,' Tiago commented as they jogged to a halt.

'You mean you couldn't catch me?' she fired back dryly.

'I caught you.'

Her body thrilled at Tiago's warrior glance. She was on a high. If there was anything better than riding out with Tiago Santos she was eager to try it. The fact that she'd given him a run for his money was an added bonus— though she could do without her body purring with approval every time he looked at her. She had to keep her head cool and her thoughts confined solely to horses.

'Have you ever thought of going back to Brazil, Danny?'

Well, that good intention had lasted all of one second. Why did he have to remind her about Brazil, when seeing him had been the highlight of each day? Her thoughts had instantly slipped to the dark side and that fantasy world she inhabited, where she spent nights with Tiago too.

'Maybe,' she admitted. 'It's hard to forget my time in Brazil. All those top-class horses and state-of-the-art training facilities—I can't say I'd turn down an opportunity to go back. Why? Are you offering me a job?'

Tiago remained silent, his considering stare on her face. Maybe she'd overdone it. She was supposed to be exercising Lizzie's horse, not touting for work.

'Shall we get back?' she suggested, wondering if he'd had enough of her company.

'I'm in no hurry.'

And then she understood. He was staring out at the silver river rushing to the sea, beyond which lay a dense and mysterious forest that seemed to beckon them into its hidden interior. There were standing stones that held secrets from ancient times to one side of them, while purple heather spread out like a carpet, leading them home. It was so magical. Who in their right mind would leave?

For a while they sat on their horses in companionable silence. She had loved this vantage spot since she was a little girl. She was at her most relaxed here—until she became aware of Tiago staring at her. What was he thinking? she wondered.

Closing her eyes, she turned her face to the sky and inhaled deeply. Just here, just now, in this one perfect moment, she felt strong and sure—as if things were changing for the better and anything was possible.

'Are you ready to go back now?' Tiago asked.

She was ready for anything. But then she remembered he was heading home to Brazil. That was life. Up one moment; down the next.

'Last one back to the house makes the coffee?' she suggested.

The last sound she heard as she galloped away from him was Tiago's laughter, carried on the wind.

'You're shivering.' he commented when they dismounted in the yard.

'You must be made of iron,' she countered. 'Aren't you

aware that it's a million degrees below freezing today?' She blew on her hands to make her point.

'Here—let me warm you.'

Before she had a chance to object Tiago had opened his arms and drawn her inside his jacket. She tensed, and then reminded herself that Latin men were demonstrative, that she shouldn't make anything of it. All he was doing was preventing a mild case of hypothermia setting in.

'Mmm…much better.' Her cheeks were burning as she pulled away—which she had to do before she grew used to the addictive feeling of hard, hot man.

'Go inside and warm up in front of the fire,' Tiago suggested. 'I'll take care of the horses.'

'I'm not leaving it all to you,' she protested. 'We'll do it together. It will take half the time, and then we can both take a shower,' she insisted when Tiago seemed about to refuse. 'You're wet through too,' she reasoned.

Sleeting rain had started to fall at the end of their ride, in an unrelenting curtain. It showed no sign of easing any time soon.

When the horses were settled they ran for the house. She screamed as a clap of thunder coincided with Tiago grabbing hold of her hand to help her run faster, and was laughing and panting by the time they reached the door. Just for a moment, as they faced each other and Tiago stilled, she wondered if he was going to kiss her.

'Come on—let's go inside.'

She spun round before he had a chance. It was a most unlikely event that he was going to kiss her. She didn't want to be disappointed. There was nothing worse than turning your face up for a kiss and receiving nothing.

'Take a shower and warm up,' he told her. 'Then come back downstairs and we'll talk.'

About what? she wondered. A job? Her heart thundered as she waited for Tiago to reply, but he said nothing.

Brazil.

The thought of returning to Brazil was enough to make her heart race with excitement. The thought of returning to Brazil with Tiago was off the scale. The pampas, the horses, the starry nights, the vibrant music, the warm and friendly people—what she'd give for a chance to go back…

Brazil with Tiago?

Okay. Don't even go there. The thought was so exhilarating she wondered if she'd ever think straight again. But she was never going to make a fool of herself over a man again.

When she came downstairs she found Tiago in the library, where he was standing by the window, staring out into the darkness, seeing nothing as it was so black out there. So he was thinking. But about what? She closed the door quietly behind her, but the click made him turn around. Even now, when she was used to the sight of him again, seeing Tiago Santos here—so tall, so dark, so powerful—she felt her senses flood with heat.

'So, what's this chat you want to have with me?' she said briskly, not wanting to appear too eager. And she had to set her expectations at a reasonable level. Not every interview ended with the offer of a job.

'Sit down, Danny. You're right. I *do* have a business proposition for you.'

She frowned. A business proposition? That sounded a bit formal. What could he mean? She had no money. He must know that. She had no land. He must know that too. She didn't own any breeding stock. She rode whichever horse needed exercise. What could she possibly offer Tiago Santos that he didn't have already in abundance?

Something didn't feel right.

Tiago sat on the sofa facing hers and came right to it. 'I've got a problem—you have too. You need a job,' he said, before she could comment. 'And you need a job that pays a lot more than your work here if you're to have any chance at all of saving to start up your own place.'

'Of course I do—but I'm realistic.' Her laugh was short and sounded false. She didn't like being reminded that her career ambition was probably a hopeless fantasy.

'The type of training stable you envisage running is going to cost a lot of money.'

'I would have to begin small,' she said.

'*Very* small,' Tiago agreed dryly. 'But what would you say if I told you that you don't have to wait, that you don't have to start small? What if I told you that you could do pretty much anything you want?'

'I'd think you were mad—or lying.' She laughed it off, but then something occurred to her. 'You're not saying you'd back me, are you?'

When Tiago had mentioned a business proposition she had never imagined he was considering investing in her skills.

'Yes, that's exactly what I'm suggesting,' he admitted. 'I'd help you to draw up a business plan and I would fund your business.'

She was briefly elated—but then common sense kicked in. 'And what would I have to do for this—beyond training horses and hopefully making a profit eventually?'

She knew full well that establishing a reputation in equine circles would take years. There would be no quick or easy profits for the type of venture Tiago was suggesting.

'You would have to put your faith in me.'

Sitting back, he crossed one booted foot over the other

and with half-closed eyes regarded her lazily, with just the hint of a smile on his mouth.

'What do you mean?' For some reason, instead of feeling excited by Tiago's suggestion, she suddenly felt chilled.

'I'd offer you a contract—a fair contract—that would give us both an out in one year's time.'

'So I could be left high and dry without a job if you felt like it?'

'That would never happen.'

'How can I be sure? What *is* this job?'

Tiago hesitated, and then said, 'As the wife of Tiago Santos you would never be left "high and dry", as you put it.'

'Your *wife*?' She couldn't have been more shocked, and her lips felt like pieces of wood as she spoke the words. 'What on earth are you talking about, Tiago?'

'I need a wife,' he said bluntly, with a careless gesture. 'And I need a wife fast. I'm telling you this because I won't pretend otherwise. I'm going to be absolutely honest with you, so that you know exactly where you stand. The terms of my grandfather's will have left me with no option. I must marry—and soon. Before the trustees find some excuse to take over the ranch. They know nothing of its history—nothing of its people—'

Tiago's passion scorched her. He didn't just care about this ranch and its people—they were his life. That was the only reason she stayed to listen and didn't get up and stamp out of the room. But she was still running his words over in her head. *His wife? Tiago's wife?* She couldn't take it in.

'I'll give you a moment,' he said. 'I can see this has come as a shock to you.'

Tiago was half out of his seat, but she gestured for him to sit down again. 'Please...'

'Don't look so apprehensive, Danny, so alarmed. I mean what I say. You would have everything you've ever wanted—ever dreamed about—right now, rather than waiting, and you'll be secure for the rest of your life.'

Secure? She would be rich enough to own and run her own training establishment—that was a dream come true, just for a start, to someone who had grown up penniless, believing her dreams to be as distant and unachievable as any fairytale. Tiago was offering her the golden chalice.

Yes, but he was keeping it just out of her reach. He could grant her everything—including security for her increasingly unpredictable mother—but at what cost? she wondered.

'I'd be selling out,' she said flatly.

'I'm sorry you see it that way.' Tiago's tone hardened. 'I think if you take a more critical look around you'll see that every marriage is a bargain of some sort.'

'What about love?' She couldn't help herself. She'd always been a romantic. 'Where does love fit into this?' She was as impassioned on the subject as Tiago had been when he'd talked about his ranch. 'I refuse to believe there aren't *some* marriages, at least, based solely on love without thought of gain by either party.'

She could tell he thought her naïve, but she *did* care about love. To love and to be loved was the most important thing in the world as far as Danny was concerned.

'I think we've made a good start,' Tiago continued calmly, as if there'd been no outburst from her.

'And a couple of days in my company is enough time for you to decide you want to *marry* me?'

'We've known each other a lot longer than that, Danny,' he reminded her.

'Yes, but as sparring partners in Brazil—nothing more.'

It had always been a lot more on her part, but she wasn't going to confess that now. She had wanted Tiago from the first moment she saw him, but he had been an international polo player, while she'd been a lowly student living on a grant for young people with troubled home lives. They hardly had anything in common, she'd thought at the time, though that hadn't stopped her standing up to him when he had sought her out. He had loved teasing her, she knew that, and she had loved answering back. It had excited her to confront a man like Tiago Santos and give back as good as she got.

'We've always got on, Danny. If we give this a chance I can see no reason why it can't work.'

'Is that any basis upon which to found a marriage?'

'Better than some,' he said.

Brushing the attraction she felt for him to one side, she challenged him again. 'And is that what you really want, Tiago?'

'I want the ranch.'

Well, that was clear enough.

'I'm proposing you remain married to me for one year, to make it seem genuine. I'm being completely honest with you, Danny. I *have* to get married if I'm to stop those idiots ruining all the good work that's been done on the ranch. Our marriage must be seen as genuine—hence the term I'm putting on it. And, no, I don't want to be tied down. Is that frank enough for you?'

'It *is* honest,' she admitted. 'You want to give me money to induce me to marry you, but you want to carry on your bachelor ways. Is that a fair summary?'

'It sounds rather calculating when you put it that way.'

'How else would you put it? It i*s* calculating. And my answer is no.'

'No?' Tiago's eyes narrowed in disbelief.

'You're suggesting a cold-blooded contract, and yet I have no say in it because you've thought it all through for me. That's right, isn't it, Tiago? You've anticipated what you think it is I want out of the agreement, but you've judged those demands through your own eyes. It must have been very convenient for you, finding me here at the wedding—a brood mare waiting for her stallion. How long have you been sizing me up? Since you found me outside in the mud? Did I look like a victim to you? Did you think I'd be grateful for the crumbs from your table?'

'I never thought that. I would never take advantage of you in that way. I remembered you from Brazil. You were always strong, always determined—'

'And I'm just as determined now to say no.'

Tiago's jaw worked as he mulled over her flat refusal.

'Can I say anything to change your mind?'

She hesitated. Her feelings for Tiago cut too deep for her not to want to help him. She understood that he cared for the ranch, and she couldn't deny that the chance to get to know him better was appealing. But did she have to marry him?

There was something else nagging at the back of her mind—and it was something that was weighted in his favour. The business opportunity Tiago was offering would allow her to *work*—and that was so far removed from anything her mother might do that it did hold appeal. She tried to measure everything she did in life by asking herself: would her mother do it? And if the answer was yes, Danny would do the opposite.

This was her one chance to fulfil her dream, Danny

reasoned. If she could do that, surely she could guard her heart for a year by burying herself in work?

'Well?' Tiago pressed impatiently.

'*If* we go ahead with this—and I'm only saying if—I have certain conditions,' she explained.

His expression turned grim. He wasn't used to bargaining when he had decided what he wanted to do, she gathered, but he could see that she wasn't going to change her mind.

'Name them,' he grated out.

'For one year I'm the only woman in your life. I mean it, Tiago,' she said quickly, when he started to speak. 'I won't take any more humiliation. I've seen my mother make a fool of herself and I don't need anyone to tell me that I was fast following in her footsteps. I won't go down that road again—not for you, not for anyone. If you want this deal you will have to put my terms in that contract too.'

Tension soared as she waited for his reply. She guessed Tiago hadn't expected her to put any obstacles in his way, but she wasn't prepared to back down.

'All right,' he said eventually. 'But if you're putting conditions on this then so am I. This will be a proper marriage, and you will be in my bed.'

Her throat constricted. She couldn't have answered him if she'd wanted to. The expression in Tiago's eyes had turned cold and hard. This was the deal-breaker, delivered by a man determined to have his way. Tiago was like a coin with two sides, she decided. There was the strong and compassionate man on one side of the coin, and the ruthless playboy on the other. Surrendering her body to a man like that was a heart-stopping thought.

But her body betrayed her now by melting. Her mind burned with confusion. It was like drowning in a sweet honey bath of desire, even while everything about Tiago in this frame of mind was a warning to her not to fall for him unless she wanted to be hurt. But how was she going to remain detached from her feelings when she was lying in his arms?

She would have to, Danny determined, but there were one or two more points she wanted to clear up first. 'If this is to be a marriage in every sense, as you suggest it will be, then we have to consider the potential consequences.'

'For instance?' he pressed without warmth.

'How will we explain this love-match of ours to any children we might have? And I use the term "love-match" in its most cynical form.'

Tiago shrugged. 'I must admit I have never thought of this as a permanent arrangement.'

'Clearly,' she said, shrinking a little inside. Was this the one thing in his life that Tiago Santos hadn't thought through? she wondered.

'Finding a wife is uppermost in my mind,' he said, as if he could read hers. 'Perhaps I am guilty of not considering every possibility. I can only tell you that when I found you yesterday outside the stable block I wasn't thinking about this at all. My one thought was your safety. I hope that reassures you? As for this contract— I can't have been planning it for long, *chica*, since I've only been here for a couple of days!'

Calling her *chica* threw her. It was so intimate—too intimate. Endearments from Tiago were unsettling, as was his cold-blooded approach to marriage. When she kept him at a distance she could handle her feelings for him. Jibing at him verbally in Brazil had been fun, but this was a very different situation.

She wasn't about to roll over and become his convenient wife, Danny concluded. Tiago would have to consider her terms and conditions. They were a deal-breaker for her.

'You've only been here for a couple of days,' she agreed, 'but that's long enough for you to negotiate a business contract, I imagine?'

'True,' Tiago agreed. 'But this is particularly important to me.'

'And to me,' she said. 'It's quite a commitment you're asking me to make.' She felt a cold hand clutch her heart as she said this.

Tiago was quick to reassure her, 'The agreement between us will be drawn up by my lawyers to include your demands. It will be absolutely watertight. I assure you of that.'

'I have no doubt.'

'You'll be protected, Danny. You'll be safe. You'll be secure for the rest of your life.'

'You make it sound like a prison sentence.'

'It will be what we make it,' Tiago told her with calm assurance. 'You can have your own lawyers look over the contract. I'll pay for them.'

'But you don't *know* me.' She shook her head, still racked with doubt. 'We don't know each other.'

'How long does it take to know someone? I saw you nearly every day for a year on Chico's ranch. It will be the same. You struck sparks off me with your banter then—'

'Do you mean I stood up for myself?' she asked wryly.

He relaxed, and his mouth curved in the familiar winning smile. 'That's why I like you, Danny. I'm not looking for a push-over. I'm not interested in taking advantage of you. I want this to be fair. And when we're married—'

'I haven't said yes to your outlandish proposal yet,' she pointed out.

'But you will,' he said confidently. 'I will expect you

to stand up to me. I expect you to tell me when something doesn't make you happy. I expect to enjoy a healthy, outspoken relationship.'

'You can depend on that,' she assured him. 'But a year sharing a bed with a man without love...?'

'I'm sorry you see it that way. I wish I had more time to persuade you that this will work really well for both of us, but I don't have that luxury. I can only promise you that you'll have everything you need and that I will always respect you and treat you well.' He shrugged. 'I can't think of anyone I would rather enter into this agreement with—anyone I can imagine seeing on a daily basis and getting on with half as well as I get on with you.'

'So long as we do get on well,' she said dryly.

'Danny—'

'I know. You have a flight plan filed, no doubt, and you don't have time to waste selling love's young dream to me.'

'Don't be such a cynic. It doesn't suit you. Your choice is simple. Stay here and nothing changes, or come with me on the biggest adventure of your life. Which is it to be, Danny?'

CHAPTER FIVE

DANNY TOOK A firmer grip of her suitcase when Tiago threatened to swoop on it. Half an hour ago, over breakfast, he'd shown her the contract his lawyers had drawn up on the screen of his phone. When she had expressed surprise that he had been able to rouse his team at such short notice just before the holidays, he'd set the tone by telling her that holidays were for wimps and that he didn't take them.

Money bought everything, she thought. And now here they were, in the hall, about to leave the house on their way to Brazil. She'd called her mother, but there had been no reply. She hadn't wanted to disturb Lizzie, so she had sent her an email. And her wedding to Tiago...? That lay some time in the future and still didn't feel real.

Just as Tiago had promised, the terms of the contract were solid enough. She'd been given everything she'd asked for, and to build her confidence before she took this final step Tiago had pressed an open first-class airline ticket home into her hands, and told her she could bail out at any time. Yet even now she felt she'd sold out.

Or, as Tiago had so romantically put it, 'Congratulations, *chica*! You've got the guts to seize the opportunity of a lifetime *and* share my bed.'

Yes, she knew he'd been teasing her, in that old, tormenting way, but this time she hadn't fired back. The reality of intimacy with Tiago was only just dawning on her. Yes, of course she knew that intimacy was part of *any* married couple's life, and Tiago had said that their marriage would be as close to normal as it could be for a year, but she was certain that sharing his bed would be very different from her fantasies.

'I said I'd carry it,' she insisted now, attempting to wrestle back her case.

'Too late,' Tiago told her.

Five minutes into the trip and they were already at odds. What did that say about her decision to do this? Tiago was holding the car door open, waiting for her impatiently. There was no going back now. She was leaving everything familiar behind.

Yes, but to embark on an adventure. If she wasn't up to it she had better decide now.

She hurried down the steps to join him.

The car dropped them off at the side of a sleek executive jet, which Tiago and his team would pilot to Brazil, he'd explained. And just in case she was still uncertain as to her status, 'Santos Inc' was written in bold blood-red down the side of the fuselage. She really was entering another world—and it was a faster moving world than she was used to.

'There's no time to hang around,' Tiago insisted, seizing her arm. 'My take-off slot is non-negotiable.'

He wasn't joking. He indicated left rather than right once they were inside the cabin.

'Into the cockpit?' she queried.

'I thought you might like to sit with me when we take off. If you prefer you can sit in the back?'

'No. This is good.' Normally she was a nervous passenger, but since everything else had changed why not this too? 'Thank you…'

Thankfully, she sounded so cool, so certain—but her emotions were in a riot. 'I've always wanted to sit next to the pilot.'

'You won't be sitting next to me. That's the co-pilot's job. But you will still see everything.'

Probably a lot more than she wanted to, Danny thought ruefully, hoping some of Tiago's confidence would wash off on her.

'If you're having second thoughts…it's too late.' He slanted her that dangerous smile that flooded his eyes with amusement and reached all parts of her too. 'There's a bedroom in the back,' he added, 'if you need it.'

'Hopefully not. And I'm not having second thoughts,' she assured him.

'Not yet,' he said dryly. 'It's a long flight, Danny, so go to bed if you have to.'

'What about you?'

'Don't worry about me,' he murmured, with one last look.

They took off smoothly, with Tiago handling the jet with the same easy skill he employed on his horses. When they reached cruising height and levelled off he handed over control of the plane to his co-pilot and came to ask Danny how she'd liked the new experience.

Having turned at just the wrong moment, he caught her chewing her lip as she tried to work out if this was the best decision of her life, or the biggest screw-up ever. It didn't help when she looked at the man who would shortly be her husband. Her body thrilled at the thought, though she still had major concerns.

Flying a jet was all in a day's work for Tiago—as was running a multi-national business and playing polo at international level—while *she* had a neat line in handing out pony nuts, and not a clue when it came to negotiating contracts, let alone those with a marriage clause involved.

She would just have to be a fast learner, Danny concluded as Tiago smiled down at her.

A couple of hours later she was glad to take him up on his offer to use the bedroom in the back of the plane, and was surprisingly snug between crisp white sheets in a very comfortable bed when the door opened.

'Coffee?'

She shot up, and only belatedly remembered to yank the covers to her chin. Having stripped off her clothes, she was naked, while Tiago had rolled back the sleeves of his crisp white shirt, leaving his powerful forearms bare. Her body clenched with pleasure at the sight. There should be a law against being so attractive.

'Sit up,' he urged, putting the coffee down on the nightstand at her side. 'Drink your coffee before it gets cold. Do you have everything you need?'

She wasn't sure she could answer him honestly, and confined herself to a prim 'Thank you for the coffee.'

His lips slanted in a smile. 'Aren't you going to invite me to sit down?'

'No.' When he looked at her like that? Absolutely not.

He sat down anyway. She held her breath as he made himself comfortable. Kicking off his boots, he arranged the pillows to his liking and lay down.

'Are you quite comfortable there?' she enquired sarcastically.

Tiago turned his head to shoot her an amused glance. 'Very. Why?'

Sitting up in bed, she drew her knees up to her chin.

Sipping the steaming coffee, she allowed her hair to cover her face like a curtain, to hide her burning cheeks.

'Am I keeping you?' he growled.

She have him a look. 'From drinking my coffee?'

'I don't know, *chica.* You seem tense to me. Are you naked under those sheets?'

Tiago reached out to hook some hair behind her ear and she exhaled with shock. But then, just as she relaxed, he touched her naked thigh.

'You *are* naked…' His mouth tugged in a lazy smile. 'Silky smooth skin and silky hair.' He wound a strand of her hair around his finger, and then, taking the coffee mug from her hands, placed it safely on the nightstand out of reach.

'Relax,' he murmured, his mouth curving in a smile. 'This is a long flight. Why not enjoy it?'

Because…

Her throat closed down before she could say anything. Tiago's touch was so exciting. He aroused her. He made her want more. Much more.

He took his time to soothe and stir her, and before long she had eased down in the bed as he continued to stroke and kiss her…her arms, her neck, the top of her chest above the swell of her breasts. It all seemed so safe and innocent. He had that down to a tee.

When she opened her eyes it was to find Tiago turned on his side, watching her. To have him monitor her responses aroused her even more, and a shaking breath shivered out of her as his big hand cupped her breast. His palm was so warm and firm, and a little roughened from his work with horses. He had intuitive hands, intuitive fingers, and when he shifted position to move over her, and his dangerous, swarthy dark face blocked out the light—blocked out everything but Tiago—she was more conscious than ever of his size and his strength. And also his willpower, and his control, and that aroused her too.

She held her breath with excitement when he stopped, wondering what would come next.

Making her comfortable on the pillows, he drew the covers back and stared down at her body, and for once in her life she didn't rush to cover herself. She *wanted* Tiago to look at her. She didn't want any secrets between them. She wanted him to see her body respond to him. Exposed like this.

His touch when he stroked her breasts was on another level. She tried to stay still but found it impossible, and with a whimper of need she reached out for him.

Tiago smiled. His dark eyes burned with hunger but he had more control than she had, and even as she writhed beneath him, trying to urge him on, he only dipped his head to brush her lips with his. That was almost enough, that kiss, but he denied her the weight of his body. His kisses fired her, his fingers teased her, and she was agonisingly responsive to his touch, but nothing she could do would make him do more.

He curved a smile. 'I'm the luckiest man on earth.'

She was aching—really aching. She needed his firm touch *now*.

She gasped with relief as he returned to the assault on her senses, using firm strokes across her belly and down her thighs. And all the time he held her gaze in his.

She cried out when his hand finally found its destination. Easing her legs apart, he teased around her clitoris with a touch that was indescribable, while she lifted her hips in a hunt for more contact, crying out in desperation, not caring what he thought. She needed this—needed him. She needed this *now*.

At first she thought he was only going to tease her

and leave her aching, but as if he could sense the level of her need he relented. Using one gloriously roughened finger-pad, he applied just the right amount of pressure, just the right amount of friction, at just the right speed.

Exclaiming at the intensity of sensation, she lost control. Tiago held her firmly in place, using his hand to increase her pleasure and make it last. Even when the pleasure waves began to fade she was incapable of speech, and could only grab a breath as he murmured with amusement, 'I think you needed that.'

He had no idea. Sex as sport might be second nature to him, but she was a novice and would have to put these feelings in her heart to one side.

She laced her fingers through Tiago's hair. His hair was so thick and strong. She loved the feel of it beneath her hands, just as she loved the rasp of his stubble against her neck.

Pressing kisses against her breasts, he eased her down in the bed and at last gave her what she longed for: the weight of his body pressing into hers.

She lost control again. That was all it took. She had imagined this moment for so long that now it was here she could only ride the sensation, while Tiago held her firmly in his arms, dropping kisses on her mouth.

'Good?' he murmured, knowing very well that it was.

'Stop,' she whispered, 'or I won't be held responsible for my actions.'

'Don't be,' he said, finding this amusing. 'Let *me* be responsible for your actions.'

She responded instantly as he teased her into a state of readiness and fell happily into wild release. Tiago's kisses thrilled her. *He* thrilled her. She hadn't realised how fierce she would be when it came to her need for this man. They were a fierce couple. Their hungry kisses spoke of mutual need. Tiago's tongue claimed her. *He* claimed her. He challenged her in a way she welcomed. He made her fight him. He made her test him. He made her feel alive.

When he surprised her by standing up she actually groaned, her disappointment was so extreme, but he didn't lose eye contact with her for a moment, and smiled as he reached for the buckle on his belt.

Folding her arms beneath her head, she rested back, watching him, enjoying the sight of his deft, pleasure-dealing fingers working to free him of the clothes that stood between them. His torso was hard and tanned, muscular, and magnificent, and her body was ready for him. She had never needed Tiago more.

CHAPTER SIX

PLUCKING THE PAGER on his belt off the bed, Tiago scanned it impatiently. 'I'm needed on the flight deck.'

'You have to go *now*?'

He laughed. 'Yes, *chica*—I have to go now. Patience. Put this on the back burner. Save it for our wedding night.'

Once he was dressed he left her, the door closing quietly behind him. She felt like wailing—and not just with frustration. She was angry she had let things go this far. Tiago was so hard to resist, but she needed something more than a quick coupling in the back of his jet. She might not be heading for a proper marriage, as other people understood the term, but retaining some vestige of pride was important to her.

She had lost all semblance of self-respect after her affair with Carlos Pintos, and she knew what a long walk it was back. This time she wanted to come out of it with her head held up high.

Collapsing on the pillows, she groaned. It would be hard coming back from this. Not only would Tiago expect more from her in the physical sense, but the way she felt inside her heart gave 'aching with need' a whole new meaning. Her body ached too, but even that couldn't compare with the inner pain.

Tiago had awoken dreams and thoughts and feelings inside her—more than she'd known she had.

Tossing and turning, she curled up into a ball and tried to sleep. It was useless. Nothing worked. And it wasn't just thinking about what might have happened with Tiago that was keeping her awake. There was so much she didn't know about him, so much she wanted to know. Maybe in Brazil they'd get the chance to talk—hopefully before their wedding night. She didn't even have a clue when that would be. She really had jumped in with both feet this time.

If Danny had thought Chico's ranch in Brazil was fantastic she was in for a surprise when they arrived at Fazenda Santos, where *everything* was impressive—from the immaculately maintained fencing, stretching as far as the eye could see over rolling green pampas, to the state-of-the-art buildings that comprised the stud. Tiago's ranch was situated in one of the wildest regions on earth, allowing her to gain a far better understanding of the scale of his work.

Tiago seemed not to need anything as mundane as sleep, and after a shower said he would be checking round the ranch. Or at least that part of it closest to the house, he explained, as surveying all of it would take a month or more.

'When I return I will have a hard copy of our contract with me,' he promised, leaving her in the capable hands of his friendly housekeeper, Elena.

She was alone now in her bedroom, with time to reflect on the rapidly unfolding events of the past few days. She made a start on investigating the suite of rooms, knowing she should unpack and bathe, take the chance to go to bed for a few hours, but she just couldn't. She was too tightly wound.

Seeing Tiago's home for the first time was like opening a box of surprises, and she'd soaked up every detail greedily. She wasn't sure what she had expected. Not some grungy living quarters on a ranch devoted to raising ponies, because Tiago's playboy side would never allow it. But not glitz and glamour either, as that wouldn't be appropriate for a working ranch, and for all his society polish Tiago was a surprisingly down-to-earth man.

The reality was a happy mix between comfort and luxury. The ranch house was a large, rambling building, and when they'd first driven up to it Danny wondered if he lived in just a small part of it—perhaps a bachelor pad, stark and functional, with just the high-end accessories of life to keep him company. She had pictured high-tech gadgets jostling with spurs and boots, fast cars parked outside, maybe a Harley. She wouldn't have been surprised to see saddle soap and tins of hoof oil on the kitchen table, or bridles slung over the banister in the hall.

She couldn't have been further off-beam. Tiago's home was a stunning example of an old-style ranch house, though it certainly boasted every conceivable modern facility. In spite of its size he had managed to make his home cosy. Mellow wood predominated, along with all the colours of the earth—russet, ochre, claret and dusky blue—which, with the wooden floors and ethnic wall hangings, gave the old house a prosperous look and an ambience she found as alluring as Tiago.

She should have known he would live comfortably, Danny reflected as she walked to the window to stare out down the long, impressive drive. The gates had been the first giveaway that she was entering somewhere really special. They were impressive, carved out of centuries-old wood, and they had opened on to a scene of well-ordered prosperity. The drive up to the house was broad and long, and impeccably groomed, with paddocks full of horses either side. Immaculate farm buildings stood in the distance, together with a host of other facilities she had yet to name.

But even the buildings hadn't impressed her as much as Tiago's wonderfully welcoming staff. They'd shown her nothing but warmth and enthusiasm since the moment she'd arrived, and she had noticed Tiago's face lighting up like a flame when he had received their smiling welcome to his home.

'These are my people, Danny,' he had told her, with such pride in his voice.

She'd never seen him so animated. And then he'd made the introductions, leading her by the hand as if they were already married. Whatever reservations she'd had about their unusual arrangement had faded then. How was she supposed to keep her heart out of this, surrounded by such warmth?

But she wasn't an employee, and she wasn't Tiago's fiancée either. She was in an odd position, Danny mused as she continued to explore her accommodation. There was a lavish dressing room that had obviously been equipped in anticipation of visitors with a far more sophisticated lifestyle than she had. She wondered again what Tiago's staff must make of her, and then put it out of her mind. It was up to her to form a bond with this place, and with its people, and an arbitrary title wouldn't help her to do that.

What she loved most, Danny decided, turning full circle, was the lack of ostentation. There was just sheer quality everywhere she looked. Inside, the house was perfect, while outside the emerald-green pampas beckoned.

Her bathroom wouldn't have been out of place in the most sumptuous hotel. The cream marble was veined with honey, and there were more fluffy towels than she could count. She paused to stare out of the bathroom window, from where she had a good view of the rolling paddocks and the formal gardens surrounding the house. They had flown over Tiago's ranch for miles, he had explained, before he'd brought the jet in to land.

She had been shipwrecked on a desert island fit for a queen.

Her upbeat mood changed abruptly when she remembered Tiago's parting words. Even here, in this cosy suite of rooms, a shiver ran through her. She had been telling him how much she loved his home when he'd replied, 'This is what money can buy, *chica*. This is what *you* can buy now.'

It all came down to the ranch for Tiago, and he thought she felt the same about money.

When Tiago returned from his tour of the ranch everything moved towards the wedding at breakneck speed.

'I had wanted time for you to get used to your surroundings,' he explained the next morning with a careless gesture, 'but there *is* no time. The clock is ticking. I must marry before the week is out if I am to fulfil the terms of my grandfather's will.'

And there was no chance he would risk reneging on that, Danny thought, though now she'd met the people on the ranch she could understand why.

'Will there be enough time to arrange everything?' she asked with concern.

'You knew the terms of our agreement before you left Scotland,' Tiago said impatiently, ruffling his thick black hair.

'Yes, but—' She pulled herself up. 'I hadn't expected it to be quite so soon.'

'I factored in the inconvenience element when I calculated your payment.'

His words hurt. Tiago could be charm personified, or he could be as he was now—a warrior, ruthless and driven, a man who had paid a lot for his bride. And now it was payback time.

She had to remind herself that this wasn't a love-match but a marriage of convenience—for expediency, and to ensure her mother's future as well as her own.

They were standing in a field where foals were grazing, and she guessed Tiago had brought her here on purpose, so she would be relaxed when he dropped the bombshell of their marriage happening by the end of the week. He must have known how quickly they would have to be married before they'd left Scotland, but had chosen not to tell her. Perhaps because he'd been worried that she'd change her mind.

Her hope for a happy-ever-after future had always been slim, but now it drained away into the ground.

Sensing her tension, Tiago wheeled around to pin her with a stare. 'I thought I had explained quite clearly the urgency of this situation?'

'You did.' She was a 'situation' now.

'We should get the contract signed.'

'Yes.'

She would sign. She wouldn't go back on her word. She would make the best of this *situation*, and commit to a life she couldn't imagine. It would be a life with the man who had won her heart in Brazil, but a life in which she neither belonged, nor would be able to distance herself.

When Tiago started walking back towards the house his face was set. 'Let's get this thing done. I want you to check the contract over carefully—make sure you agree with all the terms before you sign.'

How cold-blooded could a wedding be?

She was about to find out.

She had always had such soft, romantic dreams about her wedding day…the wildflowers she would wear in her hair. Everyone would walk to the kirk in the village of Rottingdean and there would be a party afterwards in the village hall. Everyone would help out and contribute something. It would be such a happy day—a simple day, a precious day full of memories…the type of memories she would treasure for a lifetime.

That was her dream. The facts were somewhat different. It sounded as if there was going to be a rushed ceremony—possibly with witnesses she didn't even know.

Tiago was striding ahead of her. His transformation into gaucho was complete. The unforgiving pampas had carved him. Even his clothes had changed. There was nothing designer about his clothes now—nothing of the playboy. He wore threadbare jeans with worn leather chaps over them, and a red bandana secured his wilful hair. His boots were tooled leather, and he carried a lethal-looking *facón*—the vicious knife that gauchos wore—hanging from their belt.

It was hardly possible to believe that this rock-like individual was the same sophisticate who had joked and laughed and made her feel good about herself on Chico's ranch.

Tiago had stopped abruptly—but not to wait for her. He was staring at some horses in the field—evaluating them, counting them, maybe, though she suspected he knew every head of stock. Compared to his ranch, she was nothing. There were no sacrifices Tiago would not make, no lengths he would not go to, to keep this land.

She could always change her *mind.*

Could she? Signing this contract was a way forward for her—the best and perhaps the only way to secure her mother's future.

'Now you understand why I must do this,' Tiago said with confidence as he laid the contract down in front of Danny on his desk. 'You've only seen a fragment of the ranch, but enough to know that it must be saved.'

She wouldn't disagree with him, Danny thought as she took her time to check the contract, line by line. It was everything she had asked for, everything she had read on the screen of his phone—not a line had been changed.

'A year...' she murmured, wondering if it would be a happy year, or a year of torment for them both. And then something mischievous occurred to her, right out of the blue. 'How many relationships have you had that have lasted a year, Tiago?'

He narrowed his eyes and she could practically see his hackles rise. 'I don't understand what that's got to do with this.'

'How many?' she pressed.

Raking his hair with an impatient gesture, he decided to ignore her question. 'Are you going to sign this or not?'

She guessed he had *never* stayed with a woman for as long as a year. Tiago was sailing into uncharted waters as much as she was. If he had ever enjoyed a long-term relationship the press would have seized on it. What the press would make of their marriage she didn't know—and didn't care, either. This was a private arrangement between the two of them. The world would have to make of it what it wanted.

He held out his pen. She took it and signed her name, and Tiago countersigned the document after her. She stared at their signatures and felt cold inside. She had no idea what Tiago felt. Relief, certainly, but she doubted whether he felt anything more.

What had made him this way? she wondered. The polished playboy of the polo circuit seemed far happier and more relaxed here on his ranch, working alongside the gauchos. The thought that she had just contracted to marry a man she didn't know did nothing to reassure her. She should have listened to those rumours of the lone wolf. If she had she wouldn't be here now, with her heart yearning for a man who thought of her only as the means to an end.

'So you're rich now,' he said. 'How does that feel?'

'Strange,' she admitted.

Stranger still was the fact that she had never felt more impoverished in her life.

What had she done? Danny wondered as she watched Tiago cross the yard. She had to shake off this feeling of doom. She was about to join one of the finest horsemen in the world and work alongside him. What could be better than that? The wedding would happen when it happened, and in the meantime she would concentrate on everything Tiago could teach her about the ranch.

Maybe that would bring them closer. If not love, then maybe they could pick up their friendship and make the year ahead bearable for them both. That shouldn't be too hard when they shared so many interests.

Deciding to act as if this were just a new and exciting day in Brazil, rather than the start of a new and uncertain life, she leaned over the fence of the corral where Tiago was working, telling herself that she would get through this, and would learn a lot along the way.

'Would you like to try?' Tiago called to her softly.

He didn't take his attention off the young colt he was training for a moment. The pony was trembling with awareness, and it was one of the most valuable animals on the ranch, Tiago had explained.

'You'll let me work with him?' Danny asked with surprise.

'Why not? You're good.'

She couldn't pretend that didn't thrill her.

Taking care to shut the gate silently, she joined one of the best horse-trainers in the world. Working alongside Tiago would be the greatest opportunity of her life.

'Now, watch how I do this,' he said after a few moments.

Watching Tiago was no hardship. She watched his lips move when he spoke. She watched the muscles flex in his arms as he worked with the pony. She watched his hands soothe and stroke with exquisite sensitivity—

'Concentrate,' he said softly.

She hated it that he knew what she was thinking.

'That's good, Danny.'

He came to stand behind her. She held her breath as his body brushed hers, and tensed when his hands came around her, allowing Tiago to use his hands to direct hers.

'Bring your face closer,' he advised in an undertone. 'Share the same air as your pony.'

His husky voice was hypnotic, and his touch made both Danny and the pony relax.

'He's starting to trust you,' Tiago murmured. 'I'm going to move away now, while you carry on. Caress him, speak to him and build his confidence. Who knows? One day he might be yours.'

Danny smiled, knowing she would never be able to afford the young colt, and then felt a spear of surprise, knowing that with Tiago's marriage settlement in the bank she could.

'What would you call him?' he asked.

'Firefly.' She turned, expecting to find Tiago behind her, but he was already with the gauchos on the other side of the fence.

He was on the same wavelength as Danny, Tiago reflected as he watched her work. He never allowed bystanders into the corral when he was working with young ponies fresh to training, but he trusted Danny. He'd seen her work on Chico's ranch.

And on the personal front...?

He trusted her on the personal front too. He couldn't say that about any other woman apart from Elena, his housekeeper. His mother had been a socialite—a butterfly who had fallen in love with the son of a rough working man who'd happened to own a valuable ranch. His mother had seen an opportunity.

Tiago had been pampered and petted as a boy—a situation he'd refused to tolerate as a teen. By that time his father had been a drunk and his mother an ageing beauty who had refused to accept that her day in the sun was over. There had to be more pills, more potions, more clothes, more visits to the beauty salon, and then eventually to the plastic surgeon. She had ruined his father, who had ended up stealing from the ranch, leaving Tiago's grandfather with nothing.

It had taken Tiago to return—a changed man—and rescue things to the point where Fazenda Santos had become no longer a broken-down ranch that existed solely to feed the greed of his parents, but a highly successful concern he had dedicated his life to.

Did he *want* to get married, with a family history like that?

No. But a year with a woman as lithe and lovely as Danny might just be tolerable—especially when she was in his bed.

CHAPTER SEVEN

TIAGO WAS IN a good mood after working with the colt, and as they walked back to the house it seemed as good a moment as any for Danny to ask him about the details of the wedding. She might not be having the idyllic country wedding she had imagined as a girl, but arrangements would still have to be made. It might be a hastily arranged formality, or—and she desperately hoped this wouldn't be the case—a full-blown society wedding for the type of people Tiago mixed with when he was on the polo circuit.

'So…our wedding…' she began.

'Friday,' he said.

'Friday?' She looked at him blankly.

'Friday is the end of the week,' he said impatiently. 'I did tell you it would have to be this week.'

Yes, but talking about something was very different from facing the reality of the situation. She was already running through a checklist in her mind.

'There's too much to do in the time available.'

Even if a wedding could be arranged at such short notice, she had to consider the demands of the ranch, as well as the Thunderbolts' polo fixtures.

'Did you check on the team's games?'

'Of course.' Tiago drilled a stare into her eyes, as if

the choice between a polo match and their wedding was no contest. 'All we need for this wedding is you and me and a couple of witnesses.'

'I never expected anything more,' she said, angry to think Tiago imagined she craved some sort of grand ceremony to accompany her pay-out.

Nothing could be further from the truth. It was bad enough knowing she had to make promises that she would only keep for a year, without attempting to fool wedding guests into believing theirs was a romantic love match.

'We'll get married here on the ranch,' Tiago said, to her relief. 'But I want everyone to share the celebrations. This won't be a quiet wedding. I'm not ashamed of what we're doing, and neither should you be. When Chico and Lizzie return from their honeymoon we'll fly to Scotland and have a blessing at the kirk in the village, with a party afterwards. You can have whatever you want, then—ten dresses and a dozen bridesmaids, if you like.'

Tiago knew so little about her, she thought, chilled by his casual attitude. 'I just want to get it over with,' she said, speaking her thoughts out loud. She was uncomfortable discussing the charade they were about to take part in.

'I am not trying to cheat you, but I do want you to understand this situation for what it is. It's a short-term solution that will benefit both of us enormously.'

'I know that. I've made a bargain and I'll stick to it,' she confirmed.

Tiago relaxed. 'Thank you, Danny.' And then his eyes became slumberous, and a half-smile curved his wicked mouth. 'Our wedding must be soon. I don't *do* waiting.'

For anything, she remembered, thinking about their encounter on his jet.

'I suggest you get some rest between now and Friday, *chica*. It will be a big day for you.'

And an even bigger night, she thought, shivering in a very different way.

'Will I see you before then?' She tried to sound casual, and only succeeded in making Tiago impatient.

'I hope you're not trying to tie me down even before we're married?'

'No.' She took him on. 'I'm asking you a question.'

'Will the fire of South America sit well with the frost of Scotland?' he mocked.

She raised a brow. 'Let's be quite clear. I've got no intention of becoming your doormat.'

'Well said,' he approved, curving her another smile. 'And now I have business to attend to. You'll see me when I get back.' His powerful shoulders eased in a careless shrug. 'I can't tell you how long that will be.'

'So long as you're back for our wedding, I imagine that will be time enough,' she said coolly.

Tiago huffed a laugh. 'I wouldn't miss it for the world,' he assured her.

Those eyes, that smile—she was glad he couldn't feel the heat surging through her veins. To say Tiago was arrogant would be vastly understating the case, but he was also bone-meltingly hot, and she was in no way immune to his appeal.

'Shall I spread the word about our wedding?' she suggested mildly.

'Tell anyone you like.'

'Fine. Goodbye, then,' she said coolly. 'Enjoy your trip.'

Tiago stared at her as if he expected something more —a longing look, perhaps, or a flaccid wave. She gave him a steely look as he walked away, and then—not for the first time—wondered what on earth she had got herself into.

It wasn't as if she couldn't arrange a wedding, Danny reasoned, now that she was alone, but for all Tiago's interest in the matter it was clear to her that the groom intended to carry on as usual, with no interruption to his schedule. She could challenge him all she liked, but Tiago wouldn't change his life for anyone.

He would be back by Wednesday, thought Tiago. She could like it or not. He *would* be back—because the gauchos were holding a party on Wednesday night, and he would take the opportunity to introduce Danny formally as his intended bride. And then he would take her to bed.

Everyone would know by then, as she would have told them, and waiting until their wedding night on Friday was too long for him to wait to claim a woman he'd already tasted and been denied.

He'd made a good deal with Danny and he was confident she would stick to it. It pleased him to think the people on the ranch already liked her. And the gauchos wouldn't have crowded around to watch her training the colt if she hadn't been good. The sketchy character he'd drawn in his mind of the wife he would be forced to take had acquired an appealing reality in Danny, and if their brief encounter on the jet had been anything to go by she would be a willing pupil outside the training ring too.

Tiago was a saint. That much she had learned while he'd been away. As she crossed the yard on Wednesday morning, heading for the house, she was still thinking about her conversation with one of the elderly gauchos, who had told her that Tiago rarely took time off. He knew every family by name, and all the names of generations past.

He'd saved them from ruin, having plucked his grandfather's property from the brink of disaster. His parents had both been fools, who hadn't been able to spend Tiago's grandfather's money fast enough. They had been more interested in funding their lavish lifestyle than in saving the ranch.

The old man's face had lit up at this point as he'd told her, 'But Tiago is different. Tiago is one of us.'

Tiago was overly generous to everyone who worked for him, and one of the most highly regarded horse-trainers and horse-breeders of his time. He was also a world-famous polo international.

Basically, he had no flaws—though Danny suspected the world's women might disagree, because Tiago had never recovered from his mother's spendthrift ways and so didn't trust women. This was what Elena, who had a far better command of English than anyone else on the ranch, had explained, after hugging Danny when she'd heard about their impending wedding.

Tiago's mother had been the sophisticated type, Elena had confided, and she had groomed her son to be a playboy. This was a mask Tiago still wore when it suited him, but he was gaucho through and through—like his grandfather before him.

Danny took all this information and added it to what she already knew about Tiago, but whether it would give her more confidence regarding the next year or less, she wasn't sure. Tiago was a product of his upbringing, and *she* was hardly a child from a stable home. Perhaps together they stood a chance of building something worthwhile?

They might, but that wasn't why she was here. In a year's time there would be no Tiago and Danny together. What was the point of building anything beyond an understanding between them?

Hearing rotor blades, she stopped in the middle of the yard to stare up at the sky. *He was back.* Her heart thundered. She tightened her grip on the parcel in her hand. She had bought him a wedding gift—had it made for him by one of the gauchos on the ranch. It was only a small gesture, but it was something. She didn't want to go to Tiago empty-handed on Friday.

Now she began to wonder why she'd done it at all, and what he'd make of the gift—this man who could buy anything, and who travelled to town in his helicopter.

She glanced at the bulky package and at the white knuckles on her hand. Sucking in a deep, steadying breath, she firmed her resolve. Why go for half-measures?

Plucking a flower from one of the pots in the yard, she tucked it beneath the string on the parcel. Whether Tiago wanted her or not, he'd got her for a year—and she'd got him.

And he took her breath away.

Tiago's air of purpose and energy seemed redoubled as he strode into the yard. He didn't waste time. Dragging her close, he stared into her face for a heartbeat, and then kissed her as if he would never let her go.

'I've missed you,' he growled. 'Where's Elena?'

Still recovering from his sensory assault, she somehow found the breath to tell him that the housekeeper had gone home about an hour ago.

'Excellent.'

Maintaining eye contact, Tiago backed her towards the house. Removing the parcel from her hands, he left it on the hall table along the way. He grabbed her hand when they reached the foot of the stairs.

'No!'

He stopped abruptly and stared down at her, frowning. 'No? What do you mean, *no*?'

'I mean no.' She had to tell him how she felt about this. 'I don't want to.'

'You don't want to what?' Tiago demanded, his expression darkening.

'I don't want to make love to you. Not today. Not now.'

He seemed incredulous, and laughed. He certainly wasn't used to rejection. 'Explain,' he said coldly.

Stiffening her resolve, she went ahead and told him. 'I have decided to save myself for our wedding night.'

His frown deepened, and then he laughed again. 'You've *what*?'

'You heard me. I'm not going to bed with you until our wedding night. I want to make it special,' she explained, starting to feel awkward as Tiago stared at her as if she were mad.

'I have to keep my pride, Tiago. Surely you understand that?'

'Your pride?' His eyes narrowed.

'Yes, my pride,' she insisted more forcefully.

Tiago lifted his hands away from her, as if the last thing he wanted now was to touch her.

'Please don't be angry.'

He stepped back. 'Is this some sort of power-play?' He stared down at her suspiciously. 'Are you using sex as a weapon?'

'Hardly. I'm not using sex at all.'

He was incredulous. He didn't have a clue what could be motivating this. Danny had been so different on the jet. But as he advanced towards her she paled, and put her hands flat against his chest.

'Please…' she said, staring up at him.

What had he been thinking? Was he no better than

Pintos? Had his desire for Danny blunted his brain entirely?

The world he inhabited was brutal and unforgiving. The brand of polo he played was more than competitive, it was aggressive. But aggression had no place when he was with Danny. Losing had never been an option for him, whether that be in the game of polo or the game of life. But Danny was different, and she required different rules. He'd been drawn to her in Brazil because she'd been fun to be around, but the more time he spent with her the more he realised just how badly she'd been hurt, and how well she hid that hurt.

And now he was going to add to it?

They stared at each other, and then he said, with a reluctant shrug, 'I guess waiting until our wedding night could be a good idea.'

'Liar,' she whispered, smiling now. But then she added softly, 'Thank you, Tiago. Thank you for understanding.'

'Me?' He smiled into her eyes. 'Understand pride? I'm surprised at you, Danny. You should know I'm an expert on the subject.'

She exhaled raggedly and, having surmounted that hurdle, went on to the next. 'I've got something for you,' she revealed.

'For me?' Tiago couldn't have looked more surprised. 'Why have you bought something for me?'

Was she the first woman ever to buy him a gift?

'Why shouldn't I buy something for you?' She was genuinely bewildered. 'I wanted to thank you.'

'*Thank* me?' Tiago's lips pressed down in puzzlement as he stared at her. 'For what?'

'For the chance to work alongside you—the chance to live here on your ranch for a year.'

Danny's heart filled as she spoke. There were so many

reasons to thank Tiago, starting with right back at the stables in Scotland, when he had saved her from Carlos Pintos. And now he had understood why waiting until they were married before having sex mattered so much to her.

Even further back, in Brazil the first time, when she had still been raw from her disillusionment with Pintos the first time around, it had been Tiago she'd always looked for—and not just because he was the most attractive man on the ranch…though that fact had been hard to ignore. He'd always been able to lift her spirits. He had made her feel relevant again when Pintos had called her a waste of space, and she had believed him. Tiago had never seemed less than pleased to see her, and he had made her feel like someone worth seeking out for a chat.

'Watching you work has been a revelation for me,' she said honestly. 'Having this chance to meet the people you work with, to learn how they live, will be a privilege.' She shook her head as she struggled to find the right words. 'I'd work here for nothing for the chance to learn from you.'

'You haven't mentioned money once,' he said—more as an observation than a criticism.

'Why would I?' Her elation dwindled as she remembered that this had always been about money for her. No wonder he was cynical. They both had a long way to go to build any trust between them.

'So what did you buy me?' he wanted to know.

She was glad of the change of focus, but embarrassed that her gift was small in comparison to the riches Tiago was used to. 'I think you can safely call it a job-appropriate gift.'

'What?' he demanded. 'A tin of hoof oil?'

Danny smiled. 'Not exactly.' Leaving his side, she

went to collect the bulky parcel he'd taken out of her hands. 'I just hope it's okay.'

The gaucho who had made the special coin belt for her had explained that in the olden days these traditional belts decorated with silver coins had been used almost as portable bank accounts for gauchos, as they moved from place to place in search of work.

'Now I'm curious,' Tiago admitted as she pressed the package into his hands.

'So open it.' She stood back, relieved that the tension between them had eased—at least for now.

'*Deus*, Danny, this is really special.' Tiago handled the belt reverently, the silver coins chinking in a smooth riff as they passed through his fingers. 'I can't thank you enough.'

'Do you really like it? It's not too much?'

'I love it. It's perfect,' he insisted. 'And I love you for thinking of it.'

He loved her.

No. Tiago didn't love her, Danny reasoned, losing patience with her romantic self for allowing that thought to slip through. He loved her for thinking of him and for choosing the belt.

'Manuelo said you'd like it.'

'Manuelo helped you with your choice?' He seemed impressed by this. 'Manuelo must like you. He and his family have been making these belts for generations, but he won't make them for just anyone. These traditions are another reason why this ranch is so special to me.'

'You don't have to tell me how much this ranch means to you.'

Catching her close, Tiago kissed her—first on each cheek and then, after a pause, on her mouth. He had never kissed her like that before. It was a tender, lingering kiss that made her eyes sting with tears, and when he pulled back there was a look in his eyes that thrilled her. It was warm and assessing and thoughtful.

'What?' she prompted when he didn't speak.

He slanted her a smile. It planted that attractive crease in his cheek. 'I bought something for *you*,' he revealed. 'I hope you like it. I went shopping in town.'

She smiled back at him as she imagined Tiago battling with the crowds. 'Now, *that* I would like to have seen.'

'I bought you this…' Reaching into the back pocket of his jeans, he brought out the most astonishing diamond ring. 'Do you like it?'

She was too stupefied to speak. And when she did find her voice she could only blurt, 'You kept *that* in your back pocket?'

'The boxes were boring,' Tiago said, frowning. 'They were all the same. What's the point of them? Everyone has them. I'm not everyone—and neither are you. If you don't like it I'll change it.'

She turned the fabulous ring over in her hand, hypnotised by the prisms of light flashing from it.

'What?' he said. 'You don't seem keen. Is it too big? Too small? Too sparkly?'

Relaxing at last, she laughed. 'I'm sorry. I don't seem very grateful, do I? It's absolutely beautiful, Tiago, but I can't accept it.'

'Rubbish,' he flashed. 'But just in case…' He reached into his jeans again. 'I bought a few more, in case you didn't like that one.'

She gasped as he tipped a selection of rings into her hand to join the first. Each was a fabulous jewel in its own right, and there was every possible style, colour of stone and variety of cut.

'Take your time,' he said with a shrug, as if he had

given her a selection of candy to choose from. 'Or keep them all, if you prefer.'

Wealth on this scale was incomprehensible to Danny. 'But I don't understand…'

'What's to understand?' Tiago demanded. 'We're getting married. I want my wife to have the best.'

'Yes, but…' She hesitated, knowing she would rather have a tender word from him, or a teasing look like those they'd used to share in Brazil. This felt like another payment—a bonus to secure the deal.

'This is a gift,' Tiago said, as if reading her mind. 'My gift to you.'

She still wasn't convinced. Had all his mistresses received similar gifts? Suddenly the rings felt cold and heavy in her hand.

'I can't keep them.'

'Of course you can.' Tiago closed her hand around them. 'Keep them all. Swap them round from day to day, and then you'll never be tired of them.'

'I can't do that.' She was genuinely shocked. 'I can't casually swap these rings around as I might change my clothes. Any ring you give me is going to be a precious keepsake and full of meaning. Its value will lie in more than the stone.'

He frowned. 'So you don't like my gift?'

'I didn't say that. I love them. But all these are too much. You don't have to do this, Tiago. Under the circumstances, wouldn't it be more appropriate if you gave me something simple? Or nothing at all. I don't *have* to have a ring.'

'I want you to have a ring,' he insisted.

'Because of what other people might think?' she suggested.

'I don't give a damn what other people think,' he

flared. 'Take the rings. Sell them if you don't want to wear them—put the money towards stock for your new premises, if that's what you want to do.'

His voice had turned cold. She could tell she had hurt him. Her heart shrank at the thought. They were so close, and yet miles apart.

'You're a very generous man, Tiago' she said quietly, closing her hand around the rings. 'Thank you.'

'Good,' he said briskly, as if he were glad to have the matter dealt with.

CHAPTER EIGHT

SHE WAS FALLING in love with this man, Danny realised as they rode out side by side later that day. But how could she ever relax totally with Tiago, the gaucho who made her laugh and who had taught her so many things about horses, when she had to handle his cold-blooded playboy side too?

That would have to be a problem for another day, she concluded as he looked at her.

He glanced at their horses. 'Shall we test them?'

'Why not?'

His dark force was irresistible. Tiago's love of challenge and risk and danger was fast becoming her secret pleasure. The heat and passion of Brazil must have infected her, she realised as they urged their horses on. The sun was warm, the breeze was cool, and scent from the flowers they were trampling saturated the air she breathed. There surely could be nothing more exhilarating than this. Nothing that could release the tension inside her faster.

Except for one thing, she thought as she flashed a glance at Tiago, who looked so relaxed, and yet so dark and dangerous in the saddle—and that would have to wait until their wedding night.

Tiago reined in beside the river that watered his land,

and for a moment she allowed herself to believe she needed nothing more out of life than this. She could work alongside Tiago for a year without wanting him to feel the same way she did.

Couldn't she?

He had never looked better than here, where there were no pretensions, no dress shirts, no tailored suits— just Tiago in the raw, in ripped and faded jeans, with battered leather chaps over them, a faded top clinging to his hard-muscled torso, and a bandana tied carelessly around his wild black hair.

She was rapt as he pointed things out to her. The giant-sized Rhea bird, disappearing into the long grass, and a wild cat that surprised her by diving into the river as Tiago explained that this particular breed of cat ate frogs.

He turned to her. 'This is a nature reserve. All the animals are safe here. My vets are responsible for them just as they are for my horses.'

She was learning a lot—and not just about the animals. Hearing about Tiago's interests and his active concern for this land told her more about him than anyone could.

'Last one to the house makes the coffee?' he suggested as he turned his horse.

'You don't frighten me,' she called back, laughing.

She went ahead, but Tiago caught up with her easily and for a few strides they rode side by side. But he couldn't resist taking the lead. She let him go, just for the sheer pleasure of watching him with one hand on the reins and his hips working effortlessly to a lazy rhythm. Arousal lodged deep inside her at the sight of him, and she finally admitted to herself that Friday couldn't come quickly enough.

Clattering into the yard after him, she dismounted.

Tiago's dark eyes were wicked, and there was a smile

on his lips as she started untacking her pony. 'Make sure you sleep tonight. There won't be much sleeping on Friday.'

Hefting his tack, he walked past her.

She stilled with her hand resting on the saddle. She had to take a deep breath before she could continue. She wanted him. His deep, husky voice had sent heat coursing through her. She wanted to marry Tiago. Worse, she wanted to live with him and share his life. But every time that thought slipped through she had to remind herself that theirs was a marriage of convenience, with a time limit of one year. Any fantasies on her part were just that: fantasies.

It seemed surreal to be standing in the middle of a dance floor at Tiago's side. They were at the gauchos' party and he was calling for silence with his arms raised.

Everything was moving at breakneck speed. In two days they would be married.

So? What was her problem? The wedding on Friday was no surprise, so why the jitters?

She was decked out in her one and only dress, with her hair neatly tied back and hardly any make-up, trying to make a good impression. She was at ease around these people in the corral, or in the kitchen, but here, at Tiago's side, it all seemed so improbable. He was like a god to them, and she had just sprung out of nowhere. What must they think?

Never mind what anyone thought—for the sake of these people she had to make a go of this. Why cause problems when Tiago had worked so hard to save the ranch?

'Danny?'

Tiago's voice held a note of command and her eyes

flashed open. How could she live with this man, love him, and then leave him without a backward glance?

She couldn't.

Glancing round the smiling faces, she felt like the worst kind of confidence trickster. The only way she could get through this was by concentrating on the fact that her marriage to Tiago would secure the future of everyone here. Meanwhile, Brazil's most eligible bachelor—the man she adored—was announcing their wedding to cries of excitement from the crowd.

'I realise that Danny will have already told some of you, and you may think that this has all happened at the speed of light, but Danny and I have known each other for quite some time, and recently our friendship has turned into something more.'

Everyone cheered at this romantic interpretation of their cold-blooded contract, and when Tiago turned to look at her she could almost believe it too.

Putting his arm around her shoulder, he led her out of the spotlight to a crescendo of cheers, and then his men distracted him, coming up to shake his hand, while the women and children of the ranch clustered around Danny.

'And now I have a special gift for my bride,' he announced.

Taking hold of her hand, he led her through the crowd to the space beyond the dance floor.

'Another gift?' Danny stared up into Tiago's rugged face. 'You don't have to.'

'But I want to.'

His sharp whistle of command caused a commotion in the crowd, and everyone fell back at the sound of thundering hooves. Danny gasped as the young colt galloped towards them.

'Is there anything else you'd rather have?'

'Nothing,' she said. 'But—'

'Then accept him and be gracious,' Tiago advised. 'You have to think like a businesswoman now, Danny. This colt will be a valuable stud one day.'

It would have been better if she could have thought like a businesswoman from the start, Danny reflected, stunned by Tiago's gift. Her marriage was an advantageous merger for them both, nothing more—just as this young colt, Firefly, was an advantageous acquisition.

'Thank you.' She moved quickly to the young horse's head, to soothe him and to speak to him gently, wanting him to focus on her and be calm, rather than focus on the noisy crowd.

'I'm glad he gives you pleasure.'

'There's nothing you could have given me that I would treasure more.' Nestling her face against the colt's warm neck, she breathed in the familiar scent and wished, just for a moment, that one day she would ride him with Tiago at her side.

The colt was led away to a round of appreciative applause. Everyone on the ranch understood the significance of such a gift. It was a pledge from Tiago to his people that this marriage would be good for them.

But they didn't know the ins and outs of it, Danny fretted as she smiled to show that she couldn't have been happier with her gift. There could be no certainties in life, she told herself firmly as Tiago spoke to some of the men. Surely every bride-to-be felt this way—that to be so happy must come at a cost?

'It's official, Danny.'

She tried to close her heart to Tiago, but when he took hold of her hands to draw her close she failed miserably. Even when he dipped his head to kiss her she suspected it was for the sake of the crowd.

'We've made everyone happy tonight,' he said.

'Yes,' she agreed.

Sensing her unease, Tiago led her out of the crowd. 'Is that all you have to say?'

He had every right to expect her to be bouncing with happiness after his announcement of their engagement, the upcoming wedding, and now his wonderful gift, but she couldn't fake it.

Why must she always pick holes in perfection? Why wouldn't the fairytale work for her?

He ground his jaw, seeing the tension in Danny's back as she walked away with a group of women who were keen to help her organise their wedding. Nothing must go wrong now. His lawyers were standing by. Full ownership of the ranch was a matter of hours away.

He was as tense as he had ever been, Tiago realised as a group of his fellow gauchos encouraged him to stay and spend the night celebrating with them. His determination to build on what he'd started with these people had never been stronger than it was today.

And Danny?

Deus! A million things could go wrong between now and their wedding day. Suddenly Friday seemed an eternity away.

This could work, Danny thought on Thursday morning as she waved goodbye to the women who had helped her to design the menu for their wedding banquet. She had left them late last night, after discussing plans for the wedding, and had felt much calmer after spending time with them. She had slept well for the first time in ages.

Maybe because there had had been no sign of Tiago, she thought now with amusement, as he stood at her

side in the middle of the courtyard, supposedly surveying the decorations when he was clearly itching to go on
his morning ride.

'Happy?' Tiago asked as the lively group trooped
home.

'Yes,' Danny said. 'I am now I know that this is the
type of wedding we're having. I honestly couldn't think
of anything better.'

'Everyone wants to help because they think a lot of you.'

'I hope that's true.'

'Didn't I tell you everything would be all right?'

'Yes,' she murmured, wondering if once they were
married she'd even see him.

It was too late to worry about that now, Danny concluded, heading for the house as Tiago turned for the
stables—or so she thought.

She hadn't realised but he was coming after her, and
she exclaimed with surprise.

'Not long now.' He cupped her chin, and his eyes
blazed into her own. 'Is there anything that could make
this better for you, *chica*?'

If you loved me, she thought, *that would make it better. If this marriage of ours were not a sham, that would
make it better still.*

'Your friends from Rottingdean?' he suggested.

'Lizzie and Chico are still on honeymoon, and with
Hamish and Annie in charge of the house in their absence—'

'What about your mother?'

'If you can find her.' Danny's mouth twisted with regret. 'I'm afraid I don't even know where she is. I keep
trying to contact her, but—'

'She's in the South of France,' Tiago revealed, shocking her.

'What's she doing there?'

'Spending the last of the money you sent her, I imagine.'

'Did you speak to her?' she asked urgently.

Hope soared inside her. She'd always been a dream-weaver, and if there was the slightest chance she could speak to her mother, make her understand, reassure her about this marriage...

'Yes. I've spoken to her,' he confirmed. 'I wanted everything to be perfect for you—or as perfect as it can be. You're doing so much for me, Danny. I don't think you even realise what you're doing. I would have flown your mother out here for the wedding, but there are some things even I can't control.'

'What did she say to you?' She couldn't hide her eagerness. 'Did she get my messages?'

'She got all of them, apparently.'

Tiago's grim look warned her to be brave.

'What did she say?'

'She said they were blocking up her phone, and could you please stop?'

CHAPTER NINE

'Oh.' Danny's voice was flat. The shock of what Tiago had told her cut deep. She couldn't blame him for his candour after she'd pressed him for an answer. She guessed he'd thought a clean cut would be the best. The news that her mother wasn't interested in Danny was old, but it hurt all the same. The fact that her mother didn't even care that she was getting married was brutal.

'You tried, Danny. At least you tried.'

Yes, she was certainly a trier, Danny reflected dryly. How stupid she felt now, imagining her mother would want to wish her well.

'I can't honestly say I expected her to be here for the wedding,' she admitted, pinning a smile to her face.

She glanced up to find Tiago staring down at her with concern. Maybe she was wrong about him. Maybe he did have feelings but, having spent a lifetime hiding them, now found them impossible to express.

'Don't feel sorry for me, Tiago. I'm not a child.'

'Maybe not,' he agreed, 'but my people show you more affection than your own mother. If she had been born with a title, and then squandered an old man's fortune, I would say that your mother and mine must have been twins.'

The bitterness in his voice told her that Tiago had experience of loving someone and being rejected. She knew that that could lead down one of two roads: the road *she* trod, where she never stopped trying, or the road Tiago had taken, where he simply turned his back. It was another thought to unsettle her.

'I can't bear to see you hurt like this,' he raged.

'I'm not hurt. I'm—'

'Accustomed to it?' he spat out. 'Why *should* you be accustomed to it? This is wrong, Danny. You should cut her out of your life.'

'She's my mother. I can't.'

'She's no mother to you.'

With an impatient gesture, Tiago ground his jaw, but thankfully said nothing more on the subject.

'Don't worry,' he said at last. 'Everyone on the ranch will be here to cheer you on.'

'And that's all that matters,' she said with conviction.

She only had to remember how touched she'd been when a selection of treasured veils and wedding dresses had been brought out of lavender-scented storage for her to choose from to know how much Tiago's people meant to her.

'They're your people now, Danny,' he said, reading her.

'*Our* people.'

That thought made her feel strong. Whatever happened in the future, the bond she was building here with the people of Fazenda Santos would support her as surely as any strong family could.

'They've done so much in the short time they've known me to make me feel welcome,' she said, glancing round the courtyard, which was already dressed for the wedding, 'and I'm honoured to have been accepted here.'

'You'll be happy. I'll make sure of it,' he said.

But when Tiago put his arm around her shoulders and drew her close she thought, *Yes, but for just one year.*

She was certain that Tiago would do his best to make her time in Brazil trouble-free. It wasn't in his interest to do otherwise. He would never risk this marriage of convenience being challenged by anyone.

'One last drink before we part?' he suggested.

'Why not?' She smiled.

Tomorrow was their wedding day. It hardly seemed possible. Closing her eyes briefly, she drank in his strength, wishing with all her heart that they were a normal couple, with a normal relationship. But what *was* normal? Could any couple enter into marriage with complete certainty?

Shaking off her doubts, she walked with him towards the outdoor area at the back of the ranch house, where Tiago loved to stand and look out across his property. She reminded herself that for some married couples it wasn't even possible to guarantee a happy year.

The hunter had become the protector. His cold-blooded plan to marry Danny at all costs had been brought to its knees by the way she was treated by her mother. No one should be treated like that. Hot blood surged through his veins as Danny stood beside him. There was anger, and there was lust—and something else he refused to name. Twenty-four hours ago he had held her in his arms—and that seemed too long.

Glancing down, he saw how pale she was. The conversation he'd had with her about her mother had hit her hard. He should have found some gentler way to break it to her. He shouldn't have been surprised by her resilience, but he was. He poured her a drink—orange juice, as she'd requested. She was determined to keep a clear head, he concluded, quelling his disappointment at the thought that temptation would have to be resisted for another night.

'Why are you smiling?' she asked him when he took the empty glass from her hand.

'You're wearing a dress, and I don't think I've ever seen your legs before.'

'Liar. You saw me at the wedding in a bridesmaid's dress.'

'Which trailed around your ankles.' He tipped the neck of his bottle of beer in Danny's direction.

She shook her head. 'It did not trail.' And then she said, 'Shall we drink a toast to your grandfather?'

'My grandfather? I'm surprised you're even thinking about him.'

'Why wouldn't I? We wouldn't be here without him,' she pointed out.

His lips pressed down with amusement as he shook his head. She was right. His grandfather might have done a lot of things he disagreed with, but he had given Tiago the chance to change his life.

Easing onto one hip, he told her a little more about his history. 'I never imagined my grandfather would deny me full ownership of the ranch, but he was cunning, and he never liked my playboy antics. He said it reminded him too much of my mother—the feckless socialite, as he called her. That's why he constructed his will as he did. He knew how much I loved this place. He knew I wouldn't let the people down.'

'Whatever it took?' Danny observed dryly.

'Whatever it took,' he agreed, meeting her stare head-on. The one thing he would never do was lie to her.

'To your grandfather,' she said softly, chinking her glass against his bottle. 'Manuelo told me your parents were never around, and that when they were they only came here to beg for money from your grandfather. Once they got that, he said they left—sometimes without even seeing you. So what's the sequel to this story, Tiago? I know there must be one, because Manuelo thinks the world of you—as does everyone else on this ranch.'

He was reluctant to get into it, but from the look in her eyes Danny wasn't giving up. 'My grandfather bailed me out of a juvenile correctional facility—said he'd give me a trial on the ranch. He said I could live with him if I worked for the privilege.'

'And you fought him every step of the way?' she guessed.

He didn't deny it. 'I didn't want to work for anyone except myself. And when I saw this place in the middle of nowhere—' He grimaced. 'I didn't feel as I do now about it, that's for sure. It held no appeal for my teenage self.'

'But you stayed?' she pressed, her eyes filled with concern.

'Yes, because I came to love the people. And now you've met them I'm sure you understand why.'

'I do.' She spoke softly and touched his arm.

He had to pause and hold himself in check for a moment, or he would have responded for sure.

'I try never to be away from them for long,' he went on then. 'Because they and my grandfather opened my eyes to a different way of life—*their* way of life. And I could relate to it—to them. The passion they have for the country and their animals is the same as mine, and as soon as the gauchos discovered I had a way with horses, that was it—I was one of them. It was enough for me for a time, and then—like everyone else when they're growing up—I had to get away. I was desperate to expand my horizons—to explore that other side of me, bequeathed to me by my mother.'

He laughed as he thought about it.

'And then?' Danny asked.

'My grandfather was wise enough to back off and leave me to it.'

'Where did you go?'

'I hitched my wagon to whichever polo player was fashionable at the time.' He shrugged. 'By watching and learning I somehow managed to save up enough from my wages to buy my first pony. She was an old girl, on the point of retirement, but I was eager to try the game myself, and I made a passable polo pony out of her. Thanks to that mare I could take part in at least one chukka during amateur matches, where not every rider owned a string of ponies and we all did the best we could.'

'Which brought your riding skills to the attention of those that mattered?'

'Correct.'

She was standing close enough to touch, and that distracted him for another few moments.

'Eventually I was entrusted with training a few medium-grade ponies.' He cast his mind back to those uncertain days. 'Then my grandfather became ill, but I was having too much of a good time to come home. I should have come. I owe everything I have to him. I just couldn't see it at the time. Now do you understand why I am so committed to this place?'

'Yes,' she said quietly. 'It explains a lot about you.'

'Like why I'm such a selfish bastard?' He laughed.

'Like why you belong here,' Danny argued. 'And why you believe you can never do enough for this ranch or for the people who live here. You think you deserted your grandfather when he needed you most, but he had let you go, knowing you'd come back. He wanted you to see how wide your horizons could be. You haven't let him down, Tiago—anything but.'

'Some of the decisions I've had to make to keep this ranch haven't been easy.'

She shook her head and laughed. 'I think I know that.' She looked into his eyes and hers darkened.

The pain in his groin increased. Taking hold of her wrist, he led her around the side of the house, and with the utmost self-control he held her away from him at the door.

'Goodnight, Danny. The next time I see you will be at our wedding.'

Could there be anything more beautiful than his bride on their wedding day? He couldn't hold back a smile as Danny walked slowly towards him down the petal-strewn aisle. She was coming to join him through packed rows of people whose smiling faces meant the world to him.

The fact that they were fast adopting Danny as one of their own was the icing on the cake for him, but he didn't need anyone to tell him that he'd made a wonderful choice of bride. Danny had so much to offer the ranch and its people. When they were married he hoped she would play an even bigger role, adding the human touch he'd never had time to bring to the ranch.

The outdoor ceremony beneath an archway of flowers passed quickly, in a series of softly spoken words on Danny's part and brisk assertions on his. He would take away a series of sensory memories, together with the relief of being married.

Danny was small and soft and fragrant—and so keyed-up, so alert she was almost trembling. Her close-fitting lace dress was rustling, though she wasn't moving. It rustled when she breathed and her breasts rose above the confining fabric, and it rustled when she turned to him to speak her wedding vows, and through all this they were standing close, but not touching, and that tiny space keeping them apart was charged with electricity.

'You may kiss the bride.'

At last he could breathe freely. He was married. He owned the ranch. The relief of having the caveat in his grandfather's will fulfilled was indescribable. His people sensed it too and cheered wildly, standing to applaud as he cupped Danny's face in his hands. The future security of everyone here was assured now. This was his gift to his guests. He had an aide on hand, waiting to make a copy of the wedding certificate, as well as a courier standing by to deliver a hard copy to the lawyers as soon as this ceremony was over.

This was more romantic than she had dared to hope. Surrounded by fragrant blossoms in front of the registrar, she could feel love swelling all around her. She knew she was doing the right thing. Tiago's steady gaze was all it took to convince her that her doubts before the wedding had been based on nothing more than pre-wedding nerves.

Surely Tiago must feel the magic too? How could he not? Danny wondered as he dipped his head and kissed her. She closed her eyes, knowing she'd never been so happy. Even the cruel barbs in the press couldn't touch her now. She remembered some of them, and smiled as Tiago stared deep into her eyes.

'Can a small-town girl rein in a man like Tiago Santos?'

Yes, she could.

'Does a leopard change his spots?'

Yes, he had.

'Will the Playboy be curbed by Miss Whiplash?'

That remark had made her laugh. Nothing mattered now except the fact that Tiago Santos and Danny Cameron were husband and wife. The reporters didn't know him as she did. No one who hadn't seen Tiago Santos on this ranch had seen the real man.

'Well, Senhora Santos, are you ready to start your new life with me?'

'I am.'

'When you look at me like that,' Tiago murmured, 'all I can think about is taking you to bed. Is that bad?'

'I like you bad. Tonight I think I'm going to be very bad too.'

'I'm counting on it,' Tiago assured her.

He excited her. She trembled in an entirely pleasurable way at the thought of their wedding night. She'd asked for this delay, and could hardly believe how long she'd waited—not long in actual terms of this week, but if she counted in her feverish erotic daydreams from that first moment she saw him in Brazil, that was quite a build-up to tonight.

She was about to find out if her imagination was equal to their wedding night. Pleasure thrummed through her at the thought that she might not even be close.

But they had guests to entertain first, Danny remembered as Tiago was distracted by some of his polo-playing friends.

While he was talking she stared at the jewel-encrusted band on her hand, sitting snugly next to the enormous diamond engagement ring. How incongruous they looked on her work-worn hands. Silk purse and sow's ear came to mind.

She flashed a glance at Tiago—blisteringly hot, unreasonably handsome, sleekly tailored and unimaginably successful—and in spite of all the encouragement she'd been giving herself before the wedding she shrank a little inside her beautiful borrowed wedding dress.

The wedding party might have been last-minute but, as he had expected, everyone had pulled together to make it special. It was the best party he'd been to in a long time, and every time he looked at his bride he knew he'd made a good choice.

His groin was straining, begging for him to do something about it, but he was beginning to enjoy the agony—and he wanted to show off his beautiful wife. So many people were waiting to congratulate them that any chance of their being alone was slim, at least for now, but hearing tributes from the heart from his people made it easy to stay.

'It's thrilling to feel part of such a wonderful extended family,' Danny told him. 'I feel closer than ever to this ranch.'

Covering her hand with his, he linked their fingers. 'Are you frustrated?'

Her eyes cleared as she took his meaning, and then she held his gaze and smiled. 'Of course I am.'

Heat swept over him. He wanted her *now*.

'Do you think me too obvious? Too unsophisticated?'

'No. I think you're a normal healthy woman, with a normal healthy appetite.'

He smiled into her eyes, but she pulled back.

'*Deus*, Danny. You look as if I have you by the throat. You can't be frightened of your wedding night?'

'I'm not,' she said, not entirely convincingly.

Putting his arm around her shoulder, he stared into her eyes. 'So if it isn't that, what is it?' He thought of Pintos and the pain she'd suffered. 'You *do* know I'd never hurt you, don't you?'

She laughed—a little sadly, he thought. 'Of course I do. At least not for a year,' she joked, and was soon smiling again.

'You will be secure for the rest of your life,' he reminded her. 'I promise you, Danny, I'll never forget what you've done for me. You will never need to worry again.'

Her eyes clouded. 'Do we have to talk about that now?'

'No.' He slanted a smile. 'What would you rather talk about, *chica*?'

Would Tiago ever understand that this wasn't about the money? Or that she hurt because they had not once said they loved each other? But why should they? It wouldn't be right. It wouldn't be appropriate. She might love Tiago, but even on their wedding day it wouldn't be right to tell him how she felt. They had a contract—nothing more. She had payment. He had the ranch. This wasn't about love. This wedding was for public consumption, to put a seal of approval on the secret they held between them that would bind them together for no more than a year.

She moved restlessly, and was rewarded by the lift of his ebony brow. It didn't help her composure when she wanted him so badly in every way there was. She ached to be held in his arms and made love to in every sense. Their faces were so close she could see the glint of tiger-gold in his eyes, and that look…that darkening slumberous look.

'Is there anything I can do to help you?' he murmured, teasing her into an even higher state of arousal with those words. 'Bearing in mind that we may be here for some time…?'

CHAPTER TEN

HER BODY PULSED with need while her mind screamed at her to hold back. 'Help me with what?' She frowned, pretending ignorance—anything rather than give way to Tiago and be lost.

He shared none of her inhibitions. 'Help you with that ache,' he said frankly, holding her gaze.

'I'm not sure what ache you're talking about.'

'Think back to the jet.'

'Here?'

Now he had shocked her. She was no prude, but what had happened between them in Tiago's bedroom on his private jet couldn't possibly happen here at their wedding party.

His expression grew darker. 'No one will notice,' he said, with the hint of a smile.

'You *are* joking?' Danny answered, looking around the room.

They were somewhat secluded from the other guests, but might be interrupted at any time. The idea was both shocking and thrilling for Danny.

'Am I?' He was already moving her skirts aside. 'Stop finding reasons not to, and concentrate on why you should.' His mouth was still curving wickedly—and so confidently. 'Look at me, Danny,' he murmured. 'Just keep looking at me, and let me do the rest...'

She gasped as his hand found her. It felt so warm and big and strong and sure as he cupped her. Tiago was so wicked, but she couldn't stop herself edging forward just a little to help him. She was already lost, her senses in chaos, and her body was tuned to his smallest touch. She had been well trained by Tiago on the flight over, to respond to pleasure this way, and she instantly concentrated on that one place to the exclusion of everything else.

The noise of the party, the chatter and laughter of their guests, even the band playing loudly, couldn't compete with the thundering of her heart or the rasp of her breathing as Tiago's lightest touch brought wave after wave of pleasure washing over her.

'Tell me to stop if you want to,' he said in a matter-of-fact tone as she lost it completely.

She could only answer him with a soft groan when the fiercest waves had subsided—and then he began to move his hand with more intent. She sucked in a sharp breath as his fingers worked their magic. Tiago knew just what to do, what she liked, and how to administer pleasure in a leisurely fashion, so she could savour every moment and make it last.

His fingers were so sensitive to her needs, so skilful as they went about their work. At first he avoided the place where she needed him most, and teasing her this way made her mad for him. By moving a little further forward in her chair she managed to increase the pressure of his hand, and then he passed his forefinger lightly over her straining clitoris until she gasped—only to moan with disappointment when he pulled away.

'Not for long, *chica*,' he whispered, his breath warm against her face.

His hand quickly found the ribbons holding her bridal thong in place. It was a wisp of lace, nothing more, but he took his time unlooping the bow; unwrapping her slowly, like the revealing of a gift he was in no mood to rush.

'Move to the very edge of the chair,' he instructed, 'and lean back.'

She was quick to do as he said, her excitement intensified by the risk involved as their guests milled all around them.

'There's so much noise no one will notice what you do, but try not to cry out too loudly,' Tiago advised. 'Now, open your legs a little wider for me.'

She opened them as wide as she could, wanting that plump, needy place to be the centre of his universe.

'Oh, yes...'

Excited by the risk, and by the promise in Tiago's lazy tone, she rested back and waited.

'Relax... Enjoy...' he murmured, as if she needed prompting. 'Just leave everything to me.'

Oh, she would... She *would*...

'Ah...' The touch of his slightly roughened finger-pad was exquisite.

'I'll catch you when you fall,' he promised. 'Just keep looking into my eyes and I'll tell you when.'

'You'll *know*?' she somehow managed to gasp out.

'I'll know.'

'Oh...' She grabbed a breath and concentrated.

Tiago's finger was circling repeatedly, maintaining just the right amount of friction... 'Wide,' he reminded her, pressing her legs apart. 'And keep looking at me.'

She grabbed a shuddering breath. 'I'm not sure how long I can hold on...' Her eyes widened as she stared at him.

'I know,' he soothed.

Those eyes—that touch...

She whimpered as he began to rub faster, and with just the right pressure. 'I can't—'

'Then don't,' he said in a different tone. 'Let go now...'

Tiago drowned her cries of pleasure against his chest and held her firmly as she lost control.

'And that's just the start of our wedding night,' he promised, smiling down at her as she sank into his arms.

He strolled back with Danny to the house, making painfully slow progress as everyone who hadn't yet congratulated them seized their chance. He welcomed their good wishes, telling himself that if control was good for him it was even better for Danny.

The women on the ranch had asked him if they could prepare a scented bath for her, and he had agreed, hoping this would please and reassure her. He wouldn't risk anything going wrong now—not with so many witnesses on the ranch. His representative had already left to take the marriage certificate to the lawyers. The ranch was his, thanks to Danny.

When they reached the door he swept her into his arms and carried her across the threshold.

'I didn't know if you would do that,' she said, laughing up at him, her face alive with happiness as he lowered her to her feet

'I don't forget anything where you're concerned. Would you like me to help you out of your dress?'

Suddenly, she was shy. 'If you could just unbutton it for me, please?'

Her voice was tight with nerves.

'Whatever you want.'

This wasn't the Danny he had enjoyed getting to know all over again—the girl who had already become an essential cog in the wheel that was Fazenda Santos. This was a girl who still harboured doubts and it was up to him to resolve them.

He had barely unfastened the last button when she picked up her skirts and fled up the stairs.

'First on the right,' he called after her. 'The women have made a surprise for you.'

She paused and turned, hovering on the stairs. 'Aren't you coming up?'

'Of course I am. This is our wedding night.'

Their eyes locked for a moment, and then she carried on, running to the first floor, while he held back. She reminded him of a wild pony—trapped and uncertain in its new circumstances.

'Take your time…relax,' he called up the stairs.

She disappeared out of sight without answering him.

The silence was heavy in the hall. Maybe that was why the shadow of doubt fell over him. He had been so certain that for this one year he could make Danny happy, and that when that year was over she would have everything she could possibly need and he would be free. But she was proving as elusive as a wisp of smoke that kept slipping through his fingers, which left him in the unique position of wondering if he could hold her for as long as a year.

Danny exclaimed with pleasure when she walked into the bathroom. The women had gone to so much trouble for her, with scented candles and fresh flowers strewn everywhere. She turned full circle, knowing that she didn't deserve this. How could she, when her marriage was a charade? But to waste their preparations for her would be throwing their generosity back in their faces.

Releasing the hem of her dress, she let it fall to the floor and stepped out of it. Climbing into the bath, she sank into the warm, sudsy water and lay back, closing her eyes. She could hear a shower running somewhere close by. When it stopped she pictured Tiago stepping out, grabbing a towel and winding it around his body. She waited a few more seconds and then sat up.

Just in time. The door opened and he was there. Just as she had imagined, his powerful torso was naked, while his body was gleaming and barely dry.

'You're lucky,' he said, smiling as he glanced around her fairy dell. 'The women have really gone to town for you.'

Her heart beat faster as he strolled deeper into the room. He picked up a towel, unfolded it and held it out. She climbed out of the bath, naked and transfixed by his eyes. She had no doubts left. This had nothing to do with the contract. This was what she wanted.

Tiago wrapped her in a towel and lifted her into his arms. He carried her into his bedroom and laid her down on the bed. Unlooping the towel from his waist, he let it drop. The room was silent apart from her breathing. The bed yielded to his weight with a sigh.

His muscles were formidable close up. She had never seen him naked before. His skin was deeply tanned to a rich bronze, and scarred from a lifetime of taking riding to the limits—maybe scarred from his youth too, she remembered, knowing he'd been wild.

She traced his tattoos, those brutal reminders of the Thunderbolts polo team, with an exclamation mark for emphasis—intended, no doubt, to strike fear into the team's opponents. His stubble was thick, his hair was thick too, and his gold earring glinted in the light. He was like no man she'd ever seen before. He was the perfect barbarian. And he was *her* barbarian.

'Slowly, *chica*,' he advised as she pressed against him. 'I'm big and you're small.'

'No...' She smiled cheekily up at him.

But, yes, he *was* big—and she was small by comparison and she loved that. She loved the weight of his erection pressing against her thigh, and exclaimed softly when his hand found her.

'Are you surprised?' she murmured, when he raised a brow at how ready she was.

'Not surprised,' he growled as he moved over her, to start teasing her with his velvet-smooth tip.

'You can't do that,' she complained. 'You can't tease me like that.'

'Really?' He smiled faintly. 'I think you'll find I can.'

A cry escaped her when he probed deeper, but he took his time and waited until he'd built her confidence. Then he moved a little more, a little deeper, stretching her beyond imagining, but his knowing fingers made her forget the shock of it.

'Do you want me?'

'You know I do,' she forced out shakily

'Deep?'

'Yes,' she confirmed.

'Firmly?' Tiago suggested, smiling, his lips brushing hers.

'Please...'

'Now?'

She cried out with pleasure as this big man, who looked so brutal but was so careful with her, took her smoothly until he was lodged deep. Then he rested, giving her a chance to recover from the invasion and catch her breath. She hung on to him, her hands clutching as she gasped with excitement. And then he cupped her buttocks, and that felt so good. It turned her on to think of those big, strong hands controlling her. He lifted her onto him and began to move with regular, dependable strokes, until she was whimpering in time with every one.

She reached her climax fast—too fast—and lost control with a throaty scream of shock. And then she was all melting, soaring, gliding on thunderclaps of sensation.

'More?' Tiago suggested when she was finally reduced to astonished sobs.

'Please...' She only needed that one word in her vocabulary, Danny concluded as she stared into Tiago's eyes.

She pressed her mouth against his shoulder as he began to move again, faster now. She clung on tightly as the primal imperative to move with him, to work with him, claimed her.

'Let me pleasure you,' he encouraged huskily, opening her legs wider still.

'Yes...' she agreed. This was everything she had ever wanted, and it thrilled her all the more to know that Tiago needed her too.

She exclaimed with disappointment when he withdrew, and then laughed when she realised that he was teasing her. When he sank deep again she moaned and pressed her mouth against his neck.

'More?'

'As much as you can give me?' she suggested. Her whole world was sensation now, and he had centred it in that one place.

He thrust deep and pulled out, then thrust deep again. Her heart cried out to him to give her everything, to find his release. Grabbing hold of his buttocks, so firm and muscular, she moved with him. She was demanding now, claiming her mate and moving as strongly as he was with every stroke. They were both ravenous for this, and she could be as fierce as Tiago.

It was only a matter of moments before she felt the pressure building again and, seeing the mist of pleasure reflected in Tiago's eyes, she knew he was close too.

'I'll tell you when,' he cautioned.

'Now,' she said fiercely.

He could do nothing to stop her—to stop himself—as she tightened her muscles around him. They were both lost, both swept up in a fire storm of sensation, and when she found release he did too.

If only she hadn't read the screen on Tiago's computer. She had come downstairs for two glasses of water while Tiago was in the shower, and she hadn't been able to wait to get back to bed. But now she was squatting on the kitchen floor with her arms over her head, pressing—pressing hard—as she tried to make the words on the screen go away.

If she hadn't come down to the kitchen she wouldn't have nudged his computer and the screen wouldn't have flashed on. It was too late now. She'd seen it. And, short minutes after crying with happiness, she had tears of desperation pouring down her face.

She never learned. She always trusted. She always hoped for the best. And now she was a ridiculous bride in a skimpy outfit that one of the young girls had left out for her to wear on her wedding night. The decorated bathroom, with its candles and scent bottles and flowers, had been wasted on her. The women on the ranch had wanted her to feel like a treasured bride, when in fact she was a complete idiot.

Burying her head again, she hugged it harder. But the words on the screen still flashed in front of her eyes.

'You will never hear anything good about yourself if you eavesdrop, Danny,' her grandmother had used to say.

And you wouldn't read anything good about yourself either—as she had just discovered. Tiago had been in the middle of writing an email back to Lizzie when he had broken off—presumably because the gauchos had arrived to escort him to their wedding. And once she had started reading the screen she hadn't been able to stop. She had even scrolled back to read the rest of Lizzie's messages.

It had been about then that she had ended up on the floor. Her legs must have given way as her world had shattered.

It was all lies. Tiago had lied to her by omission.

The subject line on Lizzie's email had been enough without the rest: Chico told me. That sounded so accusatory. What could Chico possibly have told Lizzie to make Danny's best friend so angry?

Reading on, she'd found out.

I know you'll stop at nothing to secure the ranch, because I know *you*, Tiago, but your plan smacks of desperation to me. And if you hurt her—if you force Danny to do anything she doesn't want to do—you might be Chico's friend, but I swear I'll never forgive you.

Danny's *my* friend, and I *will* protect her. You can't marry someone simply because you need a wife and a baby fast. When I challenged Chico about it he said you would keep the child, but not the mother. How *could* you, Tiago? I refuse to believe my friend would agree to this unless you've lied to her—and when she finds out her heart will be broken again.

Please send her home. The work on the roof is nearly finished, so the house is safe to live in, and we'll be back from honeymoon soon. Please tell Danny she always has a home here—

Tiago would keep her baby?

Danny shook her head in desperation. It wasn't so much the fact that Lizzie obviously believed Danny's marriage to Tiago was doomed but the thought of having her child taken from her that had stopped her in her tracks.

Tiago had never mentioned anything about a baby. Even when she had confronted him about the possibility of their having a child he had shrugged it off. No system of birth control was absolutely reliable, and they had used none today, but if Tiago thought he could take her child away from her—he didn't know her at all. She would fight to defend her child to her dying breath.

What was *wrong* with him? The terms of his grandfather's will had been unreasonable. Tiago had acknowledged that. His grandfather had wanted him to found a dynasty that carried his name, but they had both agreed how outdated that was.

Saving the ranch was something she could support—but tearing a child from its mother?

A chill of dread swept over her. Tiago believed he had to comply exactly with the terms of his grandfather's will or risk losing everything: the community he'd built, the wonderful people… Everything he cared about would be destroyed. And she had entered into this arrangement with her eyes wide open. But did an unborn child deserve to be a pawn in their game?

It wasn't going to happen. She wouldn't *let* it happen. She couldn't change him. She had to get that through her head. Tiago's childhood experience had been with utterly selfish parents and he'd built a carapace of steel around his heart. *Her* past had made her determined to survive anything—and she would survive this.

CHAPTER ELEVEN

'DANNY?'

She could hear him coming down the stairs, and his purposeful stride heading towards the kitchen. She was on her feet, leaning over the kitchen counter with her arms braced and her fists planted. She didn't move when he came into the room. She couldn't bear to look at him. She didn't respond in any way.

'Are you okay? Danny—what's wrong?'

Tiago was at her side in moments, still warm and damp from the shower. She could smell soap on him, she registered numbly as she pushed his hand away.

She stepped to one side, but he stood in front of her.

'Speak to me, Danny.' Dipping his head, Tiago searched her eyes.

She turned her face away. 'I think it's better if I don't talk now.'

He straightened up. 'What do you mean?'

'I'm angry, Tiago, and I don't want to say anything in the heat of the moment to make it worse.'

'To make what worse?' he demanded. Raking his hair, he shook his head impatiently. 'I'm in the dark, here. Can you help me?'

Danny didn't know if she could. 'I owe you an apology.'

'What are you *talking* about?' Tiago flared.

'I read your email. I know I shouldn't have, but I came to get us both some water and I nudged your laptop by mistake. The screen flashed on and I read it. I read your exchanges with Lizzie.'

A shiver gripped her as Tiago swore softly under his breath.

'Can you explain them?' she asked quietly. 'Can you tell me why you didn't think to tell me that a baby was part of our deal?'

'You must have known—'

'That there was a possibility I could have a child? Of course I knew. I tried to discuss it with you, but you brushed it off.'

'I didn't brush it off,' he defended.

'Well, let me tell you this, so there can be no misunderstanding. If I'm lucky enough to have a child, no one on this earth is going to rip that child from my arms.'

'Let me explain—'

'You're going to explain *now*?' She shook her head. 'It's too late. Don't you see that? I don't think you were ever going to tell me, Tiago. I think you hoped nature would take its course and that it wouldn't be necessary to tell me that a baby was part of the deal. And then— and I can't imagine how you came to *this* conclusion— you must have thought I'd be content to leave with my money and without my baby at the end of our allotted year. How could you think that, Tiago? Why didn't you say something? Didn't you think I was strong enough to hear the truth?'

'That rubbish in my grandfather's will means nothing. It would never stand up in law.'

'But it must have crossed your mind at some point that it might be a good idea, or why would Chico have mentioned it to Lizzie? Come on, Tiago—say something to make me believe I've misread this, that I've misunder-stood your intentions. *Please!*'

'It was a talking point and nothing more.'

'A *talking point*?'

'It was careless talk with Chico about a ridiculous demand by my grandfather that I had no intention of pursuing.'

'Really? Careless talk?' Firming her lips angrily, she shook her head. 'Would that be "careless talk" back in the days when you were a playboy? Let me see—how many days ago would that be? And I'm supposed to be-lieve you've changed?' She made a contemptuous sound.

'Danny, I *have* changed.'

'Have you, Tiago?'

'You've changed me.'

'I'm supposed to believe that, am I?'

'I would have told you everything—but not today. I didn't want to spoil our wedding day.'

'But you *have* spoiled it. You might as well tell me everything now.'

She twirled the fabulous engagement ring and the jewelled wedding band next to it round and round her finger, until the rings threatened to cut into her skin.

'Shall I summarise for you?' she suggested, when Tiago said nothing. 'You bought me, and you think you've bought any baby I might have too. That's why you gave me so much money. I understand now. It all makes sense. They do it in supermarkets—buy one, get one free.'

'Danny—'

'Well, how would *you* put it?' she flared, her shoulders braced, ready to confront him. 'To add insult to injury, you not only transferred an obscene amount of money into my bank account, you tried to pretend our relation-ship was close to normal with gifts—these rings and that fabulous horse. And to make things even worse I gave *you* gifts—chief amongst which was my heart.'

Almost crying from all the furious emotion inside her, she snatched off the rings and threw them across the counter at him.

'And when I get home I'll be transferring your money back too.'

Tiago snapped alert. 'What are you talking about? When you get home?'

'You can't expect me to stay *now*?'

'I *do* expect you to stay. Of course I do.' His expression grew fierce. 'You're my wife. Where else would you be but with me?' When she laughed incredulously he insisted, 'Come with me, Danny. Come with me now and let me explain.'

'Explain?' She snatched her arm from his grasp. 'I always *knew* this was wrong. Anything you have to say to me can be said right here, right now.'

'This wasn't meant to happen.'

'I'm sure it wasn't,' she agreed.

With an impatient sound, Tiago raked his hair. 'Not tonight—'

'Not ever, I'm guessing.'

'You're wrong, Danny. I know this sounds bad—'

'*Bad?*' she said over him. 'It doesn't just sound bad—it *is* bad. I'm an adult, Tiago, quite capable of making my own decisions, but it would have helped if I'd known *all* the facts before I agreed to this marriage deal. Now let's be clear. I will not involve an innocent child in this. I can't get past that. Any arrangement we might have had is over. I'm going home.'

She held his blazing stare unflinching, certain that neither of them had expected their marriage to end on their wedding night. She was equally sure that Tiago

had never seen her like this before—so cold, so determined, the equal of him. But her childhood hadn't been
so very different from his, and she could switch off *her*
feelings too.

'If you won't allow me to explain, at least let me get
you a robe.'

'Oh, *please*,' she exploded. 'Don't pretend you're concerned about my appearance *now*.'

'But I *am* concerned about you,' Tiago insisted, in a
much more collected tone.

He had realised she was serious about leaving him,
Danny guessed as she gazed down at her flimsy outfit.
It was so inappropriate for what was happening, and it
upset her to think that it had been so carefully chosen
for her by a young girl who had wanted nothing but the
best for Tiago's bride.

'Do I need to be more suitably dressed when you explain your way out of this?' she suggested bitterly.

'For God's sake, Danny— If you'd just listen to me.'

'I have been listening to you. I've heard everything
you've said. It's what you haven't said that's upset me.
You've upset Lizzie—and on her honeymoon too. I
shouldn't have had to read those things, Tiago. I believed
you. I trusted you.'

Moving past him, she snatched his riding jacket down
from the hook on the back of the door and pulled it on.
It drowned her, but the jacket served its purpose in that
it covered her completely.

'You've always been my number one concern, Danny.'

'Save it,' she said coldly. 'I suppose it was only a matter of you choosing the right time to explain?'

'As a matter of fact, it was,' he agreed. 'Husbands
and wives talk. I did say those things to Chico, but that
was when I was still formulating a plan. Of course I was

going to tell you. I knew there was a risk Lizzie might say something, and I knew it was up to me to reassure you that my grandfather's demands were, and are, completely unacceptable.'

'And when would you have done that, Tiago? In the delivery ward? Or one year from today when our contract was at an end?' She shook her head in despair. 'What type of woman do you think I am?'

'It's precisely because of the type of woman you are that I married you. Yes, this started out as a business deal, but you mean so much more to me than that.'

'Lucky me,' she scoffed. 'And now I suppose you *love* me?' She raised a brow. 'Is that what you're saying?'

'Yes, I do,' Tiago admitted quietly.

'How convenient. Let me tell you something, Tiago. There can be no love without trust. And you've destroyed my trust completely. I don't think you have a clue what love is. I think you've shut yourself off from feelings for so long you'll never understand.'

'I didn't want to hurt you.'

'So you were going to sit me down like a little girl to explain? How patronising. And I thought we entered this marriage as equals.'

'We *are* equals.'

'But some are more equal than others, it seems to me,' she said coldly. 'I was a convenient bride. I get that. But don't think any child of mine is going to be a convenient baby.'

'I've never thought that and I never will.' He blocked her way out of the kitchen. 'There is no small print in our contract that you don't know about. There was talk in my grandfather's will of a child, but that was all part of his delusion and cannot be upheld in law.'

'How disappointing for you.'

'Don't,' he said. 'Please don't be bitter and angry. You never used to be like this—'

'You mean I used to be a mug?'

'No!' Tiago exclaimed.

'Just unlucky, then?' she said. 'Maybe I could have swallowed this too, if you hadn't stirred my maternal instincts—but you have. I fell in love with you, Tiago. That was my mistake. I thought this was going to be the best night of my life—not the worst. And, worst of all, I thought I could change you.'

'You *have* changed me.'

'Have I, Tiago?' Drawing in a shaking breath, she lifted her head to look at him. 'Why can't polo players ever be straight with a woman? Are you all too busy and important to consider the feelings of your fellow human beings? Do we exist only for your convenience?'

'If you're referring to Pintos, I'll take that—because I should have been straight with you from the start. But I was trying to protect you, Danny, and I got it wrong. I would have done anything to protect you. Nothing you've read on that screen suggests that I agree with my grandfather. It's old talk. And he can't enforce his demands from the grave. Nor would I allow him to if he were alive today. And in spite of what you must think of him he wasn't a bad man. He'd just fought so hard for what he had, and he'd lost it once. He couldn't bear to lose it again.'

With an exhausted gesture, he shook his head.

'All I can say is that I wish those emails had never been sent, because then I could reassure you. But, whatever you think of me now, I will always protect you. Maybe I went too far this time, but that's only because I love you.'

'You love me? You don't even know the meaning of the word.'

'Stop it, Danny—this is your insecurity. You're not so different from me. We can work this out.'

'Can we? Why drag it out for a year, Tiago? You have the ranch. My job is done. Why keep up the pretence any longer?'

'Because I love you. Because I'm happier than I've ever been.'

'I don't know what to think any more,' Danny admitted. 'I feel as if every time I put down foundations something comes along to shake them loose.'

'Not this time—I promise you,' Tiago insisted fiercely. 'That's your past talking. Just because your mother's never been there for you. That's not me—that's not now.'

Drawing his jacket tightly around her shoulders, she shook her head. 'I can't give you the answer you want. I'm sorry, Tiago. Maybe it *is* my past getting in the way, but I need time to think this through.'

'Danny—'

'Please…' She backed away. 'I need space to think, and I can't think when I'm close to you.'

He slept the rest of the night in the guest bedroom, while Danny slept in his room. He couldn't say he blamed her for doubting him. A lifetime of blanking out his feelings hadn't helped him to handle the situation better. He could have dealt with Danny angry and hot-tempered more easily, but when she'd turned cold, had spoken to him so bleakly, he had known she was right. The past had a lot to answer for, and she did need time.

But he wasn't ready to give up. Swinging out of bed, he showered and dressed, and then knocked on her door.

'Come on. Get up—we're going riding.'

He wasn't even sure she'd heard him, let alone that she would join him. But she did. He should have known

Danny was a survivor, and that she would be every bit as tough this morning as she had been last night, when she had told him what he could do with his gifts and his money.

They saddled up in silence and rode out together. They didn't speak until they reached the river, where he dismounted.

Danny joined him. 'So?' she said.

'So,' he echoed, staring out across the river. 'When are you leaving?'

'Soon.'

He ground his jaw, but acknowledged this. 'This is not how I expected to spend the first day of my married life—but then I didn't expect to get married at all,' he admitted. 'My parents put me off marriage when I was a child, with their shouting and squabbling over what was left of my grandfather's money.'

'You were put off marriage until you were forced to marry. Isn't that it, Tiago?'

'Yes,' he admitted bluntly.

'Were you hunting for a bride at Lizzie's wedding, when I practically ran into you?'

'You were so angry and shocked—I seem to remember you almost knocked me over. You would probably have liked to, anyway. As for hunting for a bride... Yes, I did scan the pool for likely candidates, and you were close to the top of my list.'

'Only close?' Danny said dryly, staring out across the river.

'I judged you too vulnerable to be drawn into my plan.'

'And now, Tiago?' She swung around to face him, but there was no warmth in her eyes.

'I was wrong about you,' he admitted. 'I should have known you were strong enough to take up any challenge.'

'And more than willing,' she remembered, smiling faintly.

He made no comment.

'And then I made the mistake of falling in love with you. We got close so fast that even our crazy wedding made sense.'

'It wasn't so fast,' he argued, frowning. 'We were close in Brazil.'

'Friends,' she conceded. 'You liked teasing me.'

'Yes, I did. And, as I remember it, you liked it too.'

She shrugged, slanting him a smile, but refused to comment.

'My grandfather was delusional, Danny. Don't you think after the childhood I experienced I would want to do something better for my children? I certainly wouldn't risk any child of mine growing up thinking I'd *bought* it. And you...' He paused and looked at her steadily. 'You're a very special woman, and someone I'm proud to call my wife.'

'If you could pull out of our deal, though, would you?'

He frowned. 'This is no longer a deal, Danny.'

'But it still feels like one to me.'

'So what can I do to change that?'

'I don't know,' she said honestly. 'I've never wanted anything from you in the material sense, but it was part of the deal. Maybe I can't live with that. Maybe my problem is with me and my judgement, not you. My only thought was to secure my mother's future and buy my own establishment. I couldn't see further than that. I didn't once think about the true cost...'

'You wanted to spread your wings,' he argued hotly. 'There's nothing wrong with that, and you still can. You want to taste adventure? It's right here.'

He had thought he was getting through to her, but instead of moving towards him she moved back towards her horse and mounted up.

'I need more,' she said softly. 'I need to prove myself before I have anything to offer you.'

He opened his arms in a gesture of surrender. 'You're so wrong. You don't have to prove anything to me. But, please, keep the money. You're going to need it if you go. Take it for your mother—make her secure. Give yourself a future, Danny.'

'I wanted you,' she said. 'I wanted your love. I wanted a life together.'

'And you can have it.'

'But how can I be sure that there won't be another time when you hide something from me in the mistaken belief that you're protecting me?'

'You can't,' he said bluntly, resting his hand on the neck of her horse. 'I won't commit to a promise I'm not certain I can keep. If you need protecting I'm going to do that, whatever you have to say about it.'

He tensed as she turned her horse for home.

'So you're just going to give up? You're not even going to fight for us?'

'For *us*?' she said, gathering up her reins. 'There is no "us", Tiago. There never has been. And, as you say, I have a life to lead and so do you.'

'But I love you.'

Tiago loved her. But her own feelings were in turmoil. She owed it to both of them to sort herself out... Would this *ever* work out?

'At least think it through,' Tiago insisted. 'You don't have to go right away. You've been just as cut off from emotion as I have, but if the last half-hour is anything to go by we've unlocked something in each other. Don't throw that away, Danny.'

She'd hurt him and she didn't know how to make it right, Danny thought as Tiago brought his horse alongside hers. She blamed herself. She should never have agreed to such a cold-blooded agreement. It had never been going to turn out well. She should have been content to stay where she was, with her heart in one piece.

'Where will you go? What will you do?' he said.

'I'll go back to Scotland and get a job.'

'Your qualifications are excellent,' Tiago agreed, as if he thought it was a good idea—or was that her insecurity talking again? 'With your experience it shouldn't be hard to find work. But don't settle for just anything.'

'Stop worrying about me, Tiago. My decisions aren't all flawed. I'll rebuild my life and move forward.'

'I have no doubt you will, but I can't see how going back to Rottingdean is moving forward.'

'Maybe you're right. But I'm never going backwards again.'

CHAPTER TWELVE

HE RODE OUT with his collar turned up against the persistent drizzle, his jaw tightly clenched at the prospect of returning to an empty house.

Why hadn't he filed a flight plan? Any day without Danny was a damp, drizzly day, and she had been gone for over a month. In all that time no one had asked him about his missing bride. No one had dared to question him.

He had dealt with the yawning gap in his life by working longer hours and playing more polo. He had made improvements to the ranch and that had made him even angrier, wondering if Danny would like what he'd done. What did anything matter now?

She would always matter.

His security team had reported that, preferring to stand on her own feet rather than return to her old job at Rottingdean, Danny was now working as a Jack of all trades at a local stable close by the house in Scotland where she had worked for Lizzie's family. He respected Danny's wish to find herself, to be her own person, but respect didn't mean he was giving up on their relationship.

Yes. *Relationship.* They might have been married for only five minutes, but the bond between them was stron-

ger than any piece of paper they had signed to silence his
grandfather's lawyers.

Reining in, he turned for home. If he cared so much
about Danny why was he still here?

He piloted the jet, but even he couldn't make it fly
faster. He swore viciously at the thought of the time he'd
wasted. But they were both stubborn, and Danny was
still locked in the past. He appreciated that she needed
time, but when had he ever hesitated before when he'd
cared about something as much as this? He should have
told her every detail from the start. Then she would not
only have known the facts, she would also have known
how he intended to deal with them. Instead he had tried
to protect her, when what Danny needed was love and
respect—not coddling.

He touched down in Scotland and leapt into the four-
wheel drive he'd hired. He didn't wait. He didn't rest. He
didn't sleep. Anticipation at the thought of seeing Danny
was all it took to keep him wide awake.

He drove straight from the airport to the farm where
she was working. He might have guessed it would be in
a remote glen. Was she going to hide away here for the
rest of her life?

His heart gripped tight when he spotted her. He hadn't
expected it to be so easy, but she was working with a
young colt in an outdoor arena. He climbed out of the vehicle and stood watching. He smiled, noticing how much
she had learned from his training methods. He felt good
about that, though standing back like this was an acute
type of torture. And it was no more than he deserved.

The rampaging polo player the press talked about—
the man who collected women like fine wine, drank
deep and moved on—was in love. He'd only had to see

Danny again to know how deeply he loved her. His life was meaningless without her. He'd missed her every waking hour, and had lain awake each night thinking about her.

There'd been gossip since they'd parted. He couldn't expect the press to ignore the facts. *'Marriage is not for Tiago Santos!'* one of the reporters for a red-top had crowed, no doubt rejoicing in his misery. Danny must have read that article. And, yes, their marriage was unusual, but Danny wasn't just any bride—she was *his* bride. She was the only bride he could ever want. The only *woman* he would ever want.

He tensed as she stilled, and wondered if she'd sensed him. Whatever Danny liked to think, they were keenly tuned to each other. Did she know he'd come to find her?

She turned slowly and stared straight at him. The wealth of feeling inside him as their stares held was indescribable. He stood motionless, absorbing every detail of her as she turned back to the pony and, saying something, stroked its ears. Leaving the arena, she closed the gate and walked towards him. With every step she took he grew more certain that they belonged together, and that he would do anything it took to make this right.

He slanted her a smile as she walked up to him. 'How are you?'

'Good.'

She was pale, he thought as she studied his face intently.

'How are you, Tiago?'

'I'm fine.'

She didn't sound fine, and instead of taking the single step that would bring her into his arms she remained a few paces back, staring at him as if she couldn't believe her eyes.

'What brings you to the Highlands?'

Her voice, with its soft Scottish burr, rolled over him like a familiar pleasure—one he'd missed more than he could say. He had never felt so alert or more aware of Danny, more *alive*.

'I'm visiting old friends.'

'Chico and Lizzie?' She frowned. 'I didn't realise there were any upcoming polo matches.'

'Do I need an excuse?'

'So you've come here to train with Chico?' she guessed, searching his face.

'I'm here to see *you*, Danny.'

She collected her breath quickly and exhaled raggedly. Her breath clouded in front of her face as they faced each other.

'I've stayed away for as long as I'm prepared to.'

'I thought we agreed—?'

'I didn't agree to anything,' he cut in. 'You left me. Remember? You wanted time to get your head together. I've given you time.'

'Are you here because of what they've started saying about us in the press?'

'Don't insult me.'

Biting her lip, she replied, 'They're saying our marriage was on the rocks before it began. But if you think I started that rumour—'

'I don't think that. And I'm not worried about what people think. Our marriage is our business. And, before you ask, no one can touch the ranch. The deeds are in my vault and that's where they will stay. So, you see, I am no longer in the market for a "convenient bride".'

She smiled a little, hearing her own words thrown back at her. 'So why are you here?'

'We've been apart long enough. Everyone on the ranch

misses you. Lizzie and Chico wonder why they don't see more of you. You've shut yourself away here. Lizzie misses you, Annie misses you—*Deus*, Danny, *I* miss you.'

He hadn't realised how much.

'Come back to us,' he said softly.

She remained silent and he looked around the rundown farm, with its broken fencing, peeling paintwork and neglected yard.

'I don't know what this proves. You must be working an eighteen-hour shift just to keep things on an even keel here.'

She firmed her jaw, but didn't deny anything he'd said.

'No one doubts you can stand on your own two feet, but why isolate yourself like this? Why are you punishing yourself, Danny?'

'I'm making a life,' she said simply. 'And I'm doing it without your money. I'm sure Lizzie understands why I must do this.'

'Lizzie might understand, but it doesn't stop her worrying about you. Is that fair? I don't understand you, Danny. I don't understand why you've separated yourself from people who care so much about you. I don't understand why you're pushing us all away.'

'You've no right to discuss me with Lizzie.'

'I've got every right. We care about you. Is that such an alien concept to you?'

'It is where you're concerned. I've never known you to express your feelings before.'

'And you're so open with *yours*?'

She turned, restless, uncertain, hovering, as if she wanted to go but also wanted to stay. 'Thank you for coming to see me,' she said at last. 'I do appreciate your concern—'

'For God's sake, Danny, I'm not the local doctor. I'm your *husband*.'

'Of one night,' she said. 'And I know this farm doesn't look much, but I enjoy my work here.'

'You'd enjoy any job with a horse attached to it. Is this a permanent position?'

Lifting her chin, she peeled off her riding gloves and blew onto her cold red hands. 'Nothing's permanent— is it, Tiago?'

Shaking his head, he ignored the jibe. At any other time he would have seized those hands and put them inside his jacket, so his blood could heat hers, but Danny was like an edgy colt that might bolt if he made any sudden movement.

Undaunted, he asked, 'How about lunch in town?'

She looked at him as if he were mad.

He shrugged. 'I'm hungry. It's nearly lunchtime. And it's far too cold to hold our reunion here.'

'But what would we have to talk about?'

He had to remind himself that he had vowed to take this slowly.

'I'm sure we'll think of something.'

The only possible reason she could come up with for sitting in the sedate hush of the Rottingdean tea rooms with a barbarian, whose face was coated in thick black stubble and whose brilliant smile made the elderly waitress primp and simper, was that it wasn't possible to ignore her husband when he was in town. Tiago had come all the way from Brazil, she reminded herself, and she owed him the common courtesy of a conversation—if only in the hope that they could find some sort of closure.

'Do you *have* to do that?' she demanded—an unreasonable demand, she registered a split second after the words left her mouth, as Tiago removed his jacket.

Just revealing the powerful spread of his shoulders was enough for her awareness of him to soar into the stratosphere. She would challenge anyone to spend the night with Tiago and then just blank it from their mind.

'You take it off, laddie,' one of the elderly waitresses advised, endorsing Danny's opinion that in this sun-starved land Tiago Santos was a rare treat. 'You'll never feel the benefit when you go outside if you don't take your jacket off,' she commented approvingly, and a dozen or so more women turned their heads to stare at the splendid sight of Tiago, whose powerful frame was clad in the finest black Scottish cashmere.

With a warm smile at the waitress, Tiago raised a brow as he turned to Danny.

'You wanted to hear about my place of work?' She judged that a safe enough topic to start off with.

'Go ahead.' Smiling faintly, he looked down as he attempted to ease his legs beneath the dainty table without sending it crashing to the floor.

'You're too big for here,' she said as she steadied the teapot.

'Too big for civilised company?'

She buried her face in her teacup.

'So?' he pressed with a faint strand of amusement in his voice when she failed to answer him. 'This farm where you're working…?'

'It's a tenancy,' Danny revealed, looking up now they were back on safe ground. 'The landlord lives off-site. He owns several similar properties, and he has asked if I would consider managing all of them for him.'

'Has he indeed?' Tiago's jaw tightened.

'There's no need to sound so suspicious. He's old

enough to be my grandfather and due to retire any time now. More tea?'

Tiago's eyes narrowed at her prim tone, drawing her attention to the fact that he was twice the size of any man in the tea room. His hair was thicker, blacker, wavier and more unruly. And you could take it as a flat-out fact that there wasn't another man in the place wearing a gold earring. Local skin was blue-white—freckled, in her case—while Tiago's skin was swarthy, and she was quite sure there wasn't a man in a fifty-mile radius who could boast anything close to his physique.

'I feel like a giant, trying to fit my frame into this chair.'

She was forced to smile when he eased his position gingerly. 'You'll break it if you move too suddenly,' she warned.

Dipping his head, he stared up at her in a way that sent heat to every part of her body. It was impossible to remain immune to Tiago's particular brand of charm, and impossible to forget how it felt to be held in his arms. And now every woman in the place was staring at him.

'I won't catch you if you fall,' she warned him when he tipped his chair back.

'You've already caught me, *chica.*'

Tiago's murmur and that black stare fixed onto hers made her think of one thing only—and it wasn't tea.

'Are you ready to go?' he said.

She was about to leave when the bell tinkled over the door and Hamish, the gamekeeper, and his crew walked in. She was glad of the distraction, and surprised when Hamish acknowledged Tiago as if they were old friends—but then she remembered that they would have met at Chico's.

'Are you okay, Danny?' Hamish asked gruffly.

'Yes. Thank you.'

After the two men had exchanged greetings, and Hamish had gone to find a table, Tiago turned to her. 'Come to dinner with me tonight.'

'I'm sorry?'

'You will be if you refuse me,' he threatened with a wicked smile.

She gave him a warning look that didn't deter him at all. 'Are you asking me out?'

'That's exactly what I'm doing,' Tiago confirmed.

His lips pressed down, drawing her attention to the fact that he was badly in need of a shave—as usual. Imagining that stubble scraping her skin was a breath-stealing reminder of how it had felt when he kissed her.

'It's harmless,' he said. 'We're married, and I'm in town.'

Nothing was harmless where Tiago was concerned, but she couldn't bring herself to let him go yet. 'I have to eat, and so do you. Why not?'

Why not? She could think of a thousand reasons why not. Discarding them all, she allowed her imagination to run riot for a moment... Screaming with pleasure in Tiago's arms would be preferable to sitting across a table from him...

'Danny?'

She pulled herself round fast and smiled into his eyes. 'So you're asking me out on a *date*?'

Tiago frowned slightly. 'I suppose I am.' But his eyes were dancing with laughter too.

It would be all right. She would confine herself to chatting about people they knew. She would keep the conversation, as well as everything else, on safe ground.

'Stop frowning, Danny. It's a meal and a catch-up, and then I'll take you home.'

Now she just had to convince herself that that was exactly what she wanted. 'That sounds good,' she agreed. 'Yes,' she said softly.

Tiago smiled his bad-boy smile. 'You *do* know that a candlelit dinner is usually a prelude to sex?'

'If you think that's going to tip the balance—' She stopped, noticing that the respectable townsfolk at the tables surrounding them were listening in with avid interest.

'I think they like me,' Tiago murmured, with amusement in his dark eyes.

She sucked in a sharp breath as he lifted her hand to his lips.

'Stop,' she warned him, pulling her hand back. 'I've agreed to supper—nothing more.'

'That's all I'm offering,' Tiago assured her. 'Sex isn't on the menu tonight.'

Now she was hit by doubt. *Why* didn't he want sex? Had Tiago found someone else? She felt sick at the thought.

'If this is another of your games...'

Leaning across the table until their faces almost touched, he whispered, 'The only game I play is polo.'

'Is it?' She was still tense.

'Although I do have a repertoire of games that don't require a horse and a mallet to make them fun.'

She made an incredulous sound as Tiago sat back with a confident smile on his face. He continued to regard her steadily, his amused black stare warming her, and even when he looked away to call for the bill a sweet pulse of desire throbbed deep inside her.

CHAPTER THIRTEEN

DANNY WAS ALWAYS CALM, always measured—at least that was what she told herself—except for tonight, when she was catapulting from one side of her room to the other, trying on clothes and trying to decide how she should wear her hair.

Finally she stood back, arms folded, wondering how it was possible for one person to buy so many sale rejects in the hope that one day she would find just the right accessory to pull the hopelessly mismatched set of items together. She had never pulled an outfit together in her life. She had always been a tomboy in jeans.

And she had around five minutes before Tiago was due to arrive to pick her up and take her to supper.

Why had she left things to the last minute?

She blamed it on the shortbread.

In the spirit of keeping things platonic, and to show Tiago some true Scottish hospitality, she had used her small worktop oven and her grandmother's secret recipe—sure to melt all but the stoniest heart—to bake him a tray of the traditional Scottish cookies, so he didn't think she was accompanying him tonight solely in the expectation of a free meal.

Tied up with a tartan ribbon, the small cellophane

packet was a humble offering, but it was the best she'd been able to come up with in the time available.

Tiago took a shower, shaved, and tamed his hair in as much as it could be tamed. He even put on a jacket and tie with his jeans for the occasion. He checked himself over in the mirror. He looked like an undertaker. Ruffling his hair, he ditched the tie, opened a couple of buttons at the neck of his shirt and tugged on a sweater. *Better.*

Danny was waiting for him in the biting cold outside her front door. Because she didn't want him to see where she lived, he suspected. The farm seemed even more dilapidated and unappealing to him on second viewing. He didn't like the thought of her living here on her own.

'You didn't have to wait out here.' He ushered her towards the four-wheel drive

'I didn't want to keep you waiting,' she said, standing back as he opened the door for her. 'Where are we going?'

'I can't say.'

'You can't say or you won't say?'

He smiled. 'You decide.'

'Maybe I won't come with you.'

'You'll come,' he said confidently. 'You never could resist an adventure.'

He would forgive her anything tonight. Just the fact that she had gone to some trouble with her appearance was enough for his groin to tighten with appreciation— though he would take her straight from mucking out a stable if he had to. Fortunately, that wasn't necessary. Her hair was shining and she was wearing the familiar wildflower scent, and make-up—just a touch, but enough to suggest she wasn't completely switched off.

'You'd better not be teasing me with this supper,' she warned him, frowning in a way that made him want to grab her close and kiss her hard. 'You tell me where we're going or I'm not moving another step.'

Maybe the signs weren't *all* good, he amended, hiding his amusement. 'I'm taking you somewhere new.'

'Tiago,' she said patiently, 'there is nowhere new. This is the Highlands of Scotland, where nothing has changed for a thousand years.'

His lips curved with amusement, but he wouldn't be drawn. Strolling round to the driver's side, he got into the vehicle.

'Where *is* this?' Danny demanded a short time later, as he swung the wheel to turn the four-wheel drive onto a recently resurfaced driveway lined with majestic snow-frosted pines.

'You tell me. You've lived in Rottingdean all your life—where nothing ever changes,' he reminded her dryly.

'But this place has been derelict for years.' She frowned as she stared out of the window.

'Not any longer.'

'When did it become a hotel?'

'Never, as far as I'm aware.'

She turned ninety degrees to stare at him. 'What do you mean?'

'I live here. At least I'm planning to spend a good part of the year here.'

A stunned silence greeted this remark.

'I apologise if this comes as a shock to you, Danny, but as you haven't been talking to me lately...' He shrugged. 'It's better that you know. I can hardly be your neighbour and spend time at a house down the road without you noticing at some point.'

'Let me get this straight. Are you telling me that you've bought the Lochmaglen estate?'

'And the whisky distillery.'

'You're going into business here?' Danny's eyes widened.

'I like Scotch.'

'Tiago!'

'Lochmaglen will form part of my business empire, but I won't allow any investment to be a drain on my finances. Everything I put money into has to earn its keep.'

'Is that what you thought about me?' she asked him lightly.

'You sent the money back.'

'Yes, I did.' She sounded pleased about that.

Tiago continued without comment. 'I mostly bought this place for the excellent pasture—or it will be excellent once I've reclaimed it from the weeds. I'm going to build a new training facility for my horses.'

'But you've got excellent training facilities in Brazil.'

'On the other side of the world,' he pointed out. 'But now I'm setting up in Scotland—to service my European interests.'

This made perfect sense to him, but Danny was shaking her head.

'Don't think I'm coming to work for you. I'm very happy where I am.'

'Good,' he said flatly. 'You couldn't have said anything to please me more.'

Was that a flash of disappointment on her face?

'Ah, there's Annie!' he exclaimed as he stopped the vehicle at the foot of the steps leading up to the sturdy front door of the ancient manse.

Hamish's wife, Annie, the housekeeper at Rottingdean, had offered her services for the night, and was standing ready on the steps, waiting to welcome them.

'You leave no stone unturned, do you, Tiago?' Danny threw at him as she waved at Annie.

'No,' he admitted. 'Annie's missed you. It's time you two were brought together. So, what do you think I have in mind for tonight?'

She firmed her jaw and refused to answer.

'You do remember what *isn't* on the menu for tonight?'

'Sex,' she said, turning her cool stare on his amused face.

'That's right.' Tiago's mouth curved in a smile. 'Whatever you want, whatever you need—you're not going to get it tonight.'

'You are such an arrogant barbarian.'

'But you knew that from the start.'

'What makes you think—?'

'Danny, please…' He gave her a look and saw her eyes darken. 'We should go in. Annie's waiting to spoil you.'

'I don't need spoiling.'

'Don't you?' He reached across to open her door and paused. 'You've got shadows under your eyes. Have you been working all hours?'

'What's it to you?'

She turned away, shutting him out. He'd done his research and knew without her telling him that she was trying to shore up a failing stable on her own, with no financial input from the landlord whatsoever. Danny was too proud to take money from anyone—even when she'd earned it. She'd seen difficulty and hardship, and instead of turning her back had responded by throwing her heart and soul into the job. No wonder she looked so tired. She had to be exhausted.

'What are your hours?' he demanded as he helped her down from the four wheel drive

'Whatever's required,' she said.

He believed her.

'I'm building a nest egg. Remember that?'

'You're not going to build it at that place—there's not even the money to pay you a fair wage.'

She didn't answer this.

Taking hold of her hand, he helped her down. She let go of him at the first opportunity.

'I hope I'm dressed appropriately tonight?'

He smiled. She never could resist making a teasing barb. He took it as a good sign.

'You're dressed perfectly.'

However tired she was, Danny would always look beautiful to him. However limited her budget, she looked like a queen. Tonight, in a simple dress of moss-green wool, and a pair of shoes that—well, the best that could be said for them was that they weren't riding boots—she had a natural elegance that would put the society women he'd used to date to shame.

'Let's get one thing straight,' she said at the foot of the steps.

'By all means,' he said pleasantly.

'I only agreed to come to supper with you tonight be-cause—'

'Because...?' He prompted with an amused stare.

'Because you're a stranger in town, and because it would be rude to ignore you.'

'Extremely rude, considering you're my wife,' he agreed. 'Come on. Let's not keep Annie waiting.'

Annie swept Danny into a hug, and then chivvied her up the steps and into the welcoming warmth beyond the sturdy front door.

'I've prepared you both a lovely supper and left it in the library, where you'll be snug,' the housekeeper was telling Danny breathlessly as she ushered them down the newly redecorated hall.

Tiago followed the two women into the library, glad to see them so close and Danny so happy. Asking Annie to come was a masterstroke. Danny had relaxed instantly in the older woman's company.

'This is a beautiful room,' she said, turning to him now.

'Thank you.'

He was very proud of the library. He had dreamed of a room like this—of the adventures contained within the covers of a book—ever since he was a child, and had created a library exactly to that dream design. He'd recoiled at his designer's suggestion that he buy books 'by the yard', and had handpicked each one and had them shipped to Scotland.

The room was perfection, in his eyes, and never more so than now, with a fire burning lustily in the hearth, a feast prepared by Annie spread out on the table, and the woman he loved standing in the centre of the room. gazing around with wonder at the walls filled with books.

Yes. He loved her—more than anything on this earth.

'I can't believe how stupid I was not to realise all this was going on down the road!'

'Not stupid,' he argued as Annie smiled and left them to it. 'My people are the best, and they were under strict instructions not to create any upheaval with their heavy vehicles in the village—and I didn't exactly run a banner across the sky.'

'But still,' she argued, running her hand across the newly refurbished mantelpiece. 'You've restored everything to its original state. This is wonderful, Tiago.'

'I'm glad you like it.'

He had wanted to bring the old place back to life again, and now Danny was standing here he felt he had succeeded. The library was large and airy, with French doors leading out onto the newly reformed gardens, and there was a large oak table in the centre of the room, where he could sit and spread out his papers, but it was Danny who held his attention now.

As she shook her head in surprise at one new discovery after another her hair caught the light and gleamed as if it were coated with gold dust. All the suspicion had gone from her face and all that was left was happiness. He could almost believe they had never been apart.

'What?' he asked as her head shot up and she turned round to look at him.

'I'm such a fool. I almost forgot.'

'Will you stop saying that? You are *not* a fool,' he insisted as she hurried back to the chair where she'd left her bag. Goodness knew what her mother had called her in the past, but he could imagine.

She delved inside her bag and rummaged around, before handing him a scrunched-up pack of biscuits. Taking care not to touch his hand, she said, 'I'm afraid they're a bit broken, but I made them for you. It's traditional Scottish shortbread. We hand it out to visitors to encourage them to come back.'

'Is that what you're doing now, Danny?'

Her cheeks flushed red as he stared into her eyes. Her gift thrilled him. He had been given a full-blood Arabian stallion by the daughter of a sheikh, and a watch beyond price by a princess—both of which he had returned. Well, he had bought the horse for a fair price later, at auction… But nothing in his life had meant more to him than this packet of broken biscuits.

Broken? They looked as if they had been pulverised between Danny's wringing hands.

'You *do* eat carbs?' she asked worriedly.

He raised an amused brow. 'Please...'

'Okay.' She risked a smile. 'Only some sportsmen—'

Danny had stopped talking, as if something in his face had made her think he was going to kiss her. It was sad to think his wife knew so little about him—but then they were both to blame for that.

'We should eat,' he said, moving away to give her space. 'Annie's made a feast for us. I'll show you round later, if you like?'

'I'd like...' Danny's brows drew together, as if she was trying to figure him out. 'If this library is anything to go by, I suspect you've worked wonders on the rest of the house.'

'You can judge for yourself after supper.'

She had seriously underestimated the effect of being close to Tiago after having spent so much time apart from him. When he didn't look at her, her heart thundered with disappointment. And when he did look at her she could hardly breathe. And through all this she was supposed to appear cool and detached...

It shouldn't be hard, when Tiago was so calm, but keeping her own counsel was proving almost impossible when she longed to ask him about so many things. Like what was left between them now Tiago no longer needed a wife?

Maybe the answer was in his manner. He was behaving more like an old friend keen to show her round his new house than a lover—let alone a husband. She would just have to adapt to this new situation between them, and fall into a similar role.

* * *

They took the tour after supper. He had to try very hard not to notice the soft dark green wool stretching over the plump swell of Danny's buttocks as she walked in front of him, or her nipples pressing against the soft fabric through the fine lace of her bra. He concentrated instead on his wife's animated face and the brilliance of her eyes, and relished the fact that it was thanks to Danny that he had learned so much about himself. He knew now that he wasn't wholly gaucho *or* playboy, but a man determined to do his best. And if that meant curbing his playboy ways...

'I like you here,' Danny murmured as she looked around his home. 'You seem more real.'

He laughed. 'Do you mean I'm a hologram in Brazil?'

'No. A barbarian,' she said without hesitation.

'Would you have me any other way?'

From the blush on her cheeks, he guessed not.

She started making thoughtful comments about the décor, but all he could think about was taking her to bed, pleasuring her through the night, and not even bothering to muffle her screams of pleasure.

Yes, he had aimed for discreet but sumptuous country casual, he agreed distractedly. And, yes again, he was glad she approved of the colour scheme. But frankly he wasn't interested in jewel colours and expensive art when he had a living, breathing work of art standing in front of him, waiting to be undressed.

'Nothing too obviously billionaire chic?'

He laughed at her comment. 'I suppose you could say that.'

'So, who did you use?'

He frowned. He knew whose *body* he'd like to use— right after he'd pleasured it into a state of erotic euphoria. 'No one.'

Her gaze dropped to his lips. 'You mean you designed this all by yourself?'

'All except the library. Would you like to see the rest of it?' He led the way to the stairs.

'Why not?'

CHAPTER FOURTEEN

Tiago's bedroom was full of mellow wood and rich coloured drapes—a necessity in the Highlands, where the wind could be cruel and even well-insulated houses could be gripped in a frozen chill for months on end. There were tasteful accessories in a variety of muted honey colours, and crisp white linen on the bed. Two elegant lamps stood one either side of the bed on nightstands covered in books.

Feeling him close behind her, she turned and almost collided with him. From the way he was looking at her it was as if he knew everything she had been thinking... dreaming. Gathering herself quickly, she ignored the glint of understanding, and, yes, even humour in his eyes.

'Are you ready to go home, Danny?'

The way he was prompting her didn't leave her with much option. He had even stood back to clear her way to the door.

'Thank you for showing me around.' She sketched a smile. She couldn't pretend she wasn't disappointed that the evening was over so soon, but what had she expected? 'You have a beautiful home,' she said truthfully. 'I wish you every happiness living here. And in Brazil too, of course.'

He escorted her to the door and helped her on with

her jacket. He'd been the perfect gentleman throughout the entire evening. She knew she shouldn't hope for anything more, but having Tiago back in her life, even in a new way, was disturbing…upsetting. He was a complex man who demanded life on his own terms—as she demanded life on *her* terms. How had she ever imagined they could meet in the middle?

They couldn't, she concluded as Tiago helped her into the car and closed the door.

Why had he bought a Scottish estate? It couldn't be Chico's influence. No one influenced Tiago. She could understand him falling in love with the Highlands. Who wouldn't? This rugged setting was a scenic feast and, as he'd said, this was a perfect base for him. But how would she feel with her estranged husband living down the road? What if he found someone else? What if Tiago had children with that person? Could she look on and feel nothing?

'Are you all right?' he asked, flashing a concerned glance at her after a long silence.

'Yes. Thank you.' If he had been trying to jolt her into feeling passionately about him—about life, about everything—he couldn't have planned this evening better. And now she couldn't resist asking him… 'How long do you think you'll spend here each year?'

'That all depends.'

She waited, but Tiago revealed nothing more. His attention was fixed on the icy road. How could they have become so distant? Had she really thought she could handle this? How wrong she'd been.

'We'll go riding on the estate tomorrow.'

Her head shot up, but then she remembered her job. 'I'm afraid I can't.'

'Your work?'

'Yes.'

'You can take time off. I've spoken to your employer.'

She frowned. 'You didn't think to ask me first?'

'Forgive me.'

Tiago was mocking her a little bit, but she would forgive him anything for one of those smiles.

'It was a spur-of-the-moment impulse,' he admitted.

'You can't just walk back into my life and take over.'

'Shall I see you to your front door?' he asked, unfazed by this.

'That's not necessary—'

Ignoring her, he came round anyway and helped her out of the car. His touch was electric. She pulled back, still annoyed at the thought of her employer's likely reaction when a world-famous polo player had knocked on his door, demanding that one of his staff have time off.

'Thank you very much for tonight,' she said formally, turning to face Tiago at the front door. 'But please don't interfere in the life I'm making here in future.'

Inclining his head in a way that might have meant yes, or no, he smiled. Taking the key from her hand, he opened the front door. She flinched when he took hold of her shoulders, and then softened beneath his touch. She couldn't help herself. Her reaction was automatic. The bond between them could survive anything, and nothing she could do or think would change that.

'Goodnight, Danny...' Dipping his head, Tiago brushed a chaste kiss against her cheek.

'Goodnight...'

Her stomach clenched with disappointment as he walked away.

He stood beneath a shower turned to ice, and then rubbed himself down roughly before falling naked into bed.

Cursing viciously, he punched the pillows. Turning this way and that, he felt like a frustrated wolf that would be better off howling at the moon.

He'd get no sleep tonight. Seeing Danny again had thrown him completely. He had thought he was ready for it—ready for *her*—and that the time for their reunion had come and he'd be able to handle it. Now he wasn't sure of anything—except that his love for her had grown. And he wanted her more than ever.

Every wasted second was a second too long. He was in the most acute agony of his life. Mental frustration and physical frustration had combined to torture him.

He turned restlessly as his cell phone pinged. Picking it up, he scanned the number, then closed it down. He would not talk to Danny tonight—not over the phone. Nothing but having her in bed beside him would do. They belonged together.

But he'd waited for her this long and he could wait a little longer. What was pain?

He rejoiced in her strength, and in the fact that she had built a life for herself here. He even, however begrudgingly, had to admit that she was doing very well without him. So whatever she wanted from him tonight would have to wait until tomorrow morning.

The air was blue by the time Danny had pulled the bed-covers up to her chin. How *dared* Tiago come back into her life and interfere?

Had he found someone else?

Why else would he be so distant with her?

Had he lost all feeling for her?

Clearly he had.

How dared he refuse to take her call? She had wanted to warn him off one last time.

She had wanted to hear his voice before falling asleep.

How dared he speak to her employer without her express permission?

She took out her frustration on the pillow.

And how was everyone on the ranch?

Why hadn't he told her? Did that mean she was never going to see them again?

She picked up the phone to call him again but it went straight to voicemail. Again!

Damn the man! She didn't need him anyway!

She didn't need anyone!

Burying her head between the pillows, as if Tiago might hear her noisy sobs of anger and frustration, failure, longing and loneliness all the way over at the big house at Lochmaglen, she dragged the jacket of her flannelette pyjamas a little closer and curled up tightly in a ball.

She must have fallen asleep almost immediately, but woke feeling as if she hadn't slept at all. She had been dreaming about Tiago all night, Danny realised groggily. She'd been telling him how glad she was that he was back. And then they'd made love. She would never forget that dream. Her body would never forget that dream. She would always remember Tiago kissing her as if they'd spent a lifetime apart, rather than a matter of weeks. And then, when they had been resting, she'd told him she loved him, and Tiago had said he loved her too.

Dreams!

And now she had work to do. But first she had to speak to her employer and reassure him that she wouldn't be taking any time off—contrary to whatever he might have been told by their new and forceful neighbour.

She showered and dressed, and then ate breakfast. With a piece of buttered toast clamped between her teeth she hurried over to the stable block, and soon she was immersed in the work she loved.

But not for long.

Hooves clattering across the cobblestones reminded her that Tiago still expected them to ride out together this morning.

And what Tiago wants, Tiago gets...

Not on her watch.

That thought couldn't stop her heart going crazy. Whatever she thought of him—or of herself, or of the way she had handled their relationship up to now—Tiago would always make her world a brighter place. Just more annoying, she reflected with amusement as he rode into the yard.

'Nice horse,' she commented mildly.

Colossal understatement. Tiago was riding a fancy stallion that must have cost a king's ransom, and he was leading an equally fine grey at his side.

'Good morning, Danny.'

His voice played her like a violin, reverberating all the way through her.

'I trust you slept well?'

As well as he had, apparently. He had dark circles under his eyes too.

'Very well, thank you,' she said primly, while her body went on a rampage of lust.

With his swarthy skin, his unshaven face, and a bandana barely keeping his wild black hair under control, Tiago looked like every woman's answer to lonely nights. His relaxed way of riding suggested the master of the sexual universe had arrived. He was dressed in jeans and boots, and a rugged black jacket with the collar turned up against the wind, but it was his dark eyes that held her.

This was ridiculous. She was in no mood for his nonsense this morning. Planting her hands on her hips, she confronted him. 'Have you forgotten that I told you I was working this morning?'

'I remembered.'

Dismounting, he secured both horses to a post, while she tried very hard not to notice the width of his shoulders, his lean frame... And she definitely refused to notice his tight butt, along with the familiar bulge in his jeans.

'I left a message for my employer to let him know I will be working as usual this morning,' she announced crisply.

'I know you did.'

'You know?'

Tiago turned to face her and his expression was distinctly amused.

It took her a moment, and then the penny finally dropped. *'You!'*

He shrugged. 'Had you forgotten that this farm belongs to the Lochmaglen estate? Don't look so horrified, Danny. I made a very generous offer. Your ex-employer had no difficulty accepting it.'

'So you've bought up everything in sight?'

'Not quite. Chico and Lizzie still own Rottingdean.'

'So between you and Chico you've bought up half the Highlands?' She shook her head. 'You're incredible!'

'Glad you think so,' Tiago observed wryly, utterly unfazed.

'This isn't funny, Tiago. You could have told me last night, but instead you chose to dangle me on the end of your line. I won't let that happen again.'

'Mount up,' he suggested calmly. 'We can discuss this on the ride. And don't pretend you can resist checking out such a fabulous horse.'

True. He'd caught her looking at the mare. 'You've got a damn cheek.'

'I'm still trialling her,' he said, ignoring this, 'and I'd like to know what you think. I value your opinion, Danny. Is that so strange? You *have* had the best training in the world, after all.'

'And you can stop mocking me, and smiling like that, right now.'

Narrowing her eyes, she'd made the mistake of meeting Tiago's dark stare to say this, and now it was impossible to look away. His eyes held far too many wicked messages—messages that her body was all too eager to receive.

Tearing herself away from that distraction, she checked the tack and mounted up. 'You could have told me all of this last night.'

'I never show my hand on a first date.'

'A first date?' she queried, bending to flick the latch on the gate with her crop. 'Is that what you'd call it?'

'What would *you* call it?'

'You don't want to know.'

Tiago shrugged and then followed her through. 'Shall we just enjoy the ride and find out where it takes us?' he suggested, closing the gate behind them.

'I would need to erase the past for that.'

Danny urged her horse into a relaxed canter, but as Tiago rode alongside all the hurt came welling back.

'I would need to forget that you persuaded me to marry you without telling me what was involved. I would have to blank out the fact that you arranged a wonderful evening for us last night at a house you forgot to tell me you owned. And you even drew Annie into it—'

'Stop.' Tiago shifted position in the saddle so he could stare directly at her. 'Annie was eager to be part of last

night, and I thought you were eager to be there. You were
obviously pleased to see Annie—and you were eager to
marry me, I seem to recall.'

'I *was* eager,' Danny admitted. 'I was eager and stupid and gullible. But not now. I gave you my heart and
my trust in Brazil, but that was before I woke up. And
I thought you knew me better than to imagine I could
ever, *ever* involve a child.'

'Danny—'

'No,' she flashed, and with a click of her tongue she
urged the grey mare to gallop away from him.

He wasn't staying back this time. This time he gave chase.
They rode neck and neck at a flat-out gallop across the
purple heather before finally reining in on the riverbank.

'What do you think of her?' he asked.

Danny looked at him as if she couldn't believe he
could change tack so easily.

'The horse?' he prompted.

'I know what you're talking about,' she assured him.
'The horse is great.'

'She's great—but we're not?' he suggested, raising
a brow.

Danny's face reflected her conflicting emotions. 'You
had to find a wife—any wife—and there I was.'

'Yes,' he admitted. 'But I fell in love with you.'

'You fell in love with me?' she said. Her mouth slanted.
'If you'd loved me you would have told me the truth.'

'Maybe I didn't know what love was, but you taught
me. I married you for the worst of reasons, but *graças a
Deus* I saved the ranch. I'll make no apologies for that. Do
I love you now? God help me, yes. Now more than ever.'

Swinging his leg over the horse, he dismounted. Running up his stirrups, he turned to stare at her.

'Do I ask you to forgive me? No. There's nothing for you to forgive. I will always love you, and I have never lied to you—'

'Except by omission,' she interrupted.

He shrugged. 'If I'd told you everything last night you would have thought, *The playboy is back. He thinks he can buy up everything in sight, including me.* I didn't want you to think that, Danny. I wanted the chance to speak to you and win your trust. I wanted to ride with you, out here in the open, where we have nothing to lose and everything to gain. I wanted to see your face when you saw the new mare. I rebuilt the house with you in mind, and I chose everything in it for you. Maybe I was wrong to believe there were some things it was better for you not to know, but I did it out of the best of reasons. I wanted last night to be special, unthreatening. I wanted to give us another chance. I didn't want what I can buy getting in the way of our reunion.'

'Like this horse?' Dipping her head, she nuzzled her face against the mare's silky neck.

'I wanted us to start afresh—just you and me last night, and then a new start for us this morning.'

Danny didn't say anything for a long time as they watched their horses drink, and then she said, 'You look tired.'

'So do you. Bad night?'

She curbed a smile. 'I didn't sleep much,' she admitted. 'But we can't just erase the past and start again, Tiago.'

'Why not?' He mounted up.

'Because your plan is redundant. You own Fazenda Santos and you don't need a wife.'

'But I need *you*. And what if I have a new plan? One that includes you? I'm going to turn this estate around,

Danny. I'm going to base it on my success in Brazil. You can help me, if you like. Unless that's a problem for you?'

'I couldn't possibly work fast enough to meet *your* exacting standards,' she commented.

'Really?' He pretended surprise. 'I found you satisfactory in Brazil.'

'Satisfactory?' she exclaimed. 'Watch it! I might be transparent when it comes to horses, but—'

'Not just horses,' he said.

'I'm certainly not vulnerable where you're concerned.'

'I don't think you're vulnerable at all,' he argued. 'I think you're strong—though you're far too trusting.'

'Tell me about it,' she said. And then a new thought occurred to her and she frowned. 'If this is your way of asking for my resignation…?'

'Certainly not,' he assured her. 'I'm going to put you to work.'

She held up her hand. 'Not so fast. If I do stay on I should warn you I'm unlikely to agree with you on most things.'

'Should I act surprised?'

'I won't be easy to work with,' she warned him, mounting up.

'Now I *am* surprised,' he murmured dryly as they both turned for home.

On the brow of the hill overlooking the old house of Lochmaglen, they stopped and reined in. They could see broken fencing stretching for miles from there.

He turned to Danny and smiled. 'I've always loved a challenge, haven't you?'

CHAPTER FIFTEEN

'I'VE NOT BOUGHT this place to see it fail,' Tiago told her as their horses clattered into the yard.

'But casualties are unavoidable?' Danny suggested as she dismounted.

'I hope not, but I can't afford to be weak. Weakness destroyed my family and almost destroyed Fazenda Santos. My parents were like yours—weak and easily led. I could never live through that again. So if you think I'm hard, understand why.'

'And if I find it hard to trust, understand why,' she countered.

'I do,' he assured her wryly. 'But luckily my main interest in life is rescuing and rebuilding.'

She laughed. 'I remember.'

He turned serious. 'But sometimes it's the tender things that get trampled—which is where you come in.'

'Me?'

'You brought the human touch to the ranch. I want you to do the same here'

'So what exactly is the job you're offering me?'

'The hardest job of all—the job of being my wife,' Tiago said as he hefted the saddle off his horse. 'And not just in name only, or for a year, but for a lifetime.'

'As long as that?' she said.

She turned to look at him and their stares met and held, and then they both laughed. It had been a long time coming, but they were finally back to their tormenting best—in a way they hadn't been since those early days of their friendship on Chico's ranch.

And now Tiago was in hunting mode, his firm mouth curving.

'You need to accept that I love you,' he said. 'You need to understand that when you walked out I was hurting too.' His lips pressed down as he thought back. 'But maybe I needed that wake-up call. I certainly got one when I almost lost you.'

'And now?' she said.

Tiago shrugged. 'Now I just want to know if I'm wasting my time here. Has your life moved on?'

'Has yours?'

Neither of them answered. Maybe they didn't need to. They had entered the stillness and shade of the stable block, and made swift work of settling their horses.

'So I've still got a job?' Danny confirmed as they walked outside.

'Yes. Of course.'

They stopped walking. Tension was rising. Did she move closer, or did he? Closing her eyes, she inhaled deeply, glutting herself on the sweet tang of leather and hot, clean man.

'What are you doing?' he asked as she stood on tiptoe.

'I'm going to kiss you.'

'That's my job.'

'You're too slow. This is just something else you're going to have to get used to. Barbarian mates tend to be as fierce as each other.'

She kissed him.

Tiago didn't move. 'Are you always going to be so forceful with me?'

'Always,' she promised.

'Then we are going to have a very interesting life together, Senhora Santos.'

'I certainly hope so.'

'I've missed you, Danny...' He stared into her eyes.

'I've missed you too.'

'Let's never fight again.'

'Unless we're in bed?' she suggested.

Tiago laughed, his breath clouding with hers in the frigid air. 'I will always love you, always protect you, always care for you—for as long as you will allow me to. And I will always support you in anything you decide to do.'

'Stop.' Reaching up, she placed her fingers on his lips. 'In your position I would have done exactly the same. We're like two halves of the same coin.'

'What are you saying, Danny?'

'Is it wrong to have sex on a second date?'

'Deus! I need a bed,' Tiago said huskily as he slammed her against the wall. 'Why is there never a bed when I need one?'

'Let me!' Danny insisted fiercely. 'Why do you always wear so many clothes?'

'It's winter?'

'Stop making excuses.'

She tugged at his shirt, exclaiming when she got down to hot, hard skin. She threw her head back and rubbed her body against him, purring deep in her throat like a contented kitten.

'Not here—not like this,' Tiago insisted, plucking reason from the air when it was lost to both of them. 'We've waited too long for this, and I've no intention of breaking such a long fast in a tack room.'

'All right,' Danny agreed grudgingly. 'But be quick—'

Tiago strode across the yard with her in his arms, into the house and up the stairs, without pausing. Reaching the bedroom, he kicked the door shut behind them and they fell on each other. Clothes flew left and right. Words were unnecessary. When they were naked she was ready to scramble up him, but Tiago held her still and brought her in front of him.

'No,' he said, speaking softly and intently as he stared into her face. 'This has to be special for you.'

Carrying her to the bed, he laid her down gently. Stretching out his powerful length beside her, he brought her into the circle of his arms and proceeded to give lovemaking a new meaning.

Keeping her arms above her head in one fist, he maintained eye contact as he built her pleasure with strokes and gentle teasing, until she was wild for him and it was all she could do to keep still. She had never felt like this before—so full of love, so abandoned, so free. Free to trust, to give, and to receive as Tiago introduced her to a new and extraordinary level of pleasure.

A groan escaped her as he stroked her buttocks, encouraging her to open her legs for him. And then, after teasing her with just his tip, he allowed himself to catch inside her, but then moved away again, making her sob with frustration.

'More…'

'More?' he queried in a low, husky voice.

'Don't tease me,' she begged him. 'I've waited too long for this.'

She gasped with relief when he allowed her another exquisite inch.

But then he pulled back again.

'Are you trying to drive me crazy with frustration?'

'No. I'm making sure you trust me. Completely and for ever this time.'

He took her again, by a couple of inches, and then he rested, allowing her to savour how good it was. Then he began to move, slowly and steadily, thrusting his hips to a dependable rhythm that had her screaming his name within seconds.

'Again,' she gasped as the strongest of the pleasure waves rolled over her and subsided. 'I must have more—please…please…more…again…'

Her fingers dug into him as she fell a second time, even more strongly than the first.

'Again, and again, and again,' Tiago promised her as he worked steadily to bring her more pleasure.

And this time when she quietened he murmured her name against her mouth and told her that he loved her.

They rode out the next morning, after a night of no sleep, but neither of them was tired for some reason. Tiago glanced at Danny and smiled. Life was too precious to waste a moment sleeping. They had done more than make love last night—constantly and vigorously; they had reached a new understanding built on trust and the realisation that neither of them was perfect, but they were better together than they could ever be apart.

The horses seemed to sense their exhilaration and it was a fast ride out and an even faster ride back. The horses were keen to get to their oats and hay nets, while Danny and he couldn't wait to go back to bed.

They went about the business of settling the horses as thoroughly as they always did, but with a careful speed. They didn't speak—they didn't have to—but each time they brushed against each other in the confined space he knew they felt the same bolt of electricity.

'So what do you think of the grey?' he demanded as they strode briskly across the courtyard to the house.

'I'd keep her, if I were you.'

'Really?' he said, opening the door and standing back to let her in.

'Definitely—she's responsive and intelligent. What more could you want?'

'What are you saying, Danny?' There was laughter in his voice. 'Are we still talking about the horse?'

Dragging her close, he stared deep into her eyes.

'That didn't require an answer, by the way,' he said as he led her towards the stairs.

She was breathless by the time they reached the bedroom, and that had nothing to do with the speed at which she'd climbed the stairs. Catching hold of her, Tiago swung her round and eased her down gently onto the coverlet.

'Are you sore after our excesses? Do you need me to go easy on you?'

She smiled. 'What do you think?'

Grabbing hold of Tiago by the front of his shirt, she pulled him down beside her. He didn't lose eye contact for a moment as he tugged off his shirt and quickly unlatched the buckle on his belt.

'You're beautiful,' she said as he pulled off his jeans.

'And you're overdressed. No—let me,' Tiago insisted.

He undid each of her buttons slowly, and after unfastening the zipper on her jeans eased them down. Each brush of his fingertips was surely intentional; each pulse of pleasure was certainly real.

'Let me touch you,' he whispered, holding her gaze. 'Let me pleasure you, Danny.'

'Don't you always?'

Tiago's mouth curved, and she was already so very sensitive that she exclaimed with excitement the moment he touched her.

'Don't look away. I want you to look at me, Danny, and I'll tell you when—'

'Now!' she wailed, unable to hold on.

'Greedy.' He laughed as he held her in his arms and she convulsed with pleasure. 'We do have all day and all night,' he reminded her as he kissed her.

'Is that all?' she complained.

'Believe me—I'm here for as long as you want. And I have no complaints.' He swallowed the last of her satisfied groans in a kiss. 'We have a lot of time to make up.'

'For every night apart?' she suggested.

'And every night going forward,' Tiago said.

It was a long time later, when they were stretched out dozing, with their limbs entwined, that Tiago murmured something Danny wasn't sure she'd heard correctly.

'Say again?' she murmured groggily.

'I said I love you, Danny, and I want to spend the rest of my life with you—so will you marry me?'

'No can do,' she said sleepily.

'Why not?' Tiago prompted huskily.

'I'm already married…my husband wouldn't like it.'

'Would he approve of a blessing in the local kirk?'

She stirred, properly awake now. 'You're serious?'

'I'm absolutely serious. I was thinking we could have our blessing at Rottingdean, so everyone can share the day. That is what you wanted, isn't it?'

'Yes… Yes, of course is it. But I do have one condition.'

'Name it,' Tiago growled.

'We spend our entire honeymoon in bed.'

'I'm sure that can be arranged,' he agreed as he gathered her into his arms.

EPILOGUE

THE TINY CHAPEL in the Highland village of Rotting-dean was filled to capacity for the blessing of Danny and Tiago's marriage vows. Tiago had flown everyone who mattered over from Brazil, and had even persuaded Lizzie's mother to make an appearance—though she had scooted off to meet up with her toy-boy some time before the end of the ceremony.

That apart, he was determined nothing would stand in the way of Danny's happiness. He had left nothing to chance—even buying Danny a more 'job-appropriate' ring to jostle alongside the jewels he loved to lavish on her.

'I intend to work you very hard,' he murmured as he slipped the simple platinum band on to Danny's wed-ding ring finger.

'I love it,' she whispered, glancing at the ring and then meeting and sharing the humour in his eyes. 'And as for working me hard—both in and out of the bedroom—I wouldn't have it any other way. Though I may have to take some time off...'

'Why?'

'Shh...' she warned him as the minister began to ad-dress the congregation once more.

'Are you going to make me wait before you explain that comment?' Tiago demanded, with his usual force.

'Tiago, I am going to make you a daddy. Now, please be quiet.'

She had never seen Tiago so happy. He couldn't wait to tell everyone their news when they arrived at the hotel where they were holding their reception.

'So you tamed the playboy?' Lizzie commented, giving Danny a hug. 'And I couldn't be more thrilled that we're both expecting our babies in the same month.'

'Hello, you two!'

'Emma?'

Danny couldn't have been more surprised to see a chirpy young girl with the same bright red hair as Lizzie wearing a chambermaid's uniform.

But why was she surprised, when Lizzie's cousin Emma had always worked hard and had always loved working with people? Danny only had to think back to the garden parties the three of them had used to organise under Lizzie's grandmother's supervision, to raise money for local charities, to remember that. With her bubbly personality, Emma Fane would be an asset wherever she worked.

'No wonder you hardly recognised me,' Emma exclaimed, giving Danny an enthusiastic hug. 'It has been almost ten years since I last visited Rottingdean.'

Emma had been little more than a child then. 'Of course I recognise you...' Danny was still computing the information. 'But I thought you were at college...?'

'I was—hotel management,' Emma confirmed, 'but then this—'

She stroked her stomach lovingly, which caused Danny to exchange a fast concerned glance with Lizzie.

Emma was a lot younger than they were, and seemed too young to be having a baby.

'And now I need the money,' Emma admitted bluntly. 'But don't worry about me,' she added brightly. 'This job at the hotel is great experience, and I love it here. Lizzie told me about the vacancy for a chambermaid, and here I am.'

Emma opened her arms wide, as if embracing the world and everything in it, with the infectious *joie de vivre* Danny had always associated with the young girl.

'I hope you don't mind me crashing your blessing,' she went on, 'but I'm just about to finish my shift and I couldn't resist peeping in.'

'Of course I don't mind,' Danny insisted. 'You're more than welcome to join us.'

'Oh, no,' Emma protested. 'I couldn't do that.'

'Why not?' Danny frowned. 'I'll speak to the manager for you.'

'If you're sure…?' Emma's face lit up.

'I'm certain. It will be good to catch up. I had no idea you were married—'

Danny stopped—blanched—wanted to cut out her tongue. She knew immediately from the look on Emma's face and Lizzie's sudden tension that she'd said the entirely wrong thing.

'Sorry—I didn't mean to infer anything.'

'It's an easy mistake to make,' Emma insisted. 'But please don't be embarrassed—I'm not. I couldn't be happier.'

'That's obvious,' Danny said warmly. 'So the three of us are going to share this exciting trip into motherhood together? You *are* sticking around?' she confirmed with Emma.

Emma was just about to answer when Tiago strolled

up to introduce them to a man—presumably another polo player, from the look of him—who might safely be called intimidating if you were of a nervous disposition.

Thankfully, Danny was not. She was used to daunting men, she thought as she glanced at Tiago, but for some reason she clutched Emma's hand a little tighter. She felt protective towards the young girl—and not just because Tiago's timing was so badly off. The little she knew about Emma's family suggested there would be no support for the young girl there, and Emma must be barely out of college—if she had even finished college at all.

There was a mystery here, Danny suspected. Emma had been such a promising student, and so serious about her career.

'Don't look so worried,' Emma whispered discreetly, before pulling away to leave Danny to mingle with her guests. 'I'm a lot tougher than I look.'

She would have to be, Danny concluded with concern as she noticed the daunting polo player staring after Emma. A vivacious, pretty girl like Emma would always attract plenty of male attention.

She turned back to Tiago, who was waiting to introduce her.

'Danny, this is Lucas Marcelos—another reprobate on the polo circuit.'

'I'm very pleased to meet you, Lucas,' she said politely. 'Welcome to Scotland.'

Danny's heart plummeted when she noticed that Lucas's attention was still fixed on Emma—though he covered his distraction fast, turning to face Danny with a stare that was piercing in its intensity.

'Tiago warned me you were beautiful,' he said, 'but now I see he was understating the case.'

Lucas's voice was deep and accented, and for some

reason it sent shivers down Danny's spine. She was glad when Tiago moved to stand between them.

'You're a lucky man,' Lucas told Tiago. 'I don't know what you've done to deserve such a woman, but you should give me your secret.'

'I love her. It's as simple as that and as complicated,' Tiago admitted as he looped a protective arm around Danny's shoulders. 'And she keeps me in line.'

'Which you *like*?' Lucas sounded incredulous at this.

'Which I adore,' Tiago insisted, in a way no man in his right mind would choose to argue with. 'You should try it some day, Lucas—find out for yourself.'

'That, my friend, is never going to happen.'

'You'd be surprised,' Tiago murmured, turning back to Danny as Lucas strolled away.

'Wow!' Danny released her pent-up tension in a gust of relief. 'Was I just scorched by an overload of testosterone, or was that a hologram of a very angry and frustrated man?'

'That, *chica*, was a good friend of mine who has taken more hits from life than he should have done. But I don't want to talk about Lucas now. I want to concentrate on you—if you don't mind?'

'I don't mind at all.'

Danny shook off the feeling of unease Lucas had given her as Tiago drew her into the shadows, where they could be alone for a moment, but she did feel sorry for Lucas. To be alone was not an enviable position to be in. She just hoped Lucas wouldn't decide to take out his bitter energies on young Emma tonight—because Emma was also alone, and a good deal more defenceless than a successful polo player like Lucas Marcelos.

'Danny?'

She gazed up at her husband, rejoicing that they were

together. No one and nothing would ever part them again, and soon there would be a new addition to the Santos family.

'I love you with all my heart,' Tiago whispered against her mouth, kissing her tenderly and repeatedly. 'And I can't bear to share you with anyone. Is that terrible of me?'

'Not at all.' Standing on tiptoe, she kissed him back.

'And now we're going to be three—'

'Or four—who knows?' she teased him.

'You've made me very happy,' Tiago growled, staring deep into her eyes. 'And that was before you gave me the news of our baby.'

Danny's gaze dropped to the firm, sexy mouth of the man she loved. 'Did you say you had taken a suite at the hotel, so we could freshen up after the blessing if we needed to?'

'That's right. I have,' Tiago confirmed.

'I need to freshen up.' She looked at him.

'Strange,' Tiago murmured, brushing her mouth with his. 'So do I…'

* * * * *

IT STARTED WITH A DIAMOND

TERI WILSON

For Brant Schafer, because naming a polo pony after me will guarantee you a book dedication.

And for Roe Valentine, my dear writing friend and other half of the Sisterhood of the Traveling Veuve Clicquot.

Chapter One

"It's hard to be a diamond in a rhinestone world."
—Dolly Parton

Diana Drake wasn't sure about much in her life at the moment, but one thing was crystal clear—she wanted to strangle her brother.

Not her older brother, Dalton. She couldn't really muster up any indignation as far as her elder sibling went, despite the fact that she was convinced he was at least partially responsible for her current predicament.

But Dalton got a free pass. For now.

She owed him.

For one thing, she'd been living rent free in his swanky Lenox Hill apartment for the past several months. For another, he was a prince now. A literal Prince Charming. As such, he wasn't even in New York anymore. He was somewhere on the French Riviera polishing his crown or sitting on a throne or doing whatever it was princes did all day long.

Dalton's absence meant that Diana's younger brother, Artem, was the only Drake around to take the full brunt of her frustration. Which was a tad problematic since he was her boss now.

Technically.

Sort of.

But Diana would just have to overlook that minor point. She'd held her tongue for as long as humanly possible.

"I can't do it anymore," she blurted as she marched into his massive office on the tenth floor of Drake Diamonds, the legendary jewelry store situated on the corner of 5th Avenue and 57th Street, right in the glittering center of Manhattan. The family business.

Diana might not have spent every waking hour of her life surrounded by diamonds and fancy blue boxes tied with white satin bows, as Dalton had. And she might not be the chief executive officer, like Artem. But the last time she checked, she was still a member of the family. She was a Drake, just like the rest of them.

So was it really necessary to suffer the humiliation of working as a salesperson in the most dreaded section of the store?

"Engagements? *Really?*" She crossed her arms and glared at Artem. It was still weird seeing him sitting behind what used to be their father's desk. Gaston Drake had been dead for a nearly a year, yet his presence loomed large.

Too large. It was almost suffocating.

"Good morning to you, too, Diana." Artem smoothed down his tie, which was the exact same hue as the store's trademark blue boxes. *Drake* blue.

Could he have the decency to look at least a little bit bothered by her outburst?

Apparently not.

She sighed. "I can't do it, Artem. I'll work anywhere in this building, except *there*." She waved a hand in the direction of the Engagements showroom down the hall.

He stared blithely at her, then made a big show of looking at his watch. "I see your point. It's been all of three hours. However have you lasted this long?"

"Three *torturous* hours." She let out another massive sigh. "Have you ever set foot in that place?"

"I'm the CEO, so, yes, I venture over there from time to time."

Right. Of course he had.

Still, she doubted he'd actually helped any engaged couples choose their wedding rings. At least, she hoped he hadn't, mainly because she wouldn't have wished such a fate on her worst enemy.

This morning she'd actually witnessed a grown man and woman speaking baby talk to each other. Her stomach churned just thinking about it now. Adults had no business speaking baby talk, not even to actual babies.

Her gaze shifted briefly to the bassinet in the corner of her brother's office. She still couldn't quite believe Artem was a dad now. A husband. It was kind of mind-boggling when she thought about it, especially considering what an abysmally poor role model their father had been in the family department.

Keep it professional.

She wouldn't get anywhere approaching Artem as a sibling. This conversation was about business, plain and simple. Removing herself from Engagements was the best thing Diana could do, not just for herself, but also for Drake Diamonds.

Only half an hour ago, she'd had to bite her tongue when a man asked for advice about choosing an engagement ring and she'd very nearly told him to spend his money on something more sensible than a huge diamond when the chances that he and his girlfriend would live happily ever after were slim to none. *If* she accepted his proposal, they only had about an eighty percent chance of making it down the aisle. Beyond that, their odds of staying married were about fifty-fifty. Even if they remained husband and wife until death did them part, could they reasonably expect to be happy? Was *anyone* happily married?

Diana's own mother had stuck faithfully by her husband's side after she found out he'd fathered a child with their housekeeper, even when she ended up raising the boy herself. Surely that didn't count as a happy marriage.

That boy was now a man and currently seated across the desk from Diana. She'd grown up alongside Artem and couldn't possibly love him more. He was her brother. Case closed.

Diana's problem wasn't with Artem. It was with her father and the concept of marriage as a whole. She didn't like what relationships did to people...

Especially what one had done to her mother.

Even if she'd grown up in a picture-perfect model family, Diana doubted she'd ever see spending three months' salary on an engagement ring as anything but utter foolishness.

It was a matter of logic, pure and simple. Of statistics. And statistics said that plunking down $40,000 for a two-carat Drake Diamonds solitaire was like throwing a giant wad of cash right into the Hudson River.

But she had no business saying such things out loud since she worked in Engagements, now, did she? She had no business saying such things, period. Drake Diamonds had supported her for her entire life.

So she'd bitten her tongue. Hard.

"I'm simply saying that my talents would be best put to use someplace else." *Anyplace* else.

"Would they now?" Artem narrowed his gaze at her. A hint of a smile tugged at the corner of his mouth, and she knew what was coming. "And what talents would those be, exactly?"

And there it was.

"Don't start." She had no desire to talk about her accident again. Or ever, for that matter. She'd moved on.

Artem held up his hands in a gesture of faux surrender. "I didn't say a word about your training. I'm simply pointing out that you have no work experience. Or college education, for that matter. I hate to say it, sis, but your options are limited."

She'd considered enrolling in classes at NYU, but didn't bother mentioning it. Her degree wasn't going to materialize overnight. *Unfortunately.* College had always been on her radar, but between training and competing, she hadn't found the time. Now she was a twenty-six-year-old without a single day of higher education under her belt.

If only she'd spent a little less time on the back of a horse for the past ten years and a few more hours in the classroom...

She cleared her throat. "Do I need to remind you that I own a third of this business? You and Dalton aren't the only Drakes around here, you know."

"No, but we're the only ones who've actually worked here before today." He glanced at his watch again, stood and buttoned his suit jacket. "Look, just stick it out for a while. Once you've learned the ropes, we'll try and find another role for you. Okay?"

Awhile.

Just how long was that, she wondered. A week? A month? A year? She desperately wanted to ask, but she didn't dare. She hated sounding whiny, and she *really* hated relying on the dreadful Drake name. But it just so happened that name was the only thing she had going for her at the moment.

Oh, how the mighty had fallen. Literally.

"Come on." Artem brushed past her. "We've got a photo shoot scheduled this afternoon in Engagements. I think you might find it rather interesting."

She was glad to be walking behind him so he couldn't see her massive eyeroll. "Please tell me it doesn't involve a wedding dress."

"Relax, sister dear. We're shooting cuff links. The photographer only wanted to use the Engagements show-room because it has the best view of Manhattan in the building."

It did have a lovely view, especially now that spring had arrived in New York in all its fragrant splendor. The air was filled with cherry blossoms, swirling like pink snow flurries. Diana had lost herself a time or two staring out at the verdant landscape of Central Park.

But those few blissful moments had come to a crashing end the moment she'd turned away from the show-room's floor-to-ceiling windows and remembered she was surrounded by diamonds. Wedding diamonds.

And here I am again.

She blinked against the dazzling assault of countless engagement rings sparkling beneath the sales floor lights and followed Artem to the corner of the room where the photographer was busy setting up a pair of tall light stands. A row of camera lenses in different sizes sat on top of one of glass jewelry cases.

Diana slid a velvet jeweler's pad beneath the lenses to protect the glass and busied herself rearranging things. Maybe if she somehow inserted herself into this whole photo-shoot process, she could avoid being a part of anyone's betrothal for an hour or two.

A girl can dream.

"Is our model here?" the photographer asked. "Because I'm ready, and we've only got about an hour left until sundown. I'd like to capture some of this nice view before it's too late."

Diana glanced out the window. The sky was already tinged pale violet, and the evening wind had picked up, scattering pink petals up and down 5th Avenue. The sun was just beginning to dip below the skyscrapers. It would be a gorgeous backdrop...

...if the model showed up.

Artem checked his watch again and frowned in the direction of the door. Diana took her time polishing the half-dozen pairs of Drake cuff links he'd pulled for the shoot. Anything to stretch out the minutes.

Just as she reached for the last pair, Artem let out a sigh of relief. "Ah, he's here."

Diana glanced up, took one look at the man stalking toward them and froze. Was she hallucinating? Had the blow to the head she'd taken months ago done more damage than the doctors had thought?

Nothing is wrong with you. You're fine. Everything *is fine.*

Everything didn't feel fine, though. Diana's whole world had come apart, and months later she still hadn't managed to put it back together. She was beginning to think she never would.

Because, deep down, she knew she wouldn't. She couldn't pick up the pieces, even if she tried. No one could.

Which was precisely why she was cutting her losses and starting over again. She'd simply build a new life for herself. A normal life. Quiet. Safe. It would take some getting used to, but she could do it.

People started over all the time, didn't they?

At least she had a job. An apartment. A family. There were worse things in the world than being a Drake.

She was making a fresh start. She was a jeweler now. Her past was ancient history.

Except for the nagging fact that a certain man from her past was walking toward her. Here, now, in the very real present.

Franco Andrade.

Not him. Just...no.

She needed to leave. Maybe she could just slink over to one of the sales counters and get back to her champagne-sipping brides and grooms to be. Selling engagement rings had never seemed as appealing as it did right this second.

She laid her polishing cloth on the counter, but before she could place the cuff links back inside their neat blue box, one of them slipped right through her fingers. She watched in horror as it bounced off the tip of Artem's shoe and rolled across the plush Drake-blue carpet, straight toward Franco's approaching form.

Diana sighed. This is what she got for complaining to Artem. Just because she was an heiress didn't mean she had to act like one. Being entitled wasn't an admirable quality. Besides, karma was a raging bitch. One who didn't waste any time, apparently.

Diana dropped to her knees and scrambled after the

runaway cuff link, wishing the floor would somehow open up and swallow her whole. Evidently, there were indeed fates worse than helping men choose engagement rings.

"Mr. Andrade, we meet at last." Artem deftly side-stepped her and extended a hand toward Franco.

Mr. Andrade.

So it *was* him. She'd still been holding out the tiniest bit of hope for a hallucination. Or possibly a doppelganger. But that was an absurd notion. Men as handsome as Franco Andrade didn't roam the Earth in pairs. His kind of chiseled bone structure was a rarity, something that only came around once in a blue moon. Like a unicorn. Or a fiery asteroid hurtling toward Earth, promising mass destruction on impact.

One of those two things. The second, if the rumors of his conquests were to be believed.

Who was she kidding? She didn't need to rely on rumors. She knew firsthand what kind of man Franco Andrade was. It was etched in her memory with excruciating clarity. What she didn't know was what he was doing here.

Was he the model for the new campaign? Impossible.

It had to be some kind of joke. Or possibly Artem's wholly inappropriate attempt to manipulate her back into her old life.

Either way, for the second time in a matter of hours, she wanted to strangle her brother. He was the one who'd invited Franco here, after all. Perhaps joining the family business hadn't been her most stellar idea.

As if she had any other options.

She pushed Artem's reminders of her inadequate education and employment record out of her head and concentrated on the mortifying matter at hand. Where was that darn cuff link, anyway?

"Gotcha," she whispered under her breath as she caught sight of a silver flash out of the corner of her eye.

But just as she reached for it, Franco Andrade's ridiculously masculine form crouched into view. "Allow me."

His words sent a tingle skittering through her. Had his voice always been so deliciously low? The man could recite the alphabet and bring women to their knees. Which would have made the fact that she was already in just such a position convenient, had it not been so utterly humiliating.

"Here." He held out his hand. The cuff link sat nestled in the center of his palm. He had large hands, rough with calluses, a stark contrast to the finely tailored fit of his custom tuxedo.

Of course that tuxedo happened to be missing a tie, and his shirt cuffs weren't even fastened. He looked as if he'd just rolled out of someone's bed and tossed on his discarded Armani from the night before.

Then again, he most likely had.

"Thank you," she mumbled, steadfastly refusing to meet his gaze.

"Wait." He balled his fist around the cuff link and stooped lower to peer at her. "Do we know each other?"

"Nope." She shook her head so hard she could practically hear her brain rattle. "No, I'm afraid we don't."

"I think we might," he countered, stubbornly refusing to hand over the cuff link.

Fine. Let him keep it. She had better things to do, like help lovebirds snap selfies while trying on rings. Anything to extricate herself from the current situation.

She flew to her feet. "Everything seems in order here. I'll just be going…"

"Diana, wait." Artem was using his CEO voice. Marvelous.

She obediently stayed put, lest he rethink his promise and banish her to an eternity of working in Engagements.

Franco took his time unfolding himself to a standing position, as if everyone was happy to wait for him, the Manhattan sunset included.

"Mr. Andrade, I'm Artem Drake, CEO of Drake Diamonds." Artem gestured toward Diana. "And this is my sister, Diana Drake."

"It's a pleasure to meet you," she said tightly and crossed her arms.

Artem shot her a reproachful glare. With no small amount of reluctance, she pasted on a smile and offered her hand for a shake.

Franco's gaze dropped to her outstretched fingertips. He waited a beat until her cheeks flared with heat, then dropped the cuff link into her palm without touching her.

"El gusto es mio," he said with just a hint of an Argentine accent.

The pleasure is mine.

A rebellious shiver ran down Diana's spine.

That shiver didn't mean anything. Of course it didn't. He was a beautiful man, that was all. It was only natural for her body to respond to that kind of physical perfection, even though her head knew better than to pay any attention to his broad shoulders and dark, glittering eyes.

She swallowed. Overwhelming character flaws aside, Franco Andrade had always been devastatingly handsome... emphasis on *devastating.*

It was hardly fair. But life wasn't always fair, was it? No, it most definitely wasn't. Lately, it had been downright cruel.

Diana's throat grew thick. She had difficulty swallowing all of a sudden. Then, somewhere amid the sudden fog in her head, she became aware of Artem clearing his throat.

"Shall we get started? I believe we're chasing the light." He introduced Franco to the photographer, who practically swooned on the spot when he turned his gaze on her.

Diana suppressed a gag and did her best to blend into the Drake-blue walls.

Apparently, any and all attempts at disappearing proved futile. As she tried to make an escape, Artem motioned her back. "Diana, join us please."

She forced her lips into something resembling a smile and strode toward the window where the photographer was getting Franco into position with a wholly unnecessary amount of hands-on attention. The woman with the camera had clearly forgiven him for his tardiness. It figured.

Diana turned her back on the nauseating scene and raised an eyebrow at Artem, who was tapping away on his iPhone. "You needed me?"

He looked up from his cell. "Yes. Can you get Mr. Andrade fitted with some cuff links?"

She stared blankly at him. "Um, me?"

"Yes, you." He shrugged. "What's with the attitude? I thought you'd be pleased. I'm talking to the same person who just stormed into my office demanding a different job than working in Engagements, right?"

She swallowed. "Yes. Yes, of course."

She longed to return to her dreadful post, but if she did, Artem would never take her seriously. Not after everything she'd said earlier.

"Cuff links." She nodded. "I'm on it."

She could do this. She absolutely could. She was Diana

Drake, for crying out loud. She had a reputation all over the world for being fearless.

At least, that's what people used to say about her. Not so much anymore.

Just do it and get it over with. You'll never see him again after today. Those days are over.

She squared her shoulders, grabbed a pair of cuff links and marched toward the corner of the room that had been roped off for the photo shoot, all the while fantasizing about the day when she'd be the one in charge of this place. Or at least not at the very bottom of the food chain.

Franco leaned languidly against the window while the photographer tousled his dark hair, ostensibly for styling purposes.

"Excuse me." Diana held up the cuff links—18-carat white-gold knots covered in black pavé diamonds worth more than half the engagement rings in the room. "I've got the jewels."

"Excellent," the photographer chirped. "I'll grab the camera and we'll be good to go."

She ran her hand through Franco's hair one final time before sauntering away.

If Franco noticed the sudden, exaggerated swing in her hips, he didn't let it show. He fixed his gaze pointedly at Diana. "You've come to dress me?"

"No." Her face went instantly hot. Again. "I mean, yes. Sort of."

The corner of his mouth tugged into a provocative grin and he offered her his wrists.

She reached for one of his shirt cuffs, and her mortification reached new heights when she realized her hands were shaking.

Will this day ever end?

"Be still, *mi cielo*," he whispered, barely loud enough for her to hear.

Mi cielo.

She knew the meaning of those words because he'd whispered them to her before. Back then, she'd clung to them as if they'd meant something.

Mi cielo. My heaven.

They hadn't, though. They'd meant nothing to him.

Neither had she.

"I'm not yours, Mr. Andrade. Never have been, never will be." She glared at him, jammed the second cuff link into his shirt with a little too much force and dropped his wrist. "We're finished here."

Why did she have the sinking feeling that she might be lying?

Chapter Two

Diana Drake didn't remember him. Or possibly she did, and she despised him. Franco wasn't altogether sure which prospect was more tolerable.

The idea of being so easily forgotten didn't sit well. Then again, being memorable hadn't exactly done him any favors lately, had it?

No, he thought wryly. *Not so much.* But it had been a hell of a lot of fun. At least, while it had lasted.

Fun wasn't part of his vocabulary anymore. Those days had ended. He was starting over with a clean slate, a new chapter and whatever other metaphors applied.

Not that he'd had much of a choice in the matter.

He'd been fired. Let go. Dumped from the Kingsmen Polo Team. Jack Ellis, the owner of the Kingsmen, had finally made good on all the ultimatums he'd issued over the years. It probably shouldn't have come as a surprise.

Franco knew he'd pushed the limits of Ellis's tolerance. More than once. More than a few times, to be honest.

But he'd never let his extracurricular activities affect his performance on the field. Franco had been the Kingsmen's record holder for most goals scored for four years running. His season total was always double the number of the next closest player on the list.

Which made his dismissal all the more frustrating, particularly considering he hadn't actually broken any rules. This time, Franco had been innocent. For probably the first time in his adult life, he'd done nothing untoward.

The situation dripped with so much irony that Franco was practically swimming in it. He would have found the entire turn of events amusing if it hadn't been so utterly frustrating.

"Mr. Andrade, could you lift your right forearm a few inches?" the photographer asked. "Like this."

She demonstrated for him, and Franco dragged his gaze away from Diana Drake with more reluctance than he cared to consider. He hadn't been watching her intentionally. His attention just kept straying in her direction. Again and again, for some strange reason.

She wasn't the most beautiful woman he'd ever seen. Then again, beautiful women were a dime a dozen in his world. There was something far more intriguing about Diana Drake than her appearance.

Although it didn't hurt to look at her. On the contrary, Franco rather enjoyed the experience.

She stood at one of the jewelry counters arranging and rearranging her tiny row of cuff links. He wondered if she realized her posture gave him a rather spectacular view of her backside. Judging by the way she seemed intent on ignoring him, he doubted it. She wasn't posing for his benefit, like, say, the photographer seemed to be doing. Franco could tell when a woman was trying to get his attention, and this one wasn't.

He couldn't quite put his finger on what it was about her that captivated him until she stole a glance at him from across the room.

The memory hit him like a blow to the chest.

Those eyes…

Until he'd met Diana, Franco had never seen eyes that color before—deep violet. They glittered like amethysts. Framed by thick ebony lashes, they were in such startling contrast with her alabaster complexion that he couldn't quite bring himself to look away. Even now.

And that was a problem. A big one.

"Mr. Andrade," the photographer repeated. "Your wrist."

He adjusted his posture and shot her an apologetic wink. The photographer's cheeks went pink, and he knew he'd been forgiven. Franco glanced at Diana again, just in time to see her violet eyes rolling in disgust.

A problem. Most definitely.

He had no business noticing *any* woman right now, particularly one who bore the last name Drake. He was on the path to redemption, and the Drakes were instrumental figures on that path. As such, Diana Drake was strictly off-limits.

So it was a good thing she clearly didn't want to give him the time of day. What a relief.

Right.

Franco averted his gaze from Diana Drake's glittering violet eyes and stared into the camera.

"Perfect," the photographer cooed. "Just perfect."

Beside her, Artem Drake nodded. "Yes, this is excellent. But maybe we should mix it up a little before we lose the light."

The photographer lowered her camera and glanced around the showroom, filled with engagement rings. You couldn't swing a polo mallet in the place without hitting a dozen diamond solitaires. "What were you thinking? Something romantic, maybe?"

"We've done romantic." Artem shrugged. "Lots of times. I was hoping for something a little more eye-catching."

The photographer frowned. "Let me think for a minute."

A generous amount of furtive murmuring followed, and Franco sighed. He'd known modeling wouldn't be as exciting as playing polo. He wasn't an idiot. But he'd been on the job for less than an hour and he was already bored out of his mind.

He sighed. Again.

His eyes drifted shut, and he imagined he was someplace else. Someplace that smelled of hay and horses and churned-up earth. Someplace where the ground shook with the thunder of hooves. Someplace where he never felt restless or boxed in.

The pounding that had begun in his temples subsided ever so slightly. When he opened his eyes, Diana Drake was standing mere inches away.

Franco smiled. "We meet again."

Diana's only response was a visible tensing of her shoulders as the photographer gave her a push and shoved her even closer toward him.

"Okay, now turn around. Quickly before the sun sets," the photographer barked. She turned her attention toward Franco. "Now put your arms around her. Pull her close, right up against your body. Yes, like that. Perfect!"

Diana obediently situated herself flush against him, with her lush bottom fully pressed against his groin. At last things were getting interesting.

Maybe he didn't hate modeling so much, after all.

Franco cleared his throat. "Well, this is awkward," he whispered, sending a ripple through Diana's thick dark hair.

He tried his best not to think about how soft that hair felt against his cheek or how much her heady floral scent reminded him of buttery-yellow orchids growing wild on the vine in Argentina.

"Awkward?" Diana shot him a glare over her shoulder. "From what I hear, you're used to this kind of thing."

He tightened his grip on her tiny waist. "And here I thought you didn't remember me."

"You're impossible," Diana said under her breath, wiggling uncomfortably in his arms.

"That's not what you said the last time we were in this position."

"Oh, my God, you did *not* just say that." This was the Diana Drake he remembered. Fiery. Bold.

"Nice." Artem strode toward them, nodding. "I like it. Against the sunset, you two look gorgeous. Edgy. Intimate."

Diana shook her head. "Artem, you're not serious."

"Actually, I am. Here." He lifted his hand. A sparkling diamond and sapphire necklace dangled from it with a center stone nearly as large as a polo ball. "Put this around your neck, Diana."

Diana crossed her arms. "Really, I'm not sure I should be part of this."

"It's just one picture out of hundreds. We probably won't even use it. The campaign is for cuff links, remember? Humor me, sis. Put it on." He arched a brow. "Besides, I thought you were interested in exploring other career opportunities around here."

She snatched the jewels out of his hands. "Fine."

Career opportunities?

"You're not working here, are you?" Franco murmured, barely loud enough for her to hear.

Granted, her last name was Drake. But why on earth would she give up a grand prix riding career to peddle diamonds?

"As a matter of fact, I am," she said primly.

"Why? If memory serves, you belong on a medal stand. Not here."

"Why do you care?" she asked through clenched teeth as the photographer snapped away.

Good question. "I don't."

"Fine."

But it wasn't fine. He *did* care, damn it. He shouldn't, but he did.

He would have given his left arm to be on horseback right now, and Diana Drake was working as a salesgirl when she could have been riding her way to the Olympics. What was she thinking? "It just seems like a phenomenal waste of talent. Be honest. You miss it, don't you?"

Her fingertips trembled and she nearly dropped the necklace down her blouse.

Franco covered her hands with his. "Here, let me help."

"I can do it," she snapped.

Franco sighed. "Look, the faster we get this picture taken, the faster all this will be over."

He bowed his head to get a closer look at the catch on the necklace, and his lips brushed perilously close to the elegant curve of her neck. She glanced at him over her shoulder, and for a sliver of a moment, her gaze dropped to his mouth. She let out a tremulous breath, and Franco could have sworn he heard a kittenish noise escape her lips.

Her reaction aroused him more than it should have, which he blamed on his newfound celibacy.

This lifestyle was going to prove more challenging than he'd anticipated.

But that was okay. Franco had never been the kind of man who backed down from a challenge. On the contrary, he relished it. He'd always played his best polo when facing his toughest opponents. Adversity brought out the best in Franco. He'd learned that lesson the hard way.

A long time ago.

Another time, another place.

"You two are breathtaking," the photographer said. "Diana, open the collar of your blouse just a bit so we can get a better view of the sapphire."

She obeyed, and Franco found himself momentarily spellbound by the graceful contours of her collarbones. Her skin was lovely. Luminous and pale beside the brilliant blue of the sapphire around her neck.

"Okay, I think we've got it." The photographer lowered her camera.

"We're finished?" Diana asked.

"Yes, all done."

"Excellent." She started walking away without so much as a backward glance.

"Aren't you forgetting something, *mi cielo*?" he said.

She spun back around, face flushed. He'd seen her wear that same heated expression during competition. "What?"

He held up his wrists. "Your cuff links."

"Oh. Um. Yes, thank you." She unfastened them and

gathered them in her closed fist. "Goodbye, Mr. Andrade."

She squared her shoulders and slipped past him. All business.

But Franco wasn't fooled. He'd seen the tremble in her fingertips as she'd loosened the cuffs of his shirt. She'd been shaking like a leaf, which struck him as profoundly odd.

Diana may have pretended to forget him, but he remembered her all too well. There wasn't a timid bone in her body, which had made her beyond memorable. She was confidence personified. It was one of the qualities that made her such an excellent rider.

If Diana Drake was anything, it was fearless. In the best possible way. She possessed the kind of tenacity that couldn't be taught. It was natural. Inborn. Like a person's height. Or the tone of her voice.

Or eyes the color of violets.

But people changed, didn't they? It happened all the time.

It had to. Franco was counting on it.

Chapter Three

Diana was running late for work.

Since the day of the mortifying photo shoot, she'd begun to dread the tenth-floor showroom with more fervor than ever before. Every time she looked up from one of the jewelry cases, she half expected to see Franco Andrade strolling toward her with a knowing look in his eyes and a smug grin on his handsome face. It was a ridiculous thing to worry about, of course. He had no reason to return to the store. The photo shoot was over. Finished.

Thank goodness.

Besides, if history had proven anything, it was that Franco wasn't fond of follow-through.

Still, she couldn't quite seem to shake the memory of how it had felt when he fastened that sapphire pendant around her neck…the graze of his fingertips on her collarbone, the tantalizing warmth of his breath on her skin.

It had been a long time since Diana had been touched in such an intimate way. A very long time. She knew getting her photo taken with Franco hadn't been real. They'd been posing, that's all. Pretending. She wasn't delusional, for heaven's sake.

But her body clearly hadn't been on the same page as her head. Physically, she'd been ready to believe the beautiful lie. She'd bought it, hook, line and sinker.

Just as she'd done the night she'd slept with him.

It was humiliating to think about the way she'd reacted to seeing him again after so long. She'd practically melted into a puddle at the man's feet. And not just any man. Franco Andrade was the king of the one night stand.

Even worse, she was fairly sure he'd known. He'd noticed the hitch in her breath, the flutter of her heart, the way she'd burned. He'd noticed, and he'd enjoyed it. Every mortifying second.

Don't think about it. It's over and done. Besides, it wasn't even a thing. It was nothing.

Except the fact that she kept thinking about it made it feel like something. A very big, very annoying something.

Enough. She had more important things to worry about than embarrassing herself in front of that polo-playing lothario. It hadn't been the first time, after all. She'd made an idiot out of herself in his presence before and lived to tell about it. At least this time she'd managed to keep her clothes on.

She tightened her grip on the silver overhead bar as the subway car came to a halt. The morning train was as crowded as ever, and when the doors slid open she wiggled her way toward the exit through a crush of commuters.

She didn't realize she'd gotten off at the wrong stop until it was too late.

Perfect. Just perfect. She was already running late, and now she'd been so preoccupied by Franco Andrade that she'd somehow gotten off the subway at the most crowded spot in New York. Times Square.

She slipped her messenger bag over her shoulder and climbed the stairs to street level. The trains had been running slow all morning, and she'd never be on time now. She might as well walk the rest of the way. A walk would do her good. Maybe the spring air would help clear her head and banish all thoughts of Franco once and for all.

It was worth a shot, anyway.

Diana took a deep inhale and allowed herself to remember how much she'd always loved to ride during this time of year. No more biting wind in her face. No more frost on the ground. In springtime, the sun glistened off her horse's ebony coat until it sparkled like black diamonds.

Diana's chest grew tight. She swallowed around the lump in her throat and fought the memories, pushed them back to the farthest corner of her mind where they belonged. *Don't cry. Don't do it.* If she did, she might not be able to stop.

After everything that had happened, she didn't want to be the pitiful-looking woman weeping openly on the sidewalk.

She focused, instead, on the people around her. Whenever the memory of the accident became too much, she tried her best to focus outward rather than on what was going on inside. Once, at Drake Diamonds, she'd stared at a vintage-inspired engagement ring for ten full minutes until the panic had subsided. She'd counted every tiny diamond in its art deco pavé setting, traced each slender line of platinum surrounding the central stone.

When she'd been in the hospital, her doctor had told her she might not remember everything that had led up to her fall. Most of the time, people with head injuries suffered memory loss around the time of impact. They didn't remember what had happened right before they'd been hurt.

They were the lucky ones.

Diana remembered everything. She would have given anything to forget.

Breathe in, breathe out. Look around you.

The streets were crowded with pedestrians, and as Diana wove her way through the crush of people, she thought she caught a few of them looking at her. They nodded and smiled in apparent recognition.

What was going on?

She was accustomed to being recognized at horse shows. On the riding circuit she'd been a force to be reckoned with. But this wasn't the Hamptons or Connecticut. This was Manhattan. She should blend in here. That was one of the things she liked best about the city—a person could just disappear right in the middle of a crowd. She didn't have to perform here. She could be anyone.

At least that's how she'd felt until Franco Andrade had walked into Drake Diamonds. The moment she'd set eyes on him, the dividing line between her old life and her new one had begun to blur.

She didn't like it. Not one bit. Before he'd shown up, she'd been doing a pretty good job of keeping things compartmentalized. She'd started a new job. She'd spent her evening hours in Dalton's apartment watching television until she fell asleep. She'd managed to live every day without giving much thought to what she was missing.

But the moment Franco had touched her she'd known the truth. She wasn't okay. The accident had affected her more than she could admit, even to herself.

There'd been an awareness in the graze of his fingertips, a strange intimacy in the way he'd looked at her. As if she were keeping a secret that only he was privy to. She'd felt exposed. Vulnerable. Seen.

She'd always felt that way around Franco, which is why she'd been stupid enough to end up in his bed. The way she felt when he looked at her had been intoxicating back then. Impossible to ignore.

But she didn't want to be seen now. Not anymore. She just wanted to be invisible for a while.

Maybe she wouldn't have been so rattled if it had been someone else. But it had been *him*. And she was most definitely still shaken up.

She needed to get a grip. So she'd posed for a few pictures with a handsome man she used to know. That's all. Case closed. End of story. No big deal.

She squared her shoulders and marched down the street with renewed purpose. This was getting ridiculous. She would *not* let a few minutes with Franco ruin her new beginning. He meant nothing to her. She was only imagining things, anyway. He probably looked at every woman he met with that same knowing gleam in his eye. That's why they were always falling at his feet everywhere he went.

It was nauseating.

She wouldn't waste another second thinking about the man. She sighed and realized she was standing right in front of the Times Square Starbucks. Perfect. Coffee was just what she needed.

As soon as she took her place in line, a man across the room did a double take in her direction. His face broke into a wide smile. Diana glanced over her shoulder, convinced he was looking at someone behind her. His wife, maybe. Or a friend.

No one was there.

She turned back around. The man winked and raised his cardboard cup as if he were toasting her. Then he turned and walked out the door.

Diana frowned. People were weird. It was probably just some strange coincidence. Or the man was confused, that was all.

Except he didn't look confused. He looked perfectly friendly and sane.

"Can I help you?" The barista, a young man with wire-rimmed glasses and a close-cropped beard, jabbed at the cash register.

"Yes, please," Diana said. "I'd like a…"

The barista looked up, grinned and cut her off before she could place her order. "Oh, hey, you're that girl."

That girl?

Diana's gaze narrowed. She shook her head. "Um, I don't think I am."

What was she even arguing about? She didn't actually know. But she knew for certain that this barista shouldn't have any idea who she was.

Unless her accident had somehow ended up on You-Tube or something.

Not that. Please not that.

Anything but that.

"Yeah, you are." The barista turned to the person in line behind her. "You know who she is too, right?"

Diana ventured a sideways glance at the woman, who didn't look the least bit familiar. Diana was sure she'd never seen her before.

"Of course." The woman looked Diana up and down. "You're her. Most definitely."

For a split second, relief washed over her. She wasn't losing it, after all. People on the sidewalk really had been staring at her. The triumphant feeling was short-lived when she realized she still had no idea why.

"Will one of you please tell me what's going on? What girl?"

The woman and the barista exchanged a glance.

"The girl from the billboard," the woman said.

Diana blinked.

The girl from the billboard.

This couldn't be about the photos she'd taken with Franco. It just couldn't. Artem was her brother. He wouldn't slap a picture of her on a Drake Diamonds billboard without her permission. Of course he wouldn't.

Would he?

Diana looked back and forth between the woman and the barista. "What billboard?"

She hated how shaky and weak her voice sounded, so she repeated herself. This time she practically screamed. *"What billboard?"*

The woman flinched, and Diana immediately felt horrible. Her new life apparently included having her face on billboards and yelling at random strangers in coffee shops. It wasn't exactly the fresh start she'd imagined for herself.

"It's right outside. Take two steps out the front door and look up. You can't miss it." The barista lifted a brow. "Are you going to order something or what? You're holding up the line."

"No, thank you." She couldn't stomach a latte right now. Simply putting one foot in front of the other seemed like a monumental task.

She scooted out of line and made her way to the door. She paused for a moment before opening it, hoping for one final, naive second that this was all some big mistake. Maybe Artem hadn't used the photo of her and Franco for the new campaign. Maybe the billboard they'd seen wasn't even a Drake Diamonds advertisement. Maybe it was an ad for some other company with a model who just happened to look like Diana.

That was possible, wasn't it?

But deep down she knew it wasn't, and she had no one to blame but herself.

She'd stormed into Artem's office and demanded that he find a role for her in the company that didn't involve Engagements. She'd practically gotten down on her knees and begged. He'd given her exactly what she wanted. She just hadn't realized that being on a billboard alongside Franco Andrade in the middle of Times Square was part of the equation.

She took a deep breath.

It was just a photograph. She and Franco weren't a couple or anything. They were simply on a billboard together. A million people would probably walk right past it and never notice. By tomorrow it would be old news. She was getting all worked up over nothing.

How bad could it be?

She walked outside, looked up and got her answer.

It was bad. Really, really bad.

Emblazoned across the top of the Times Tower was a photo of herself being embraced from behind by Franco. The sapphire necklace dangled from his fingertips, but rather than looking like he was helping her put it on, the photo gave the distinct impression he was removing it.

Franco's missing tie and the unbuttoned collar of his

tuxedo shirt didn't help matters. Neither did her flushed cheeks and slightly parted lips.

This wasn't an advertisement for cuff links. It looked more like an ad for sex. If she hadn't known better, Diana would have thought the couple in the photograph was just a heartbeat away from falling into bed together.

And she and Franco Andrade were that couple.

What have I done?

Franco was trying his level best not pummel Artem Drake.

But it was hard. Really hard.

"I didn't sign up for this." He wadded the flimsy newsprint of *Page Six* in his hands and threw it at Artem, who was seated across from Franco in the confines of his Drake-blue office. "Selling cuff links, yes. Selling sex, no."

Artem had the decency to flinch at the mention of sex, but Franco was guessing that was mostly out of a brotherly sense of propriety. After all, his sister was the one who looked as though Franco was seducing her on the cover of every tabloid in the western hemisphere.

From what Franco had heard, there was even a billboard smack in the middle of Times Square. His phone had been blowing up with texts and calls all morning. Regrettably, not a single one of those texts or calls had included an offer to return to the Kingsmen.

"Mr. Andrade, please calm down." Artem waved a hand at the generous stack of newspapers fanned across the surface of his desk. "The new campaign was unveiled just hours ago, and it's already a huge success. I've made you famous. You're a household name. People who've never seen a polo match in their lives know who you are. This is what you wanted, is it not?"

Yes…

And no.

He'd wanted to get Jack Ellis's attention. To force his hand. Just not like this.

But he couldn't explain the details of his reinvention to Artem Drake. His new "employer" didn't even know he'd been cut from the team. To Franco's knowledge, no one did. And if he had anything to say about it, no one would. Because he'd be back in his jersey before the first game of the season in Bridgehampton.

That was the plan, anyway.

He stared at the pile of tabloids on Artem's desk. Weeks of clean living and celibacy had just been flushed straight down the drain. More importantly, so had his one shot at getting his life back.

He glared at Artem. "Surely you can't be happy about the fact that everyone in the city thinks I'm sleeping with your sister."

A subtle tension in the set of Artem's jaw was the only crack in his composure. "She's a grown woman, not a child."

"So I've noticed." It was impossible not to.

A lot could happen in three years. She'd been young when she'd shared Franco's bed. Naive. Blissfully so. If he'd realized how innocent she was, he never would have touched her.

But all that was water under the bridge.

Just like Franco's career.

"Besides, this—" Artem gestured toward the pile of newspapers "—isn't real. It's an illusion. One that's advantageous to both of us."

This guy was unbelievable. And he was clearly unaware that Franco and Diana shared a past. Which was probably for the best, given the circumstances.

Franco couldn't help but be intrigued by what he was saying, though. *Advantageous to both of us...*

"Do explain."

Artem shrugged. *Yep, clueless.* "I'm no stranger to the tabloids. Believe me, I understand where you're coming from. But there's a way to use this kind of exposure and make the most out of it. We've managed to get the attention of the world. Our next step is keeping it."

He already didn't like the sound of this. "What exactly are you proposing?"

"A press tour. Take the cuff links out for a spin. You make the rounds of the local philanthropy scene—black-tie parties, charity events, that sort of thing—and smile for the cameras." His gaze flitted to the photo of Franco and Diana. "Alongside my sister, of course."

"Let me get this straight. You want to pay me to publically date Diana." No way in hell. He was an athlete, not a gigolo.

"Absolutely not. I want to pay you to make appearances while wearing Drake gemstones. If people happen to assume you and Diana are a couple, so be it."

Franco narrowed his gaze. "You know they will."

Artem shrugged. "Let them. Look, I didn't plan any of this. But we'd all be fools not to take advantage of the buzz. From what I hear, appearing to be in a monogamous relationship could only help your reputation."

Ah, so the cat was out of the bag, after all.

Franco cursed under his breath. "How long do you expect me to keep up this farce?"

He wasn't sure why he was asking. It was a completely ludicrous proposition.

Although he supposed there were worse fates than spending time with Diana Drake.

Don't go there. Not again.

"Twenty-one days," Artem said.

Franco knew the date by heart already. "The day before the American polo season starts in Bridgehampton. The Kingsmen go on tour right after the season starts."

"Precisely. And you'll be going with them. Assuming you're back on the team by then, obviously." Artem shrugged. "That's what you want, isn't it?"

Franco wondered how Artem had heard about his predicament. He hadn't thought the news of his termination had spread beyond the polo community. Somehow the fact that it had made it seem more real. Permanent.

And that was unacceptable.

"It's absolutely what I want," he said.

"Good. Let us help you fix your reputation." Artem shrugged as if doing so was just that simple.

Maybe it is. "I don't understand. What would you be getting out of this proposed arrangement? Are you really this desperate to move your cuff links?"

"Hardly. This is about more than cuff links." Artem rummaged around the stack of gossip rags on his desk until he found a neatly folded copy of the *New York Times*. "Much more."

He slid the paper across the smooth surface of the desk. It didn't take long for Franco to spot the headline of interest: Jewelry House to be Chosen for World's Largest Uncut Diamond.

Franco looked up and met Artem's gaze. "Let me guess. Drake Diamonds wants to cut this diamond."

"Of course we do. The stone is over one thousand carats. It's the size of a baseball. Every jewelry house in Manhattan wants to get its hands on it. Once it's been cut and placed in a setting, the diamond will be unveiled at a gala at the Metropolitan Museum of Art. Followed by a featured exhibition open to the public, naturally."

Franco's eyes narrowed. "Would the date for this gala possibly be twenty-one days from now?"

"Bingo." Artem leaned forward in his chair. "It's the perfect arrangement. You and Diana will keep Drake Diamonds on the front page of every newspaper in New York. The owners of the diamond will see the Drake name everywhere they turn, and they'll have no choice but to pick us as their partners."

"I see." It actually made sense. In a twisted sort of way.

Artem continued, "By the time you and Diana attend the Met's diamond gala together, you'll have been in a high-profile relationship for nearly a month. Monogamous. Respectable. You're certain to get back in the good graces of your team."

Maybe. Then again, maybe not.

"Plus you'll be great for the team's ticket sales. The more famous you are, the more people will line up to see you play. The Kingsmen will be bound to forgive and forget whatever transgression got you fired." Artem lifted a brow. "What exactly did you do, anyway? You're the best player on the circuit, so it couldn't have been related to your performance on the field."

Franco shrugged. "I didn't do anything, actually."

He'd been cut through no fault of his own. Even worse, he'd been unable to defend himself. Telling the lie had been his choice, though. His call. He'd done what he'd needed to do.

It had been a matter of honor. Even if he'd been able to go back in time and erase the past thirty days, he'd still do it all over again.

Make the same choice. Say the same things.

Artem regarded him through narrowed eyes. "Fine.

You don't need to tell me. From now on, you're a reformed man, anyway. Nothing else matters."

"Got it." Franco nodded.

He wasn't seriously considering this arrangement. It
was borderline demeaning, wasn't it? To both himself
and Diana.

Diana Drake.

He could practically hear her breathy, judgmental
voice in his ear. *From what I hear, you're used to this
kind of thing.*

She'd never go along with this charade. She had too
much pride. Then again, what did he know about Diana
Drake these days?

He cleared his throat. "What happens afterward?"

"Afterward?"

Franco nodded. "Yes, after the gala."

Artem smiled. "I'm assuming you'll ride off into the
sunset with your team and score a massive amount of
goals. You'll continue to behave professionally and eventually you and Diana will announce a discreet breakup."

They'd never get away with it. Diana hadn't even set
eyes on Franco or deigned to speak a word to him in the
past three years until just a few days ago. No one would
seriously believe they were a couple.

He stared down at the heap of newspapers on Artem's desk.

People already believed it.

"You'll be compensated for each appearance at the
rate we agreed upon under the terms of your modeling
contract. You can start tonight."

"Tonight?"

Artem gave a firm nod. "The Manhattan Pet Rescue
animal shelter is holding its annual Fur Ball at the Waldorf Astoria. You and Diana can dress up and cuddle with

a few adorable puppies and kittens. Every photographer in town will be there."

The Fur Ball. It certainly sounded wholesome. Nauseatingly, mind-numbingly adorable.

"I'm assuming we have a deal." Artem stood.

Franco rose from his seat, but ignored Artem's outstretched hand. They couldn't shake on things. Not yet. "You're forgetting something."

"What's that?"

Not what. Who. "Diana. She'll never agree to this."

Artem's gaze grew sharp. Narrow. "What makes you say so?"

Franco had a sudden memory of her exquisite violet eyes, shiny with unshed tears as she slapped him hard across the face. "Trust me. She won't."

"Just be ready for the driver to pick you up at eight. I'll handle Diana." Artem offered his hand again.

This time, Franco took it.

But even as they shook on the deal, he knew it would never happen. Diana wasn't the sort of person who could be handled. By anyone. Artem Drake had no idea what he was up against. Franco almost felt sorry for him. Almost, but not quite.

Some things could only be learned the hard way.

Like a slap in the face.

Chapter Four

Diana called Artem repeatedly on her walk to Drake Diamonds, but his secretary refused to put her through. She kept insisting that he was in an important business meeting and had left instructions not to be disturbed, which only made Diana angrier. If such a thing was even possible.

A billboard. In Times Square.

She wanted to die.

Calm down. Just breathe. People will forget all about it in a day or two. In the grand scheme of life, it's not that big a deal.

But there was no deluding herself. It was, quite literally, a big deal. A huge one. A whopping 25,000-square-foot Technicolor enormous deal.

Artem would have to take it down. That's all there was to it. She hadn't signed any kind of modeling release. Drake might be her last name, but that didn't mean the family business owned the rights to her likeness.

Or did it? She wasn't even sure. Drake Diamonds had been her sponsor on the equestrian circuit. Maybe the business did, in fact, own her.

God, why hadn't she gone to college? She was in no way prepared for this.

She pushed her way through the revolving door of Drake Diamonds with a tad too much force. Urgent meeting or not, Artem was going to talk to her. She'd break down the door of his Drake-blue office if that's what it took.

"Whoa, there." The door spun too quickly and hurled her toward some poor, unsuspecting shopper in the lobby who caught her by the shoulders before she crashed into him. "Slow down, Wildfire."

"Sorry. I just…" She straightened, blinked and found herself face-to-face with the poster boy himself. Franco. "Oh, it's you."

What was he doing here? *Again?* And why were his hands on her shoulders? And why was he calling her that ridiculous name?

Wildfire.

She'd loved that song when she was a little girl. So, so much.

Well, she didn't love it anymore. In fact, Franco had just turned her off it for life.

"Good morning to you too, Diana." He winked. He was probably the only man on planet Earth who could make such a cheesy gesture seem charming.

Ugh.

She wiggled out of his grasp. "Why are you here? Wait, don't tell me. You're snapping selfies for the Drake Diamonds Instagram."

He was wearing a suit. Not a tuxedo this time, but a finely tailored suit, nonetheless. It was weird seeing him dressed this way. Shouldn't he be wearing riding clothes? He adjusted his shirt cuffs. "It bothers you that I'm the new face of Drake Diamonds?"

"No, it doesn't actually. I couldn't care less what you do. It bothers me that *I'm* the new face of Drake Diamonds." A few shoppers with little blue bags dangling from their wrists turned and stared.

Franco angled his head closer to hers. "You might want to keep your voice down."

"I don't care who hears me." She was being ridiculous. But she couldn't quite help it, and she certainly wasn't going to let Franco tell her how to behave.

"Your brother will care," he said.

"What are you talking about?" Then she put two and two together. Finally. "Wait a minute…were you just upstairs with Artem?"

He nodded. Diana must have been imagining things, because he almost looked apologetic.

"So you're the reason his secretary wouldn't put my calls through?" Unbelievable.

"I suppose so, yes." Again, something about his expression was almost contrite.

She glared at him. He could be as nice as he wanted, but as far as Diana was concerned, it was too little, too late. "What was this urgent tête-à-tête about?"

Why was she asking him questions? She didn't care what he and Artem had to say to each other…

Except something about Franco's expression told her she should.

He leveled his gaze at her and arched a single seductive brow. Because, yes, even the man's eyebrows were sexy. "I think you should talk to Artem."

She swallowed. Something was going on here. Something big. And she had the distinct feeling she wasn't going to like it. "Fine. But just so we're clear, I'm talking to him because I want to. And because he's my brother and sort of my boss. Not because you're telling me I should."

"Duly noted." He seemed to be struggling not to smile.

She lifted her chin in defiance. "Goodbye, Franco."

But for some reason, her feet didn't move. She just kept standing there, gazing up at his despicably handsome face.

"See you tonight, Wildfire." He shot her a knowing half grin before turning for the door.

She stood frozen, gaping after him.

Tonight?

She definitely needed to talk to Artem. Immediately.

She skipped the elevator and took the stairs two at a time until she reached the tenth floor, where she found him sitting at his desk as if it was any ordinary day. A day when Franco Andrade wasn't wandering the streets of Manhattan wearing Tom Ford and planning on seeing her tonight.

"Hello, sis." Artem looked up and frowned as he took in her appearance. "Why do you look like you just ran a marathon?"

"Because I just walked a few miles, then sprinted up the stairs." She was breathless. Her legs burned, which was just wrong. She shouldn't be winded from a little exercise. She was an elite athlete.

Used to be an elite athlete.

He gestured toward the wingback chair opposite him. "Take a load off. I need to talk to you, anyway."

"So I've heard." She didn't want to sit down. She wanted to stand and scream at him, but that wasn't going to get her anywhere. Besides, she felt drained all of a sudden. Being around Franco, even for a few minutes, was exhausting. "Speaking of which, what was Franco Andrade doing here just now?"

"About that…" He calmly folded his hands in front of him, drawing Diana's attention first to the smooth surface of his desk and then to the oddly huge stack of newspapers on top of it.

She blinked and cut him off midsentence. "Is that my picture on the front page of the *New York Daily News*?"

She hadn't thought it possible for the day to get any worse, but it just had. So much worse.

And the hits kept on coming. As she sifted through the stack of tabloids—all of which claimed she was having a torrid affair with "the drop-dead gorgeous bad boy of polo"—Artem outlined his preposterous idea for a public relations campaign. Although it sounded more like an episode of *The Bachelor* than any kind of legitimate business plan.

"No, thank you." Diana flipped the copy of *Page Six* facedown so she wouldn't have to look at the photo of herself and Franco on the cover. If she never saw that picture again, it would be too soon.

Artem's brow furrowed. "No, thank you? What does that mean?"

"It means no. As in, I'll pass." What about her answer wasn't he understanding? She couldn't be more clear. "No. N.O."

"Perhaps you don't understand. We're talking about the largest uncut diamond in the world. Do you have any idea what this could mean for Drake Diamonds?" There was Artem's CEO voice again.

She wasn't about to let it intimidate her this time. "Yes. I realize it's very important, but we'll simply have to come up with another plan." *Preferably one that doesn't involve Franco Andrade in any way, shape or form.*

"Let's hear your suggestions, then." He leaned back in his chair and crossed his arms. "I'm all ears."

He wanted her to come up with a plan *now*?

Diana cleared her throat. "I'll have to give it some thought, obviously. But I'm sure I can come up with something."

"Go ahead. I'll wait."

"Artem, come on. We can take the owners of the diamond out to dinner or something. Wine and dine them."

"You realize every other jeweler in Manhattan is doing that exact same thing," he said.

Admittedly, that was probably true. "There's got to be a better way to catch their attention than letting everyone believe I'm having a scandalous affair with Franco."

Please let there be another way.

"Not scandalous. Just high profile. Romantic. Glamorous." Artem gave her a thoughtful look. "He told me you'd refuse, by the way. What, exactly, is the problem between you two?"

Diana swallowed. Maybe she should simply tell Artem what happened three years ago. Surely then he'd forget about parading her all over Park Avenue on Franco's arm just for the sake of a diamond. Even the biggest diamond in the known universe.

But she couldn't. She didn't even want to think about that humiliating episode, much less talk about it.

Especially to her brother, of all people.

"He's a complete and total man whore. You know that, right?" Wasn't that reason enough to turn down the opportunity to pretend date him for twenty-one days? "Aren't you at all concerned about my virtue?"

"The last time I checked, you were more than capable of taking care of yourself, Diana. In fact, you're one of the strongest women I know. I seriously doubt I need to worry about your virtue." He shrugged. "But I could have a word with Franco…do the whole brother thing and threaten him with bodily harm if he lays a finger on you. Would that make you feel better?"

"God, no." She honestly couldn't fathom anything more mortifying.

"It's your call." Artem shrugged. "He's rehabilitating his image, anyway. Franco Andrade's man-whore days are behind him."

Diana laughed. Loud and hard. "He told you that? And you believed him?"

"When did you become such a cynic, sis?"

Three years ago. Right around the time I lost my virginity. "It seems dubious. That's all I'm saying. Why would he change after all this time, unless he's already had his way with every woman on the eastern seaboard?"

It was a distinct possibility.

"People change, Diana." His expression softened and he cast a meaningful glance at the bassinet in the corner of his office. A pink mobile hung over the cradle, decorated with tiny teddy bears wearing ballet shoes. "I did."

Diana smiled at the thought of her adorable baby niece.

He had a point. Less than a year ago, Artem had been the one on the cover of *Page Six*. He'd been photographed with a different woman every night. Now he was a candidate for father of the year.

Moreover, Diana had never seen a couple more in love than Artem and Ophelia. It was almost enough to restore her faith in marriage.

But not quite.

It would take more than her two brothers finding marital bliss to erase the memory of their father's numerous indiscretions.

It wasn't just the affairs. It was the way he'd made no

effort whatsoever to hide them from their mother. He'd expected her to accept it. To smile and look away. And she had.

Right up until the day she died.

She'd been just forty years old when Diana found her lifeless body on the living room floor. Still young, still beautiful. The doctors had been baffled. They'd been unable to find a reason for her sudden heart attack. But to Diana, the reason was obvious.

Her mother had died of a broken heart.

Was it any wonder she thought marriage was a joke? She was beyond screwed up when it came to relationships. How damaged must she have been to intentionally throw herself at a man who was famous for treating women as if they were disposable?

Diana squeezed her eyes shut.

Why did Franco have to come strutting back into her life *now*, while she was her most vulnerable? Before her accident, she could have handled him. She could have handled anything.

She opened her eyes. "Please, Artem. I just really, really don't want to do this."

He nodded. "I see. You'd rather spend all day, every day, slaving away in Engagements than attend a few parties with Franco. Understood. Sorry I brought it up."

He waved a hand toward the dreaded Engagements showroom down the hall. "Go ahead and get to work."

Diana didn't move a muscle. "Wait. Are you saying that if I play the part of Franco's fake girlfriend by night, I won't have to peddle engagement rings by day?"

She'd assumed her position in Engagements was still part of the plan. This changed things.

She swallowed. She still couldn't do it. She'd never

last a single evening in Franco's company, much less twenty-one of them.

Could she?

"Of course you wouldn't have to do both." Artem gestured toward the newspapers spread across his desk. "This would be a job, just like any other in the company."

She narrowed her gaze and steadfastly refused to look at the picture again. "What kind of job involves going to black-tie parties every night?"

"Vice president of public relations. I did it for years. The job is yours now, if you want it." He smiled. "You asked me to find something else for you to do, remember? Moving from the sales floor to a VP position is a meteoric rise."

When he put it that way, it didn't sound so bad. Vice president of public relations sounded pretty darn good, actually.

Finally. This was the kind of opportunity she'd been waiting for. She just never dreamed that Franco Andrade would be part of the package.

"I want a pay increase," she blurted.

What was she doing?

"Done." Artem's grin spread wide.

She wasn't seriously considering accepting the job though, was she? No. She couldn't. Wouldn't. No amount of money was worth her dignity.

But there was one thing that might make participating in the farce worthwhile…

"And if it works, I want to be promoted." She pasted on her sweetest smile. "Again."

Artem's brows rose. "You're going to have to be more specific. Besides, vice president is pretty high on the food chain around here."

"I'm aware. But this diamond gala is really important. You said so yourself."

Artem's smile faded. Just a bit. "That's right."

"If I do my part and Drake Diamonds is chosen as the jewelry house to cut the giant diamond and if everything goes off with a hitch at the Met's diamond gala, I think I deserve to take Dalton's place." She cleared her throat. "I want to be named co-CEO."

Artem didn't utter a word at first. He just sat and stared at her as if she'd sprouted another head.

Great. She'd pushed too far.

VP was a massive career leap. She should have jumped at the opportunity to put all the love-struck brides and grooms in the rearview mirror and left it at that.

"That's a bold request for someone with no business experience," he finally said.

"Correct me if I'm wrong, but wasn't vice president of public relations the only position you held at Drake Diamonds before our father died and appointed you his successor as CEO?" Did Artem really think she'd been so busy at horse shows that she had no clue what had gone on between these Drake-blue walls the past few years?

Still, what was she saying? He'd never buy into this.

He let out an appreciative laugh. "You're certainly shrewd enough for the job."

She grinned. "I'll take that as a compliment."

"As you should." He sighed, looked at her for a long, loaded moment and nodded. "Okay. It works for me."

She waited for some indication that he was joking, but it never came.

Her heart hammered hard in her chest. "Don't tease me, Artem. It's been kind of a rough day."

And it was about to get rougher.

If she and Artem had actually come to an agreement,

that meant she was going out with Franco Andrade tonight. By choice.

She needed to have her head examined.

"I'm not teasing. You made a valid point. I didn't know anything about being a CEO when I stepped into the position. I learned. You will, too." He held up a finger. A warning. "But only if you deliver. Drake Diamonds must be chosen to cut the stone and cosponsor the Met Diamond gala."

"No problem." She beamed at him.

For the first time since she'd fallen off her horse, she felt whole. Happy. She was building a new future for herself.

In less than a month, she'd be co-CEO. No more passing out petit fours. No more engagement rings. She'd never have to look at another copy of *Bride* magazine for as long as she lived!

Better yet, she wouldn't have to answer any more questions about when she was going to start riding again. Every time she turned around, it seemed someone was asking her about her riding career. Had she gotten a new horse? Was she ready to start showing again?

Diana wasn't anywhere close to being ready. She wasn't sure she'd *ever* be ready.

Co-CEO was a big job. A huge responsibility—huge enough that it just might make people forget she'd once dreamed of going to the Olympics. If she was running the company alongside Artem, no one would expect her to compete anymore. It was the perfect solution.

She just had to get through the next twenty-one days first.

"Go home." Artem nodded toward his office door. "Rest up and get ready for tonight."

Tonight. A fancy party. The Waldorf Astoria. Franco.

She swallowed. "Everything will be fine."

Artem lifted a brow.

Had she really said that out loud?

"I know it will, because it's your job to make sure everything is fine," Artem said. "And for the record, there's not a doubt in my mind that your virtue is safe. You can hold your own, Diana. You just talked your way into a co-CEO job. From where I'm standing, if there's anyone who has reason to be afraid, it's Mr. Andrade."

He was right. She'd done that, hadn't she?

She could handle a few hours in Franco's company.

"I think you're right."

God, she hoped so.

Chapter Five

Franco leaned inside the Drake limo and did a double take when he saw Diana staring at him impassively from its dark interior.

"Buenas noches."

He'd expected the car to pick him up first and then take him to Diana's apartment so he could collect her. Like a proper date. But technically this wasn't a date, even though it already felt like one.

He couldn't remember the last time he'd dressed in a tuxedo and escorted a woman to a party. Despite his numerous exploits, Franco didn't often date. He arrived at events solo, and when the night was over he left with a woman on his arm. Sometimes several. Hours later, he typically went home alone. He rarely shared a bed with the same woman more than once, and he never spent the night. Ever.

In fact, the last woman who'd woken up beside him had been Diana Drake.

"Good evening, yourself," she said, without bothering to give him more than a cursory glance.

That would have to change once they arrived at the gala. Lovers looked at each other. They touched each other. Hell, if Diana was his lover, Franco wouldn't be able to keep his hands off her.

This isn't real.

He slid onto the smooth leather seat beside her.

It wasn't real, but it felt real. It even looked real.

Diana was dressed in a strapless chiffon gown, midnight blue, with a dangerously low, plunging neckline. A glittering stone rested between her breasts. A sapphire. *The* sapphire necklace from the photo shoot.

"Please stop staring." She turned and met his gaze. At last.

Franco's body hardened the instant his eyes fixed on hers. As exquisite as the sapphire around her neck was, it didn't hold a candle to the luminescent violet depths of those eyes. "You're lovely."

She stared at him coldly. "Save it for the cameras, would you? There's no one here. You can drop the act."

"It's not an act. You look beautiful." He swallowed. Hard. "That's quite a dress."

He was used to seeing her in riding clothes, not like this. He couldn't seem to look away.

What are you, a teenager? Grow up, Andrade.

"Seriously, stop." The car sped through a tunnel, plunging them into darkness. But the shadows couldn't hide the slight tremor in her voice. "Just stop it, would you? I know we're supposed to be madly in love with each other in public. But in private, can we keep things professional? Please?"

Something about the way she said *please* grabbed Franco by the throat and refused to let go.

Had he really been so awful to her all those years ago? Yes. He had.

Still, she'd been better off once he'd pushed her away, whether she'd realized it or not. She was an heiress. The real deal. And Franco wasn't the type of man she'd bring home.

Never had been, never would be.

"Professional. Got it," he said to the back of her head. It felt more like he was talking to himself than to Diana.

She'd turned away again, keeping her gaze fixed on the scenery outside the car window. The lights of the city rushed past, framing her silhouette in a dizzying halo of varying hues of gold.

They sat in stony silence down the lavish length of Park Avenue. The air in the limo felt so thick he was practically choking on it. Franco refrained from pointing out that refusing to either look at him or speak to him in something other than monosyllables was hardly professional.

Why the hell had she agreed to this arrangement, anyway? Neither one of them should be sitting in the back of a limo on the way to some boring gala. They both belonged on horseback. Franco knew why he wasn't training right now, but for the life of him, he couldn't figure out what Diana was doing working for her family business.

He was almost grateful when his phone chimed with an incoming text message, giving him something to focus on. Not looking at Diana was becoming more impossible by the second. She was stunning, even in her fury.

He slid his cell out of the inside pocket of his tuxedo jacket and looked at the screen.

A message from Luc. Again.

Ellis still isn't budging.

Franco's jaw clenched. That information wasn't exactly breaking news. If he'd held out any hope of the team owner changing his mind before the end of the day, he wouldn't be sitting beside the diamond ice princess right now.

Still, he didn't particularly enjoy dwelling on the dismal state of his career.

He moved to slip the phone back inside his pocket, but it chimed again.

This has gone on long enough.

And again.

I can't let you do this. I'm telling him the truth.

Damn it all to hell.
Franco tapped out a response…

Let it go. What's done is done. I have everything under control.

Beside him, Diana cleared her throat. "Lining up your date for the evening?"

Franco looked up and found her regarding him through narrowed eyes. She shot a meaningful glance at his phone.

So, she didn't like the thought of him texting other women? Interesting.

"You're my date for the evening, remember?" He wasn't texting another woman, obviously. But she didn't need to know that. He hardly owed her an explanation.

She rolled her eyes. "Don't even pretend you're going home alone after this."

He powered his phone down and glanced back up at Diana. "As a matter of fact, I am. Didn't Artem tell you? You and I are monogamous."

She arched a brow. "Did he explain what that meant, or did you have to look it up in the dictionary?"

"You're adorable when you're jealous. I like it." He was goading her, and he knew it. But at least they were speaking.

"If you think I'm jealous, you're even more full of yourself than I thought you were." In the darkened limousine, he could see two pink spots glowing on her cheeks. "Also, you're completely delusional."

He shrugged. "I disagree. Do you know why?"

"I can't begin to imagine what's going on inside your head. Nor would I want to." She exhaled a breath of resignation. "Why?"

"Because nothing about this conversation—which *you* initiated—is professional in nature." He deliberately let his gaze drop to the sapphire sparkling against her alabaster skin, then took a long, appreciative look at the swell of her breasts.

"You're insatiable," she said with a definite note of disgust.

He smiled. "Most women like that about me."

"I'm not most women."

"We'll see about that, won't we?"

The car slowed to a stop in front of the gilded entrance to the Waldorf Astoria. A red carpet covered the walkway from the curb to the gold-trimmed doors, flanked on either side by a mob of paparazzi too numerous to count.

"Miss Drake and Mr. Andrade, we've arrived," the driver said.

"Thank God. I need to get out of this car." Diana reached for the door handle, but her violet eyes grew wide. "Oh, wait. I almost forgot."

She opened her tiny, beaded clutch, removed a Drake-blue box and popped it open. The black diamond cuff links from the photo shoot glittered in the velvety darkness.

She handed them to Franco as the driver climbed out of the car. "Put these on. Quickly."

He slid one into place on his shirt cuff, but left the other in the palm of his hand.

"What are you doing? Hurry." Diana was borderline panicking. The back door clicked open, and the driver extended his hand toward her and waited.

"Go ahead, it's showtime." Franco loosened his tie and winked. "Trust me, Wildfire."

She stretched one foot out of the car, aimed a dazzling smile at the waiting photographers and muttered under her breath, "You realize that's asking the impossible."

Franco gathered the soft chiffon hem of her gown and helped her out of the limo. They stepped from the quiet confines of the car into a frenzy of clicking camera shutters and blinding light.

He dropped a kiss on Diana's bare shoulder and made a show of fastening the second cuff link in place. A collective gasp rose from the assembled crowd of spectators.

He lowered his lips to Diana's ear. "I have everything under control."

I have everything under control.

Maybe if he repeated it enough times, it would be true.

The man is an evil genius.

Diana hadn't been sure what Franco had up his sleeve until she felt his lips brush against her shoulder.

The kiss caught her distinctly off guard, and as her head whipped around to look at him, she saw him fastening his cuff link. He curved his arm around her waist, murmured in her ear and she finally understood. He'd purposely delayed sliding the diamonds into position on his shirt cuff so it looked as though he was only just getting dressed, no doubt because their arrival at the gala had caught them in flagrante delicto.

The press ate it up.

Evil genius. Most definitely.

"Diana, how long have you and Franco been dating?"

"Diana, who are you wearing?"

"Look over here, Diana! Smile for the camera."

Photographers shouted things from every direction.

She didn't know where to look, so she bowed her head as Franco steered her deftly through the frenzied crowd with his hand planted protectively on the small of her back.

"What's the diamond heiress like in bed, Franco?" a paparazzo yelled.

Diana's head snapped up.

"Don't let them get to you," Franco whispered.

"I'm fine," she lied. The whole scene was madness. "But if you answer that question, I will murder you."

"A gentleman doesn't kiss and tell."

Their eyes met briefly in the chaos, and if Diana hadn't known better, she would have believed he was being serious.

Suddenly, the thought of doing this for twenty-one straight days seemed absurd. Absurd and wholly impossible.

"Good evening, Miss Drake, Mr. Andrade." The doorman nodded and swept the door open for them. "Welcome to the Waldorf Astoria."

"Gracias," Franco said. *Thank you.* He gave her waist a gentle squeeze. "Shall we, love?"

His voice rumbled through her, deliciously deep.

She swallowed. *It's all pretend. Don't fall for it. Don't fall.*

She'd told herself the same thing three years ago. A fat lot of good that had done her.

Everything was moving too fast. Even after they finally made it inside the grand black-and-white marble lobby, Diana felt as if she'd been caught up in a whirlwind. A glittering blur where everything was too big and too bright, from the mosaic floor to the grand chandelier to the beautiful man standing beside her.

"Miss Drake and Mr. Andrade, I'm Beth Ross, director of Manhattan Pet Rescue. We're so pleased you could make it to our little gathering this evening."

"Ah, Beth, we wouldn't have missed it for the world," Franco said smoothly, following up his greeting with a kiss on the cheek.

Beth practically swooned.

He was so good at this it was almost frightening. If Artem had really known what he was doing, he would have made Franco the new vice president of public relations.

Say something. You're not the arm candy. He is.

"Thank you for having us. We're so pleased to be here." Diana smiled.

From the corner of her eye, she spotted someone holding up a cell phone and pointing toward her and Franco. He must have seen it too, because he deftly wrapped his arm around her waist and rested his palm languidly on her hip. Without even realizing it, she burrowed into him.

Beth sighed. "You two are every bit as beautiful

as your advertising campaign. It's all anyone can talk about."

"So we've heard." Diana forced a smile.

"Our party is located upstairs in the Starlight Ballroom. I've come to escort you up there, and if you don't mind, we'd love to snap a few pictures of you with some of the animals we have up for adoption later this evening."

Diana stiffened. "Um…"

Franco gave her hipbone a subtle squeeze. "We'd be happy to. We're big animal lovers, obviously."

We're big animal lovers.

We.

Diana blinked. Franco seemed to be staring at her, waiting for her to say something. "Oh, yes. Huge animal lovers."

They moved from the glitzy, gold lobby into a darkly intimate corridor walled in burgundy velvet. Beth pushed a button to summon an elevator.

"That doesn't surprise me a bit," she said. "I just knew you must be animal lovers. Drake Diamonds has always been one of our biggest supporters. And, of course, both of you are legendary in the horse world."

The elevator doors swished open, and the three of them stepped inside.

"Diana has a beautiful black Hanoverian. Tell Beth about Diamond, love." Franco looked at her expectantly.

Diana felt as though she'd been slapped.

She opened her mouth to say something, anything, but she couldn't seem capable of making a sound.

"Are you all right, dear? You've gone awfully pale." Beth eyed her with concern.

"I just… I…" It was no use. She couldn't talk about Diamond. Not now.

For six months, she'd managed to avoid discussing her beloved horse's death with anyone. Not even her brothers. She knew she probably should, but she couldn't. It just hurt too much. And after so much silence, the words wouldn't come.

"She's a bit claustrophobic," Franco said.

Another lie. Diana was beginning to lose track of them all.

"Oh, I'm so sorry." Beth's hand fluttered to her throat. "I didn't realize. We should have taken the stairs."

"It's fine." Franco's voice was like syrup. Soothing. "We're almost there, darling."

The elevator doors slid open.

Diana burrowed into Franco as he half carried her to the entrance to the ballroom. She couldn't remember leaning against him in the first place.

Breathe in, breathe out. You're fine.

She took a deep inhale and straightened her spine, smiled. "So sorry. I'm okay. Really."

Her heart pounded against her rib cage. She desperately wished she were back at Dalton's apartment, watching bad reality television and curled up under a blanket on the sofa.

Don't think about Diamond. Don't blow this. Say something.

She glanced up at the stained-glass ceiling strung with twinkling lights. "Look how beautiful everything is."

Beth nodded her agreement and launched into a description of all the work that had gone into putting together the gala, a large part of which had been funded by Drake Diamonds. Diana smiled and nodded, as did Franco, although at times she could see him watching her with what felt like too much interest.

She was dying to tell him he was laying it on a little

thick. They were supposed to be dating, not engaged, for crying out loud. Besides, she'd shaken off the worst of her panic.

She was fine. She just hadn't expected him to mention Diamond. That's all. She'd assumed that Franco had known about her accident. Apparently, he hadn't. Otherwise, he never would have brought up Diamond.

She'd been shocked, and probably a little upset. But it had passed.

He didn't need to be worried about her, and he definitely didn't need to be watching her like that. But an hour into the gala they were still shaking hands and chatting with the other animal shelter donors. She and Franco hadn't had a moment alone together.

Not that Diana was complaining.

The limousine ride had provided plenty of one-on-one time, thank you very much.

"If we could just ask you to do one last thing…" Beth guided them toward the far corner of the ballroom where guests had been taking turns posing for pictures. "Could we get those photos I mentioned before you leave?"

Diana nodded. "Absolutely."

Franco's hand made its way to the small of her back again. She was getting somewhat used to it and couldn't quite figure out if that was a bad thing or a good one.

It's nearly over. Just a few more minutes.

One night down, twenty to go. Almost.

She allowed herself a subtle, premature sigh of relief. Then she noticed a playpen filled with adorable, squirming puppies beside the photographer's tripod, and any sense of triumph she felt about her performance thus far disintegrated. She couldn't handle being around animals again. Not yet.

"Well, well. What do we have here?" Franco reached

into the playpen and gathered a tiny black puppy with a tightly curled tail into his arms.

The puppy craned its neck, stuck out its miniscule pink tongue and licked the side of Franco's face. He threw his head back and laughed, which only seemed to encourage the sweet little dog. It scrambled up Franco's chest and showered his ear with puppy kisses.

Beth motioned for the photographer to capture the adoration on film. "Doesn't she just love you, Mr. Andrade?"

The puppy was a girl. Because of course.

Franco's charm appealed to females of all species, apparently.

Why am I not surprised?

"Come here, love." Franco reached for Diana's hand and pulled her toward him. "You've got to meet this little girl. She's a sweetheart."

"No, it's okay. You keep her." She tried to wave him off, but it was impossible. Before she knew what was happening, she had a puppy in her arms and flashbulbs were going off again.

"That's Lulu. She's a little pug mix."

"Franco's right. She's definitely a sweetheart." Diana gazed down at the squirming dog.

Before her brother Dalton got married and moved to Delamotte, he'd tried talking her into getting a dog on multiple occasions. At first she'd thought he was joking. Dalton didn't even like dogs. Or so she'd thought. Apparently that had changed when he met the princess. Then he'd practically become some sort of animal matchmaker and kept encouraging Diana to adopt a pet.

What had gotten into her brothers? Both of them had turned into different people over the course of the past year. Sometimes it felt like the entire world was moving forward, full speed ahead, while Diana stood completely still.

Everything was changing. Everything and everyone.

It didn't use to be this way. From the first day she'd climbed onto the back of horse, Diana had been riding as fast as she could. She'd always thought if she rode hard enough, she'd escape the legacy Gaston Drake had built. Escape everything that it meant to be part of her family. The lies, the deceit. She'd thought she could outrun it.

Now she was back in the family fold, and she realized she hadn't outrun a thing.

She swallowed hard. How could she even consider saving a dog when she wasn't even convinced she could save herself?

"Here. You take her." She tried to hand the puppy back to Franco, but he wrapped his arms around her and kept posing for the camera.

"You three make a lovely family," Beth gushed.

That was Diana's breaking point.

The touching…the endearments…the puppy. Those things she could handle. Mostly. But the idea of being a family? She'd rather die.

"It's getting late. We should probably go."

But no one seemed to have a heard a word she said, because at the exact time that she tried to make her getaway, Franco made an announcement. "We'll take her."

Beth squealed. A few people applauded. Diana just stood there, trying to absorb what he'd said.

She searched his features, but he was still wearing that boyfriend-of-the-year expression that gave her butterflies, even though she knew without a doubt it wasn't real. "What are you talking about?"

"The puppy." He gave the tiny pup a rub behind her ears with the tip of his pointer finger.

"Franco, we can't adopt a dog together," she muttered through her smile, which was definitely beginning to fade.

"Of course we can, darling." His eyes narrowed the slightest bit.

No one else noticed because they were too busy fawning all over him.

"Franco, *sweetheart*." She shot daggers at him with her eyes.

This wasn't part of the deal. She'd agreed to pretend to date him, not coparent an animal.

Besides, she didn't want to adopt a dog. Correction: she *couldn't* adopt a dog.

A dog's lifespan was even shorter than a horse's. Much shorter. She wouldn't survive that kind of heartache. Not again. *Never* again.

Franco bowed his head to nuzzle the puppy and paused to whisper in her ear. "They're eating it up. What is your problem?"

It was the worst possible time for something to snap inside Diana, but something did. All the feelings she'd been working so hard to suppress for the past few months—the anger, the fear, the grief—came spilling out at once. She gazed up at Franco through a veil of tears as the whole world watched.

"Diamond is dead. That's my problem."

Chapter Six

A *Page Six* Exclusive Report

The rumors are true! Diamond heiress Diana Drake and polo's prince charming, Franco Andrade, are indeed a couple. Tongues have been wagging all over New York since their sultry billboard went up in Times Square. The heat between these two is too hot to be anything but genuine!

Drake and Andrade stepped out last night at Manhattan's Annual Fur Ball, where witnesses say they arrived on the heels of what was obviously a romantic tryst in the Drake Diamonds limousine. During the party, Andrade was heard calling Drake by the pet name Wildfire and couldn't keep his hands off the stunning equestrian beauty.

At the end of the evening, Drake was moved to tears when Andrade gifted her with a nine-week-old pug puppy.

Chapter Seven

Franco shifted his Jaguar into Park and swiveled his gaze to the passenger seat. "I don't suppose I can trust you to stay here and let me do the talking."

Lulu let out a piercing yip, then resumed chewing on the trim of the Jag's leather seats.

"Okay, then. Since you've made no attempt at all to hide your deviousness, you're coming with me." He scooped the tiny dog into the crook of his elbow and climbed out of the car.

"Try to refrain from gnawing on my suit if you can help it."

Lulu peered up at him with her shiny, oversize eyes as she clamped her little teeth around one of the buttons on his sleeve.

Marvelous.

Franco didn't bother reprimanding her. If the past week had taught him anything, it was that Lulu had a mind of her own. Not unlike the other headstrong female in his life...

Diana hadn't been kidding when she said she didn't want anything to do with the puppy. As far as pet parenting went, Franco was a single dad. Which would have been fine, had he not known how badly she needed the dog.

She was reeling from the loss of her horse. That much was obvious. If anyone could understand that kind of grief, Franco could.

He'd had no idea that Diamond had died. But now that he knew, things were beginning to make more sense. Diana hadn't given up riding because she had a burning desire to peddle diamonds. She was merely hiding out at the family store. She was heartbroken and afraid.

But she couldn't give up riding forever.

Could she?

"Franco." Ben Santos, the coach of the Kingsmen, strolled out of the barn and positioned himself between Franco and the practice field. "What are you doing here?"

Not exactly the greeting he was hoping for.

Franco squared his shoulders and kept on walking. Enough was enough. He needed to stop worrying so much about his fake girlfriend and focus on resurrecting his career.

"Nice to see you too, coach." He paused by the barn and waited for an invitation onto the field.

None was forthcoming.

Ben squinted into the sun and sighed. "You know you're not supposed to be here, son."

Franco's jaw clenched. He'd never liked Ben's habit of calling his players *son*. Probably because the last man who'd called Franco that had been a worthless son of a bitch.

But he'd put up with it from Ben out of respect. He wasn't in the mood to do so now, though.

Seven nights of wining and dining Diana Drake at every charity ball in Manhattan had gotten him absolutely nowhere. He had nothing to show for his efforts, other than a naughty puppy and a nagging sense that Diana was on the verge of coming apart at the seams.

Not your problem.

"I was hoping we could talk. Man to man," Franco said. Or more accurately, man to man holding tiny dog.

Lulu squirmed in his grasp, and the furrow between Ben's brows faded.

"Nice pup," he said. "This must be the one I've been reading about in all the papers."

Thus far, Lulu's puppyhood had been meticulously chronicled by every gossip rag and website Franco had ever heard of, along with a few he hadn't. Just this morning, Franco had been photographed poop-scooping outside his Tribeca apartment. He supposed he had that lovely image to look forward to in tomorrow's newspapers. Oh, joy.

He cleared his throat. "So you've been keeping up with me."

Excellent. Maybe the love charade was actually working.

"It's been kind of hard not to." Ben reached a hand toward Lulu, who promptly began nibbling on his fingers.

"The publicity should come in handy when the season starts, don't you think?" Franco's gaze drifted over the coach's shoulder to where he could see a groom going over one of the Kingsmen polo ponies with a curry comb. The horse's coat glistened like a shiny copper penny in the shadows of the barn.

Diamond is dead. That's my problem.

"Except you're not on the team, so, no." Ben shook his head.

"This has gone on long enough, don't you think? You need me. The team needs me. How long is Ellis planning on making me sweat this out?"

"You were fired. And I don't think Ellis is going to change his mind. He's furious. Frankly, I can't blame him." Ben removed his Kingsmen baseball cap and raked a hand through his hair. He sighed. "You went too far this time, son. You slept with the man's wife."

Franco pretended he hadn't heard the last sentence. If he thought about it too much, he might be tempted to tell the truth and he couldn't do that. Luc had his faults— bedding the boss's wife chief among them—but he was Franco's friend. Luc had been there for him when he needed someone most.

Franco owed Luc, and it was time to pay up.

"That's over." Franco swallowed. "I'm in love."

He waited for a lightning bolt to appear out of the sky and strike him dead.

Nothing happened. Franco just kept standing there, holding the squirming puppy and watching the horses being led toward the practice field.

He missed this. He missed spending so much time with his horses. He'd been exercising them as often as possible, but it couldn't compare with team practice, day in and day out.

Diana had to miss it, too. He knew she did.

Diamond is dead. That's my problem.

Franco felt sick every time he remembered the lost look in Diana's eyes when she'd said those words.

Her vulnerability had caught him off guard. It affected him far more than her disdain ever could. He didn't mind being hated. He deserved it, frankly. But he *did* mind seeing Diana in pain. He minded it very much.

Again, not his problem. He was here to get himself, not Diana, back in the saddle.

"In love," Ben repeated. His gaze dropped to the rich soil beneath their feet. "I'm happy to hear it. I am. But I'm afraid it's going to take more than a few pictures in the paper to convince Ellis."

Franco's jaw clenched. "What are you saying?"

But the coach didn't need to elaborate, because the field was filling up with Franco's team members. They were clearly preparing for a scrimmage because, instead of being dressed in casual practice attire, they were wearing uniforms. Franco spotted Luc, climbing on top of a sleek ebony mount. But the sight that gave Franco pause was another player. One he'd never seen before, wearing a shirt with a number situated just below his right shoulder—the number 1.

Franco's number.

"Perhaps Ellis would feel differently if you were married. Or even engaged. Something permanent, you know. But right now, it looks like a fling. To him, anyway." Ben shrugged. "Surely you understand. Try to put yourself in his shoes, son. Imagine how you'd feel if another man, a man whom you knew and trusted, hopped into bed and ravished Miss Drake."

Franco's gaze finally moved away from the player wearing his number. He stared at the coach, and a nonsensical rage swelled in his chest. A thick, black rage, which he could only attribute to the fact that he'd been replaced. "Don't talk about her that way."

Ben held up his hands. "I'm not suggesting it will happen. I'm simply urging you to try and understand where Ellis is coming from."

"This isn't about Diana." Franco took a calming inhale and reminded himself that losing his cool wasn't going to do him any favors. "It's not even about Ellis and his wife. It's about the team."

The coach gestured toward the bright-green rectangle of grass just west of the barn. "Look, son. I need to get going. We've got back-to-back scrimmages this afternoon."

Franco jerked his chin in the direction of the practice field. "Who's your new number 1?"

Ben sighed. "Don't, Franco."

"Just tell me who's wearing my jersey, and I'll leave."

"Gustavo Anca."

"You can't be serious." Franco knew Gustavo. He was a nice enough guy, but an average player at best. Ellis was playing it safe. Too safe. "You know he won't bring in the wins."

"Yes, but he won't sleep with the owner's wife, either." The older man gave him a tight smile.

Franco's gaze flitted ever so briefly to Luc sitting atop his horse, doing a series of twisting stretches. He turned in Franco's direction, and their eyes met.

Franco looked away.

"Listen. Can I give you a piece of advice?"

Whatever he had to say, Franco didn't want to hear it.

"Move on. Let the other teams know you're available. Someone is bound to snap you up."

He shook his head. "Out of the question."

The Kingsmen were the best. And when Franco had worn the Kingsmen jersey, he'd been the best of the best. He'd earned his place there, and he wanted it back. His horses were there. His teammates. His heart.

Also, if the Kingsmen were already scrimmaging, it could only mean the rosters had been set for the coming season in Bridgehampton. If Franco wanted to play any-where before autumn, he'd have to go Santa Barbara. Or even as far as Sotogrande, in Spain.

He couldn't leave. He'd made a promise to the Drakes. And for the time being, his position as the face of Drake Diamonds was the only thing paying his bills.

His hesitancy didn't have a thing to do with Diana. At least, that's what he wanted to believe.

"Think about it. Make a few calls. If another team needs a reference, have them contact me." Ben shifted from one foot to the other. "But I can only vouch for your playing. Nothing else."

"Of course." The tangle of fury inside Franco grew into something dark and terrible. He clamped his mouth shut.

"It was good to see you, but please understand. The sit-uation isn't temporary." His coach gave him a sad smile. "It's permanent."

"Miss Drake, you have a visitor." The doorman's voice crackled through the intercom of Diana's borrowed apart-ment. "Mr. Andrade is on his way up."

Diana's hand flew to the Talk button. "Wait. What? *Why?*"

Franco was here? Now?

There had to be some sort of mistake. They weren't scheduled to arrive at the Harry Winston party for an-other hour and a half. She wasn't even dressed yet. Be-sides, she'd given the driver strict instructions to pick her up first. She didn't need Franco anywhere near her apartment. Their lives were already far more intertwined than she'd ever anticipated.

She'd even talked to him about Diamond. Briefly, but still. It had been the closest she'd come to admitting to anyone that she was having trouble moving past her accident. It had also been the first time she'd said Diamond's name out loud since her fall.

She'd spent the intervening days since the Fur Ball carefully shoring up the wall around her heart again. She went through the motions with Franco, speaking to him as little possible. He was the last person she should be confiding in. His casual reference to Diamond had caught her off guard. She'd had a moment of weakness.

It wouldn't happen again.

Even if the sight of him with that adorable puppy in his arms made her weak in the knees...she was only human, after all.

The doorman's voice crackled through the intercom. "I assumed it was acceptable, given the nature of your relationship, that I could go ahead and send Mr. Andrade up."

The nature of their relationship. Hysterical laughter bubbled up Diana's throat.

She swallowed it down. "It's fine. Thank you."

She took a deep breath and told herself to get a grip. She couldn't reprimand the doorman for sending the purported love of her life up to see her, could she?

The building that housed Dalton's apartment was one of the most exclusive addresses in Lenox Hill. She wholeheartedly doubted the doorman would be indiscreet. But the press was always looking for a scoop. The last thing she and Franco needed was a headline claiming she'd turned him away from her door.

Diana shook her head. Not she and Franco. She and Artem. The Drakes were the ones who were on the same team. Franco was just an accessory.

A dashing, dangerous accessory.

Three solid knocks pounded on the door and echoed

through the apartment. Diana tightened the belt of her satin bathrobe and opened the door.

"Franco, what a pleasant surprise," she said with forced enthusiasm.

"Diana," he said flatly.

That was it. No loving endearment. No scandalous quip about her state of near undress. Just her name.

She motioned for him to come inside and shut the door.

Her smile faded as she turned to face him. There was no reason for pretense when they were alone together. Although, now that she thought about it, this was the first time since embarking on their charade that they'd been alone. *Truly* alone. Everywhere they went, they were surrounded by drivers, photographers, doormen.

A nonsensical shiver passed through her as she looked up at him. His eyes seemed darker than usual, his expression grim.

"What are you doing here?"

Had something happened? Had word gotten out that they'd been faking their love affair? Surely not. Artem would have said something. She'd talked to him on the phone only moments ago, and everything had seemed fine.

"We have a date this evening, do we not?" His words were clipped. Formal.

Diana never thought she'd miss his sexually charged smile and smug attitude, but she kind of did. At least that version of Franco was somewhat predictable. This new persona seemed quite the opposite.

"We do." She nodded and waited for him to ogle her. She was wearing a white satin minibathrobe, for crying out loud.

He just stood there in his impeccably cut tuxedo with

his arms crossed. "Where are we going tonight, any-way?"

"To a party at Harry Winston."

"The jewelry store?" He frowned. "Isn't Harry Winston a direct competitor of Drake Diamonds?"

"Yes, but the Lambertis are going to be there."

"Who?" he asked blithely.

Seriously? They'd been over this about a million times. "Carla and Don Lamberti. They own the diamond, re-member? *The* diamond."

"Right." His gaze strayed to her creamy satin bath-robe. Finally. "Shouldn't you be getting dressed?"

"I *was*. Until you knocked on my door." This wasn't the night for Franco to go rogue. Absolutely not. "What's with you tonight? Is something wrong? Why are you even here?"

His eyes flashed. Something most definitely wasn't right. "You're my girlfriend." He used exaggerated air quotes around the word *girlfriend*. "Why shouldn't I be here?"

"Because the car was supposed to pick me up first, and then we were going to collect you in Tribeca. That's why."

He eyed her with an intensity that made her feel warm and delicious, like she'd been sipping red wine. "I'm tired of following orders, Diana. Surely I'm not expecting too much if I want to make my own decision regarding trans-portation to a party."

"Um…"

"A real couple wouldn't be picked up at two separate locations. Real lovers would be in bed until the moment it was time to leave. Real lovers would, at the very least, be in the same godforsaken apartment." An angry muscle twitched in his jaw. Diana couldn't seem to look away from it. "We need this to look real. *I* need it to look real."

She'd never seen Franco this serious before. It shouldn't have been nearly as arousing as it was. Especially on a night as important as this one.

Diana nodded and licked her lips. "Of course."

She hadn't realized he'd cared so much about either the company or the diamond. Wasn't this whole lovey-dovey act just a paycheck for him? A way to get a little publicity for the Kingsmen?

Why *did* he care so much?

She realized she didn't actually know why he'd agreed to participate in their grand charade. Artem had said something about Franco changing his image, but she hadn't pressed for details. She just wanted to get through their twenty-one days together as quickly and painlessly as possible.

Franco prowled through her living room with the dangerous grace of a panther. "Where's your liquor cabinet? I need something to pass the time while you're getting ready."

Clearly this wasn't the moment for a heart-to-heart.

She crossed the living room, strode into the kitchen and pulled a bottle of the Scotch that Dalton favored from one of the cabinets. She set it on the counter along with a Waterford highball glass. "Will this do?"

Franco arched a brow. "It'll work."

"Good. Help yourself." She watched as he poured a generous amount and then downed it in a single swallow.

He eyed her as he picked up the bottle again. "Is there a problem, or are you going to finish getting dressed?"

Alarm bells were going off in every corner of her mind. Franco was definitely upset about something. She should call Artem and cancel before Franco polished off the rest of Dalton's Scotch.

But that wasn't an option. Not tonight, when they were

finally going to come face-to-face with the Lambertis. Their 1,100-carat diamond was the sole reason she was in this farce of a relationship.

She took a deep inhale and pasted on a smile. "No problem at all."

Not yet, anyway.

Chapter Eight

Diana held her breath as they climbed into the Drake limousine, hoping against hope that Franco's strange, dark mood would go unnoticed by everyone at the gala.

She kept waiting for him to slip back into his ordinary, devil-may-care persona, but somehow it never happened. They made the short trip to Harry Winston in tense silence, and for the first time, the strained, quiet ride seemed to be Franco's choice rather than hers.

She kept trying to make conversation and loosen him up, but nothing worked. She was beginning to realize how badly she'd behaved toward him over the course of the past week. *This must be how he feels every night.*

She shouldn't feel guilty. She absolutely shouldn't. This wasn't a real date. Not one of the past seven nights had been real. It had been business. All of it.

It needs to look real. I need it to look real.

As the car pulled up to the glittering Harry Winston

storefront at the corner of 5th Avenue and 57th Street—
just a stone's throw from Drake Diamonds—she turned
toward Franco.

"Are you sure you're ready for this?" she asked.

He met her gaze. The slight darkening of his irises was
the only outward sign of the numerous shots of Scotch
he'd consumed back at her apartment. Last week she
wouldn't have known him well enough to notice such a
subtle change.

"Yes. Are you?"

She felt his voice in the pit of her stomach. "Yes."

*There's still time to back out. Artem will be inside. Let
him charm the socks off the Lambertis.*

But making sure the owners of the diamond chose
to work with Drake Diamonds was her responsibility.
Not her brother's. And considering it was pretty much
her *only* responsibility, she shouldn't be passing it off
to Artem.

She'd already survived a week as Franco's faux love
interest. Surely they could pull this off for another fourteen days. Franco would get himself together once they
were in public. He'd be his usual, charming self.

He had to.

But even walking past the mob of paparazzi gathered
in front of the arched entrance and gold-trimmed gate
at Harry Winston's storefront felt different. Franco felt
stiff beside her.

Diana missed the warmth of his hand on the small of
her back. She missed his playful innuendo. God, what
was happening to her? She hadn't actually enjoyed spending time with him.

Because that just wasn't possible.

The moment they crossed the threshold, Artem and
Ophelia strode straight toward them. When her brother

first told her they were coming, Diana had been filled with relief. Tonight was important. She could use all the reinforcements she could get. Now she wished he wasn't here to witness what suddenly felt like a huge disaster in the making.

"Diana." Artem kissed her on the cheek, then turned to shake Franco's hand. "Franco, good to see you."

The two men exchanged pleasantries while Diana greeted Ophelia. Dressed in a floor-length tulle gown, her sister-in-law looked every inch like the ballerina she'd been before taking the helm of the design department of Drake Diamonds. The diamond tiara Artem had given her as an engagement present was intricately interwoven into her upswept hair.

"You look stunning," Diana whispered as she embraced the other woman.

"Thank you, but my God. Look at yourself. You're glowing." Ophelia grinned. "That sapphire suits you."

Diana touched the deep blue stone hanging from the diamond and platinum garland around her neck. She'd worn it every night she'd been out with Franco as an homage to their billboard. "Well, don't get used to it. I doubt my brother is going to let me keep it once this is all over."

"He won't have to, remember? He won't be your boss anymore." Ophelia winked and whispered, "Girl power!"

Diana's stomach did a nervous flip. *Powerful* was the last thing she felt at the moment.

Franco bowed his head and murmured in her ear, "I'm going to fetch some champagne. I'll be right back." He was gone before she could say a word.

Artem frowned after him. "What's wrong with your boyfriend?"

Diana cast him a meaningful glance. *He's not my boyfriend.*

"Sis, I'm being serious. What's wrong with Franco?" Artem murmured.

So much for Franco's somber mood going unnoticed.

"He's fine, Artem. He's doing a wonderful job, as usual." Since when did she jump to Franco Andrade's defense?

"Really? Because he seems a little tense. You're sure he's all right?"

Ophelia looped her arm through her husband's. "Artem, leave Diana alone. She's perfectly capable of doing her job."

Thank God for sisters-in-law.

"I never insinuated she wasn't." Artem gave Diana's shoulder an affection little bump with his own. "My concern is about Andrade. He's letting this whole mess with the Kingsmen get to him."

Diana blinked. "What mess with the Kingsmen?"

"The fact that he's been dropped from the team. I'm guessing by his mood that he hasn't been reinstated yet. But I'm sure you know more about it than I do." Artem shrugged.

Franco had been *fired*?

So that's why he'd signed on with Drake Diamonds. He had as much to gain from their pretend courtship as she did.

But he was one of the best polo players in the world. Why would the Kingsmen let him go? It didn't make sense. She stared at him across the room and wondered what other secrets he was keeping.

Whatever the case, she wasn't about to tell Artem that she didn't have a clue Franco had been cut. This seemed like the sort of thing his girlfriend should know. Even a fake girlfriend.

"He's fine." She forced a smile. Doing so was becoming alarmingly easy. She probably shouldn't be so good at lying. "Really."

"How is it we're here, anyway? I feel like we've breached enemy territory," Ophelia whispered.

Diana looked around at the opulent surroundings— pale gray walls, black-and-white art deco tile floor, cut crystal vases overflowing with white hydrangeas—and tried not to be too impressed. She'd never set foot in Harry Winston before. As far as she knew, no Drake ever had. Their father was probably rolling in his grave.

"We were invited. All the high-end jewelers in the city are here. It's a power move on Harry Winston's part. I think it's their strategy to show the Lambertis that Harry Winston is the obvious choice to cut the diamond. It's bold to invite all your competitors. Confident. You have to admire it."

"Well, I don't." Diana rolled her eyes. "When you put things that way, the invitation is insulting. How dare they insinuate Drake Diamonds isn't good enough? We're the best in the world."

Artem winked at her. "My sister, a CEO in the making."

Franco returned to their group carrying two champagne flutes and offered them to Diana and Ophelia. "Ladies."

"Thank you," Ophelia said.

Diana reached for a glass and took a fortifying sip of bubbly. It was time to make her move.

She wasn't about to let the Lambertis be swayed by Harry Winston. If the egotistical power players behind this party thought she was intimidated, they were sorely mistaken. Drake Diamonds was about to totally steal the show.

We need this to look real.

She stole a glance at Franco and took another gulp of liquid courage. Someone needed to make it look real, and clearly it wasn't going to be him for once.

She moved closer to him, slipped her hand languidly around his waist and let her fingertips rest on his hip.

His champagne flute paused halfway to his lips. He glanced at her, and she let her hand drift lower until she was caressing his backside right there in Harry Winston in front of all of New York's diamond elite.

Franco cleared his throat and took a healthy gulp of champagne.

Another couple joined their small group. Artem introduced them, but their names didn't register with Diana. Her heart had begun to pound hard against her rib cage. All her concentration was centered on the feel of Franco's muscular frame beneath the palm of her hand.

"What are you doing?" he whispered.

"I'm doing exactly what you wanted. I'm making it look real." Her gaze drifted to his mouth.

He stared down at her, and the thunder in his gaze unnerved her. "This is a dangerous game you're playing, Diana. And in case you haven't noticed, I'm not in the mood for games."

She handed off her champagne flute to a waiter passing by with a silver tray. "Come with me."

"We're in the middle of a conversation." He shot a meaningful glance at Artem, Ophelia and the others.

"They won't even miss us, babe." She slid her arm through his and tugged him away.

They ended up in a darkened showroom just around the corner from the party. The only light in the room came from illuminated display cases full of gemstones and platinum. Diamonds sparkled around them like stars against the night sky.

"*Babe?* Really?" Franco arched a brow. "Why don't you just call me *honey bun*? Or *boo*?"

He could make fun of her all he wanted. At least she was trying. "You're blowing it out there. You realize that, don't you?"

A muscle flexed in his jaw. He looked as lethal as she'd ever seen him. "You're exaggerating. It's fine."

"Fine isn't good enough. Not tonight. You said so yourself." She couldn't let his icy composure get to her. Not now. "Talk to me, Franco. What has gotten into you? Did you have a bad day on the polo field or something? Did your polo pony trip over your massive ego?"

She crossed her arms and waited for him to admit the truth.

He raked a hand through his hair, and when he met her gaze, his dark eyes went soulful all of a sudden. If Diana had been looking at anyone else, she would have described his expression as broken. But that word was so wholly at odds with everything she knew about Franco, she was having trouble wrapping her head around it.

"I didn't ride today," he said quietly. "Nor have I ridden for the past month. So, no. My pony did not, in fact, trip over my massive ego."

"I know. Artem just told me." Her voice was colder than she'd intended.

She wasn't sure why she was so angry all of a sudden. She'd been the one to insist they keep things professional. And now was definitely not the time or place to discuss the fact that he was no longer playing polo.

But she couldn't seem to stop herself. The emotions she'd been grappling with since Artem so casually mentioned Franco was no longer playing with the Kingsmen felt too much like betrayal. Which didn't even make sense. Not that it mattered, though, because words were coming out of her mouth faster than she could think.

"Why didn't you say something? Why didn't you tell me?" The last thing she wanted was for him to know she cared, but the tremor in her voice was a dead giveaway.

He looked at her, long and hard, until her breath went shallow. He was so beautiful. A dark and elegant mystery.

Sometimes when she let her guard down and caught a glimpse of him standing beside her, she understood why she'd chosen him all those years ago. And despite the humiliation that had followed, she would have chosen him all over again.

"You didn't ask," he finally said.

She gave her head a tiny shake. "But…"

"But what?" he prompted.

He was going to make her say it, wasn't he? He was forcing her to go there. Again.

She inhaled a shaky breath. "But I told you about Diamond."

Their eyes met and held.

Tears blurred Diana's vision, until the diamonds around them shimmered like rain. Something moved in the periphery. She wiped a tear from her eye, and realized someone was coming.

Her breath caught in her throat.

Carla and Don Lamberti were walking straight toward them. Diana could see them directly over Franco's shoulder. Panic welled up in her chest.

The Lambertis couldn't find them like this. They most definitely couldn't see her crying. She was supposed to be in love.

In love.

For once, the thought didn't make her physically ill.

"Kiss me," she whispered.

Franco's eyes glittered fiercely in the shadows, drawing her in, pulling her toward something she couldn't quite identify. Something dark and familiar. "Diana..."

There was an ache in the way he said her name. It caught her off guard, scraped her insides.

A strange yearning wound its way through her as she reached for the smooth satin lapels of his tuxedo and balled them in her fists.

What was she doing?

"I said kiss me." She swallowed. Hard. "Now."

Franco's gaze dropped to her lips, and suddenly his chiseled face was far too close to hers. Her heart felt like it would pound right out of her chest, and she realized she was touching him, sliding her fingers through his dark hair.

She heard a noise that couldn't possibly have come from her own mouth, except somehow it had. A tremulous whimper of anticipation.

You'll regret this.

Just like last time.

Franco took her jaw in his hand and ran the pad of his thumb over her bottom lip as his eyes burned into her. His other hand slid languidly up her bare back until his fingertips found their way into her hair. He gave a gentle yet insistent tug at the base of her chignon, until her head tipped back and his mouth was perfectly poised over hers.

She felt dizzy. Disoriented. The air seemed too thick, the diamonds around them too bright. As her eyes drifted shut, she tried to remind herself of why this was happening. This wasn't fate or destiny or some misguided romantic notion.

She'd chosen it. She was in control.

It doesn't mean anything.

It doesn't.

Franco's mouth came down on hers, hot and wanting. Every bone in her body went liquid. Warmth coursed through her and, with it, remembrance.

Then there was no more thinking. No more denial. No more lying.

Not even to herself.

This kiss was different than their last.

Franco thought he'd been prepared for it. After all, this wasn't the first time his lips had touched Diana Drake's. They'd been down this road before. He remembered the taste of her, the feel of her, the soft, kittenish noise she made right when she was on the verge of surrender. These were the memories that tormented him as he'd lain awake the past seven nights until, at last, he'd fallen asleep and dreamed of a hot summer night long gone by.

But now that the past had been resurrected, he realized how wrong he'd been. A lifetime wouldn't have prepared him for a kiss like this one.

Where there'd once been a girlish innocence, Franco found womanly desire. Kissing Diana was like trying to capture light in his hands. He was wonderstruck, and rather than finding satisfaction in the warm, wet heat of her mouth, he felt an ache for her that grew sharper. More insistent. Just...

More.

He actually groaned the word aloud against the impossible softness of lips and before he knew what he was doing, he found himself pressing her against the cold glass of a nearby jewelry display case as his fingertips slid to her wrists and circled them like bracelets.

What the hell was happening?

This wasn't just different than the last time he'd kissed

Diana. It was different from any kiss Franco had experienced before.

Ever.

He pulled back for a blazing, breathless moment to look at her. He searched her face for some kind of indication he wasn't alone in this. He wanted her to feel it too—this bewildering connection that grabbed him by the throat and refused to let go. Needed her to feel it.

She gazed back at him through eyes darkened by desire. Her irises were the color of deep Russian amethysts. Rich and rare. And he knew he wasn't imagining things.

"Franco," she whispered in a voice he'd never heard her use before. One that nearly brought him to his knees. "I…"

Somewhere behind him, he heard the clearing of a throat followed by an apology. "Pardon us. We didn't realize anyone was here."

Not now.

Franco closed his eyes, desperate not to break whatever strange spell had swallowed them up. But as his pulse roared in his ears, he was agonizingly aware of Diana's wrists slipping from his grasp. And in the moment that followed, there was nothing but deep blue silence.

He opened his eyes and focused on the glittering sapphire around her neck rather than turning around. He needed a moment to collect himself as the truth came into focus.

"Mr. and Mrs. Lamberti." Diana moved away from him in a swish of tulle and pretense. "We apologize. Stay, please."

It had been an act. All of it. The caresses. The tears. The kiss.

He took a steadying inhale and adjusted his bow tie as he slowly turned around.

"Mr. Andrade, we'd know your face anywhere." A woman—Mrs. Lamberti, he presumed—offered her hand.

He gave it a polite shake, but he couldn't seem to make himself focus on her face. He couldn't tear his gaze away from Diana, speaking and moving about as if she'd orchestrated the entire episode.

Probably because she had.

"Franco, darling. The Lambertis are the owners of the diamond I've been telling you about." Diana turned toward him, but didn't quite meet his gaze.

Look at me, damn it.

"It's a pleasure to meet you both," he said.

"The pleasure is ours. Everywhere we turn, we see photos of the two of you. And now here you are, as real as can be." Mr. Lamberti laughed.

"Real. That's us. Isn't it darling?" Franco reached for Diana's hand, turned it over and pressed a tender kiss to the inside of her wrist.

Her pulse thundered against his lips, but it brought him little satisfaction. He no longer knew what to believe.

How had he let himself be fool enough to fall for any of this charade?

"It's nice to see a couple so in love." Mrs. Lamberti brought her hand to her throat. "Romance is a rarity these days, I'm afraid."

"I couldn't agree more." Franco gave Diana's waist a tiny squeeze.

Diana let out a tiny laugh. He'd been around her long enough now to know it was forced, but the Lambertis didn't appear to notice.

They continued making small talk about their diamond as Diana's gaze flitted toward his. At last. Franco saw an unmistakable hint of yearning in the violet depths of her eyes. He knew better than to believe in it, but it made his chest ache all the same.

"Wait until you see it." Mr. Lamberti shook his head. "It's a sight to behold."

"I hope I do get to see it someday," Diana said. "Sooner rather than later."

Good girl.

She was going in for the kill, as she should. That baseball-sized rock was the reason they were here, after all. Another polo player was wearing Franco's jersey, and the prospect of keeping up the charade alongside Diana suddenly seemed tortuous at best.

But he'd be damned if it was all for nothing.

"We'll be making an announcement about the diamond tomorrow, and I think you'll be pleased." Mrs. Lamberti reached to give Diana's arm a pat. "Off the record, of course."

Diana beamed. "My lips are sealed."

Mr. Lamberti winked. "In the meantime, we should be getting back to the party."

"It was lovely to meet you both," Diana said.

Franco murmured his agreement and bid the couple farewell.

The moment they were gone, he stepped away from Diana. He needed distance between them. Space for all the lies they'd both been spinning.

"Did you hear that?" she whispered, eyes ablaze. "They're making an announcement tomorrow. They're going to pick us, aren't they?"

Us.

He nodded. "I believe they are."

"We did it, Franco. We did it." She launched herself at him and threw her arms around his neck.

Franco allowed himself a bittersweet moment to savor

the feel of her body pressed against his, the soft swell of her breasts against his chest, the orchid scent of her hair as it tickled his nose.

He closed his eyes and took a deep inhale.

So intoxicating. So deceptively sweet.

He reached for her wrists and gently peeled her away.

"Franco?" She stood looking at him with her arms hanging awkwardly at her sides.

He shoved his hands in his pockets to prevent himself from touching her. "Aren't you forgetting something? We're alone now. There's no reason to touch me. No one is here to see it."

She flinched, and as she stared up at him, the look of triumph in her eyes slowly morphed into one of hurt. Her bottom lip trembled ever so slightly.

Nice touch.

"But I…"

He held up a hand to stop her. There was nothing to say. He certainly didn't need an apology. They were both adults. From the beginning, they'd both known what they were getting into.

Franco had simply forgotten for a moment. He'd fallen for the lie.

He wouldn't be making that mistake again.

"It's fine. More than fine." He shrugged one shoulder and let his gaze sweep her from top to bottom one last time before he walked away. "Smile, darling. You're getting everything you wanted."

Chapter Nine

A *Page Six* Exclusive Report

New York's own Drake Diamonds has been chosen by the Lamberti Mining Company as the jeweler to cut the world's largest diamond. The massive rock was recently unearthed from a mine in Botswana and weighs in at 1,100 carats. Rumor has it Ophelia Drake herself will design the setting for the record-sized diamond, which will go on display later this month at the Metropolitan Museum of Art.

No word yet on the exact plans for the stone, but we can't help but wonder if an engagement ring might be in the works. Diamond heiress Diana Drake stepped out again last night with her current flame, polo-playing hottie Franco Andrade, at a private party at Harry Winston. Cell phone photos snapped by guests show the couple engaged in some scorching hot PDA. Caution: viewing these pictures will have you clutching your Drake Diamonds pearls.

Chapter Ten

*P*_{op!}

The store hadn't even opened yet, and already the staff of Drake Diamonds was on its third bottle of champagne. The table in the center of the Drake-blue kitchen was piled with empty Waterford glasses and stacks upon stacks of newspapers.

Drake Diamonds and the Lamberti diamond were front-page news.

"Congratulations, Diana." Ophelia clinked her glass against Diana's and took a dainty sip of her Veuve Clicquot. "Well done."

"Thank you." Diana grinned. It felt good to succeed at something again. Although it probably should have felt better than it actually did.

Stop. You earned this. You have nothing to feel guilty about.

She swallowed and concentrated her attention on Ophelia. "Congratulations right back at you. Have you started sketching designs for the stone yet?"

Ophelia laughed. "Our involvement has only been official for about an hour, remember?"

Diana lifted a dubious brow. "So until now you've given the Lamberti diamond no thought whatsoever?"

Ophelia's expression turned sheepish. "Okay, so maybe I've been working on a few preliminary designs... just in case."

Diana laughed. "It never hurts to be prepared."

Artem's voice boomed over the chatter in the crowded room. "Okay, everyone. The doors open in five minutes. Party time's over."

Ophelia set her glass down on the table. "I'm off, then. Duty calls."

"Something tells me your job won't be in jeopardy if you hang out a little while longer," Diana said in a mock whisper.

"I know, but I seriously can't wait to get to work on the design now that I know I'm actually going to get my hands on that diamond. I almost can't believe it's happening. It hasn't quite sunk in yet." Her eyes shone with wonder. "This is real, isn't it?"

Diana took a deep breath.

This is real, isn't it?

The memory of Franco's touch hit her hard and fast... the dance of his fingertips moving down her spine...the way his hands had circled her wrists, holding her still as he kissed her...

She was beginning to lose track of what was genuine and what wasn't.

"Believe it. It's real." She swallowed around the lump in her throat and gave Ophelia one last smile before she found herself alone in the kitchen with Artem.

Diana reached for one of the tiny cakes they kept on hand decorated to look like Drake-blue boxes and bit into it. Ah, comfort food. She could use a sugary dose of comfort right now, although she wasn't quite sure why.

You're getting everything you wanted.

Why had she felt like crying when Franco uttered those words the night before?

"Can we talk for a moment, sis?" Artem sank into one of the kitchen chairs.

"Sure." Diana sat down beside him. She was in no hurry to get back to Dalton's empty apartment. She'd rather be here, where things were celebratory.

When she'd first read the news that the Lambertis had, indeed, chosen Drake Diamonds, she'd been propped up in bed sipping her morning coffee and reading her iPad. Seeing the official press announcement hadn't given her the thrill she'd been anticipating.

If she was being honest, it almost felt like a letdown. She didn't want to examine the reasons why, and she most definitely didn't want to be alone with her thoughts. Because those thoughts kept circling back to last night.

Kissing Franco. The feel of his mouth on hers, wet and wanting. The look on his face when he spotted the Lambertis.

"You okay?" Artem looked at her, and the smile that had been plastered on his face all morning began to fade.

Diana leaned over and gave him an affectionate shoulder bump. "Of course. I'm more than okay."

But she couldn't quite bring herself to meet his gaze, so she focused instead on the table in front of them and its giant pile of newspapers. The corner of *Page Six* poked out from beneath the *New York Times*, and she caught a glimpse of the now-familiar grainy image of herself and Franco kissing.

Her throat grew tight.

She squeezed her eyes closed.

"I hope that's true, sis. I do. Because I have some concerns," Artem said.

Diana's eyes flew open. "Concerns. About what?"

He paused and seemed to be choosing his words with great care.

"You and Franco," he said at last.

She blinked. "Me and Franco?"

Artem's gaze flitted to *Page Six*. "I'm starting to wonder if this charade has gone too far."

"You can't be serious. The whole plan was your idea." She waved a hand at the empty bottles of Veuve Clicquot littering the kitchen. "And it worked. We did it, Artem."

"Yes. So far it's been a remarkable success." He nodded thoughtfully. "For the company. But some things are more important than business."

Who was his guy and what had he done with her brother? Everything they'd done for the past few weeks had been for the sake of Drake Diamonds. "What are you getting at, Artem?"

But she didn't have to ask. Deep down, she knew.

"This." He pulled the copy of *Page Six* out from beneath the *Times* and tossed it on top of the pile.

She didn't want to look at it. It hurt too much to see herself like that.

"It was just a kiss, Artem." Her brother was watching her closely, waiting for her to crack, so she forced herself to look at the photograph.

It was worse than the enormous billboard in Times Square. So much worse. Probably because this time she hadn't been acting. This time, she'd wanted Franco to take her to bed.

Her self-control was beginning to slip. Along with her

common sense. The kiss had pushed her right over the edge. It had made her forget all the reasons she despised him. Even now, she was still struggling to remember his numerous bad qualities. It was like she was suffering from some kind of hormone-induced amnesia.

Artem lifted a brow. Thank God he couldn't see inside her head. "That looks like more than *just a kiss* to me."

"As it should." She crossed her arms, leaned back in her chair and glared at him. He was pulling the overprotective brother act on her now? *Seriously?* "The whole point of our courtship is to make people believe it's real. Remember?"

"Of course I remember. And yes, I'm quite aware it was my idea. But I never said anything about kissing." He shot her a meaningful glance. "Or making out in dark corners. Where was this picture taken? Because this looks much more like a private moment than a public relations party stunt."

It took every ounce of will power Diana possessed to refrain from wadding up the paper and throwing it at him. "I can't believe what I'm hearing. For your information, the only reason I kissed him was because the Lambertis were walking straight toward us. I had to do something. I didn't want them to think Franco and I were arguing."

"Were you?" Artem raised his brows. "Arguing?"

She sighed. "No. Yes. Well, sort of."

"If there's nothing actually going on between you and Franco, what do you have to argue about?"

Diana shifted in her chair. Maybe Artem *could* see inside her head.

Of course he couldn't. Still, she should have had a dozen answers at the ready. People who weren't lovers argued all the time, didn't they?

But she couldn't seem capable of coming up with a

single viable excuse. She just sat there praying for him to stop asking questions.

Finally, Artem put her out of her long, silent misery. "Is there something you should tell me, Diana?"

"There's nothing going on between Franco and me. I promise." Why did that sound like a lie when it was the truth?

Worse, why did the truth feel so painful?

You do not have feelings for Franco Andrade. Not again.

"You're a grown-up. I get that. It's just that you're my sister. And as you so vehemently pointed out less than two weeks ago, Franco is a man whore." Artem looked pointedly at the photo splashed across *Page Six*. "I'm starting to think this whole farce was a really bad idea."

"Look, I appreciate the concern. But I can handle myself around Franco. The kiss was my idea, and it meant nothing." It wasn't supposed to, anyway. "End of story."

She stood and began clearing away the dirty champagne flutes and tossing the empty Veuve Clicquot bottles into the recycling bin. She couldn't just sit there and talk about this anymore.

"Got it." To Diana's great relief, Artem rose from his chair and headed toward the hallway.

But he lingered in the doorway for a last word on the subject. "You know, we can stop this right now. You've proven your point. You have a lot to offer Drake Diamonds. I was wrong to put you in this position."

"What?" She turned to face him.

Surely she hadn't heard him right.

He nodded and gave her a bittersweet smile. "I was wrong. And I'm sorry. Say the word, and your fake relationship with Franco can end in a spectacular or not-so-spectacular fake breakup. Your choice."

Her choice.

But she didn't have a choice. Not really.

A week ago, she would have given anything to get Franco out of her life. Now it didn't seem right. Not when she'd gotten what she needed out of the deal and Franco apparently hadn't.

Smile, darling, you're getting everything you wanted.

He'd played his part, and she owed it to him to play hers. Like or not, they were stuck together until the gala.

"You know that's not possible, Artem. We haven't even finalized things with the Lambertis. They could take their diamond and hightail it over to Harry Winston."

"I know they could. I'm beginning to wonder if it would really be so awful if they did." Artem sighed, and she could tell just by the look on his face that he was thinking about the photo again. *Page Six*. The kiss. "Is it really worth all of this? Is anything?"

"Absolutely." She nodded, but a tiny part of her wondered if he might be right. "You're making a big deal out of nothing. I promise."

It was too late for doubts. She'd made her bed, and now she had to lie in it. Preferably alone.

Liar.

Artem nodded and looked slightly relieved, which was still a good deal more relieved than Diana actually felt. "I suppose I should know better than to believe everything I read in the papers, right?"

She picked up the copy of *Page Six*, intent on burying it at the bottom of the recycling bin. It trembled in her hand.

She tossed it back onto the surface of the table and crossed her arms. "Exactly."

How was she going to survive until the gala? She

dreaded seeing Franco later. Now that he seemed intent on not kissing her again, it was all she could think about.

Even worse, how could she look herself in the mirror when she could barely look her brother in the eye?

Franco gave the white ball a brutal whack with his mallet and watched it soar through the grass right between the goal posts at the far end of the practice field on his Hamptons property.

Another meaningless score.

His efforts didn't count when he was the only player on the field. But he needed to be here, as much for his ponies as for himself. They needed to stay in shape. They needed to be ready, even if it was beginning to look less and less like they'd be returning to the Kingsmen.

Last night had been a reality check in more ways than one. He wasn't sure what had enraged him more—seeing his number on another player's chest or realizing Diana had asked him to kiss her purely for show.

He knew his fury was in no way rational, particularly where Diana was concerned. Their entire arrangement was based on deception. He just hadn't realized he would be the one being deceived.

But even that shouldn't have mattered. He shouldn't have cared one way or another whether Diana really wanted his mouth on hers.

And yet…he did care.

He cared far more than he ever thought he would.

I'm not yours, Mr. Andrade. Never have been, never will be.

Franco wiped sweat from his brow with his forearm, rested his mallet over his shoulder and slowed his horse to an easy canter. As he watched the mare's thick muscles move beneath the velvety surface of her coat, he thought of Diamond.

He thought about Diana's dead horse every time he rode now. He thought about the way she could barely seem to make herself say Diamond's name. He thought about her reluctance to even hold Lulu. She was afraid of getting attached to another animal. That much was obvious. Only one thing would fix that.

She needed to ride again.

Of course, getting Diana back in the saddle was the last thing he should be concerned about when he couldn't even manage to get himself back on his team.

That hadn't stopped him from dropping Lulu off at Drake Diamonds before he'd headed to the Hamptons. Artem's secretary, Mrs. Barnes, had looked at him like he was crazy when he'd handed her the puppy and asked her to give it to Diana. Maybe he *had* gone crazy. But if he'd forced the dog on Diana himself, she would have simply refused.

She needed the dog. Franco had never in his life met anyone who'd needed another living creature so much. Other than himself when he'd been a boy...

Maybe that's why he cared so much about helping Diana. Despite their vastly different upbringings, he understood her. Whether she wanted to admit it or not.

Let it go. You have enough problems of your own without adding Diana Drake's to the mix.

She didn't want his help, anyway, and that was fine. He was finished with her. As soon as the gala was over and once he had his job back, they'd never see each other again. He was practically counting the minutes.

"Andrade," someone called from the direction of the stalls where Franco's other horses were resting and munching on hay in the shade.

Franco squinted into the setting sun. As he headed off the field, he spotted a familiar figure walking toward him across the emerald-green grass.

Luc.

Franco slid out of his saddle and passed the horse's reins to one of his grooms. *"Gracias."*

It wasn't until he'd closed the distance between himself and his friend that he recognized a faint stirring in his chest. Hope. Which only emphasized how pathetic his situation was at the moment. If the Kingsmen wanted him back, the coach wouldn't send Luc. Santos would be here. Maybe even Ellis himself.

He removed his helmet and raked a hand through his dampened hair. "Luc."

"Hola, mano." Luc nodded toward the goal, where the white ball still sat in the grass. "Looking good out there."

"Thanks, man." An awkward silence settled between them. Franco cleared his throat. "How was the scrimmage yesterday?"

Luc's gaze met his. Held. "It was complete and utter shit."

"I wish I could say I was surprised. Gustavo Anca. Really? He's a six-goal player." Not that a handicap of six was bad. Plenty of world-class players were ranked as such. But Franco's handicap was eight. On an average day, Gustavo Anca wouldn't even be able to give him a run for his money. On a good day, Franco would have wiped the ground with him.

Luc nodded. "Well, it showed."

Franco said nothing. If Luc was hoping for company in his commiseration, he'd just have to be disappointed.

"Look, Franco. I came here to tell you I can't let this go on. Not anymore." Franco shook his head, but before he could audibly protest, Luc held up a hand. "I don't want to hear it. We've waited long enough. The Kingsmen are going to lose every damn game this season if we don't get you back. I'm going to Jack Ellis first thing in the morning, and I'm going to tell him the truth."

"No, you're not," Franco said through gritted teeth.

He'd made a promise, and he intended to keep it. Even if that promise had sent his life into a tailspin.

"It's not up for discussion. I don't know why I let you talk me into this in the first place." Luc shook his head and dropped his gaze to the ground.

He knew why. They both did.

"It's too late to come clean." Would Ellis even believe them if they told the truth this late in the game? Would anyone? Franco doubted it, especially in Diana's case. She'd made up her mind about him a long time ago.

But why should her opinion matter? She had nothing to do with this. Their lives had simply become so intertwined that Franco could no longer keep track of where his ended and hers began.

"I don't believe that. It's not too late. I love you like a brother. You know I do. You don't owe me a thing, Franco. You never did, and you certainly don't owe me this." Luc looked up again with red-rimmed eyes.

Why was he making this so difficult? "What's done is done. Besides, what's the point? If you tell the truth, you know what will happen."

"Yeah, I do. You'll be in, and I'll be out, which is precisely the way it should be." Luc blew out a ragged exhale. "This is bigger than the two of us, Franco. It's about the team now."

He was hitting Franco where it hurt, and he knew it. The team had always come first for Franco. Before the women, before the partying, before everything.

Until now.

Some things were bigger. Luc was family. Without Luc, Franco would never have played for the Kingsmen to begin with. He would have never even left Buenos Aires. He'd probably still be sleeping in a barn at night, or worse. He might have gone back to where he'd come from. Barrio de la Boca.

He liked to think that horses had saved him. But, in reality, it had been Luc.

He exhaled a weary sigh. "What's the point anymore? The Kingsmen can't lose you, either. If you do this, the team will suffer just as much as it already has."

"No. It won't." A horse whinnied in the distance. Luc smiled. "You're better than I am. You always were."

Franco's chest grew tight, and he had the distinct feeling they weren't talking about polo anymore.

"I came here as a courtesy, so you'd be prepared when Ellis calls you tomorrow. This is happening. Get ready." Luc turned to go.

Franco glared at the back of his head. "And if things change between now and tomorrow?"

Luc turned around. Threw his hands in the air. "What could possibly change?"

Everything.

Everything could change.

And Franco knew just how to make certain it would.

Chapter Eleven

Diana was running out of ball gowns, but that wasn't her most pressing problem at the moment. That notable distinction belonged to the problem that had four legs and a tail and had peed on her carpet three times in the past two hours.

As if Franco hadn't already made her life miserable enough, now he'd forced the puppy upon her. After Diana's awkward encounter with Artem in the Drake Diamonds kitchen, Mrs. Barnes had waltzed in and thrust the little black pug at her. She'd had no choice but to take the dog home. Now here they sat, waiting for Ophelia to show up with a new crop of evening wear.

Diana had never needed so many gowns, considering thus far she'd spent the better part of her life in riding clothes. But she'd worn nearly every fancy dress she owned over the course of her faux love affair with Franco, and she wanted to make an impression tonight. More than ever before.

The Manhattan Ballet's annual gala at Lincoln Center was one of the most important social events on the Drake Diamonds calendar. Ophelia had once been a prima ballerina at the company. Since coming to Drake Diamonds, she'd designed an entire ballet-themed jewelry collection. Naturally, the store and the Manhattan Ballet worked closely with each other.

Which meant Artem and Ophelia would be at the gala. So would the press, obviously. Coming right on the heels of the Lamberti diamond announcement, the gala would be a big deal. Huge.

It would also be the first time Diana had seen Franco since The Kiss.

But of course that had nothing to do with the fact that she wanted to look extra spectacular. Then again, maybe it did. A little.

Okay, a lot.

She wanted to torture him. First he'd had the nerve to get upset that she'd asked him to kiss her, and now he'd dropped a puppy in her lap. Who behaved like that?

Lulu let out a little yip and spun in circles, chasing her curlicue tail. The dog was cute. No doubt about it. And Diana didn't completely hate her tiny, velvet-soft ears and round little belly. If she'd had any interest in adopting a puppy, this one would definitely have been a contender.

But she wasn't ready to sign on for another heartbreak in the making. Wasn't her heart in enough jeopardy as it was?

Damn you, Franco.

"Don't get too comfortable," she said.

Lulu cocked her head, increasing her adorable quotient at least tenfold.

Ugh. "I mean it. You're not staying."

One night. That was it. Two, tops.

The doorbell rang, and Lulu scrambled toward the door in a frenzy of high-pitched barks and snorting noises. Somehow, her cuteness remained intact despite the commotion.

"Calm down, you nut." Diana scooped her up with one hand, and the puppy licked her chin.

Three nights...maybe. Then she was absolutely going back to Franco's bachelor pad.

"A puppy!" Ophelia grinned from ear to ear when Diana opened the door. "This must the one I read about in the paper."

Diana sighed. She'd almost forgotten that every detail of her life was now splashed across *Page Six*. Puppy included. "The one and only."

"She's seriously adorable. Franco has good taste in dogs. He can't be all bad." Ophelia floated through the front door of Diana's apartment with a garment bag slung over her shoulder. She might not be a professional ballerina anymore, but she still moved liked one, even with a baby strapped to her chest.

Diana rolled her eyes and returned Lulu to the floor, where she resumed chewing on a rawhide bone that was three times bigger than her own head. "I'm pretty sure even the devil himself can appreciate a cute puppy."

"The last time I checked, the devil wasn't into rescuing homeless animals." Point taken.

Ophelia tossed the garment bags across the arm of the sofa. "Enough about your charming puppy and equally charming faux boyfriend. I've come with fashion reinforcements, as you requested."

"And you brought my niece." Diana eyed the baby.

There was no denying she was precious. She had Artem's eyes and Ophelia's delicate features. Perfect in every way.

Diana just wasn't one of those women who swooned every time she saw a baby. Probably because she'd never pictured herself as a mother. Not after the nightmare of a marriage her own mother had endured.

"Here, hold her." Ophelia lifted little Emma out of the baby sling and handed her to Diana.

"Um, okay." She'd never really held Emma before. She'd oohed and aahed over her. Plenty of times. But other than the occasional, affectionate pat on the head, she hadn't actually touched her.

She was lighter than Diana had expected. Soft. Warm.

"Wow," she said as Emma took Diana's hand in her tiny grip.

"She growing like a weed, isn't she?" Ophelia beamed at her baby.

Diana studied the tender expression on her face. It wasn't altogether different from the one she usually wore when she looked at Artem. "You're completely in love with this baby, aren't you?"

"It shows?"

"You couldn't hide it if you tried." Diana rocked Emma gently from side to side until the baby's eyes drifted closed.

"It's crazy. I never pictured myself as a mother." Ophelia shrugged one of her elegant shoulders.

Diana gaped at her. "You're kidding."

"Nope. I never expected to get married, either. Your brother actually had to talk me into it." She grinned. "He can be very persuasive."

"I had no idea. You and Artem are like a dream couple."

"Things aren't always how they appear on the outside. But I don't need to tell you that." Ophelia gave her a knowing look.

Diana swallowed. "I should probably be an expert on the subject by now."

"I love your brother, and I adore Emma. I've never been so happy." And it showed. Bliss radiated from her sister-in-law's pores. "This life just isn't one I ever imagined for myself."

Maybe that's how it always worked. Maybe one day Diana would wake up and magically be ready to slip one of those legendary Drake diamonds onto her ring finger.

Doubtful, considering she was terrified of keeping the puppy currently making herself at home in Diana's borrowed apartment. "Can I ask you a question?"

"Sure. That's what sisters are for," Ophelia said.

"What changed? I mean, I know that sounds like a difficult question..."

Ophelia interrupted her with a shake of her head. "No. It's not difficult at all. It's simple, really. Love changed me."

"Love," Diana echoed, as the front-page image of herself being kissed within an inch of her life flashed before her eyes.

Please. That wasn't love. It wasn't even lust. It was pretend.

Keep telling yourself that.

"I fell in love, and that changed everything." Ophelia regarded her for a moment. "I may be way off base here, but do these questions have anything to do with Franco?"

"Hardly." Diana laughed. A little too loudly.

She couldn't ignore the truth anymore...she had a serious case of lust for the man. Everyone in New York knew she did. It was literally front-page news.

But she would have to be insane to fall in love with him. She didn't even like him. When she'd had her accident, she hadn't hit her head so hard that she lost her memory.

The day after she'd lost her virginity to Franco had been the most humiliating of her life. She'd known what she'd been getting into when she slept with him. Or thought she had, anyway.

She'd been all too aware of his reputation. Franco Andrade was a player. Not just a polo player...a *player* player. In truth, that was why she'd chosen him. His ridiculous good looks and devastating charm hadn't hurt, obviously. But mainly she'd wanted to experience sex without any looming expectation of a relationship.

She'd been twenty-two, which was more than old enough to sleep with a man. It hadn't been the sex that frightened her. It had been the idea of belonging to someone. Someone who would cheat, as her father had done for as long she could remember.

Franco had been the perfect candidate.

She'd expected hot, dirty sex. And she'd gotten it. But he'd also been tender. Unexpectedly sweet. Still, it was her own stupid fault she'd fallen for the fantasy.

She'd rather die than make that mistake again.

"Nothing at all? If you say so. There just seems to be a spark between you two," Ophelia said. "I'm pretty sure it's visible from outer space."

Diana handed the baby back to her sister-in-law. "Honestly, you sound like Artem. Did he put you up to this?"

Ophelia held Emma against her chest and rubbed her hand in soothing circles on the back of the baby's pastel pink onesie. Her brow furrowed. "No, actually. We haven't even discussed it."

Diana narrowed her gaze. "Then why are you asking me about Franco?"

"I told you. There's something special when you're together." She grinned. "Magic."

Like the kind of magic that made people believe in relationships? Marriage? *Family?* "You're seeing things. Seriously, Ophclia. You're looking at the world through love-colored glasses."

Ophelia laughed. "I don't think those are a thing."

"Trust me. They are. And you're wearing them." Diana slid closer to the garment bag and pulled it onto her lap. "A big, giant pair."

Ophelia shook her head, smiled and made cooing noises at the baby. Which pretty much proved Diana's point.

"By the way, there's only one dress in there." Ophelia nodded at the garment bag. "It's perfect for tonight. You'll look amazing in it. I was afraid if I brought more options, you wouldn't have the guts to wear this one. And you really must."

"Why am I afraid to look at it now?" Diana unzipped the bag and gasped when she got a glimpse of silver lamé fabric so luxurious that it looked like liquid platinum.

"Gorgeous, isn't it? It belonged to my grandmother. She wore it to a ballet gala herself, back in the 1940s."

Diana shook her head. "I can't borrow this. It's too special."

"Don't be silly. Of course you can. That's why I brought it." Ophelia bit her lip. "Franco is going to die when he sees you in it."

First Artem. Now Ophelia. When had everyone started believing the hype?

"Not if I kill him first," she said flatly.

The more she thought about his reaction last night, the angrier she got. How dare he call her out for doing exactly the same thing he'd been doing every night for a week?

Did he think the nicknames, the lingering glances and the way he touched her all the time didn't get to her? Newsflash: they did.

Sometimes she went home from their evenings together and her body felt so tingly, so alive that she had trouble sleeping. Last night, he'd even shown up in her dreams.

Her head spun a little just thinking about it. "I have no interest in him whatsoever."

"Yeah, you mentioned that." Ophelia smirked.

A telltale warmth crept into Diana's cheeks. "I'm serious. I'm not interested in marriage or babies, either. Certainly not with him."

"I believe you." Ophelia nodded in mock solemnity.

Even the puppy stopped chewing on her bone to stare at Diana with her buggy little eyes.

"Stop looking at me like that. Both of you. I assure you, it will be a long time before you see an engagement ring on my finger. And *if* that ever happens, the ring won't be from Franco Andrade."

He was about as far from being husband material as she was from being wife material. Diana should know...

She'd spent an embarrassing amount of time thinking it through.

Dios mío.

A little under twenty-four hours had hardly been enough time to rid Franco of the memory of kissing Diana. But the moment he set eyes on her in her liquid silver dress, everything came flooding back. The taste of her. The feel of her. The sound of her—the catch of her breath in the moment their lips came together, the tremble in her voice when she'd asked him to kiss her.

No amount of willful forgetting would erase those

memories. Certainly not while Diana was standing beside him in the lobby of Lincoln Center looking like she'd been dipped in diamonds.

A strand of emerald-cut stones had been interwoven through the satin neckline of her gown and arranged into a glittering bow just off-center from the massive sapphire draped around her neck. She looked almost too perfect to touch.

Which made Franco want to touch her all the more.

"You're staring," she said, without a trace of emotion in her voice. But the corner of her lush mouth curved into a grin that smacked of self-satisfaction.

Franco had a mind to kiss her right there on the spot.

He smiled tightly, instead. She hadn't said a word yet about the puppy stunt, which he found particularly interesting. But she was angry with him. For what, exactly, he wasn't quite sure. He was beginning to lose track of all the wrongs he'd committed, and tomorrow would be far worse. She just didn't know it yet.

He cleared his throat. "I can't seem to look away. Forgive me."

She shrugged an elegant shoulder. The row of diamonds woven through the bodice of her dress glittered under the chandelier overhead. "You're forgiven."

Forgiven.

The word and its myriad of implications hung between them.

He raised a brow. "Am I?"

He knew better than to believe it.

"It's a figure of speech. Don't read too much into it." She shifted her gaze away from him, toward the crowd assembled in the grand opera-house lobby.

Franco slipped an arm around her and led her down the red-carpeted stairs toward the party. He'd been dreading the Manhattan Ballet gala since the moment he'd woken up this morning. He'd lost his head at the Harry Winston party. He couldn't make a mistake like that again. Not now. Not when there was so much riding on his fake relationship. The Drakes may have gotten what they wanted, but Franco hadn't.

He would, though.

By tomorrow morning, everything would change.

"Diana, nice to see you. You look beautiful." Artem greeted his sister with a smile and a kiss on the cheek. When he turned toward Franco, his smile faded. "Franco."

No handshake. No small talk. Just a sharp look that felt oddly like a warning glare.

"Artem." Franco reached to shake his hand.

Something felt off, but Franco couldn't imagine why. Artem Drake should be the happiest man in Manhattan right now. His family business was front-page news. Everywhere Franco turned, people were talking about the Lamberti diamond. A few news outlets had even rechristened it the Lamberti-Drake diamond.

Would the Lambertis have even chosen Drake Diamonds if not for the pretend love affair? Franco wholeheartedly doubted it. The Lambertis had looked awfully comfortable at Harry Winston.

Until the kiss.

The kiss had been the deciding factor. Or so it seemed.

The way Franco saw things, Artem Drake should be high-fiving him right now.

Maybe he was just imagining things. After all, last night had been frustrating on every possible level. Most notably, sexually. Franco still couldn't think straight. Especially when Diana's silvery image was reflected back at him from all four walls of the mirrored room. There was simply no escaping it.

"Nice to see you again, Franco," Ophelia said warmly.

"Thank you. It's a pleasure to be here." He moved to give Ophelia a one-armed hug. Artem's gaze narrowed, and he tossed back the remainder of the champagne in his glass.

"I'm sure it is," Artem muttered under his breath.

Franco cast a questioning glance at Diana. He definitely wasn't imagining things.

"Shall we go get a drink, darling?" she said.

"Yes, let's." A drink was definitely in order. Possibly many drinks.

Once they'd taken their place in line at the bar, Franco bent to whisper in Diana's ear, doing his best not to let his gaze wander to her cleavage, barely covered by a wisp of pale gray chiffon fabric. It would have been a tall order for any man. "Are you planning on telling me what's troubling your brother? Or do I have to remain in the dark since I'm just a pretend boyfriend?"

Diana's bottom lip slipped between her teeth, a nervous habit he'd spent far too much time thinking about in recent days. After a pause, she shrugged. "I don't know what you're talking about."

"Do you really think I can't tell when you're lying?" He leaned closer, until his lips grazed the soft place just below her ear. "Because I can. I know you better than you think, Diana. Your body betrays you."

Her cheeks flared pink. "I'm going to pretend you didn't just say that."

"I'm sure you will." He looked pointedly at her mouth. "We both know how good you are at pretending."

"May I help you?" the bartender asked.

"Two glasses of Dom Pérignon, please," Franco said without taking his eyes off Diana.

"You're impossible," she said through gritted teeth.

"So you've told me." He handed her one of the two saucer-style glasses of champagne the bartender had given him. "Multiple times."

Her eyes flashed like amethysts on fire. "You've had your hands all over me for weeks, and I'm not allowed to be affected by it. But I kiss you once, and you completely lose it. You're acting like the world's biggest hypocrite."

The accusation should have angered him. At the very least, he should have been bothered by the fact that she was one hundred percent right. He was definitely acting like a hypocrite, but he couldn't seem to stop.

He'd thought the kiss was real. He'd *wanted* it to be real. He wanted that more than he'd wanted anything in a long, long time.

But he was so shocked by Diana's startling admission that he couldn't bring himself to be anything but satisfied at the moment. Satisfied and, admittedly, a little aroused.

"You like it when I touch you," he stated. It was a fact. She'd said so herself.

"No." She let out a forced laugh. "Hardly."

Yes.

Definitely.

"It's nothing to be ashamed of," he said, reaching for her with his free hand and cupping her cheek. "Would you like it if I touched you now?"

He lowered his gaze to her throat, where he could see the flutter of her pulse just above her sapphire necklace. In the depths of the gemstone, he spied a hint of his own reflection. It was like looking into a dark and dangerous mirror.

"Would *you* like it if I kissed you?" She lifted an impertinent brow.

Franco smiled in response. If she wanted to rattle him, she'd have to try harder.

"I'd like that very much. I see no need to pretend otherwise." He sipped his champagne. "I'd just prefer the kiss to be genuine."

"For your information, that kiss was more genuine than you'll ever know. Which is exactly why Artem is angry." Her gaze flitted toward her brother standing on the other side of the room.

Franco narrowed his gaze at Artem Drake. "Let me get this straight. Your brother wanted us to make everyone believe we were a couple, and now he's angry because we've done just that?"

Diana shook her head. "Not angry. Just concerned."

"About what exactly?"

She cleared her throat and stared into her champagne glass. "He thinks we've taken things too far."

Too far.

As irritating as Franco found Artem Drake's assessment of the situation, Diana's brother might be on to something.

He and Diana had crossed a line. Somewhere along the way, they'd become more to each other than business associates with a common goal.

Perhaps they'd been more than that all along. Every time Franco caught a glimpse of that massive billboard in Times Square he found himself wondering if they were somehow finishing what they'd started three years ago. Like time had been holding its breath waiting for the two of them to come together again.

He knew it was crazy. He'd never believed much in fate. Was it fate that he'd been born into the worst slum in Buenos Aires? No, fate wouldn't be so cruel. He was in control of his life. No one else.

But kissing Diana had almost been enough to make a believer out of him.

They weren't finished with each other. Not yet.

"And what about you, Diana? Do you think we've taken things too far?" He leveled his gaze at her, daring her to tell the truth.

Not far enough. Not by a long shot.

Chapter Twelve

When had things gotten so confusing?

A month ago, Diana had been bored out of her mind selling engagement rings, and now she was standing in the middle of the biggest society gala of the year being interrogated by Franco Andrade.

He shouldn't be capable of rattling her the way he did. The questions he was asking should have had easy answers.

Had they taken things too far?

Absolutely. That had happened the instant he'd fastened the sapphire around her neck. She should never have agreed to pose with him. That one photo had set things in motion that were now spinning wildly out of control.

Then she'd gone and exacerbated things by agreeing to be his pretend girlfriend. Worse yet, since she'd asked him to kiss her, she'd begun to doubt her motivation.

Did she really want to be co-CEO of Drake Diamonds? Had she ever? Or had the promotion simply been a convenient excuse to spend more time with Franco?

Surely not. She hated him. She hated everything about him.

You like it when I touch you.

Damn him and his smug self-confidence. She would have loved to prove him wrong, except she couldn't. She loved it when he touched her. The barest graze of his fingertips sent her reeling. And now she'd gone and admitted it to his face.

She lifted her chin and met his gaze. "Of course we haven't taken things too far. We're both doing our jobs. Nothing more."

"I see. And last night your job included kissing me." The corner of his mouth curved into a half grin, and all she could think about was the way that mouth had felt crashing down on hers.

"You seriously need to let that go." How could she possibly forget it when he kept bringing it up? "Besides, *you* kissed *me*."

"At your request." He lifted a brow.

Her gaze flitted to his bow tie. Looking him in the eye and pretending she didn't want to kiss him again was becoming next to impossible. "Same thing."

"Hardly. When I decide to kiss you, you'll know it. There will be no mistaking my intention." There was a sudden edge to his voice that reminded her of Artem's offer to end this farce once and for all.

Say the word, and your fake relationship with Franco can end in a spectacular or not-so-spectacular fake breakup. Your choice.

Her choice.

She'd had a choice all along, whether she wanted to admit it or not. And she'd chosen Franco. Again.

She was beginning to have the sinking feeling that she always would.

She'd tried her best to keep up her resistance. She really had. The constant onslaught of his devastating good looks paired with the unrelenting innuendo had taken its toll. But his intensity had dealt the deathblow to her defenses.

He cared. Deeply. He cared about Diamond. He cared about why she refused to ride again. That's why he'd forced her hand about the puppy. She'd known as much the moment that Mrs. Barnes had dropped the wiggling little pug into her arms.

Despite his playboy reputation and devil-may-care charm, Franco Andrade cared. He even cared about the kiss.

A girl could only take so much.

"What are you waiting for, then?" she asked, with far more confidence than she actually felt. She reminded herself that she knew exactly what she was doing. But she'd thought the same thing three years ago, hadn't she? "Decide."

A muscle tensed in Franco's jaw.

Then, in one swift motion, he gathered their champagne glasses and deposited them on a nearby tray. He took her hand and led her through the crowded lobby, toward a shadowed corridor. For once, Diana was unaware of the eyes following them everywhere they went. She didn't care who saw them. She didn't care about the Lambertis. She didn't care about the rest of the Drakes. She didn't even care about the press.

The only thing she cared about was where Franco was taking her and what would happen once they got there.

Decide, she'd implored. And decide he had.

"Come here," he groaned, and the timbre in his voice seemed to light tiny fires over every exposed surface of her skin.

He pushed through a closed door, pulling her alongside him, and suddenly they were surrounded on all sides by lush red velvet. Diana blinked into the darkness until the soft gold glow of a dimly lit stage came into focus.

He'd brought her inside the theater, and they were alone at last. In a room that typically held thousands of people. It felt strangely intimate to be surrounded by row upon row of empty seats, the silent orchestra pit and so much rich crimson. Even more so when Franco's hand slid to cradle the back of her head and his eyes burned into hers.

"This is for us and us alone. No one else." His gaze dropped to her mouth.

Diana's heart felt like it might beat right out of her chest. *You can stop this now. It's not too late.*

But it was, wasn't it? She'd all but dared him to kiss her, and she wasn't about to back down now.

She lifted her chin so that his mouth was perfectly poised over hers. "No one else."

He grazed her bottom lip with the pad of his thumb, then bent to kiss her. She expected passion. She expected frantic hunger. She expected him to crush his mouth to hers. Instead, the first deliberate touch of his lips was gentle. Tender. So reverent that she knew within moments it was a mistake.

She'd fought hard to stay numb after her fall. The less she felt, the better. So long as she kept the world at arm's length, she'd never have to relive the nightmare of what she'd been through. But tenderness—especially coming from Franco—had a way of dragging her back to life, whether or not she was ready.

"Diana," he whispered, and his voice echoed throughout the room with a ghostly elegance that made her head spin.

She'd wanted him to kiss her again since the moment their lips parted the night before. She'd craved it. But as his tongue slid into her mouth, hot and hungry, she realized she wanted more. So much more.

Was it possible to relive only part of the past? Could she sleep with him again and experience the exquisite sensation of Franco pushing inside her without the subsequent heartache?

Maybe she could. She wasn't a young, naive girl anymore. She was a grown woman. She could take him to bed with her eyes wide open this time, knowing it was purely physical and nothing more.

My choice.

He pushed her against a velvet wall and when his hands slid over the curves of her hips, she realized she was arching into him, pressing herself against the swell of his arousal. She could spend all the time in the world weighing the consequences, but clearly her body knew what it wanted. And it had made up its mind a long time ago.

Your body betrays you.

He'd been right about that, too, damn him.

"Franco," she murmured against his mouth. Was that really her voice? She scarcely recognized herself anymore.

But that only added to the thrill of the moment. She was tired of being Diana Drake. Disciplined athlete. Diamond heiress and future CEO. Perpetual good girl.

She wanted to be bad for a change.

"Yes, love?" His mouth was on her neck now, and his hands were sliding up the smooth silver satin of her dress to cup her breasts.

She was on fire, on the verge of asking him to make love to her right there in the theatre.

No. If she was going to do this, she wanted it to last. And she wanted to be the one in control. She refused to get hurt this time. She couldn't. Wouldn't.

But as she let her hands slip inside Franco's tuxedo jacket and up his solid, muscular back, she didn't much care about what happened tomorrow. How much worse could things get, anyway?

"Come home with me, Franco."

Franco half expected her to change her mind before they made it back to her apartment. If she did, it would have killed him. But he'd honor her decision, obviously.

He wanted her, though. He wanted her so much it hurt.

By the time they reached the threshold of her front door, he was harder than he'd ever been in his life. Diana gave no indication that she'd changed her mind. On the contrary, she wove her fingers through his and pulled him inside the apartment. The door hadn't even clicked shut behind them before she draped her arms around his neck and kissed him.

It was a kiss full of intention. A prelude. And damned if it didn't nearly drag him to his knees.

"Diana," he groaned into her mouth.

Everything was happening so fast. Too fast. He'd waited a long time for this. Three excruciating years. Waiting...wanting.

"Slow down, love." He needed to savor. And she needed to be adored, whether she realized it or not.

She pulled back to look at him, eyes blazing. "Just so you know, this is hate sex."

He met her gaze. Held it, until her cheeks turned a telltale shade of pink.

Keep on telling yourself that, darling.

He drew his fingertip beneath one of the slender straps of her evening gown, gave it a gentle tug and watched as it fell from her shoulder, baring one of her breasts. He didn't touch her, just drank in the sight of her—breathless, ready. Her nipple was the palest pink, as delicate as a rose petal. When it puckered under his gaze, he finally looked her in the eye.

"Hate sex. Obviously." He gave her a half smile. "What else would it be?"

"I'm serious. I loathe you." But as she said those words, she slid the other spaghetti strap off her shoulder and let her dress fall to the floor in a puddle of silver satin.

I don't believe you. He stopped short of saying it. Let her think she was the one in control. Franco knew better. "I don't care."

History swirled in the air like a lingering perfume as she stood before him, waiting. Naked, save for the dark, sparkling sapphire resting against her alabaster skin.

She was gorgeous. Perfect. More perfect than he remembered. She'd changed in the years since he'd seen her this way. There was a delicious curve to her hips that hadn't been there before, a heaviness to her breasts. He wouldn't have thought it possible for her to grow more beautiful. But she had.

Either that, or this meant more than he wanted to admit.

Hate sex. Right.

She gathered her hair until it spilled over one shoulder,

then reached behind her head to unfasten the sapphire-and-diamond necklace.

"Leave it." He put his hands on the wall on either side of her, hemming her in. "I like you like this."

"Is that so?" She reached for the fly of his tuxedo pants and slipped her hand inside.

Franco closed his eyes and groaned. He was on the verge of coming in her hand. As much as he would have liked to blame his lack of control on his recent celibacy, he knew he couldn't. It was her. Diana.

What was happening to him? To them?

"Diana," he whispered, pushing her bangs from her eyes.

He searched her gaze, and he saw no hatred there. None at all. Only desire and possibly a touch of fear. But wasn't that the way it should be? Shouldn't they both be afraid? One way or another, this would change things.

His chest felt tight. Full. As if a blazing sapphire like the one around Diana's neck had taken the place of his heart and was trying to shine its way out.

"I need you, Franco." Not want. *Need.*

"I know, darling." He grazed her plump bottom lip with the pad of his thumb. She drew it into her mouth, sucked gently on it.

Holy hell.

"Bedroom. Now." Every cell in his body was screaming for him to take her against the wall, but he wanted this to last. If they were going to go down this road to-gether…again…he wanted to do it right this time. Diana deserved as much.

She released her hold on him and ducked beneath one of his arms. Then she sauntered toward a door at the far end of the apartment without a backward glance.

Franco followed, unfastening his bow tie as his gaze

traveled the length of her supple spine. She moved with the same feline grace that haunted his memory. He'd thought perhaps time had changed the way he remembered things, as time so often did. Surely the recollection of their night together shone brighter than the actual experience.

But he realized now that he'd been wrong. She was every bit as special as he remembered. More so, even.

He placed his hands on her waist and turned her around so she was facing him. She took a deep, shuddering inhale. The sapphire rose and fell in time with the beating of her heart.

She was more bashful now, with the bed in sight. Which made it all the more enticing when her hands found his belt. But her fingers had started trembling so badly that she couldn't unfasten the buckle.

"Let me," he said, covering her hands with his own.

He took his time undressing. He needed her to be sure. More than sure.

But once he was naked before her, her shyness fell away. She stared at his erection with hunger in her gaze until Franco couldn't wait any longer. He needed to touch her, taste her. Love her.

He hesitated as he reached for her.

This isn't love. It can't be.

The line between love and hate had never seemed so impossibly small. As his hands found the soft swell of her breasts, he had the distinct feeling they were crossing that line. He just didn't know which side they'd been on, which direction they were going.

He lowered his head to draw one of her perfect nipples into his mouth, and she gasped. An unprecedented surge of satisfaction coursed through him at the sound of her letting go. At last.

That's it, Wildfire. Let me take you there.

He teased and sucked as she buried her hands in his hair, shivering against him. He reached to part her thighs, and she let out a soft, shuddering moan. As he slipped a finger inside her, he stared down at her, fully intending to tell her they were just getting started. But when she opened her eyes, he said something altogether different.

"You have the most beautiful eyes I've ever seen. Like amethysts."

The words slipped out of his mouth before he could stop them. He loved her eyes. He always had. But this wasn't the sort of thing people said during hate sex. Even though he wasn't at all convinced that's what they were doing.

Still. This wasn't the time to turn into a romantic. If she needed to pretend this was nothing but a meaningless release, fine. He'd give her whatever she needed.

"There's a legend about amethysts, you know," she whispered, grinding against him as he moved his finger in and out.

"Tell me more."

He guided her backward until her legs collided into the bed and she fell, laughing, against the down comforter. He stretched out beside her and ran his fingertips in a leisurely trail down the perfect, porcelain softness of her belly.

Then he was poised above her with his erection pressing against her thigh, and her laughter faded away. Her eyes turned dark, serious.

"According to legend, they're magic. The ancient Romans believed amethysts could prevent drunkenness. Some still say they do."

Franco didn't believe it. Not for a minute. He felt

drunk just looking into the violet depths of those eyes. "Nonsense. You're intoxicating."

"Franco."

He really needed to stop saying such things. But he couldn't seem to stop himself.

If the circumstances had been different, he would have said more. He would have told her he'd been an idiot all those years ago. He would have admitted that this charade they'd both been dreading had been the most fun he'd had in ages. He might even have told her exactly what he thought of her breathtaking body...in terms that would have made her blush ruby red.

But circumstances weren't different. They'd been pretending for weeks. He'd just have to pretend the words weren't floating around in his consciousness, looking for a way out.

There was one thing, however, he definitely needed to say. Now, because come morning it would be too late. "Diana, there's something I need to tell you."

She shook her head as her hands found him and guided him toward her entrance. "No more words. Please. Just this."

Then he was pushing into her hot, heavenly center, and he couldn't have uttered another word if he tried.

What am I doing?

Diana's subconscious was screaming at her to stop. But for once in her life, she didn't want to listen. She didn't want to worry about what would happen tomorrow. Her entire life had been nothing but planning, practice, preparation. Where had all of that caution gotten her?

Nothing had gone as planned.

She was supposed to be on her way to the Olympics.

And here she was—in bed with Franco Andrade. Again. By her own choosing.

On some level, she'd known this was coming. She might have even known it the moment he'd first strolled into Drake Diamonds. She most definitely had known it when he'd kissed her at Harry Winston.

But the kiss had been her idea, too, hadn't it?

Oh, no.

"Oh, yes," she heard herself whisper as he slid inside her. "Yes, please."

It doesn't mean anything. It's just sex. Hate sex.

"Look at me, Wildfire. Let me see those beautiful eyes of yours." Franco's voice was tender. So tender that her heart felt like it was being ripped wide open.

She opened her eyes, and found him looking down at her with seriousness in his gaze. He kept watching her as he began to move, sliding in and out, and Diana had to bite her bottom lip to stop herself from crying out his name.

After months and months of working so hard to stay numb, to guard herself against feeling anything, she was suddenly overwhelmed with sensation. The feel of his body, warm and hard. The salty taste of his thumb in her mouth. The things he was saying—sweet things. Lovely things. Things she'd remember for a long, long time. Long after their fake relationship was over.

It was all too much. Much more than she could handle. The walls she'd been so busy constructing didn't stand a chance when he was watching her like that. Studying her. Delighting in the pleasure he was giving her.

"That's it, darling. Show me." Franco smiled down at her. It was a wicked smile. A knowing one.

He didn't just want her naked. He wanted her exposed

in every way. She could see it in the dark intent in his gaze, could feel it with each deliberate stroke.

This didn't feel like hate sex. Far from it. It felt like more. Much more.

It felt like everything.

It felt…real.

"Franco." His name tasted sweet in her mouth. Like honey. But as it fell from her lips in a broken gasp, something inside her broke along with it.

She shook her head, fighting it. She couldn't be falling for him. Not again.

It's all pretend. Just make believe.

But there was nothing make believe about his lips on her breasts as he bowed his head to kiss them. Or the liquid heat flowing through her body, dragging her under.

She arched into him, desperate, needy. He gripped her hips, holding her still as he tormented her with his mouth and his cock, with the penetrating awareness of his gaze.

This was all her doing. He knew it, and so did she.

They hadn't been destined to fall into bed together. Not then. Not now. She'd wanted him. For some nonsensical reason, she still did. Every time he touched her, every time he so much as glanced in her direction, she burned for him.

She'd made this happen. She'd seduced him. Not the other way around.

It wasn't supposed to be this way. It was supposed to be quick. Simple. But every time her climax was in reach, he slowed his movements, deliberately drawing things out. Letting her fall.

And fall.

Until everything began to shimmer like diamond dust, and she could fall no farther.

She began to tremble as her hips rose to meet his,

seeking release. Franco reached for her hands and pinned them over her head, their fingers entwined as he thrust into her. Hard. Relentless.

"My darling," he groaned, pressing his forehead against hers.

I'm not yours.

She couldn't make herself say it. Because if she did, it would feel more like a lie than any of the others she'd told in recent days. Whether she liked it or not, he held her heart in his hands. He always had, and he always would.

The realization slammed into her, and there was no use fighting it. Not now. Not when everything seemed so right. For the first time in as long as she could remember, she felt like herself again.

Because of him.

He paused and kissed her, letting her feel him pulse and throb deep inside. It was exquisite, enough to make her come undone.

"This is what you do to me, Diana." His voice was strained, pierced with truth. She felt it like an arrow through the heart. "No one else. Only you."

In the final, shimmering moment before she came apart, her gaze met his. And for the first time it didn't feel as though she was looking at the past.

In the pleasured depths of his eyes, she could see a thousand tomorrows.

Chapter Thirteen

Diana woke to a familiar buzzing sound. She blinked, disoriented. Then she turned her head and saw Franco asleep beside her—*naked*—and everything that had transpired the night before came flooding back.

They'd had sex. Hot sex. Tender sex. Every sort of sex imaginable.

She squeezed her eyes shut. Maybe it had all been a dream. A very realistic, very *naughty* dream.

The buzzing sound started again, and she sat up. Something glowed on the surface of her nightstand. Her cell phone. She squinted at it and saw Artem's name illuminated on the tiny screen.

Why was Artem calling her at this hour?

She couldn't answer the call. *Obviously.* But when she grabbed the phone to silence it, she saw that this was his third attempt to reach her.

Something was wrong.

"Hello?"

"Diana?" Artem's CEO voice was in overdrive...at six in the morning. Wonderful. "Why are you whispering?"

"I'm not," she whispered, letting her gaze travel the length of Franco's exposed torso. God, he was beautiful. *Too beautiful.*

Had her tongue really explored all those tantalizing abdominal muscles? Had she licked her way down the dark line of hair that led to his manhood?

Oh, God, she had.

She yanked one of the sheets from the foot of the bed and wrapped it around herself. She couldn't be naked while she talked to her brother. Not while the face of Drake Diamonds was sexually sated and sleeping in her bed.

"Diana, what the hell is going on?" She couldn't think of a time when she'd heard Artem so angry.

He'd found out.

Oh, no.

She slid out of bed, tiptoed out of the room and closed the door behind her. Her confusion multiplied at once when she saw heaps of feathers all over the living room. The air swirled with them, like she'd stepped straight from the bedroom into a snowfall.

A tiny black flash bounded out of one of the piles.

Lulu.

The puppy had disemboweled every pillow in sight while Diana had been in bed with Franco. Now her life was a literal mess as well as a metaphorical one. Perfect.

"Look, I can explain," she said, scooping the naughty dog into her arms.

Could she explain? Could she really?

I know I told you there was nothing going on between Franco and me, but the truth is we're sleeping together.

Slept together. Past tense. She'd simply had a bout of temporary insanity. It wouldn't happen again, obviously. It couldn't.

Hate sex. That's all it was. She'd made that very clear, and she'd stick to that story until the day she died. Admitting otherwise would be a humiliation she just couldn't bear.

"You can explain? Excellent. Because I'd really like to hear your reasoning." Artem sighed.

This was weird. And overly intimate, even by the dysfunctional Drake family standards.

"Okay…well…" She swallowed. How was she supposed to talk about her weakness for Franco's sexual charms to her *brother*? "This is a little awkward…"

Lulu burrowed into Diana's chest and started snoring. Destroying Dalton's apartment had clearly taken its toll.

"As awkward as reading about my sister's engagement in the newspaper?" Artem let out a terse exhale. "I think not."

Engagement?

Diana's heartbeat skidded to a stop.

Engagement?

Lulu gave a start and blinked her wide, round eyes.

"W-w-what are you talking about?" Diana's legs went wobbly. She tiptoed to the sofa and sank into its fluffy white cushions.

She hoped Franco was sleeping as soundly as he'd appeared. The last thing she needed was for him to walk in on this conversation.

"You and Franco are engaged to be married. It's in every newspaper in the city. It's also all over the television. Look, I know I gave you free reign as VP of public relations, but don't you think this is going a bit far?"

"Yes. I agree, but…"

"But what? The least you could have done was tell me your plans. We just talked about your relationship with Franco yesterday morning, and you never said a word about getting engaged." Artem sounded like he was on the verge of a heart attack.

Diana felt like she might be having one herself. "Calm down, Artem. It's not real."

"I know that. Obviously. But when are you going to clue everyone else in on that fact? While you're walking down the aisle?"

A jackhammer was banging away in Diana's head. She closed her eyes. Suddenly she saw herself drifting slowly down a path strewn with rose petals, wearing a white tulle gown and a sparkling diamond tiara in her hair.

What in the world?

She opened her eyes. "That's not what I mean. The announcement itself isn't real. There's been a mistake. A horrible, horrible mistake."

"Are you sure?" There wasn't a trace of relief in Artem's voice. "Because the article in the *Times* includes a joint statement from you and Franco."

"I'm positive. A statement? That's not possible. They made it up. You know how the media can be." But he'd said the *Times*, not *Page Six* or the *Daily News*.

The *New York Times* had fact checkers. It was a respectable institution that had won over a hundred Pulitzer Prizes. A paper like that didn't fabricate engagement announcements.

Now that she thought about it, the weddings section of the *Times* was famous in its own right. Society couples went to all sorts of crazy lengths to get their engagement announced on those legendary pages.

Her gaze drifted to the closed bedroom door. Ice trickled up her spine.

He wouldn't.

Would he?

No way. Franco would be just as horrified at this turn of events as she was. He wouldn't want the greater population of New York thinking he was off the market.

You and I are monogamous.

She'd actually laughed when he'd said those words less than two weeks ago. But she'd never pressed for an explanation.

This can't be happening. I can't be engaged to Franco Andrade.

Sleeping with him was one thing. Letting him slip a ring on her finger was another thing entirely.

Forget Franco. Forget Artem. Forget Drake Diamonds. This was her life, and she shouldn't be reading about it in the newspapers.

She took a calming breath and told herself there was nothing to worry about. There had to be a reasonable explanation. She didn't have a clue what that might be, but there had to be one.

But then she remembered something Franco had said the night before. Right before he'd entered her. She remembered the rare sincerity in his gaze, the gravity of his tone.

I need to tell you something.

The engagement was real, wasn't it? The statement in the *Times* had come from Franco himself. He'd even tried to warn her, and she'd refused to listen.

She hadn't wanted words. She'd wanted to feel him inside her so badly that nothing else mattered.

And now she was going to kill him.

"Artem, I have to go. I'll call you back."

She pressed End and threw her phone across the room. She glared at the closed bedroom door.

Had Franco lost his mind? They could *not* be engaged. They just couldn't. Even a fake engagement was out of the question.

Of course it's fake. He doesn't want to marry you any more than you want to marry him.

That was a good thing. A very good thing.

She wasn't sure why she had to keep reminding herself how good it was over and over and over again.

The tightness in Diana's chest intensified. She pressed the heel of her palm against her breastbone, closed her eyes and focused on her breath. She was on the verge of a full-fledged panic attack. All over an engagement that wasn't even real. If that didn't speak volumes about her attitude toward marriage, nothing would.

Breathe. Just breathe.

Maybe she was losing it over nothing. Maybe whatever Franco had wanted to tell her had nothing at all to do with the press. Maybe the *Times* wedding page had, indeed, made an unprecedented error.

She looked at the dog, because that's how low she'd sunk. She was seeking validation from a puppy. "Everyone makes mistakes. It could happen, right?"

Lulu stretched her mouth into a wide, squeaky yawn.

"You're no help at all," Diana muttered, focusing once again on the closed bedroom door.

There was only one person who could help her get to the bottom of this latest disaster, and that person didn't have four legs and a curlicue tail.

Franco slept like the dead.

He opened his eyes, then let them drift shut again. He hadn't had such a peaceful night's rest in months. He forgot all about the Kingsmen, Luc's ultimatum and the overall mess his personal life had become. It was remarkable what great sex could do for a man's state of mind. Not just great sex. Phenomenal sex. The best sex of his life.

Sex with Diana Drake.

"Franco!"

He squinted, fighting the morning light drifting through the floor to ceiling windows of Diana's bedroom.

Someone was yelling his name.

"Franco, wake up. Now." A pillow smacked his face.

He opened his eyes. "It's a little early in the morning for a pillow fight, Wildfire. But I'm game if you are."

"Of course you think that's what this is. For your information, it's not." She stood near the foot of the bed, staring daggers at him. For some ridiculous reason, she'd yanked one of the sheets off the bed and wrapped it around herself. As if Franco hadn't seen every inch of that gorgeous body. Kissed it. Worshipped it. "And I've asked you repeatedly not to call me that."

"Not last night," he said, lifting a brow and staring right back at her.

What had he missed? Because this wasn't the same Diana he'd taken to bed the night before, the same Diana who'd cried his name as he thrust inside her. It sure as hell wasn't the same Diana who'd told him how much she'd needed him as she unzipped his fly.

"I'm being serious." She tugged the bedsheet tighter around her breasts.

Franco pushed himself up to a sitting position, rested his back against the headboard and yawned. When his eyes opened, he caught Diana staring openly at his erect cock. *That's right, darling. Look your fill.* "See something you like?"

Her gaze flew upward to meet his. Franco was struck once again by just how beautiful she was, even flustered and disheveled from a night of lovemaking. He preferred her like this, actually. Fiery and flushed. He just wished she'd drop the damned sheet and climb back in bed.

"Cover yourself, please," she said primly.

"Sure. So long as I can borrow your tent." He stared pointedly at her bedsheet-turned-ballgown.

"Nice try." She let out a laugh. Laughter had to be a good sign, didn't it? "But I'll keep it, thank you very much."

Franco shrugged. "Fine. I'll stay like this, then."

Her gaze flitted once again to his arousal. If she kept looking at him like that, he might just come without even touching her. "Suit yourself. Naked or not, you have some explaining to do."

"What have I done this time?"

"I think you know." She titled her head and flashed him a rather deadly-looking smile. "My dear, darling *fiancé*."

Fiancé.

Shit.

The engagement announcement. He'd meant to tell her about it before it hit the papers. He'd even tried to bring it up the night before, hadn't he? "So you've seen the *Times*, I presume?"

"Not yet. But Artem has. He's also seen the *Observer*, *Page Six* and the *Daily News*. It's probably the cover story on *USA TODAY*." She threw her hands up, and the sheet fell to the floor. But she'd worked herself into such a fury, she didn't even notice. "Explain yourself, Franco."

"Explain myself?" He climbed out of bed, strode toward her and picked up the pile of Egyptian cotton at her feet. Pausing ever so briefly to admire her magnificent breasts, he wrapped the sheet around her shoulders and covered her again.

Her cheeks went pink. "Thank you." For a brief second, he saw a hint of tenderness in her gaze. Then it vanished as quickly as it had appeared. "You heard me. I can't believe I even have to ask this question, but why does everyone on planet Earth suddenly think I'm going to marry you?"

He sighed and rested his hands on her shoulders, a sliver of relief working its way through him when she didn't pull away. He reminded himself the engagement was a sham. Their whole relationship was a sham. None of this should matter.

"Because I told them we're engaged."

"Oh, my God, I knew it." She began to tremble all over.

Franco slid his hands down her arms, took her hands in his and pulled her close. "No need to panic, Wildfire. It's nothing. Just part of the ruse."

A spark of something flared low in his gut. Something that felt far too much like disappointment. He'd never imagined he would one day find himself consoling a woman so blatantly horrified at the idea of being his betrothed. The fact that the woman was Diana Drake made it all the more unsettling.

She wiggled out of his grasp and began to pace around the spacious bedroom. The white bedsheet trailed behind her like the train on a wedding gown. "What were you thinking? I can't believe this."

She took a break from her tirade to regard him through narrowed eyes. For a moment, Franco thought she might slap him. Again. "Actually, I can. I don't know why I thought I could trust you. About anything."

He nearly flinched. But he knew he had no right.

As mornings after went, this one wasn't stellar. He wasn't sure what he'd expected to happen after last night.

The line between truth and lies had blurred so much he couldn't quite think straight, much less figure out whatever was happening between him and Diana. But he was certain about one thing—he'd seen the same fury in her gaze once before.

Of course he remembered what he'd said. He'd regretted the words the instant they'd slipped from his mouth.

He'd known he needed to do something dire the moment he'd woken up beside her, all those years ago. She'd looked too innocent, too beautiful with her dark hair fanned across his chest. Too damned happy.

Strangely enough, he'd felt almost happy, too. Sated. Not in a sexual way, but on a soul-deep level he hadn't experienced before. It had frightened the hell out of him.

He didn't do relationships. Never had. Never would. It wasn't in his blood. Franco had never even known who his father was, for crying out loud. As a kid, he'd watched a string of men come in and out of his mother's life. In and out of her bed. When the men were around, his mother was all smiles and laugher. Once they'd left— and they always left…eventually—the tears came. Days passed, sometimes weeks, when his mother would forget to feed him. Franco had gotten out the first chance he had. He'd been on his own since he was eleven years old. As far as he knew, his mother had never come looking for him.

He wouldn't know how to love a woman even if he wanted to. Which he didn't. If his upbringing had taught him anything, it was that self-reliance was key. He didn't want to need anyone. And he most definitely didn't want anyone needing him. Especially not a diamond heiress who'd opened her eyes three years ago and suddenly looked at him as if he'd hung the moon.

He'd done what he'd needed to do. He'd made certain she'd never look at him that way again.

Come now, Diana. We both know last night didn't mean anything. It was nice, but I prefer my women more experienced.

She'd had every right to slap him. He'd deserved worse.

"You can breathe easy. I have no intention of actually marrying you," he said.

"Good." She laughed again. Too lively. Too loud.

"Good," he repeated, sounding far harsher than he intended.

What exactly was happening?

He didn't want to hurt her. Not this time.

"What you fail to understand is that I don't want to be *engaged* to you, either." She held up a hand to stop him from talking, and the sheet slipped again, just enough to afford him a glimpse of one, rose-hued nipple.

His body went hard again. Perfect. Just perfect.

Diana glanced down at him, then back up. There wasn't a trace of desire in her eyes this time. "I can't talk to you about this while you're naked. Get dressed and meet me in the kitchen."

She flounced away, leaving Franco alone in a room that throbbed with memories.

He shoved his legs into his tuxedo pants from the night before and splashed some water on his face in the bathroom. When he strode into the kitchen, he found her standing at the coffeemaker, still dressed in the bedsheet. Lulu was frolicking at her feet, engaged in a fierce game of tug-of-war with a corner of the sheet. The dog didn't even register his presence. Clearly, the two of them had bonded, just as he'd hoped. He should have been happy. Instead, he felt distinctly outnumbered.

Diana poured a steaming cup, and Franco looked at it longingly.

She glanced at him, but didn't offer him any.

Not that he'd expected it.

"I'm sorry," he said quietly.

She lifted a brow. "For what, exactly?"

For everything.

He sighed. "I should have given you a heads-up."

Her expression softened ever so slightly. "You tried."

"I could have tried harder." He took a step closer and caught a glimpse of his reflection—moody and blue—in the sapphire still hanging around her neck.

She backed up against the counter, maintaining the space between them. "Just tell me why. I need to know."

A muscle flexed in Franco's jaw. This wasn't a conversation he wanted to have the morning after they'd slept together. Or ever, to be honest. "My chances of getting back on the Kingsmen will be much greater if I'm engaged."

She blinked. "That doesn't make sense."

Don't make me explain it. He gave her a look of warning. "It matters. Trust me."

"Trust you?" She set her coffee cup on the counter and crossed her arms. "You've got to be kidding."

"For the record, it would be even better if we were married." What was he saying? He was willing to go pretty far to get his job back, but not that far.

Diana gaped at him. "I can't believe this. You're a polo player, not a priest. What does your marital status have to do with anything…" Her eyes grew narrow. "Unless… oh, my God…"

Franco held up his hands. "I can explain."

But he couldn't. Not in any kind of way that Diana would find acceptable. Even if he broke his promise to

Luc and told her the truth, she'd never believe him. Not in this lifetime.

"You did something bad, didn't you? Some kind of terrible sexual misconduct." She fiddled with the stone around her neck, and Franco couldn't help but notice the way her fingers trembled. He hated himself a little bit right then. "Go ahead and tell me. What was it? Did you sleep with someone's wife this time?"

He looked at her long and hard.

"You did," she said flatly. The final sparks of whatever magic had happened between them the night before vanished from her gaze. All Franco could see in the depths of her violet eyes was hurt. And thinly veiled hatred. "How could I be such an idiot? *Again?* Who was it?"

Less than an hour ago, she'd been asleep with her head on his chest as their hearts beat in unison. How had everything turned so spectacularly to crap since then?

A grim numbness blossomed in Franco's chest. He knew exactly what had gone wrong. The past had found its way into their present.

Didn't it always?

He'd written the script of this conversation years ago.

He wanted to sweep her hair from her face and force her to look him in the eye so she could see the real him. He wanted to take her back to bed and whisper things he'd never told anyone else as he pushed his way inside her again.

He wanted to tell her the truth.

"It was Natalie Ellis," he said quietly.

"Ellis? As in *Jack* Ellis?" She pulled the bedsheet tighter around her curves, much to Franco's dismay. "You had an affair with your boss's wife? That's despicable, Franco. Even for you. You must think I'm the biggest fool you've ever met."

"I'm the fool," he said.

She shook her head. "Don't, okay? Just don't be nice to me right now. Please."

"Diana…"

Before he could say another word, the cell phone in the pocket of his tuxedo pants chimed with an incoming text message.

Damn it.

Diana rolled her eyes. Lulu barked at the phone in solidarity. "Go ahead. Look at it. It's probably from one of your married girlfriends. Don't let me stand in your way."

Franco didn't make a move. Whoever was texting him could wait.

His phone chimed again.

Diana glared at him. "You disgust me, Franco. And I swear, if you don't answer that right now, I'm going to reach into your pocket and do it for you."

Franco sighed and looked at the phone's display.

See you at practice today at 10 sharp. Come ready to play. Don't be late.

The engagement announcement had worked. He was back on the team.

And back on Diana's bad side.

She hated him.

Again.

Chapter Fourteen

Diana didn't bother returning Artem's call. Instead, she decided to get dressed and go straight to Drake Diamonds and explain things in person.

But there was no actual explanation, was there? She was engaged. *Pretend* engaged, but still. Engaged.

She had no idea what she was going to say to her brother. If she admitted she'd known nothing about the engagement, it would look like she'd lost control over her own public image. And as VP of public relations, the Drake image was pretty much the one thing she was responsible for. On the other hand, if she pretended she'd known all about the faux engagement, Artem would be furious that she'd kept him in the dark. It was a catch-22. Either way, she was screwed.

She had to face him sooner or later, though. She desperately wanted to get it over with. Maybe she'd go ahead and tell him he'd been right. The charade had gone too far. She should end it. The Lambertis would walk away, of course. And she'd never be co-CEO. She might not even be able to keep her current position. Artem had told her she'd proven herself, but that had been before the engagement fiasco. Who knew what would happen if she broke up with her fake boyfriend now? She could end up right back in the Engagements department.

But that would be better than having to walk around pretending she was going to get married to Franco, wouldn't it?

Yes.

No.

Maybe.

The only thing she knew for certain was that she shouldn't have slept with him the night before. How could she have been so monumentally stupid? She deserved to be fired. She'd fire herself if she could.

He'd carried on an affair with a married woman. That was a new low, even for a playboy like Franco. And it made him no different than her father.

So, of course she'd jumped into bed with him. God, she hated herself.

"Is he in?" she asked Mrs. Barnes, glancing nervously at the closed office door. What was her brother doing in there? He rarely kept his door closed. He was probably throwing darts at the wedding page of the *Times*. Or possibly interviewing new candidates for the VP of public relations position. She shook her head. "Never mind, I know he wants to see me. I'm going in."

"Wait!" Mrs. Barnes called after her.

It was too late, though. Diana had already flung Artem's door open and stormed inside. Artem sat behind his desk, just as she'd expected. But he wasn't alone. Carla and Don Lamberti occupied the two chairs opposite him.

Ophelia was also there, standing beside the desk with what looked like a crystal baseball.

The diamond.

It was even larger than Diana had imagined. She paused just long enough to take in its impressive size and to notice the way it reflected light, even in its uncut state. It practically glowed in Ophelia's hands.

All four heads in the office turned in her direction.

Any and all hopes she had of sneaking out the door unnoticed were officially dashed. "I'm so sorry. I didn't mean to interrupt."

She practically ran out of the office, but of course she wasn't fast enough.

"Diana, what a nice surprise!" The brightness of Carla Lamberti's smile rivaled that of her diamond.

Diana forced a smile and cursed the four-inch Jimmy Choos that had prevented her speedy getaway. Why, oh why, had she worn stilettos?

Probably because there had been a dozen paparazzi following her every move all day, thanks to Franco's little engagement announcement. The doorman had warned her about the crowd of photographers gathered outside her building before she'd left the apartment. If her picture was going to be splashed on the front page of every newspaper in town, she was going to look decent. Especially considering that Franco's walk of shame out of her building earlier in the morning had already turned up on no less than four websites.

Not only had she made the terrible mistake of sleeping with him, but now everyone with a Wi-Fi connection knew all about it.

"It looks like you're busy. I just needed to talk to Artem, but it can wait." She turned and headed for the door.

"Don't be silly. Join us. We insist. Right, Mr. Drake?" Carla glanced questioningly at Artem, who nodded his agreement. "I want to hear all about your engagement to Mr. Andrade. I can't seem to pry a word out of your brother."

The older woman turned to face Diana again. Behind her back, Artem crooked a finger at Diana, then pointed to the empty place on his office sofa.

Okay, then. Diana took a deep breath, crossed the room and sat down.

"So, tell us everything. As I said, Artem won't breathe a word about your wedding." Carla cast a mock look of reprimand in Artem's direction.

Your wedding.

Diana did her best not to vomit right there on the Drake-blue carpet.

Ever the diplomat, Ophelia jumped into the conversation. "I'm sure Diana and Franco would like to keep some things private. It's more special that way, don't you think?"

Diana released a breath she hadn't realized she'd been holding. She owed Ophelia. Big-time.

Mr. Lamberti rested a hand on his wife's knee. "Goodness, dear. Leave Diana alone. She's here to join our meeting about the plans for the diamond, not to discuss the intimate details of her personal life."

Carla let out a laugh and shrugged. "I suppose that's true. Please pardon my manners. I was just so excited to read about your engagement in the paper this morning. I knew from the moment I saw you and Franco together at the Harry Winston party that you were destined to be together. The way that man looks at you..."

Her voice drifted off, and she sighed dreamily.

Artem cleared his throat. "Shall we proceed with the

meeting? Ophelia has drawn up some beautiful designs for the stone."

"Of course. Just one more question. I promise it's the last one." Mrs. Lamberti's gaze shifted once again to Diana. She prayed for the sofa to somehow open itself up and swallow her whole, but of course it didn't. "It's true, isn't it? Are you and Mr. Andrade really engaged to be married?"

This was the opening she'd been waiting for. She could end the nonsensical charade right here and now, and she'd never even have to set eyes on Franco again. All she had to do was say no. The papers had made a mistake. She and Franco weren't engaged. In fact, they were no longer seeing each other. The Lambertis would obviously be disappointed, but surely they wouldn't pack up their diamond and leave.

Would they?

Diana swallowed. *Do it. Just do it.*

Why was she hesitating? This was her chance to get her life back. It was now or never. If she didn't fess up, she'd be stuck indefinitely as Franco's fiancée.

Speak now or forever hold your peace.

She was already thinking in terms of wedding language. Perfect. She may as well climb right into a Vera Wang.

She glanced from the Lambertis to Artem to Ophelia. This would have been so much easier without an audience. And without that ridiculously huge diamond staring her in the face. It was blinding. Which was the only rational explanation for the next words that came out of her mouth.

"Of course it's true." She smiled her most radiant, bridal grin. "We're absolutely engaged."

* * *

All the way to Bridgehampton, Franco waited for the other shoe to drop. He fully expected to arrive at practice only to be ousted again. The moment he'd left Diana's apartment, she'd no doubt picked up the phone and called every newspaper in town to demand a retraction.

He wasn't sure what to make of the fact that she hadn't. His cell phone sat on the passenger seat of his Jag, conspicuously silent.

He arrived at the Kingsmen practice field at ten sharp just as instructed, despite having to break a few traffic laws to get there on time. He still hadn't heard a word from Diana when he climbed out of his car and tossed his cell into the duffel bag that carried his gear.

He needed to quit worrying about her. About the two of them. Especially since they weren't an actual couple.

It had only been hate sex.

He slammed the door of his Jag hard enough to make the car shake.

"And here I thought you'd be thrilled to be back," someone said.

Franco turned to find Coach Santos standing behind him. "Good morning."

"Is it? Because you seem pissed as hell." His gaze swept Franco from top to bottom. "A tuxedo? At ten in the morning? This doesn't bode well, son."

Franco was lucky he kept a bag packed with his practice gear in the trunk of his car. There hadn't been time to stop by his apartment. "Relax. I wasn't out partying. You caught me at my fiancée's apartment this morning. I'm a changed man, remember?"

"Let's hope so. Ellis isn't so sure, but he's willing to give it a shot. For now." Santos looked pointedly at Franco's rumpled tux shirt. "But try not to arrive at practice looking like you just rolled out of someone's bed. It's not help-ing your cause. Got it?"

"Got it." Franco gave him a curt nod and tried not to think about that bed. Or that particular *someone*.

He needed to have his head in the game, today more than ever. But he hated the way he and Diana had left things. He'd thought this time would be different.

If he was being honest with himself though, it was for the best. Diana Drake had always been out of his league. He didn't have a thing to offer her.

Time hadn't changed who he was. It hadn't changed anything. He and Diana had ended back where they'd begun.

"We've got a scrimmage in an hour. And don't forget about Argentine Night at the Polo Club tonight. Ellis ex-pects you there with your doting fiancée on your arm."

Franco's gut churned. Getting Diana anywhere near the Polo Club would be next to impossible. It seemed as though she hadn't gotten within a mile radius of a live horse since her accident.

There was also the slight complication that she hated him. Now, more than ever.

"What are you waiting for? Get suited up." Coach Santos jerked his head in the direction of the practice field, where the grooms were already getting the horses saddled up and ready.

Before Franco had come to America—before all the championship trophies and the late-night after parties—he'd been a groom. He'd been the one who brushed the horses, running a curry comb over them until the Ar-gentine sunshine reflected off them like a mirror. He'd bathed them in the evenings, grinning as they tossed their heads and whinnied beneath the spray of the water hose. Franco had lived and breathed horses back then.

When he wasn't shoveling out stalls, he was on horse-back, practicing his swing, learning the game of polo.

Sometimes he missed those days.

But grooms didn't become champions, at least not where Franco had come from. He was one of the lucky ones. Not lucky, actually. Chosen. He owed Luc Piero everything.

"You did it, man." Luc greeted Franco with a bone-crushing hug the moment he stepped onto the field. "You're back."

"I told you there wasn't anything to worry about." Franco shrugged and fastened his helmet in place.

"Engaged, though?" Luc lifted a brow. "Tell me that's not real."

"Does it matter?" Franco planted one of his feet into a stirrup, grabbed onto the saddle and swung himself onto his horse's back. His grooms had gotten the horses to the field just in the nick of time.

"Yes, it matters. It matters a whole hell of a lot. I mean, you've never been the marrying kind."

"So I hear." He was being an ass, and he knew it. But he wasn't in the mood to discuss his marriageability. Not when he couldn't shake the memory of the hurt in Diana's gaze this morning.

He sighed. "Sorry. I just don't want to discuss Diana Drake. Or any of the Drakes, for that matter."

They had been the means to an end. Nothing more. Why did he keep having to remind himself of that fact?

Luc shrugged. "I can live with that. You're back. That's what important. Nothing else. Right?"

Franco shot him a grim smile. "Absolutely."

He rode hard once the scrimmage got underway. Fast. Aggressive.

By the close of the fourth chukker, the halfway point

of the game, the scoreboard read 11 to 0. Franco had scored each and every one of the goals. He managed four more before the end of the game. He was back, indeed.

His teammates gathered round to congratulate him. Ellis applauded from his box seat, but didn't approach Franco. And that was fine. Franco didn't feel much like talking. To Ellis or anyone. The urge he felt to check his cell phone for messages was every bit as frustrating as it was pressing. When he finally did, he had over forty voicemails, all from various members of the media.

Not a single word from Diana.

He shoved his phone in his back pocket and slammed his locker closed. What was he supposed to do now? Were he and Diana engaged? Were they over?

He had no idea.

He stopped by his apartment in Tribeca and packed a bag, just in case. No news was good news. Wasn't that the old adage? Besides, he couldn't quite shake the feeling that if Diana Drake had decided to dump him, he would have heard it first from the press…

Because that's how monumentally screwed up their fake relationship was.

But the mob of photographers outside Diana's building didn't say a word about a breakup when Franco arrived on the scene. They screamed the usual questions at him, along with a few new ones. About the wedding, of course. He kept his head down and did his best to ignore them.

The doorman waved Franco upstairs, just as he had before. That didn't necessarily mean anything. Diana probably wouldn't have broken the news first to her doorman, but Franco was beginning to feel more confident that he, indeed, had a fiancée waiting for him in the penthouse.

Sure enough, when Diana answered the door, there

was a colossal diamond solitaire situated on her ring finger. "Oh, it's you."

For some nonsensical reason, the sight of the ring rubbed Franco the wrong way. If their engagement had been real, he would have chosen a diamond himself. And it wouldn't be a generic rock like the one on her hand. He would have selected something special. Unique.

But what the hell was he thinking? *None* of this was real. The ring shouldn't matter.

It did, though. He had no idea why, but it mattered.

"Nice ring," he said through gritted teeth.

"I picked it up at Drake Diamonds today since my *fiancé* forgot to give me one." She lifted an accusatory brow. "What are you doing here, anyway?"

He gave her a grim smile and swished past her with his duffle and a garment bag slung over his shoulder. "Honey, I'm home."

She gaped at him. "I beg your pardon?"

Lulu shot toward him, all happy barks and wagging tail. At least someone was happy to see him. He tossed his bags on the sofa and gathered the puppy into his arms.

Diana frowned at Lulu, then back at Franco. *Someone looks jealous.* "What's going on? Surely you don't think you're moving in with me."

"We're engaged, remember? This is what engaged people do."

She shook her head. "Please tell me you're not serious. I've already taken in one stray. Isn't that enough?"

It was the wrong thing to say.

"You're comparing me to a stray dog now?" he said through clenched teeth.

She opened her mouth to say something, but Franco wouldn't let her. He'd heard enough.

"I've put up with a hell of a lot from you and your family in the past few weeks, Diana. But you will not speak to me that way. Is that understood, wifey?"

She blinked. "I..."

He held up a hand. "Save it. We can talk later. We have a date tonight, anyway. You should get dressed."

"A *date*?"

"We're going to Argentine Night at the Polo Club. If you have a problem with it, I don't want to hear it. I've accompanied you to every gala and party under the sun in the past few weeks. You can do one thing for me." He gave Lulu a scratch behind the ears. "Unless you'd like to kick both of the strays out of your life once and for all?"

She wouldn't dare. If she wanted him gone, she wouldn't be wearing that sparkling diamond on her ring finger. Franco honestly didn't know why she wanted to play along with the engagement, but he no longer cared.

You care. You know you do.

If he didn't, the stray dog comment wouldn't have gotten under his skin the way it had.

"Well?" he asked.

"I'll be ready in half an hour." She plucked the dog from his arms. "And Lulu isn't going anywhere."

She sauntered past him with the little pug's face peering at him over her shoulder and slammed the bedroom door.

Franco wanted to stay angry. Anger was good. Anger was comfortable. He knew a lot more about what to do with anger than about what to do with the feelings that had swirled between them last night.

But seeing her with the dog took the edge off. He'd been right to force the puppy on her. He'd done something good.

For once in his life.

Chapter Fifteen

Diana had spent the better part of her life around horses, but she'd never been to the Polo Club in Bridgehampton. Show jumping and polo were clearly two separate sports. She'd known polo players before, obviously. She'd certainly seen Franco at her fair share of equestrian events. But she'd never run in the same after-hours circles as Franco's crowd.

Even before the night she'd lost her virginity to Franco, she'd noticed a brooding intensity about those athletes that both fascinated and frightened her. They rode hard and they play hard. Deep down, she knew that was one of the qualities about Franco that had first drawn her toward him. He didn't care what anyone else had to say about him. He behaved any way he chose. Both on and off the field.

Diana had no idea what that might feel like. She was a Drake, and that name came with a myriad of expectations.

If she'd been born a boy, things would have been different. Drake men were immune to rules and expectations. At least, that had been the case with her father. He'd spent money as he wished and slept with whomever he wished, and everyone in the family had to just deal with it. Her mother included.

"You look awfully serious all of a sudden," Franco said as she stepped out of the Drake limousine at the valet stand outside the Polo Club. "What are you thinking about?"

"Nothing." *Marriage.* Why was she even pondering such things? Oh, yeah, because she was engaged now. "I'm fine. Let's just go inside."

"Very well." He lifted her hand and kissed it before tucking it into the crook of his elbow.

Diana looked around, expecting to see a group of photographers clustered by the entrance of the club. But she didn't spot a single telephoto lens.

"Good evening, Mr. Andrade and Miss Drake." A valet held the door open for them as Franco led her into the foyer.

"Wow," she whispered. "This is really something."

The stately white building had been transformed into a South American wonderland of twinkling lights and rich, red decor. Sultry tango music filled the air. Diana was suddenly very glad she'd chosen a red lace gown for the occasion.

She and Franco were situated at a round table near the center of the room, along with his coach and several other players and their wives. When she took her seat, the man beside her introduced himself as Luc Piero.

"It's a pleasure to meet you," she said.

"The pleasure's all mine, I assure you." Luc grinned from ear to ear. "I've known Franco for a long time, and

I've never seen him as captivated with anyone before as he is with you. I've told him time and again that I wanted to meet you, but he's been hiding you away."

"I've done no such thing," Franco countered.

"That's right. Your pictures have been in the newspaper every day for two weeks running. How could I forget?" Luc smiled.

Diana kind of liked him. She probably would have liked him more if she weren't so busy searching the room for Natalie Ellis. She had a morbid curiosity about the woman Franco had apparently considered worth risking his entire career over. Diana had seen the woman on a handful of occasions, but she wanted a better look. She wasn't jealous, obviously. Simply curious.

Right. You're a card-carrying green-eyed monster right now.

"I'm going to go get us some drinks, darling." Franco bent to kiss her on the cheek, which pleased her far more than it should have. "I'll be right back."

She reminded herself for the millionth time that she hated him, then turned to Luc. "You say you've known Franco a long time?"

"All our lives. We grew up together in Argentina."

"Really?" Franco had never breathed a word to her about his childhood. She couldn't help being curious about the way he'd grown up. "Tell me more."

"He's loved horses since before he could walk. You know that, right?"

She didn't. But she understood it all too well. "That's something we have in common."

"My father owned one of the local polo clubs in Buenos Aires. I used to hang out there when I was a kid, and that's where I met Franco."

"Oh, was he taking riding lessons there?"

Luc gave her an odd glance. "No, Franco's one hundred percent self-taught. A natural. He was a groom at my father's stable."

"I see." She nodded as if this wasn't stunning new information. After all, she should probably have some sort of clue about Franco's childhood since he was her fiancé.

But a groom?

In the equestrian world, grooms and riders belonged in two very different social classes. Not that Diana liked or condoned dividing people into such groups. But it was an unpleasant fact of life—she'd never known a groom who had gone on to compete in show jumping. Maybe things were different in the sport of polo.

Then again, maybe not.

"It's unusual, I know. But Franco was different, right from the start."

Indeed. Her throat grew tight.

She should be furious with him after the stunt he'd pulled. He'd strong-armed her into an engagement, plain and simple. An engagement she didn't want.

And she'd let him. She wasn't sure who she was angrier at—Franco or herself.

"Different. How so?" She glanced at Franco across the room, where he stood standing beside a man she recognized from equestrian circles as Jack Ellis, the owner of the Kingsmen.

Her breath caught in her throat. No matter how many times she looked at Franco—whether it was from the other side of a crowded room or beside him in bed—his physical perfection always seemed to catch her off guard. He was the most handsome man she'd ever seen. Ellis, on the other hand, appeared immune to Franco's charms. The expression on his face was grim. Even the woman on Jack Ellis's arm didn't seem to notice Franco's charming smile or dark, chiseled beauty. Natalie Ellis looked almost bored as she glanced around the room. When her gaze fell on Luc, her lips curved into a nearly imperceptible smile.

Odd.

"Well…" Luc continued, dragging her attention back to their conversation. "Like I said, he was a talented rider. Fearless. Instinctual. Even as a kid, I knew I was witnessing something special. He had a bond with the horses like nothing I'd ever seen. They were his life."

A chill went up Diana's spine. She had a feeling she was about to hear something she shouldn't.

"His life," she echoed.

"I found out he was sleeping in the stables and kept it a secret from my father for over year before he found out." Luc gave her a sad smile. "I thought he'd be angry and kick Franco out. Instead, he gave Franco a room in our family home."

She most definitely shouldn't be hearing this. Franco had never said a thing to her about his life in Argentina. Now she knew why. These were the sort of intimate details only a lover should know. A real lover.

She should change the subject. Delving further into this conversation would be an invasion of Franco's privacy. But she was so distraught by what she'd heard that she couldn't string together a single coherent sentence.

She'd called Franco a stray.

And he'd been homeless.

Oh, God.

"Are you all right, Diana?" Luc was watching her with guarded curiosity. "You look like you've seen a ghost."

No, just a monster. And that monster is me.

"Fine." She cleared her throat. "Is that when Franco

started playing polo? After he moved in with your family?"

Luc shrugged. "Yes and no. He was still working as a groom, but I'd begun playing. Franco was my training partner. In the beginning, he was just there to help me improve my game. That didn't last long."

"He's that good, isn't he?" She forced herself to smile like a doting bride.

What was happening? She was acting just like the nauseatingly sweet engaged couples she'd loathed so much when she worked in Engagements.

It *was* an act, wasn't it?

"He's the best. He always has been. His talent transcends any traditional rules of the game. That's why my father put him on the team." He smiled at Franco as he approached the table. "We've been teammates ever since."

A lump formed in Diana's throat. "I'm glad. Franco deserves a friend like you."

"He's more like a brother than a friend. He's always got my back. The guy's loyal to a fault, but I'm sure you know that by now."

Loyal to a fault...

Before Franco had walked through the door of Drake Diamonds a month ago, Diana would have never used those to words to describe him. Now she wasn't so sure.

She'd seen a different side to Franco in recent weeks. It all made sense now...the way he'd jumped at the chance to adopt a homeless puppy, his commitment to their fake relationship. Franco was a man of his word.

She was beginning to question everything she'd believed about him, and that wasn't good. It wasn't good at all. Their entire relationship had been built on a lie, and Diana preferred it that way. At least she knew where she stood. She operated best when she could look at the world in black and white. But things with Franco had blurred into a disturbing shade of gray.

She didn't know what she thought anymore. Worse, she wasn't sure what she felt. Because despite everything that had happened in the past, and despite the fact that just when she thought she could trust Franco he'd gone and announced to the world that they were engaged, she felt something for him. And that *something* scared the life out of her.

But he obviously had little or no regard for marriage, otherwise he wouldn't have bedded Natalie Ellis. Natalie Ellis, who seemed to have no interest in Franco whatsoever.

What was going on?

"Hello, darling. Sorry to leave you alone for so long." Franco bent and kissed her on the cheek again. "I hope Luc hasn't been boring you."

"No, not at all." Quite the opposite, actually.

She smiled up at him and tried to forget all the things she'd just heard. But it was no use. She couldn't shake the image of Franco as a young boy, sleeping on a bed of straw in a barn. What had happened to him to make him end up there? Where was his family? So many unanswered questions.

The air between them was heavy with secrets and lies, but somewhere deep inside Diana, an unsettling truth had begun to blossom.

She had feelings for Franco. Genuine feelings.

"The tango contest is about to begin." He offered her his hand. "Dance with me?"

She stared at his outstretched palm, and words began to spin in her head.

Do you take this man to love and to cherish, all the days of your life?

She was losing it.

"Yes." *I do.* She placed her hand in his. She didn't even know how to tango, but she didn't much care at this point. "Yes, please."

The music started and Franco wrapped his right arm around Diana until his hand rested squarely in the center of her back. When he lifted his left arm, she placed her hand gently in his.

"I should probably mention that I don't exactly know how to tango." She blushed.

"Not to worry. I'm a rather strong lead."

"Why am I not surprised?" she murmured. He took a step forward, and she moved with him in perfect synchrony. "Luc had some lovely things to say about you just now."

They reached the end of the club's small dance floor, and Franco spun her around. "He's probably had more than his fair share of champagne."

"Don't." Diana shook her head and slid one of her stilettos up the length of his leg. "I'm being serious. He loves you like a brother."

Franco nodded. Her leg had traveled nearly up to his hip. He pulled her incrementally closer. "You're right. He does. And I'd do anything for him."

He deliberately avoided glancing in Natalie Ellis's direction.

This wasn't the time or place for a heart-to-heart, but something about the way Diana was looking at him all of a sudden made it impossible for him to keep giving her flippant responses.

She slid her foot back to the floor and they resumed stalking each other across the floor to the strains of the accordion music.

"I had no idea you could dance like this, Franco." Diana swiveled in his arms. "You're full of surprises."

"It's an Argentine dance." He lifted her in the air, and her legs wrapped around his waist, then flared out before she landed on the floor with a whisper. For someone who claimed not to know how to tango, Diana was holding her own. Someone had clearly been watching *Dancing With the Stars*.

This was beginning to feel less like dancing and more like sex. Not that Franco was complaining.

"Tell me more about your life in Argentina," she whispered as her hand crept to the back of his neck.

Should he be this aroused at a social function? Definitely not. He was a grown man not a horny fifteen-year-old kid. "Other than the dancing?"

"Yes, although I'm a little curious about the dancing, as well."

He pulled her closer, but kept his gaze glued in the opposite direction. The quintessential tango posture. Convenient, as well, since he never discussed his family upbringing. But he'd witnessed a staggering amount of Drake family dynamics over the past few weeks. Hell, he was beginning to almost feel like a Drake himself. If she was asking questions, he owed her a certain degree of transparency.

"I grew up with a single mother in Barrio de la Boca. I never knew my father."

"I see," she murmured.

He cast a sideways glance in her direction, hoping against hope he wouldn't see a trace of pity in her gaze. Having Diana Drake look at him in such a way would have killed him. She wasn't, though. She seemed more curious than anything, and for that, Franco was grateful.

"My mother was less than attentive. I ran away when

I was eleven. Luc's father took me in. The rest is history, as they say."

They reached the end of the dance floor again, but instead of turning around, Diana slid her foot up the back of his calf. "I wish I would have known about this sooner."

He reached for the back of her thigh and ground subtly against her before letting her let go. "Would it have changed anything?"

"Yes." She swallowed, and he traced the movement up and down the elegant column of her neck. "I'm sorry, Franco. I should have never said what I did earlier."

He lowered her into a deep dip and echoed her own words back to her from the night before. "You're forgiven."

"Ladies and gentlemen, the winners of the annual tango contest are Franco Andrade and Diana Drake."

The room burst into applause.

"I can't believe this," Diana said as Franco pulled her upright. "We won!"

Franco wove his hand through hers and held on tightly as Jack Ellis approached them, holding a shiny silver trophy.

His mouth curved into a tight smile as he offered it to Franco. "Congratulations."

"Gracias." The fact that Ellis was so clearly upset by his presence probably should have bothered Franco to some extent, but he couldn't bring himself to care at the moment.

Diana was speaking to him again. They'd only exchanged a handful of words since their engagement had been announced, and somehow he'd managed to get back in her good graces. Better than that, it felt genuine. He was starting to feel close to her in a way he seldom did with anyone.

Don't fool yourself. It's only temporary, remember.

"Miss Drake, it's a pleasure to make your acquaintance." Ellis shook Diana's hand. "Will you be joining us at tomorrow's match?"

Diana went instantly pale. "Tomorrow's match?"

"The Kingsmen have a game tomorrow. Surely Franco's mentioned it." Ellis frowned.

A spike of irritation hit Franco hard in his chest. Ellis could talk to him however he liked, but he wasn't about to let his boss be anything but polite to Diana. "Of course I have. Unfortunately, Diana has a previous engagement."

She nodded. After an awkward, silent beat, she followed his lead. "I'm afraid Franco's right. I have a commitment tomorrow that I simply can't get out of."

"That's too bad," Ellis said. "Another time, perhaps."

"Perhaps." She smiled, but Franco could see the panic in her amethyst gaze. She had no intention of watching him on horseback. Not tomorrow. Not ever.

Ellis said his goodbyes and walked away. The band began to play again, and Franco and Diana were swallowed up by other couples.

"Come with me." He slid his arm around her and whispered into her hair.

"Where are we going?" She peered up at him, and he could still see a trace of fear in those luminous eyes.

Franco would have given everything he had to take her distress away. But no amount of money or success could replace what she'd lost the day she'd fallen. He'd never felt so helpless in his life. Nothing he could do would bring Diamond back to life.

But maybe, just maybe, he could help her remember what it had been like to be fearless.

If only she would let him.

* * *

"Close your eyes," Franco whispered. His breath was hot on her neck in tantalizing contrast to the cool night air on her face.

Franco's voice was deep, insistent. Despite the warning bells going off in Diana's head, she did as he asked.

"Good girl."

A thrill coursed through her and settled low in her belly. What was she doing? She shouldn't be out here in the dark, taking orders from this man. She most definitely shouldn't be turned on by it.

She inhaled a shaky breath. *Open your eyes. Just open your eyes and walk away.*

But she knew she wouldn't. Couldn't if she tried. Something had happened out there on the dance floor. She felt as if she'd seen Franco for the first time. She'd gotten a glimpse of his past, and somehow that made the dance more meaningful. Not just their tango…the three-year dance they'd been engaged in since they'd first met.

"This way." His hand settled onto the small of her back. "Keep your eyes shut."

He started walking. Slowly. Diana kept in step beside him, letting him lead her. Unable to see, her other senses went on high alert. The sweet smell of hay and horses tickled her nose. The light touch of Franco's fingertips felt decadent, more intimate than it should have.

She licked her lips and let herself remember what it had felt like to take those fingertips into her mouth, to suck gently on them while he'd watched through eyes glittering like black diamonds. She wanted to feel that way again. She wanted *him* again, God help her.

"Be careful." Franco's footsteps slowed. She heard a door sliding open.

"Can I open my eyes now?" He voice was breathy, barely more than a whisper.

Franco's hand slid lower, perilously close to her bottom. "No, you may not."

How close was his face? Close enough to kiss? Close enough for her to lean toward him and take his bottom lip gently between her teeth?

She swallowed. This shouldn't be happening. None of it. The sad reality of Franco's childhood shouldn't change the ridiculous truth of their situation. The only thing they shared was a long string of lies. This was the same man who'd called the newspapers and told them he was marrying her. It was the same man who'd so callously dismissed her the morning after she'd lost her virginity.

They were pretending.

But it no longer felt that way. Not now that she'd seen the real him.

"Franco," she whispered, reaching for him.

He caught her wrist midair. "Shhhh. Let me."

She waited for a beat and wondered what would come next. Franco slid her hand into his, intertwining their fingers. Then her hand made contact with something soft. Warm. Alive.

She stiffened.

"It's okay, Diana. Keep your eyes closed. I'm here. I've got you." Franco's other arm wrapped around her, pulling her against him. He stood behind her with his hand still covering hers, moving it in slow circles over velvety softness.

A horse. She was touching a horse. She knew without opening her eyes.

I'm here. I've got you.

Did he know this was the closest she'd come to a horse since she'd fallen? Did he know this was the first time she'd touched one since that awful day? Could he possibly?

Of course he did. Because he saw her. He always had.

She felt a tear slide down her cheek, and she squeezed her eyes shut even harder. If she opened them now and saw her fingers interlocked with Franco's, moving slowly over the magnificent animal in front of them, she wouldn't be able to take it. She'd fall apart. She'd fall...

But this time, Franco would be there to catch her.

Or not.

How could this man be the same one who'd slept with Natalie Ellis and gotten himself fired?

It didn't make sense. Especially now that she knew his background. She could see why he pushed people away. She could even see why he'd said such awful things after she'd slept with him three years ago. Intimacy—real intimacy—didn't come easily to Franco. It couldn't. Not after what he'd been through as a boy.

If anyone could understand that, Diana could. Hadn't her own childhood been filled with a similar brand of confusion? They'd each found their escape on horseback. Which is why nothing about his termination made sense.

Polo meant everything to Franco. More than she'd ever imagined. Why would he risk it for a meaningless romp with his boss's wife?

There had to be more to the story. She wished he would tell her, but she knew deep down he never would. And she didn't particularly blame him.

"I lied, Franco." She kept her eyes closed. She couldn't quite bring herself to look at him. "It wasn't hate sex."

"I know it wasn't." He pulled her closer against him. When he spoke, his lips brushed lightly against the curve of her neck, leaving a trail of goose bumps in their wake.

"I don't hate you. I never did." She was crying in earnest now. Tears were streaming down her face, but she didn't care. She was tired of the lies. So very tired.

"Don't cry, Wildfire. Please don't cry." He pressed an openmouthed kiss to her shoulder. "It kills me to see you hurting. It always did, even back then."

Her heart pounded hard in her chest. There were more things to say, more lies to correct. She wanted to set the record straight. She *needed* to. Even if she never saw him again after next week.

You won't. He's going away, and he's not coming back.

"For three years, I've been telling myself I chose you because I knew you'd let me down. It's not true. I chose you because I wanted you. I wanted you back then. I wanted you the other night. And I want you now." She opened her eyes and turned to face him.

They were standing in a barn. She'd known as much, and she'd expected to feel panicked when confronted with the sight of the horses in their stalls. But she didn't. She felt right, somehow. Safe.

She'd dreaded coming here tonight, and now she realized it had been a gift.

"How did you know this is what I needed?" she asked.

He cupped her face, tipped her chin upward so she looked him in the eyes. "I knew because, in many ways, you and I are the same. I want you, too, Diana. I want you so much I can barely see straight."

"Take me home, Franco."

Chapter Sixteen

Franco didn't dare touch Diana in the backseat of the limo on their ride back to New York. If he did, he wouldn't be able to stop himself from making love to her right there in plain view of the driver and every other car on the long stretch of highway between Bridgehampton and the city.

It was more than just an exercise in restraint. It was the longest ninety minutes of his life.

They rode side by side, each trying not to look at the other for fear they'd lose control. An electric current passed between them. If the spark had been visible, it would have filled the lux interior of the car with diamond light.

As the dizzying lights of Manhattan came into view, he allowed his gaze to roam. It wandered down Diana's elegant throat, lingering on the tantalizing dip between her collarbones—the place where he most wanted to kiss her at the moment so he could feel the wild beating of her pulse beneath his lips. He wanted to taste the decadent passion she had for life. Consume it.

Diana felt each and every one of her emotions to its fullest extent. It was one of the things he'd always loved about her. Being by her side these past weeks had caused Franco to realize the extent to which he avoided feelings. Since he'd moved to America, he'd done his level best to forget the world he'd left behind. His memories of Argentina were laden with shame. The shame of growing up without a father. The shame of the way his mother had all but abandoned him.

He'd tried to outrun that shame on the polo field. He'd tried to drown it in women and wine. But it had always been there, simmering beneath the surface, preventing him from forming any real sort of connection with anyone. At times he even kept Luc at arm's length.

Luc knew the rules. He knew not to bring up the past. He knew not to push. Why he may have done so this evening was a mystery Franco didn't care to examine too closely.

He thinks this is different. He thinks you're in love.

This *was* different.

Was it love? Franco didn't know. Didn't want to know. Because what he and Diana had together came with an expiration date. He'd known as much from the start, but for some reason it was just beginning to sink in. The date was growing closer. Just a matter of days away. And now that he was a member of the Kingsmen again, he'd be leaving just as soon as their arrangement came to an end.

He should be happy. Elated, even. This was why he'd gotten himself tangled up with the Drakes to begin with. This was what he'd wanted.

But as his gaze traveled lower, past the midnight blue

stone that glittered against Diana's porcelain skin, he had the crippling sensation that everything he wanted was right beside him. Within arm's reach.

Screw the waiting.

He pushed the button that raised the limo's privacy divider and slid toward her across the wide gulf of leather seat in under a second. Diana let out a tiny gasp as his mouth crushed down on hers, hot and needy. But then her hands were sliding inside his tuxedo jacket, pulling him closer. And closer, until he could feel the fierce beat of her heart against his chest.

Not here. Take it slow.

But he couldn't stop his hands from reaching for the zipper at her back and lowering it until the bodice of her dress fell away, exposing the decadent perfection of her breasts. He stared, transfixed, as he dragged the pad of his thumb across one of her nipples with a featherlight touch.

The gemstone nestled in her cleavage seemed to glow like liquid fire, burning blue. On some level, Franco knew this wasn't possible. But he'd lost the ability for rational thought. All he knew was that this moment was one that would stick with him until the day he died.

He'd never forget the feel of Diana's softness in his hands, the way she looked at him as the city whirled past them in a blur of whirling silver light. Years from now, when he was nothing but a distant memory in her bewitching, beguiling mind, he'd remember what it had felt like to lose himself in that deep purple gaze. He'd close his eyes and dream of radiant blue light. God help him. He'd probably never be able to look at a sapphire again without getting hard.

"Diana, darling." He groaned and lowered his lips to her breasts, drawing a nipple into his mouth.

He was being too rough, and he knew it, nipping and biting with his teeth. But he couldn't stop. Not when she was arching toward his mouth and fisting her hands in his hair. His hunger was matched by her need, which didn't seem possible.

It was like falling into a mirror.

How will this end?

Badly. No question.

He couldn't fathom walking away from Diana Drake. But he knew he would. He always walked away. From everyone.

"Mr. Andrade." The driver's voice crackled over the intercom.

Franco ignored it and peeled Diana's dress lower. He was fully on top of her now, spread over the length of the backseat. He was kissing his way down her abdomen when the driver's voice came over the loud speaker again.

"Mr. Andrade, there are photographers at the end of the block, just outside the apartment building."

Diana stiffened beneath him.

"It's okay," he whispered. "Don't worry. Everything will be fine."

He gently lifted her dress back into place, cursing himself for being such an impatient idiot.

What were they doing? They weren't teenagers on prom night, for crying out loud. He was a grown man. The choices he made had consequences. And somehow the consequences of his involvement with Diana seemed to grow more serious by the day.

Diana sat up and brushed the chestnut bangs from her eyes. Her sapphire necklace shimmered in the dark.

Franco looked away and straightened his tie from the other end of the leather seat.

"We're here, Miss Drake, Mr. Andrade," the driver announced.

"Thank you," Franco said, squinting through the darkened car window.

The throng of paparazzi gathered at the entrance to the building was the largest he'd ever seen. The press attention was getting out of hand. The wedding would be a circus.

Get a grip.

He shook his head. There wasn't going to be a wedding. Ever. The engagement was a sham, despite the massive rock on Diana's finger.

The ring was messing with Franco's head. He was having enough trouble maintaining a grasp on reality, and seeing that diamond solitaire on Diana's hand every time she reached for him, touched him, stroked him just added to the confusion.

The back door opened, and he and Diana somehow managed to find their way inside the building amid the blinding light of flashbulbs. The photographers screamed questions at them about the details of the wedding. Would it be held at the Plaza? Who was designing Diana's wedding dress?

It occurred to Franco that he would have liked to see Diana dressed in bridal white. She would look stunning walking toward her man standing at the front of a church in front of the upper echelons of Manhattan society. A lucky man. A man who wasn't him.

They managed to keep their hands off each other as they navigated the route to Diana's front door. When had touching each other become something they did in private rather than for show? And why did that seem so dangerous when that's the way it should have always been?

Diana slid her key into the lock. She pushed the door open, and they paused at the threshold.

Franco caught her gaze and smiled. "I'm sorry about what happened in the car and the close call with the photographers. That was..." He shook his head, struggling for an appropriate adjective. *Careless. Intense. Fantastic.*

They all fit.

The corners of her perfect bow-shaped lips curved into a smile that could only be described as wicked. "I'm not sorry."

Franco swallowed. Hard.

Like falling into a mirror.

But mirrors broke when they fell. They ended up in tiny shards of broken glass that sparkled like diamonds but cut to the quick.

He didn't care what happened to him next month. Next week. Tomorrow. He just knew that before the night was over, he would bury himself inside Diana again. Consequences be damned.

The moment they stepped inside the apartment and the door clicked shut behind them, Diana found herself pressed against the wall. Franco's mouth was on hers in an instant, kissing her with such force, such need that her lips throbbed almost to the point of pain.

A forbidden thrill snaked its way through her. This was different than it had been the night before. They'd been somewhat cautious with each other then, neither of them willing to fully let down their guard. But she knew without having to ask that tonight wouldn't be like that. Tonight would be about surrender.

"Take off your dress," he ordered and took a step backward. His gaze settled on her sapphire necklace as he waited for her to obey.

She stood frozen, breathless for a moment, as she tried to make sense of what was happening. She shouldn't enjoy being told what to do, but this was for her pleasure. His. Theirs. And the molten warmth pooling in her center told her she liked it, indeed.

She reached behind her back for her zipper, but her hands were already shaking so hard that they were completely ineffectual. Franco moved closer, his face mere inches from hers. Her neck went hot, her knees buckled and she desperately wanted to look away. To take a deep breath and calm the frantic beating of her heart. But she couldn't seem to tear her gaze from his.

The corner of his mouth lifted into a barely visible half smile. His eyes blazed. He knew full well the effect he had on her. In moments like this, he owned her. He knew it, and so did she.

It should have frightened her. Diana had never wanted to belong to anyone, let alone him. And she wouldn't. Not once their charade was over and they'd gone their separate ways.

But just this once she wanted it to be true. Just for tonight.

"Turn around, love." His voice was raw, pained.

She did as he said and turned to face the wall. With excruciating care, he unzipped her gown. Red lace slid down her hips and fell to the floor. Franco's hands reached around to cup her breasts as his lips left a trail of tantalizing kisses down her spine.

"Preciosa," he murmured against her bare back. *Lovely.*

His breath was like fire on her skin. She was shimmering, molten. A gemstone in the making.

She sighed and arched her back. Franco's hands slid from her breasts to her hips, where he hooked his fingers around her lacy panties and slid them down her legs. She stepped out of them, turned to face him, but he stopped her with a sharp command.

"No." He took her hands and pressed them flat against the wall, then whispered in her ear. "Don't move, Diana. Stay very still."

This was like nothing she'd ever experienced before. She'd never been with anyone besides Franco, but this was even different than the times they'd been together. The brush of his designer tuxedo against her exposed skin made her consciously aware of the fact that, once again, she was completely undressed while he remained fully clothed. She couldn't even see him, but that seemed to enhance the riot of sensations skittering through her body. She could only close her eyes and feel.

He brushed her hair aside and kissed her neck, her shoulder. His hands were everywhere—on her waist, her bottom, sliding over her belly. She was suddenly grateful for the wall and the way he'd pressed her hands against it. It was the only thing holding her up. Her legs had begun to tremble, and the tingle between them was almost too much to bear. She was so overwhelmed by the gentle assault of his mouth and the graceful exploration of his hands that she didn't even notice he'd nudged her legs apart with his knee until his fingertips reached between her thighs and found her center.

"I could touch you forever," he said and slid a finger inside her.

Forever.

It was a dangerous word, but this was a dangerous game they were playing. For all practical purposes, they were playing house. Living as husband and wife. And to Diana's astonishment, she didn't hate it.

On the contrary, she quite enjoyed it.

Especially now, bent over with Franco's fingers moving in and out of her. She moaned, low and delicious. She needed him to stop. Now, before she climaxed in this brazen posture. But she'd lost control of her body. Her hips were rocking in time with his hand, and she was opening herself up for him like a flower. A rare and beautiful orchid. Diamond white.

"Franco," she begged. "Please."

"Come," he whispered. "For me. Do it now."

Stars exploded before her eyes, falling like diamond dust as her body shuddered to its end. She collapsed into his arms, and he carried her across the apartment to the bedroom, whispering soothing words.

She'd gone boneless, yet her skin was alive. Shimmering like a glistening ruby. The King of Stones. And as he gingerly set her down and pushed inside her, she felt regal. Adored as no woman had ever been.

She was a queen, and Franco Andrade was her king.

Chapter Seventeen

Diana took her place at a reserved table situated near midfield, where Artem and Ophelia sat beneath the shade of a Drake-blue umbrella. She tried not to think too hard about the fact that this is what life would be like if she and Franco were together.

Really together.

Sundays at the Polo Club, sipping champagne with her brother and his wife, surrounded by the comforting scents of fresh-cut grass and cherry blossoms. A real family affair.

It wouldn't be so bad, would it?

Her throat grew tight. It felt quite nice, actually. Far too nice to be real.

Surrender.

It would have been so easy to give in. The past month had been more than business. It had been such a beautiful lie that she wondered sometimes if she actually believed it.

I could touch you forever.

Forever.

The word had branded itself on her skin, along with Franco's touch.

"Here he comes," Ophelia said.

Diana dragged her attention away from the night before and back to the present, where Franco was riding onto the field atop a beautifully muscled bay mare. The horse's dark tail was fashioned into a tight braid, and the bottoms of its legs were wrapped with bright red bandages. These were protective measures, necessary to guard against injury during play, rather than fashion statements. But the overall effect was striking just the same. The horse was magnificent.

But not as magnificent as its rider.

Diana had never seen Franco in full polo regalia before. Riding clothes, sure. But not like this...

He wore crisp white pants and brandy-colored boots that stretched all the way above his knees. The sleeves of his Kingsmen polo shirt strained at his biceps as he gave his mallet a few practice swings. She couldn't seem to stop looking at the muscles in his forearms. Or the way he carried himself in the saddle. Confident. Commanding. The aggressive glint in his eyes was just short of cocky.

He winked at her, and she realized he'd caught her staring. Before she could stop herself, she wiggled her white-gloved fingers in a tiny wave.

Beside her, Artem cleared his throat. "Are you ready for this, sis?"

She dropped her hand to her lap and nodded. "I am."

He was talking about the horses, of course. As far as Artem knew, she hadn't been this close to a horse since the day of her accident. She thought about telling him what Franco had done for her, but she couldn't find the words. She wasn't even sure words existed to describe what had happened when he'd taken her hands and placed them on the warmth of the gelding's back.

But the main reason she didn't try and explain was that she wanted to keep the grace of the moment to herself. To preserve its sanctity. Almost every move she and Franco had made for the past month had been splashed all over the newspapers. Every touch. Every kiss. Every lie. The truth between them lived in the quiet moments, the ones no one else had seen. And she wanted to keep it that way as long as she possibly could.

Because so long as no one knew how much he really meant to her, she could pretend the end didn't matter. She could hold her head high when the gossip pages screamed that she and Franco were over.

Right in front of her, the players were clustered together in the center of the field. The two teams faced each other, waiting for the throw-in—the moment when the umpire tossed the ball into play. Diana forced herself to watch, to concentrate on the present rather than what hadn't even happened yet. But as the bright white ball fell to the ground, she couldn't help but feel like time had begun to move at warp speed. And, with a resounding whack of Franco's mallet, it did.

The ball sailed across the grass, a startling white streak against bright, vivid green. Franco leaned into the saddle, and his horse charged forward. The ground shook beneath Diana's feet as the players charged toward the goal.

Franco led the charge, and when he hit the ball with such force that it went airborne, her heart leaped straight to her throat.

She held her breath while she waited for the official ruling. When the man behind the goal waved a flag over his head to indicate the Kingsmen had scored, she flew to her feet and cheered.

Franco caught her eye as his horse galloped toward the opposite end of the field. He smiled, and her head spun a little.

God, she was acting like an actual fiancée. A wife.

But she was supposed to, wasn't she? She was just doing her job.

It was more than that, though. There was no denying it. She wasn't acting at all.

Oh, no.

Her legs went wobbly, and she sank into her white wooden chair.

You're in love with him.

"He's amazing, isn't he?" Ophelia clapped and yelled Franco's name.

"He is, indeed." Diana felt sick.

How had she let this happen? Sleeping with Franco again—*twice*—had been stupid enough. Falling in love with him was another thing entirely. Off-the-charts idiotic.

The players flew past again in a flurry of galloping hooves and swinging mallets, and Diana's gaze remained glued to Franco. She shook her head and forced herself to look away, to concentrate on something real. The silver champagne bucket beside the table. The feathered hat situated at a jaunty angle on Ophelia's head. Anything. She counted to ten, but none of the little tricks she'd once used to stop herself from thinking about Diamond worked. She couldn't keep her eyes off Franco.

In the blink of an eye, he scored three more goals. It was a relief when the horn sounded, signaling the end of the first chukker. The break between periods was only three minutes, but she needed those three minutes. Every second of them. She needed a break from the intensity of the action on the field. Time to collect herself. Time to convince herself that she wasn't in love with the high-scoring player of the game.

Artem refilled their champagne flutes. "Franco's on fire today."

Diana watched him trot off the field toward a groom who stood by, ready and waiting, with Franco's next horse and mallet. By the time the match was finished, he'd go through at least seven horses. One for each chukker.

"Diana?" Artem slid a glass in front of her.

"Hmm?" she asked absently.

Franco had removed his helmet to rake his hand through his hair, a gesture that struck her as nonsensically sensual. Even from this distance.

"Could you peel your eyes away from your fiancé for half a second?" There was a smile in Artem's voice.

Sure enough, when she swiveled to face him, she found him grinning from ear to ear. Ophelia's chair was empty. Diana hadn't even noticed she'd left the table.

"Fake fiancé," she said. The back of her neck felt warm all of a sudden. She sipped her champagne and wished Artem would find something else to look at.

"You can stop now," Artem said. "I know."

"Know what?" But she was stalling. She knew exactly what he'd meant. He *knew*.

"About you and Andrade." His gaze flitted toward Franco climbing onto his new horse. This one was a sleek, solid-black gelding. Just like Diamond.

Diana's heart hammered in her chest. "Who told you?" Franco? Surely not.

But no one else knew.

"No one." Artem let out a laugh. "Are you kidding?

No one had to. I'm not blind, sis. It's written all over your face."

She shook her head. "No. We're not... I'm not..."

I'm not in love. I can't be.

"Don't even try to pretend it's an act. I'm not buying it this time." His gaze flitted from her to Franco and back again. "How long?"

Diana sighed. She was suddenly more exhausted than she'd ever been in her life. So many lies. She couldn't tell another one. Not to her brother. "I don't know when it happened, exactly."

Slowly. Yet, somehow, all at once.

Was it possible that she'd loved him all along, since the first night they'd been together, back when she was twenty-two?

"This is awful. Artem. What am I going to do?" She dropped her head into her hands.

Artem bent and whispered in her ear. "There are worse things in the world than falling for your fiancé."

She peered up at him from beneath the brim of her hat. "You seem to be forgetting the fact that we're not actually engaged. Also, I know for certain that you hate the thought of Franco and me."

His brow furrowed. "When exactly did I say that?"

She sat up straight and met his gaze. "The day of the Lamberti diamond announcement. And the morning the engagement was listed in the newspaper. And possibly a few other times over the course of the past four weeks."

He shook his head. "Clearly you weren't listening."

"Of course I was. You're not all that easy to ignore, my darling brother. Believe me, I've tried." She gave him a wobbly smile.

She felt like she was wearing her heart on the outside of her body all of a sudden. It terrified her to her core.

The giddy, bubbly feeling that came over her every time she looked at Franco was probably the same thing her mother had experienced when she'd looked at Diana's father. His long list of mistresses had no doubt felt the same way about him, too.

Fools, all of them.

Artem reached for her hand and gave it a squeeze. "I never said I didn't like the idea of you and Franco having a *genuine* relationship."

Could that be true? Because it wasn't the way she remembered their conversations. Then again, maybe she'd been the one who found the idea so repugnant, not Artem.

He leveled his gaze at her. "I was concerned about your pretend relationship. It seemed to be spinning out of control, far beyond what I intended when I make the mistake of suggesting it. But if it's real…"

If it's real.

That was the question, wasn't it?

She would have given anything in exchange for the answer.

Ophelia returned to the table as the next chukker began. Diana redirected her attention to the field, where Franco cut a dashing figure atop his striking black horse. Seconds after the toss-in, he was once again ahead of the other players, smacking the ball with his mallet and thundering toward the goal.

But just as he reached the far end of the field, a player from the other team cut diagonally between him and the ball.

"That's an illegal move," Artem said tersely.

Diana could hear Franco yelling in his native tongue. *Aléjate! Away!* But the player bore down and forced his horse directly in front of Franco's ebony gelding.

Somewhere a whistle sounded, but Diana barely heard

it. Her pulse had begun to roar in her ears as Franco and his horse got lost in the ensuing fray. She flew to her feet to try and get a better look. All she could see amid the tangle of horses, players and mallets was a flash of dazzling black.

Just like Diamond.

Her throat grew tight. She couldn't breathe. Couldn't speak. She reached for Artem, grabbed his forearm. The emerald grass seemed too bright all of a sudden. The sky, too blue. Garish. Like something out of a nightmare. And the black horse was a terrible omen.

No. She shook her head. *Please, no.*

There was a sickening thud, then everything stopped. There was no more noise. No more movement. Nothing.

Just the horrific sight of Franco lying facedown on top of that glaring green lawn. Motionless.

Franco heard his body break as it crashed into the ground. There was no mistaking the sound—an earsplitting crack that seemed as though it were echoing off the heavenly New York sky.

The noise was followed by a brutal pain dead in the center of his chest. It blossomed outward, until even his fingertips throbbed.

He squeezed his eyes closed and screamed into the grass.

Walk it off. It's nothing. You've been waiting for this chance for months. You can't get sidelined with an injury. Not now.

He moved. Just a fraction of an inch. It felt like someone had shot him through the left shoulder with a flame-tipped arrow. At least it wasn't his playing arm.

Still, it hurt like hell. He took a deep breath and rolled himself over with his right arm. He squeezed his eyes closed tight and muttered a stream of obscenities in Spanish.

"Don't move," someone said.

Not *someone*. Diana.

He opened his eyes, and there she was. Kneeling beside him in the grass. The wind lifted her hat, and it went airborne. She didn't seem to notice. She just stared down at him, wide-eyed and beautiful, as her dark hair whipped in the wind.

For a blissful moment, Franco forgot about his pain. He forgot everything but Diana.

If she was putting on an act, it was a damned convincing one. Something in his chest took flight, despite the pain.

"You're a sight for sore eyes, you know that?" He winced. Talking hurt. Breathing hurt. Everything hurt.

Especially the peculiar way Diana was looking at him. As if she'd seen a ghost. "Why are you sitting up? You shouldn't be moving."

"And you shouldn't be on the field. You're going to get hurt." She was on her hands and knees in the grass, too close to the horses' hooves. Too ghastly pale. Too upset.

She remembers.

He could see it in the violet depths of her eyes—the agony of memory.

"*I'm* going to get hurt? Look at you, Franco. You *are* hurt." She peered up at the other riders. "Someone do something. Get a doctor. Call an ambulance. Please."

Luc had already dismounted and stood behind her with the reins to his horse as well as Franco's in his hand. He passed the horses off to one of their other teammates and knelt beside Diana. "The medics are coming, Diana. Help is on its way. He's fine. See?"

She blinked and appeared to look right through him.

Franco wished he knew what was going on in her head. Which part of her horrific accident was she remembering?

He'd known she was having trouble coming to terms with what had happened to her...with what had happened to Diamond. But he'd never once suspected that she remembered her accident. She'd had a concussion. She'd been unconscious. Those memories should have been mercifully lost.

No wonder she'd had such a hard time moving on.

"Diana, look at me." He reached for her, and a hot spike of pain shot through his shoulder. He cursed and used his right arm to hold the opposite one close to his chest.

A collarbone fracture. He would have bet money on it.

It was a somewhat serious injury, but not the worst thing in the world. With any luck he'd be back on the field in four weeks. Six, tops.

But he didn't care about that right now. All he cared about was the woman kneeling beside him...the things she remembered...the fear shining in her luminous eyes.

He'd been such an idiot.

The list of things he'd done wrong was endless. He shouldn't have pushed her to overcome her fears. He shouldn't have ridden a jet-black horse today. He damn well shouldn't have pressured her into watching him play.

He wished he could go back in time and change the things he'd said, the things he'd done. He would have given anything to make that happen. He'd never set foot on a polo field again if it meant he could turn back the clock.

If that were possible—if he could step back in time, he'd walk...run...all the way to the first moment he'd touched her. Not last night. Not last week.

Three years ago.

"Diana, I'm fine. Everything is fine."

But his assurances were lost in the commotion as the medical team reached him. He was surrounded by medics, shouting instructions and cutting his shirt open so they could assess his injuries. Someone shone a light in his eyes. When the spots disappeared from his vision, he could see the game officials clearing the horses and riders away. Giving him space.

He couldn't see Diana anymore. Suddenly, people were everywhere. Jack Ellis loomed over him, his expression grave. The emergency medical team was carrying a stretcher out onto the field.

Franco looked up at Ellis. "Is all of this really necessary? It's a collarbone. I'll be fine."

"Let's hope so," Ellis said coldly. "We need you on the tour."

Luc cleared his throat. His gaze fixed on Franco's, and Franco felt...

Nothing.

For months this was all he'd wanted. Polo was his life. Since he'd left home at eleven, he'd lived and breathed it. Without it, he'd been lost. The thought of losing it again, even for a few weeks, combined with the look on Ellis's face should have filled him with panic.

He wasn't sure what to make of the fact that it didn't.

"Diana," he said, ignoring Ellis and focusing instead on Luc. "Where is she? Where did she go?"

"She's with her brother." Luc jerked his head in the direction of the reserved tables.

"Go find her." Franco winced. The pain was getting worse. "Bring her to the hospital. Please."

Luc nodded. "The second the game is over, I will."

The game.

Franco had all but forgotten about the scrimmage. He'd turned his life upside down to get back on the team, and in a matter of seconds it no longer mattered.

Slow down. This is your life. She's a Drake. You're not. Remember?

Diana would be fine.

She was a champion. She'd come so far in conquering her fears in recent weeks. She was close. So close. His fall had been nothing like hers. Of course she'd been rattled, but by the time he saw her again, she'd be okay.

He clung to that belief as the paramedics strapped him to a stretcher and lifted him into an ambulance.

But the look on Diana's face when she walked into his hospital room however many hours later hurt Franco more than his damned arm did. The person standing at his bedside was a ghost of the woman he'd taken to bed the night before. Memories moved in the depths of her amethyst eyes.

Painful remembrance.

And stone-cold fear.

Franco had seen that look before in the eyes of spooked horses. Horses that had been through hell and back, and flinched at even the gentlest touch. It took years of patience and tender handling to get those horses to trust a man again. Sometimes they never did.

"You're here." He shifted on the bed, and a spike of pain shot from his wrist to his shoulder. But he didn't dare flinch. "I'm glad you came."

She gave him an almost invisible smile. "Of course I came. I'm your fiancée, remember? How would it look if I weren't here?"

So they'd gone from making love to just keeping up appearances. Again. Marvelous.

"Sweetheart." He reached for her hand and forced himself to speak with a level of calmness that was in direct contrast to the panic blossoming in his chest. "It's not as bad as it looks. I promise."

She nodded wordlessly, but when she quietly removed her hand from his, the gesture spoke volumes. He was losing her. It couldn't happen again. He wouldn't let it, damn it. Not this time. Not for good.

"Diana…"

"I'm fine." There was that forced smile again. "Honestly."

He didn't believe her for a minute, and he wasn't in the mood to pretend he did. Hadn't they been pretending long enough? "You're not fine, Diana."

She stared at him until the pain in her gaze hardened. *Go ahead, get mad. Just feel something, love. Anything.* "Be real with me."

She shook her head. "We had an agreement, Franco."

"Screw our agreement." She flinched as if he'd slapped her. "There's more here than a fake love affair. We both know there is."

"Stop." She exhaled a ragged breath. "Please stop. The gala is in two days, and so is the Kingsmen tour."

"Do I look like I'm in any kind of condition to play polo right now?" He threw off the covers and climbed out of the hospital bed. There was too much at stake in this conversation to have it lying down.

"You're going on the tour. Luc said Ellis is insisting that you come along. As soon as your injury heals, you'll be right back in the saddle." Her gaze shifted to his splint, and she swallowed. Hard.

"I'll always ride. It's not just my job. It's my life." Using his good arm, he reached to cup her cheek. When she didn't pull away, it felt like a minor victory. "It's yours, too, Diana. That's one of the things that makes us so good together. You'll ride again. You will. When you're ready, and I intend to be there when it happens."

She backed out of his reach. So much for small victories. The space between them suddenly felt like an impossibly vast gulf. "Go on tour, Franco. You'll be fired again if you don't."

Franco sighed. "I highly doubt that."

"It's true. Ask Luc. Apparently your coach wants to keep an eye on you." Her gaze narrowed. "I guess he doesn't want to leave you behind with his wife."

Shit. That again.

"Natalie Ellis means nothing to me, Diana. She never did."

"That's not such a nice way to talk about a woman you slept with. A woman who was *married*, I might add."

Franco followed her gaze to her ring finger, where her Drake Diamonds engagement ring twinkled beneath the fluorescent hospital lighting. He watched, helpless, as she slid it off her hand.

No. Every cell in his body screamed in protest. "What do you think you're doing?"

"I'm breaking up with you." She opened her handbag and dropped the ring inside. Her gaze flitted around the room. She seemed to be looking anywhere and everywhere but at him.

"Why remove the ring? It's not as if I actually gave it to you." Would she have been able to remove it so easily if he had?

He hoped not, but he couldn't be sure.

"I still think it's a good idea to take it off. You know, in case the press…"

"You think I still give a damn what the press thinks? Here's a headline for you—I don't. This isn't about our agreement. It's not about Drake Diamonds or Natalie

Ellis. It sure as hell isn't about the press. What's happening in this room is about you and me, Diana. No one else."

He'd fallen off his horse—something he'd done countless times before with varying degrees of consequences. Over the course of his riding career, he'd broken half a dozen bones and survived three concussions. But never before had a fall caused so much pain.

"Diana, you're afraid. But I'm fine. I promise. Now stop this nonsense. We have a gala to attend in two days."

She shook her head. "We had a deal, and now it's over. We both got what we wanted. It's time to walk away."

"Don't do this, Wildfire." His voice broke, but he couldn't have cared less. The only thing he cared about was changing her mind.

He wasn't sure when, but somewhere along the way he'd stopped pretending. He had feelings for Diana Drake. Feelings he had no intention of walking away from.

"Marry me."

Her face went pale. "You're not serious."

"I am. Quite." He'd never wanted this. Never asked for it. But he did now. The future suddenly seemed crystal clear.

She saw it, too. He knew she did. She could close her eyes as tightly as she wanted, but it was still there. Diamond bright.

"I'll marry you right now. We could go straight to the hospital chapel. Just say yes." They could have a fancy ceremony later on. Or not. Franco didn't care. He just wanted to be with her for the rest of his life. "Come on the tour with me, Diana. I don't want to do this without you."

"No." She shook her head. "You're not. You're just confused. I am, too. But it's not real. *We're* not real. You know that as well as I do."

"All I know is that I'm in love with you, Diana."

"Is that what you told Natalie Ellis? Were you in love with her too?" Diana's gaze narrowed. "You slept with a married woman, Franco. Your boss's wife. Do you even believe in marriage?"

What was he supposed to say to that?

I never slept with her.

I lied.

She'd never believe him. "There's never been anyone else, Diana. Only you."

"That doesn't exactly answer my question, does it? I can't marry you, Franco. Don't you see that? I might be a Drake, but I'm not my mother. She stood by the man she loved, even as he slept with every other woman who crossed his path. It killed her. It would kill me, too."

Then Diana turned and walked right out the door, and Franco was left with only the devastating truth.

He knew nothing.

Nothing at all.

Chapter Eighteen

The Met Diamond gala was supposed to be the most triumphant moment of Diana's fledgling career as a jewelry executive, but she dreaded it with every fiber of her being. She should have been walking up the museum's legendary steps on Franco's arm. She couldn't face the possibility of doing so alone. Not when every paparazzo in the western hemisphere would be there, wondering what had happened to her famous fiancé. She'd rather ride naked through the streets of Manhattan, Lady Godiva-style. But she'd made a promise, and she intended to honor it.

Thank God for Artem and Ophelia. Not only did they ride with her in the Drake limo, but they also flanked her as she climbed the endless marble staircase. She didn't know what she would have done without them. Artem slipped her arm through his and effectively held her upright as she was assaulted by thousands of flashbulbs and an endless stream of questions.

"Diana, where's Franco?"

"When's the wedding?"

"Don't tell us there's trouble in paradise!"

She wanted to clamp her hands over her ears. She could hear the photographers shouting even after they'd made it inside the museum.

"Are you okay?" Artem eyed her with concern.

God, she loved her brother. This night was every bit as important for him as it was for her, but his first concern was her broken heart.

She forced a smile and lied through her teeth. "I'm fine."

"No, you're not," Ophelia whispered. "You're shaking like a leaf. Artem, call our driver back. Diana should go home."

As good as that sounded, she couldn't. She'd made it this far. Surely she could last another few hours. Besides, she couldn't hide forever. The world would find out about her breakup eventually. It was time to face the music.

She was shocked no one had learned the truth yet. Two days had passed since she'd ended things with Franco. He hadn't breathed a word to the press, apparently. Which left her more confused than ever.

"Diana, I'd like you to stay." Artem glanced at his watch. "At least for half an hour. Then you can go straight home. Okay?"

"Artem…" Ophelia implored.

He cast a knowing glance in his wife's direction, one of those secret signals that spouses used to communicate. Diana would never be on the receiving end of such a look. Obviously.

"Thirty minutes," he repeated. "That's all I'm asking."

"No problem. I told you I'm fine, and I meant it." For the thousandth time since she'd walked out the door of

Franco's hospital room, the pad of her thumb found the empty spot where her engagement ring used to be.

A lump sprang to her throat.

She wasn't fine. She hadn't been fine since the moment she'd seen Franco fall to the ground at the polo match.

She'd thought she'd been ready to be around horses again, but she hadn't. She'd thought she'd been ready for a real relationship, one that might possibly lead to a *real* engagement and a *real* marriage, but she'd been wrong about that, too.

She couldn't lose anyone again. She'd lost both her mother and her father, and she'd lost Diamond. Enough was enough. She couldn't marry Franco. Not now. Not ever. If she did and something happened to him—if she lost him, too—she'd never be able to recover.

She shouldn't even want to marry him, anyway. The man had zero respect for the sanctity of marriage. He'd been fired for sleeping with his boss's wife, which meant that Diana had somehow fallen for a man who was exactly like her dad.

She'd have to be insane to accept his proposal.

Even though she'd almost wanted to...

"Excuse me." A familiar voice broke into their trio.

Diana turned to find the last person in the world she ever expected to see. "Luc?"

What on earth was Luc Piero doing at the Met Diamond gala? Had Franco not even told his closest friend that the engagement was off?

"Luc, I'm sorry. There's been a change of plans. Franco's not with me tonight." *Or any other night.*

He shook his head. "I'm not here for Franco. I came to talk to you."

"Me?" She swallowed.

What could she and Luc possibly have to talk about?

"Yes. You." He looked around at their posh surroundings. The Met was stunning on any given day, but tonight was special. Faux diamonds dripped from every surface. It was like standing inside a chandelier. "Is there someplace more private where we can chat?"

She shouldn't leave. She had a job to do. She had to speak to the Lambertis and pose for photos. And just looking at Luc made her all the more aware of how much she missed Franco.

She shook her head, but at the same time she heard herself agreeing. "Come with me." She glanced at Artem and Ophelia, who'd been watching the exchange with blatant curiosity. "I'll be right back."

She led Luc past the spot where the Lamberti diamond, which had just been officially rechristened the Lamberti-Drake diamond, glowed in a spectacular display case in the center of the Great Hall. Her stilettos echoed on the smooth tile floor as they rounded the corner beneath one of the Met's sweeping marble archways. When they reached the darkened hall of Greek and Roman art, her footsteps slowed to a stop.

They were alone here, in the elegant stillness of the sculpture collection. Gods and goddesses carved from stone surrounded them on every side. Secret keepers.

Diana was so tired of secrets. She'd spent her entire life mired in them. No one outside the family knew the circumstances surrounding her mother's death. Diana hadn't been allowed to talk about it. Nor did the public know the identity of Artem's biological mother. To the outside world, the Drakes were perfect.

So much deception. When would it end?

She turned to face Luc. "What is it? Has something happened to him?"

She hadn't realized how afraid she'd been until she uttered the words aloud.

Luc wouldn't have sought her out if what he had to say wasn't important. The moment he'd asked to speak to her in private, her thoughts had spun in a terrible direction. She remembered what it had felt like to find her mother's lifeless body on the living room floor...the panic that had shaken her to her core. It had been the worst moment of her life. Worse than her accident. Worse than losing Diamond. Worse than watching Franco's body break.

Every choice she'd made since the day her mother died had been carefully orchestrated so she'd never feel that way again. And where had it gotten her?

Completely and utterly alone.

But that wasn't so bad. She could handle loneliness. What she couldn't handle was the way her heart had broken in two the moment she'd seen Franco's lifeless body on the ground.

She'd fought her love for him. She'd fought it hard. But she'd fallen, all the same.

"No, he's fine." Luc's brow furrowed. "Physically, I mean. But he's not fine. Not really. That's why I'm here."

Her heart gave a little lurch. "Oh?"

Franco couldn't possibly love her. Not after the way she'd treated him. He'd been real with her. Unflinchingly, heart-stoppingly real. And she'd refused to do the same.

Worse, she'd judged him. Time and again. She'd acted so self-righteously, when all along they'd both been doing the same thing—running from the past. She'd chosen solitude, and in a way, so had Franco. Neither one of them had let anyone close. Until the day Franco asked her to marry him.

He was ready to leave the past behind. He was moving

beyond it, and he'd offered to do so hand in hand with Diana. But she'd turned him down.

She'd spent years judging him, and now she knew why. Not because the things he'd done were unforgivable, but because it was convenient. So long as she believed him to be despicable, he couldn't hurt her.

Or so she'd thought.

But he hadn't hurt her, had he? She'd hurt herself. She'd hurt them both.

"He's in love with you, Diana," Luc said.

She shook her head. "I don't think so."

She'd made sure of that.

"You're wrong. I've known Franco all his life, and I've never seen him like this before." The gravity in his gaze brought a pang to her chest. "He misses you."

She shook her head. "Stop. *Please*."

Why was he doing this? She'd nearly made it. Franco was leaving with the Kingsmen in less than twenty-four hours. Once he was gone, she'd have no choice but to put their mockery of a romance behind her and move on. She just had to hold on for one more day.

A single, heartbreaking day.

She swallowed. "I'm sorry, Luc. But I can't hear this. Not now."

She needed to get out of here. She'd thought she could turn up in a pretty gown and smile for the cameras one last time, but she couldn't. All she wanted to do was climb into bed with her dog and a pint of ice cream.

She gathered the skirt of ball gown in her hands and tried to slip past Luc, but he blocked her exit. He jammed his hands on his hips, and his expression turned tortured. "You're going to make me say it, aren't you?"

Diana was afraid to ask what he was talking about. Terrified to her core. She couldn't take any more. Refusing Franco had been the most difficult thing she'd ever had to do.

But she couldn't quite bring herself to ignore the torment in Luc's gaze. "I don't know what you're talking about."

Luc shook his head. "Franco is going to kill me. But you deserve to know the truth."

The truth.

A chill ran up Diana's spine. She had the sudden urge to clasp her hands over her ears.

But she'd been turning her back on the truth long enough, hadn't she?

No more secrets. No more lies.

"What is it?" Her voice shook. And when Luc turned his gaze on her with eyes filled with regret, she had to bite down hard on the inside of her cheek to keep from crying.

His gaze dropped to the floor, where shadows of gods and goddesses stretched across the museum floor in cool blue hues. "Look, I don't know what happened between the two of you, but there's something you should know."

Diana nodded wordlessly. She didn't trust herself to speak. She couldn't even bring herself to look at him. Instead, she focused on the marble sculpture directly behind him. Cupid's alabaster wings stretched toward the sky as he bent to revive Psyche with a kiss.

A tear slid down her cheek.

"Tell me," she whispered, knowing full well there would be no turning back from this moment.

Luc fixed his gaze with hers. The air in the room grew still. Even the sculptures seemed to hold their breath.

"It was me," he said.

Diana began to shake from head to toe. She wrapped

her arms around herself in an effort to keep from falling apart. "Luc, what are you saying?"

"I was the one who had an affair with Ellis's wife, not Franco." He blinked a few times, very quickly. His eyes went red, until he stood looking at Diana through a shiny veil of tears. "I'm sorry."

Diana shook her head. "No."

She wanted him to take the words back. To swallow them up as if she'd never heard them.

"No!" Her voice echoed off the tile walls.

Luc held up his hands in a gesture of surrender. "It wasn't my idea. It was Franco's. I left my Kingsmen championship ring in Ellis's bed. He found it and knew it belonged to one of the players. Franco confessed before I could stop him."

"I can't believe what I'm hearing." But on some level, she could.

Franco loved Luc like a brother. He wanted to protect him, just as Luc had protected him when he'd been living in his barn and then his home.

She should have figured it out. From the very beginning, she'd suspected there was more to Franco's termination than he'd admitted. Then, at Argentine Night at the Polo Club, Natalie Ellis had looked right through him.

And Diana had known.

Franco had never touched her.

But Diana had been so ready to believe the worst about him, she'd pushed her instincts aside. What had she done?

"He never anticipated being cut from the team. He was too valuable. But Ellis couldn't stand the sight of him. I tried to tell the truth. Over and over again. Franco wouldn't have it."

She wanted to pound her fists against his chest. She wanted to scream. *You should have tried harder.*

But she didn't. Couldn't. Because deep down, she was just as guilty as he was. Guilty of letting the past color the way she saw her future.

I should have believed.

Franco wasn't her father. Loving him didn't make her into her mother. And she *did* love him, despite her best efforts not to.

She'd spent every waking second since her accident trying to protect herself from experiencing loss again, and it had happened anyway. She'd fallen in love with Franco, and she'd lost him. Because she'd pushed him away.

"Tell me this changes things." Luc searched her gaze. His eyes were red rimmed, but they held a faint glimmer of hope.

"I wish it could." Her heart felt like it was going to pound out of her chest. She pressed the heel of her hand against her breastbone, but it didn't make a difference. She was choking on her remorse. "He asked me to marry him, Luc. And I turned him down."

Luc's brow furrowed. "What do you mean? I thought you were already engaged. It was in all the papers."

"He didn't tell you?" Her voice broke, and her heart broke along with it. "It was never real."

"He never said a word."

The fact that Franco never told Luc their relationship was a sham meant something. Diana wasn't sure what... but it did. It had to. He'd been willing to sacrifice everything for Luc, but he'd let his closest friend believe he was in love. He'd let him think he was going to marry her.

And that made whatever they'd had seem more genuine than Diana had ever allowed herself to believe.

It was real. It had been real all along.

She needed to go to him. What was she doing standing here while he was preparing to leave? "Sorry Luc, there's something I need to do."

She turned and ran out of the sculpture gallery, her organza dress swishing around her legs as she ran toward the foyer. But when she rounded the corner, she collided hard against the solid wall of someone's chest.

A hard, sculpted chest.

She'd know that chest anywhere.

"Franco, you're here." She pulled back to look up at him, certain she was dreaming.

She wasn't. It was him. He was wincing and holding his arm in the sling where she'd banged against it, but it was him. She'd never been so happy to see an injured man in all her life.

"I am." He smiled, and if her heart hadn't already been broken, it would have split right in two.

It felt like a century had passed since she'd walked out of his hospital room. A century in which she'd convinced herself she'd never see him again. Never get to tell him the things she should have said when she'd had the chance...

"Franco, there's something I need to say." She took a deep breath. "I'll go with you on tour. Please take me with you."

His smile faded ever so slightly. "Diana..."

"I just want to be with you, Franco. *Really* be with you." She choked back a sob. "If you'll still have me."

She felt as if she'd just taken her broken heart and given it to him as an offering. Such vulnerability should have made her panic. But it was far easier than she'd expected. Natural. Right. The only thing making her panic was the thought that she'd almost let him leave Manhattan without telling him how she felt.

She took a deep, shuddering inhale and said the words

she'd tried all her life not to say. "I love you. I always have. Take me with you."

Around them, partygoers glided in the silvery light. The air sparkled with diamond dust. They could have been standing in the middle of a fairy tale.

But as Franco's smile wilted, Diana plunged headfirst into a nightmare.

"It's too late." He took her hands in his, but he was shaking his head and his gaze was filled with apologies that she didn't want to hear.

She'd missed her chance.

She should have believed.

She should have said yes when she'd had the opportunity.

"I understand." She pulled her hands away and began gathering her skirt in her fists, ready to run for the door. Just like Cinderella.

The ball was over.

Everything was over.

"It's okay." But it wasn't. It would never be okay, and it was all her fault. "I just really need to go…"

"Diana, wait." Franco stepped in front of her. "Please."

She couldn't do this. Not now. Not here, with all of New York watching. Couldn't he understand that?

But she'd fallen in love while the world watched. She supposed there was some poetic symmetry to having her heart broken while the cameras rolled.

"I can't." It was too much. More than she could take. More than anyone could.

But just as she turned away, Franco blurted, "I quit the team."

Diana stopped. She released her hold on her dress, and featherlight organza floated to the floor. "What?"

"That's what I meant when I said it's too late. You

can't go with me on the road because I'm not going."
His mouth curved into a half grin, and Diana thought
she might faint. "Did you really think I could leave you?"

He's not my father.

She'd turned him down, sent him away. And he was
still here. He'd stuck by Luc, even when it had come at
great personal cost.

Now he was sticking by her. He was loyal in a way
she'd never known could be possible.

"You're afraid," he said in a deliciously low tone that
she felt deep in her center. "Don't be."

He moved closer, cupped her face with his left hand.
She'd missed him. She'd missed his touch. So, so much.
She could have wept with relief at the feel of his warm
skin against hers.

"I'm not afraid. Not anymore." She searched his gaze
for signs of doubt, but found only rock-solid assurance.
His eyes glittered, as sharp as diamonds.

He dropped his hand, and her fingertips drifted to her
cheek, to the place where he'd touched her. She hadn't
wanted him to release her. *Too soon*, she thought. She
needed his hands on her. His lips. His tongue.

Everywhere.

"Wildfire." Franco winked, and she felt it down to
the toes of her silver Jimmy Choos. "I have something
for you."

He reached into the inside pocket of his tuxedo and
pulled out a tiny Drake-blue box tied with a white satin
ribbon. It was just like the ones she'd once sold to all the
moonstruck couples in Engagements.

Diana stared at it, trying to make sense of what was
happening. For as long as she could remember, she'd
hated those boxes. But not this time.

This time, the tears that pricked her eyes were tears of joy.

"Franco, what are you doing?" How had he even gotten that box? Or whatever was inside of it?

Her gaze flitted over Franco's shoulder, and she spotted Artem watching from afar with a huge grin on his face. So her brother was in on this, too? That would certainly explain where the tiny blue box had come from. It also explained his insistence that she stay for the beginning of the gala.

Is this really happening?

"Isn't it obvious what I'm doing?" Franco dropped down on one knee, right there in the Great Hall of the Met.

It *was* happening.

A gasp went up from somewhere in the crowd as the partygoers noticed Franco's posture. Diana could hear them murmuring in confusion. Of course they were baffled. She and Franco were supposed to be engaged already.

Let them be confused. For once, Diana didn't care what anyone was saying about her. She didn't care what kind of headlines would be screaming from the front page of the papers tomorrow morning. All she cared about was the man kneeling at her feet.

"It occurred to me that I never asked properly for you to become to my wife. Not the way in which you deserve. So I'm giving it another go." He took her hand and gently placed the blue box in it.

Her fingertips closed around it, and their eyes met. Held.

"I love you, Diana Drake. Only a fool would walk away from something real, and I don't want to be a fool anymore. So I'm asking you again, and I'm going to keep asking for as long as it takes." But there would be no more proposals, because she was going to say yes. She could barely keep herself from screaming her answer before he finished. *Yes, yes, yes.* "Will you marry me, Diana Drake?"

"I'd love to marry you, Franco Andrade."

The crowd cheered as he rose to his feet and took her into his arms. Diana was barely conscious of the popping of a champagne cork or the well-wishers who offered their congratulations. She was only aware of how right it felt to be by Franco's side again and how the tiny blue box in her hand felt like a magic secret.

She waited to open it until they were back at her apartment. The time between his proposal and the end of the party passed in a glittering blur. She needed to be alone with him. She needed to step out of her fancy dress and give herself to him, body and soul.

After they left the gala and finally arrived at her front door, Diana wove her fingers through Franco's and pulled him inside.

"Alone at last," he said, gazing down at her as the lights of Manhattan twinkled behind him.

"Sort of." Diana laughed and lifted a brow at Lulu, charging at them from the direction of the bedroom.

Franco scooped the puppy into the elbow of his uninjured arm and sat down on the sofa. Lulu burrowed into his lap, and he gave the empty space beside him a pat. "Come sit down. Don't you have a box to open?"

She sat and removed the little blue box from her evening bag. She held it in the palm of her hand, not wanting the moment to end. She wanted to hoard her time with Franco like a priceless treasure. Every precious second.

"Open it, Wildfire."

She tugged on the smooth satin ribbon and it fell onto her lap, where Lulu pounced on it with her tiny black paws. As the puppy picked it up with her mouth, she fell over onto her back between them, batting at the ribbon with her feet. The comical sight brought a lump to Diana's throat for some strange reason.

Then she realized why...

The three of them were a family.

She lifted the lid of the box, but the large rose-cut diamond solitaire nestled on top of the tiny Drake-blue cushion inside was unlike any of the rings in the shiny cases of the Engagements section of Drake Diamonds. Jewelers didn't typically style diamonds in rose cut anymore. This ring was different. Special. Familiar in a way that stole the breath from Diana's lungs.

"This was my mother's ring." She hadn't seen this diamond in years, but she would have recognized it anywhere. When she was a little girl, she used to slip it on and dream about the day when she'd wear sparkling diamonds and go to fancy black-tie parties every night, just as her parents did.

That had been in the years before everything turned pear-shaped. Before they'd all learned the truth about her father and his secret family. Back when being a wife and a mother seemed like a wonderful thing to be.

Diana had forgotten what it was like to feel that way.

Now, with breathless clarity, she remembered.

"How did you get this, Franco?" It was more than a stone. It was hope and happiness, shining bright. Diamond fire.

"I went to Artem to ask for your hand, and he gave it to me. He said it's been in the vault at Drake Diamonds for years. Waiting." Franco took the ring and slid it onto her finger. Then he lifted her hand and kissed her fingertips.

The diamond had been waiting all this time. Waiting for her broken heart to heal. Waiting for the one man who could help her put it back together.

Waiting for Franco.

At long last, the wait was over.

Epilogue

A *Page Six* Exclusive Report

Diamond heiress Diana Drake returns to New York today after winning a gold medal in equestrian show jumping at the Tokyo Olympics. The win is a shocking comeback after Drake suffered a horrific fall last year in Bridgehampton that resulted in the death of her beloved horse, Diamond. Drake's new mount—a Hanoverian mare named Sapphire—was a gift from her husband, polo-playing hottie Franco Andrade.

Andrade was on hand in Tokyo to watch his wife win the gold, where we hear there was plenty of Olympic-level PDA. We can't get enough of Manhattan's most beautiful power couple, so *Page Six* will be front row center this weekend when Andrade returns to the polo field as captain of the newly formed team, Black Diamond, which he co-owns with his longtime friend and teammate, Luc Piero.

All eyes will certainly be on Diana, who is returning to the helm of her family's empire Drake Diamonds as co-CEO. Rumor has it she declined a glass of champagne at the party celebrating her Olympic victory, and we can't help but wonder...

Might there be a baby on the horizon for this golden couple?

Only time will tell.

* * * * *

COMING SOON!

We really hope you enjoyed reading this book.
If you're looking for more romance
be sure to head to the shops when
new books are available on

Thursday 24th April

To see which titles are coming soon, please visit

millsandboon.co.uk/nextmonth

MILLS & BOON

MILLS & BOON

THE HEART OF ROMANCE

A ROMANCE FOR EVERY READER

MODERN

Prepare to be swept off your feet by sophisticated, sexy and seductive heroes, in some of the world's most glamourous and romantic locations, where power and passion collide.

HISTORICAL

Escape with historical heroes from time gone by. Whether your passion is for wicked Regency Rakes, muscled Vikings or rugged Highlanders, awaken the romance of the past.

MEDICAL

Set your pulse racing with dedicated, delectable doctors in the high-pressure world of medicine, where emotions run high and passion, comfort and love are the best medicine.

True Love

Celebrate true love with tender stories of heartfelt romance, from the rush of falling in love to the joy a new baby can bring, and a focus on the emotional heart of a relationship.

HEROES

The excitement of a gripping thriller, with intense romance at its heart. Resourceful, true-to-life women and strong, fearless men face danger and desire - a killer combination!

From showing up to glowing up, these characters are on the path to leading their best lives and finding romance along the way – with plenty of sizzling spice!

To see which titles are coming soon, please visit

millsandboon.co.uk/nextmonth

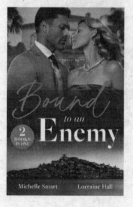
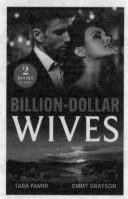

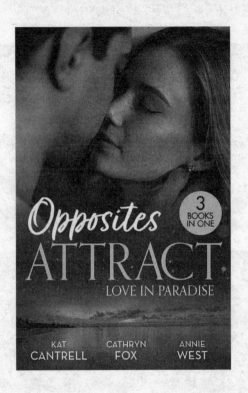

afterglow BOOKS

Afterglow Books is a trend-led, trope-filled list of books with diverse, authentic and relatable characters, a wide array of voices and representations, plus real world trials and tribulations. Featuring all the tropes you could possibly want (think small-town settings, fake relationships, grumpy vs sunshine, enemies to lovers) and all with a generous dose of spice in every story.

♪ @millsandboonuk
⊙ @millsandboonuk
afterglowbooks.co.uk
#AfterglowBooks

For all the latest book news, exclusive content and giveaways scan the QR code below to sign up to the Afterglow newsletter:

SCAN ME